"The *Oxford English Dictionary* credits SF Grand Master Williamson . . . for coining the term 'terraforming' . . . to describe an alien world altered for human habitation. With the terraforming of Earth itself, the original concept now gets an oblique and awesome twist well over half a century later. Williamson's skill at speculative fiction is once again evident in this far-future saga of mankind's destiny. . . . Throughout, poetic undercurrents permeate this masterful work by a superb chronicler of the cosmic."
—*Publishers Weekly*

"This latest novel by the grand old man of SF (his career began in 1928!) uses a timely theme—the collision of a killer asteroid with Earth—as a springboard for exploring the far-reaching consequences of such a disaster, both for Earth and for any survivors. Fans of hard science and old-fashioned SF adventure should enjoy this vividly imagined tale of life at the far end of time."   —*Library Journal*

"Williamson seems to see humanity as doomed but resilient, destined to fall and rise and fall and rise, until. . . . The final version is a science-fictional take on a traditional glory."
—*Analog*

"I have no hesitation in placing Jack Williamson on a plane with two other American giants, Isaac Asimov and Robert Heinlein."   —*Arthur C. Clarke*

BOOKS BY JACK WILLIAMSON

The Legion of Space
*Darker than You Think
The Green Girl
The Cometeers
One Against the Legion
Seetee Ship
Seetee Shock
Dragon's Island
The Legion of Time
Undersea Quest
(with Frederik Pohl)
Dome Around America
StarBridge
(with James Gunn)
Undersea Fleet
(with Frederik Pohl)
Undersea City
(with Frederik Pohl)
The Trial of Terra
Golden Blood
The Reefs of Space
(with Frederik Pohl)
Starchild
(with Frederik Pohl)
The Reign of Wizardry
Bright New Universe
Trapped in Space
The Pandora Effect
Rogue Star
(with Frederik Pohl)
People Machines
The Moon Children

H.G. Wells: Critic of
Progress (criticism)
The Farthest Star
(with Frederik Pohl)
The Early Williamson
The Power of Blackness
The Best of Jack
Williamson
Brother to Demons,
Brother to Gods
The Alien Intelligence
The Humanoid Touch
The Birth of a New
Republic
(with Miles J. Breuer)
Manseed
Wall Around a Star
(with Frederik Pohl)
The Queen of the Legion
Wonder's Child:
My Life in Science Fiction
(memoir)
Lifeburst
*Firechild
*Land's End
(with Frederik Pohl)
Mazeway
The Singers of Time
(with Frederik Pohl)
*Beachhead
*The Humanoids
*Demon Moon
*The Black Sun
*The Silicon Dagger
*Terraforming Earth

*A Tor Book

TERRAFORMING
EARTH

JACK WILLIAMSON

A TOM DOHERTY ASSOCIATES BOOK
NEW YORK

This is a work of fiction. All the characters and events portrayed in this book are either products of the author's imagination or are used fictitiously.

TERRAFORMING EARTH

Edited by James Frenkel

A Tor Book
Published by Tom Doherty Associates, LLC
175 Fifth Avenue
New York, NY 10010

www.tor.com

Tor® is a registered trademark of Tom Doherty Associates, LLC.

ISBN: 0-765-34497-1

First edition: June 2001
First mass market edition: February 2003

Printed in the United States of America

0 9 8 7 6 5 4 3 2 1

For my brother Jim

Contents

PART ONE

Impact and Aftermath

1

We are clones. A hundred years have passed since the great impact. All our natural parents lay in the cemetery on the rubble slope outside the crater rim long before the robots brought our frozen cells to life in the maternity lab. I remember the day my Robo father brought the five of us up to see the Earth, a hazy red-spattered ball in the black Moon sky.

"It looks—looks sick." Looking sick herself, Dian raised her face to his. "Is it bleeding?"

"Bleeding red-hot lava all over the land," he told her. "The rivers all bleeding iron-red rain into the seas."

"Dead." Arne made a face. "It looks dead."

"The impact killed it." His plastic head nodded. "You were born to bring it back to life."

"Just us kids?"

"You'll grow up."

"Not me," Arne muttered. "Do I have to grow up?"

"So what do you want?" Tanya grinned at him. "To stay a snot-nosed kid forever?"

"Please." My Robo father shrugged in the stiff way robots have, and his lenses swept all five of us, standing around him in the dome. "Your mission is to replant life on Earth. The job may take a lot of time, but you'll be born and born again till you get it done."

That task seemed too much for us. We were all alone, the five of us growing up together there on the Moon, the only human beings anywhere. Our world was Tycho Station, the little nest of tunnels dug below the dome into the crater rim. Our natural parents were gone forever, their world dead and left a quarter-million miles behind. I knew my natural father, the man whose frozen cells had made me, only from his image in the holo tank.

He had been Duncan Yare. I loved him and felt sorry for all he had suffered. His face was lean and haggard, furrowed deep with pain. When I looked into his eyes, I often saw a dark despair.

"Look up at Earth when you're up in the dome," he told us. "You'll see it strange and dead, all we ever knew and hoped for gone. Four billion years of evolution all wiped out. Nothing left but us." His shoulders sagged in the old brown jacket. Lips set, he shook his head. "Tycho Station. The master computer. The Robos. The live cells frozen in the cryostat.

"And you." He stopped, with his terrible eyes fixed on us. "You're the only hope that Earth can live again. That will be your job when you are grown. To restore the life the great impactor killed. You're all we have. You can't stop. You can't quit."

A ring of iron came into his rusty voice.

"Promise me that."

We raised our hands and promised.

He was only an image that flickered into the tank when the master computer wanted it there. Robos were real, the human-sized robots who had cloned us in the maternity lab and cared for us since.

Though I could feel his grief and pain, that promise often seemed impossible to keep. We were only children. Earth itself seemed unreal, only a great bright spot in our black north sky. The world of our parents was gone, all except the traces of it in the files and relics Calvin DeFort had brought to the station before the impact.

He had put us here but died too soon to record any full holo of himself. We knew him only from the videos and papers he had left, and what our other parents had to say about him. The Robos had set up a glass case in the museum to hold a few relics of him: a pocketknife, a class ring, an antique pocket watch that had been his grandfather's. There was also a diary my father tried to keep, a little handwritten book bound in cracked green leather, half the pages blank.

The dome was always wonderfully exciting when the Robos let us climb up to it. It was full of strange machines I longed to learn about. The clear quartz walls let us see the stark Earth-lit moonscape all around us. We had clone pets. Mine was Spaceman, a beagle. He growled and bristled at a black-shadowed monster rock outside and crouched against my leg. Tanya's cat had followed us.

"Okay, Cleo," she called when it mewed. "Let's look outside."

Cleo came flying into her arms. Jumping was easy, here in the Moon's light gravity. My Robo father had pointed a thin blue plastic arm at the cragged mountain wall that curved away on both sides of the dome.

"The station is dug into the rim of—"

"Tycho!" Arne interrupted him. "We know it from the globe."

"It's so big!" Tanya's voice was hushed. She was a spindly little girl with straight black hair that her mother made her keep cut short, and bangs that came down to her eyebrows. Cleo sagged in her arms, almost forgotten. "It—it's homongoolius!"

She stared out across the enormous black pit at the jagged peak towering into the blaze of sunlight at the center. Dian had turned to look the other way, at the bright white rays that fanned out from the boulder-strewn slopes far below, spreading beyond the landing pads and gantries and hangars, on across the waste of black-pocked dust and

gray broken rocks that reached away to the black and
starless sky.

"Homongoolius?" Dian mocked her. "I'd say fracta-
bulous!"

"Homon-fractabu-what?" Pepe made fun of them both.
He was short and quick, as skinny as Tanya was, and
darker. He liked to play games, and never combed his
hair. "Can't you speak English? *O posible español?*"

He was learning Spanish from his holo father.

"Better *anglais* than you." Dian was a tall pale girl who
never cared for pets and tried to know everything. The
Robos had given her dark-rimmed glasses to help her read
the old paper books in the library. "And I'm learning
Latin."

"What good is Latin?" Cloned together, we were all the
same age, but Arne was the biggest. He had pale blue
eyes and pale blond hair, and he liked to ask questions.
"It's dead as Earth."

"It's something we must save." Dian was quiet and shy
and always serious. "The new people will need everything."

"What new people?" He waved his arm at the Earth.
"If everybody's dead."

"We have the frozen cells from thousands of people
down in the cryostat," Tanya said. "We can grow them
again when we get home to Earth."

Nobody heard her. We were all looking out at the dead
moonscape. The dome stood high between the rock-
spattered desert and the ink-black shadow that filled the
crater pit. Looking down, I felt giddy for an instant, and
Arne backed away.

"Fraidy-cat!" Tanya jeered him. "You're gray as a
ghost."

Retreating farther, he flushed red and looked up at the
Earth. It hung high and huge, capped white at the poles
and swirled with great white storms. Beneath the clouds,

the seas were streaked brown and yellow and red where rivers ran off the dark continents.

"It used to be so beautiful," Dian whispered. "All blue and white and green in the old holos."

"Before the impact," my father said. "Your job is to make it beautiful again."

Arne squinted at it and shook his head. "I don't see how—"

"Just listen," Tanya said.

"Please." My Robo father's face was not designed to smile, but his voice could reflect a tolerant amusement. "Let me tell you what you are."

"I know," Arne said. "Clones—"

"Shut up," Tanya told him.

"Clones." My robot father nodded. "Genetic copies of the humans that got here alive after the impact."

"I know all that," Arne said. "My Robo told me. We were born from cells frozen before the great impact that killed the Earth. I saw the simulation on my monitor."

"I didn't," Tanya said. "I want to know."

"Let's begin with Cal DeFort." Our Robo parents were all shaped just alike, but each with a breastplate of a different color. Mine was bright blue. He had cared for me as long as I remembered, and I loved him as much as my beagle. "Cal was the man who built Tycho Station and got us here. He gave his life for your chance to go back—"

Stubbornly, Arne pushed out his fat lower lip. "I like it better here."

"You're a dummy," Tanya told him. "Dummies don't talk."

He stuck his tongue out at her, but we all stood close around my Robo father, listening.

"Calvin was born in North America, in a place called Texas. We're looking at Asia now, but you can find it on the maps. That was back before anybody knew about the asteroid, but he was used to bad things coming. He was crippled in a school bus accident, and had to learn to walk again. A tornado killed his parents—"

"Tor what?" Arne demanded.

"Look it up," Tanya told him. "Or ask your holo father."

"A wind storm," my robot father said. "They were bad in Texas."

"What's wind?" Arne wanted to know.

"Air in motion," Tanya said. "Look it up."

"Cal was buried in the wreck of their house," my Robo father went on. "When he got out of the hospital, his aunt brought him to live with her in an old city called Chicago. He grew up there. The day he was seven she took him to a museum where he saw the skeletons of the great dinosaurs that used to rule the Earth. The huge bones and great teeth frightened him.

"She tried to tell him he was safe. The dinosaurs were truly dead, she said, killed by a great object out of space that struck the coast of Mexico. A film about them frightened him more. Not to worry, she told him. Big impacts came millions of years apart. But he did worry.

"A colony on the Moon could double our chances, he thought, if something did hit the Earth. He trained for an early Moon station that was planned but never built. That's where he learned about the Robos. They were self-directed robots, designed by military engineers for rescue and repair in contaminated areas too dangerous for people. He organized the Robo Multiservice Corporation to buy the rights and reprogram them for civilian use."

My father's gray holo face had no expression and his toneless words ran on as if read from a book. Arne fidgeted, making faces at Dian's Robo where it stood motionless beside the ladder pit in the middle of the floor, teasing it to move or speak, but DeFort's story held the rest of us.

"The Robos made him a fortune, and they were perfect for the Moon. He sent them here to prepare it for the colonists. Better than the human astronauts, they require no air or food, no rest or sleep. They suffer no harm from low gravity or high radiation. They could build and repair themselves.

"But the Patagonian impactors—"

"Patawhat?" Arne broke in.

"A swarm of falling rocks," my father told him. "They blazed around half the Earth and struck the South Atlantic. None of them were huge, but they raised a tsunami that washed far into South America, drowning cities, killing millions. That woke his old dread of a greater impact. It also set off a financial panic that nearly ruined his corporation and forced him to give up his plans for any large Moon colony.

"Instead, he set his Robos to work on Tycho Station. He wanted a place where we could survive anything that happened, and keep our science and art and history safe. The Robos run on fusion power. They found water, frozen in the rubble and dust at the bottom of the polar craters where sunlight never strikes. Heavy metals are rare here, but they salvaged metal from the old spacecraft that had brought supplies. They found nickel and iron where a big meteorite had struck. They're still busy here."

"Where?" Arne asked.

"Down in the shops and hangars." My father gestured at the leveled flight field out below the crater rim. "Safe from radiation and minor impacts. Caring for the station. Caring for you. Standing by for any command from the master computer."

"Our boss machine," Arne muttered. "It thinks it knows everything and never cares what we want."

"So what?" Pepe shrugged. "It's got us here to do our job. To bring the Earth back to life."

"If we can." Very soberly, my father's image frowned.

"The station was a complex and ambitious project, expensive and difficult to build here on the Moon. DeFort set up a twelve-year plan for it. The big impactor caught him by surprise, years too soon. The station was never fully finished or supplied."

"Impactor?" Tanya stared up at him, her black eyes wide. "What was it, really?"

"A ten-mile chunk of interstellar rock. DeFort had the telescopes finished. The master computer was watching the sky, but the big bolide came out of the north sky, away from the ecliptic, where nothing should have been. It grazed the sun and got deflected toward Earth, coming down in the sun-glare where the telescopes were blind."

2

We loved our parents, but their natural bodies lay under the gray moondust the Robos had showed us, down below the crater rim. Trying to know my father, I used to watch his fleeting holo image and listen to his voice, but the best clues to his life, and the life of Calvin DeFort, were those I found in his diary.

Reading it was sometimes difficult. Even the language often baffled me with such terms as freeway, common cold, and shopping mall, whose meanings are gone forever, with whatever things they meant. Yet the holos and the Robos could answer some of our questions. We learned from the books and disks in the library, studied the precious artifacts in the museum.

My father was born in a section of old America called Kentucky. His father had been a coal miner, his mother a nurse. They saved money to put him through college, where he happened to room with DeFort. He had dreamed of being an astronaut till he found he was colorblind. He had been a news reporter and a history teacher before DeFort called him to old New Mexico to offer him a job with Robo Multiservice, when that great corporation was still no more than the name and a dream.

My father found DeFort in a temporary office near the military laboratory where the Robos had been developed. A small quick man, he walked with a slight limp from that childhood injury. He had light brown hair and blue eyes that lit when he spoke of the Robos and his plans for them.

"Look at them!" He gestured at a plastic model standing beside his desk. "The first citizens of space. They'll be at home on the Moon!"

My father was no engineer, but he became DeFort's

trusted associate, working with him as he made millions. The financial panic that followed the Patagonian impacts killed their plans to colonize the Moon. It made setting up Tycho Station a bigger challenge. Robo Multiservice itself was almost ruined. DeFort had to rove the continents, begging for private support and governmental subsidies.

"My own main task was to recruit a staff for the station," my father wrote in his diary. "People with all the essential knowledge and skills to repair the harm to Earth after any worst-case scenario. They must care enough to find time to program the master computer with all their know-how. They must give us tissue specimens to be frozen for any future need. And they must be willing to train for space and visit the Moon for life-drills there."

Not many were willing. It was sixty-five million years since the Yucatan impact wiped out the dinosaurs, one distinguished molecular biologist told my father. The next big extinction was likely just as far ahead. He had too much to do right now, here on Earth.

Yet he did convince a few. The first was Pedro Navarro, already a Multiservice employee. Trained as an astronaut, he had been a space pilot, ferrying cargo and Robos to the Moon for the planned colony. Younger than my father, likeable and easy to please, he was eager to ferry whatever we needed out to the station.

Looking for advice on things that had to be preserved in case all else was lost, he found Diana Lazard in the library of the old American congress. A lean, plain-faced woman, severe in manner and dress, she was ready enough with advice, but difficult about anything more.

She shrank from the notion of leaving her Washington apartment for the Moon, even for a few weeks of training. Most of the items she wanted for preservation were hideously expensive. My father fought with her over the price of rare books and paintings, compromised on the items

DeFort could pay for, finally filled our limited space with books and disks and art she thought might help us rekindle an extinct civilization.

"Get the best biologist you can," DeFort told my father. "A man with medical training and cloning expertise. Past disasters have almost sterilized the planet more than once. I want us to be ready to start evolution all over again."

They talked to other top people, all fighting to stay at the top, none with time for the station. The biologist who finally joined the project was a woman, Tanya Wu. She had been head of a medical research center at the old city of Baltimore. Listening to DeFort and my father, she caught some of their determination.

"A safety net for Earth!" she called it. "Our own biocosm took four billion years to evolve. It's a sacred trust. Nothing like it might ever happen again."

She quit her job to plan the maternity lab, to program the Robos with cloning skills, to fill the cryostat with seed, spores, and tissue specimens to replenish an injured planet.

DeFort wanted a terraforming specialist. They talked to Arne Linder, a distinguished geologist who had made his fortune as a mining engineer and his name with a proposal for terraforming Mars. When my father called, he shrugged the project off as "an idiot's nightmare."

Overtaken on a lecture tour, he wanted money. DeFort finally paid him a huge fee to give a tissue specimen and spend a few weeks with the master computer on the Moon.

Though money and willing recruits were hard to find, they were hoping to add space and facilities for a larger survival team. My father had spent that last week at a city on the west coast of old America, asking for more private donations and trying to enlist an astronomer who was also a computer scientist.

———

The impactor came out of nowhere, a terrible surprise. DeFort had hoped to have the station ready for something that might happen in a thousand years, or a million, or better, never. They never really dreamed that it would happen to them before they even had it finished.

The station was still manned by Robos. The small human staff was back on Earth at the White Sands base, a spot located in the arid New Mexico region of old America and named for an odd mineral formation. The warning from the Moon reached it at the worst possible moment, late on the night of December 24.

The Robos had detected the object a day or two earlier, but they were only machines. They were programmed to inform the human staff of any such event, but they seem to have delayed transmission because they had been told that the Earth office was closing for the holiday.

The coded message found my father on an airplane in flight back to the base.

"A good week," he had written in the diary the day before. "Half a million in promises, and Yamamoto wants to visit the station.

"He says he'll consider signing on with us."

A line is drawn across the page. The next entry is an undated scrawl.

"A wasted week. What's half a million now? I feel stunned. I must try to write something, just to get some sanity back. I have to shield the page from the woman beside me. She saw my Tycho button and asked what I thought about Robo intelligence.

"If she knew! I must settle my thoughts. Calm myself for the madhouse waiting ahead, as we fight to get off in time. There's nothing else I can do. A terrible moment. Worse for me, because nobody knows. Of course I can't tell them. The people seated around me, whispering, reading, watching a silly holo comedy, trying to sleep. I almost envy them, because they don't know. If they did, panic could kill us all before we get to the Moon.

"If we get there. If.

"No good to wonder. Building the station was a game. I see that now. A great game that has filled my life for years. Great friends, a noble cause, often fun. But never real. Not till now. If the dice do fall for us, future life may have a chance. But I can't feel anything but shock. Regret for too much I never did and can't do now.

"I wish I could call my mother. I wish for Ellen. I wish she were here with me, to share whatever chance I have to get away alive. I wish, yet I know that life with her was never possible. The project took too much of me. She had a world of her own. Wishes—they don't matter now.

"Landing now. To face the end of everything."

Most of what we know about the escape comes from the papers of the other team members and the words recorded in the master computer for the Robos and their holo images. As those few hours drained away, the takeoff had to be delayed and delayed again. Vital shipments for the maternity lab and the hydroponic gardens had to be found at the dock and rushed aboard. Two fuel trucks collided and burned.

Word of the warning got out. Few believed it, at least at first, but rumors spread that DeFort had a fleet of spacecraft standing ready to carry refugees to the Moon. Terror was contagious. Frightened thousands converged on our single little supply craft standing on its pad.

It was back from the Moon only a few days before, the human crew away on holiday leave and the fuel tanks empty. A cargo of vital equipment had been ordered but much of it not yet delivered. Members of the survival team were scattered everywhere.

Navarro had flown Arne Linder to Iceland, where he wanted to observe a volcano in eruption. They were hard

to locate, and they barely won a desperate race to get back
to White Sands in time to save their lives. Lazard and Wu
were in their home cities, far across the continent. Holding
a taxi till she found her pet cat, Wu nearly missed her
flight.

Most people may have been stoic enough, but the panic
brought refugees by the thousand, fighting for space on
the escape ship, which had no space. Desperate pilots ignored airport controls, crashed their planes to burn on
crowded airstrips, crashed on the desert sand beside them.
Drivers abandoned stalled vehicles and came on afoot.

But for a black-skinned night watchman named Casey
Kell, they might never have got off the ground. He saw
the danger early, raided a gun shop for weapons, organized a little group of truck drivers and other workers to
defend the ship. They parked trucks in a ring around it,
and he stood on the loading dock at the door, yelling
commands through a bullhorn.

Writing later, out in space, my father set down a final
incident. He was working with DeFort on that dock, loading Wu's last shipment of frozen tissue specimens, when
a gate in the barrier opened for the last fuel truck. A
woman broke through and fought her way up the ladder
to DeFort. She tried to thrust a baby into his arms, begging him to save it.

"A moment of anguish I can't forget," my father wrote.
"DeFort had reached instinctively to take the baby, smiling down at it, but then his face went white. He froze for
an instant, shook his head, pushed the woman away. A
choice he had to make, for the sake of all he hoped to
save."

There must have been many such moments, too painful
to be recalled.

There is one last entry in my father's diary, written at the station and dated a few months after they reached it.

"We're alive. Very efficiently, the Robos have helped us work the bugs out of the survival gear. The hydroponic gardens are thriving. Linder says we can expect to stay alive. Wu has inspected the cryostat and the maternity lab. She is confident that the Robos will remain alert, watching the Earth and watching the sky, ready and able to clone us when the master computer discovers the need.

"Safe here, we have the rest of our years ahead. We could spend them usefully. We have vehicles, space gear, the Robos to serve us. We could explore the Moon, mapping resources that some future emergency might require. We have fine telescopes. We could learn the science of astrophysics and explore the cosmos. We could study the old world's history and Dian's collected relics of it. We could be looking ahead, working on plans to restore the planet.

"We do none of those things. Linder calls us the living dead. The shock and pain of loss have numbed us to everything. We drank too much until the Robos began to restrain us. We eat the meals they serve. We work out in the centrifuge. Linder plays bridge when he can find a partner. Wu inspects the maternity lab and inspects it again, revising the programs recorded in the master computer and rehearsing the Robos on the procedures of cloning. DeFort sits long hours at the telescope, searching for holes in the dense cloud cover that hides the ruined Earth.

"Navarro spends most of his time with Kell and his woman, who got aboard in the last minutes before the takeoff. They speak Spanish, which I barely understand. They seem more content than the rest of us, keeping busy with needless chores about the station. They drink together and sing Spanish songs of unhappy love; the woman has an appealing voice. Kell tells improbable tales of his life back on Earth. He's shrewd enough to know he'll never be corrected.

"When I find any will to work, I try to record what I can of DeFort's life and the history of the station, though I see no real point to that. He himself is anxious for a look at the surface of the Earth, hoping to fly back for a look at the damage, but he doubts that we will find it recovered enough for us to land there. Any resettlement, he says, may take centuries.

"Our own work is done. The future of the planet rests now in the arms of the Robos, the master computer, and cosmic chance."

3

In our classroom on the Moon, my father's holo image flashed into the tank and out again like magic, but he looked alive while he was there. A thin little man in an old corduroy jacket with leather patches on the elbows, he used to watch us with a worried frown while he spoke, waving an empty pipe to punctuate his sentences.

He never seemed happy when we asked about the escape from the frightened mobs at the White Sands base. Sorrow and pain would cloud his face. Sometimes his image would freeze for a moment, and then he would speak of something else. But we always begged him to go on, until the story was as real in our own minds as if we had been back on Earth when the big rock came down.

It fell into the Bay of Bengal. Night had fallen over Asia, but the time was high noon there in New Mexico, halfway around the world, when the first shock wave struck the launch site. He and DeFort had spent most of the morning at their headquarters in Las Cruces, calling the scattered survival team together.

DeFort had a little private plane that took them to the site when they had to go. They drove from the airstrip, through a jam of stalled vehicles and frantic people, to the spaceplane. A muscular man on the loading dock was yelling orders though a bullhorn.

"Your natural dad." Telling us the story, my father's image gave Casey a wry little grin. "El Chino. That's what they called him, though he gave his name as K. C. Kell. Black as tar, though he had an Oriental poker face. Stripped to the waist in the heat, he wore the flags of Mexico and China tattooed across his chest. He claimed to be an ex-Marine, and we found him acting the part."

DeFort made a quick inspection of the plane and

climbed aboard. My father stayed out on the dock, helping Kell identify people and cargo to be loaded. The rumors had created chaos by then, in spite of DeFort's desperate appeals for order, appeals for assistance in getting us off the ground. The police, or at least a few of them, did try to help, but they were overwhelmed. Kell was sweating and cursing in two languages, fighting to keep a little island of order inside the ring and a safe gap open for fuel and cargo trucks.

"One by one, our people got there." My father's words in his diary and his image in the tank brought the scene to life for us. "Lazard, staggering up the ramp under a backpack loaded with books she couldn't bear to abandon. Wu with one last cryopack of tissue specimens. Finally Navarro and Linder. Delivery trucks were still arriving when DeFort came out to tell Kell to wave them away. Navarro was warming up the engines. Two minutes to takeoff."

Those two minutes are as real as if I had been there. DeFort turned to thank Kell for defending the ship and found him staring at a police car careening though the gate in the ring of trucks, siren screaming. It rammed the dock. A woman tumbled out and darted up the ramp. Linder was waiting to shut the door, shouting for my father and Defort to get aboard.

"Hold everything." Kell spoke very quietly, but he had drawn a heavy pistol. "We want to live. Me and Mona. We're coming with you."

The woman was barefoot, in a faded blue terry robe, her wet blond hair under a towel wrapped like a turban. Pale with shock, a red-nailed hand on her throat, she stood mutely gaping at the open door.

"You can't!" DeFort snapped at them. "We've got no space, no facilities—"

"Sorry, sir."

The gun in one hand, Kell caught the woman with the other arm and stalked with her toward the door. Her robe flapped open to show her own tattoo, the Mona Lisa smiling from her belly.

"Out of the way." Kell waved the gun. "We're human, too."

Hand raised, DeFort stepped to stop them. The gun crashed. A push from Kell sent him staggering across the dock. They shoved past him into the plane. Ears ringing from the shot, my father rushed to help him, but the bullet had gone into the air. In a moment he had his balance back.

"Now!" Linder was shouting. "Or never."

With a grim shrug, DeFort waved my father aboard. The door clanged shut. The jets roared. My father tumbled into his seat, feeling stunned, he said, by his sense of the world's death and grateful for that numbing thunder and the crushing rocket thrust.

They were all he knew until Navarro began easing the engines back toward free-fall flight and he could think and feel again. The dying Earth still filled the telescreens. He heard snatches of Linder's geologic jargon, narrating the stages of cataclysm, and gathered himself to make a brief pep talk. The pain of loss must be endured. They must live to restore the injured Earth.

In free fall, the engines silent, they were able to relax a little. Navarro came back from the cockpit to announce his flight plan to the Moon. Wu and Lazard handed out space rations, little self-heating packets. Few had any appetite, but Kell holstered the gun and ate heartily, whispering with the woman.

Some were still strangers to one another. DeFort gathered them for introductions and tried again to cheer them for the mission. Kell and the woman listened silently as Linder lectured on terraforming. Wu described the maternity lab where their cells would be frozen and cloned. Lazard spoke of all the treasures of art and learning still safe on the Moon.

"Now, Mr. Kell." DeFort turned at last to him, grimly grave. "Let's hear from you."

"We ain't doctors of anything." The crossed flags shining through the sweat and desert dust on his torso, Kell stood with one hand on the woman's shoulder, the other near the gun. "I don't know a flea's ass about this terra-what. But one thing I damn sure know is how to stay alive. Try to throw us off, somebody will die. Won't be me. Won't be Mona."

"We don't want violence." DeFort raised his hand uneasily. "But you are a problem."

"Your problem, sir."

"Mr. Kell—" Looking sick, DeFort gulped and blinked. "I do feel for you. I pity all the billions we left dead behind us."

My father heard the tremor of emotion in his voice and saw the sardonic quirk of Kell's lips.

"Something—" DeFort gulped again to find a stronger voice. "There's something you've got to understand. The impact was worse than anybody ever imagined. We're probably the only people left alive. Our facility on the Moon was never finished. We have no resources to support a larger staff—"

"You want us to jump off the plane?" Kell grinned unpleasantly. "You'll make room for us."

"Kill any of us," DeFort tried to warn him, "you'll kill us all. Kill our chance—"

Kell touched the gun. DeFort stopped.

"Watch 'em, Shug." Muttering to the woman, Kell swung to glance behind him. "A nest of mad rattlers. Don't let 'em strike."

The cabin went quiet till Navarro spoke.

"Cal?" He waited for DeFort's baffled nod. "I don't

want bullet holes in the fuel tanks. We'd better talk." He turned quietly to Kell. "Why don't you tell us who you are?"

"If you give a damn."

"We've got to care," Navarro said. "We all want to stay alive."

Kell scanned them one by one, meeting their eyes, waiting for signs of assent. Linder was pale and shaking, his shirt smudged dark with sweat. Wu nodded calmly. Lazard held a frozen stare. Navarro stuck up his thumb.

"Okay," DeFort muttered. "Let's hear."

Kell glanced behind him again and moved to get his back toward the wall. Following, the woman slid her arm around him.

"Like I said, I ain't no doctor. Fact is, I never went to any school. Mona says she had third grade. We don't know a rat's tit about shock waves and impacts, but we mean to stay alive." He stopped to glare at DeFort. "By God, we will."

"I hope we all can." DeFort nodded soberly. "We must try."

"We need to know each other," Navarro said. "Tell us where you come from."

"I don't know." Kell had relaxed a little, his hand straying from the gun. "I never knew my birth parents. The man I called my father said he won me in a poker game. Maybe he did, though he was not addicted to the truth. He was English, white as chalk, so he had to explain the dark freak I am. He said he'd been an actor; he liked to recite Shakespeare. Said he failed at that and found a richer role to play—" Warily, he stopped. "One he wouldn't talk about."

"No need for secrets now," Navarro urged him. "We're starting over. No need to fret about the past. If we've got to get along, we need to know each other."

"If we really are the only ones alive—" He frowned, considering.

"About your father?"

"I loved him, the father I knew." His voice softer for a moment, he glanced at the woman. "He loved me. More than his women; he must have had half a hundred women. Some tried to mother me. Some despised me. One taught me to screw. A birthday gift, the day I was nine."

"Quite a man." Navarro grinned. "How could he afford so many women?"

"He never said, but he did have money. Money for classy hotels. Money for travel, and we traveled a lot. Always another passport and some new name I had to learn. Sometimes another language. The women taught me to read and write, but I never went to school. He hated institutions, I think because he done his prison time, but he taught me most of what I know.

"Taught me weapons." Grinning at DeFort, Kell seemed to relish the recollection. "Knives, firearms, bombs. The martial arts. What he called the fine art of killing without getting caught. He used to call it erasure. Keys to life and death, he used to call the weapons. He loved them like his women.

"I used to wonder why, but I never got the truth till after he was dead. I was twelve the summer that happened. We'd checked into a Bangkok hotel with his latest woman, a saucy little beauty he called Missy Ming. He went out for lunch with a friend. No friend; he never got back.

"Missy cried when she heard he was gone, but she took me with her to bed that night and left next day before the cops got there. Local police and international agents, looking for his killer. Seems he had been a high-paid hit man in the drug trade, till he met another one grade better. That was my father."

Kell paused, with a wry shrug at DeFort.

"He made his own law, lived his own life. Call him bad if you want, but he was good to me. He made me what I am. Taught me how to stay alive."

"A skill still useful to you."

Navarro grinned. DeFort nodded at the woman, and Kell smiled down at her.

"My lady friend, Miss Mona Diamond." His tone seemed proudly fond. "A gifted singer, performing in a Juarez nightclub when we met."

"A lie."

With a long look at Kell, she shook her hair out of the towel and came to her feet. Tall for a woman, my father said, long-legged and well-breasted, with honey-colored hair falling nearly to her waist. Turning to the others, she opened the robe to show the tattoo.

"I never sang in Juarez." She shook a bright-nailed finger at Kell. "If we're all sardines in this tin can—" She paused to look around at the others. "We've got no room for lies."

"True," Navarro said. "We'll live or die together."

"I did want to sing, but I never got that good." Her voice was low and likable, my father said, and it had a ring of confidence. "I come from dirt-poor people, back in the Bluegrass county. I learned to love the music and longed for my own chance to make it, but I never had the luck.

"Hard times hit us when they outlawed tobacco. The state went bust. Pa planted pot and went to jail for it. Ma got sick, and I had to keep the house. On my own when they died, I did what I had to. Waitress, hooker, topless dancer, stripper. That's when I got the tattoo. Billed as Mona Lisa Live."

Demurely, she closed the terry robe.

"Like Casey says, I learned to stay alive. Got hard lessons all along the way. I've been rich and more often broke. Casey changed my life."

She grinned at him, affectionately.

"I'm here because he got the warning to me. You've heard my story. It's been a hard fight, but I've had good times along the way. If the old world's finished, like you say, I'm sad to see it go." She stopped to look around the cabin. "Luck to you, if you want to build it back."

"And luck to you." Navarro grinned. "I think we need you on the team."

"That's our testimony." Kell turned to DeFort. "Now let's talk about the verdict."

4

My father's world was dead. He nearly died with it. The pain haunted him through the rest of his natural life and followed him into the master computer. Though the killer object had been guided to Earth by cosmic forces far beyond human knowledge or control, he found ways to blame himself.

The diary gives a glimpse of his useless brooding. If he had given DeFort better business advice, Robo Multiservice might have earned enough to let them fund a self-sustaining colony on the Moon. Human civilization might have survived there, with no need for Tycho Station. In the holo tank, he was always ready to talk about our mission, but any question about that last day made his image dim and flicker. Sometimes it vanished altogether, but if we kept on calling, the master computer would bring it back again.

"You've got to learn how wonderful the old world was." His face grim, he used to pull his shoulders straighter in the old brown jacket and try to smile and cheer us on. "And remember your mission to let it live again. The whole future of life depends on you."

"Just us?" Arne asked him once, standing with Dian and Pepe and Tanya and me in front of the tank—we never needed chairs on the Moon. "Just us kids? What do you think we can do?"

"Grow up." Tanya stuck her tongue out at him. "Even dummies grow up."

"None of you are dummies." My father shook his head at them, with a patient little smile. "Your job's too big for dummies."

"I hope we grow up able to do it." Pepe was very solemn. "But the look of Earth scares me. I want to know how it got that way."

The image froze for a moment. Maybe the computer was searching for the data it needed to keep the image running, but my father seemed to be remembering.

"The last day." His slow voice was almost a whisper when he began to move again. "Christmas Eve had been a happy time. My married sister lived in Las Cruces, a city near the base. She had twins, two kids just five years old. I'd bought trikes for them. She was making dinner, baked turkey and dressing, yams, cranberry sauce—"

His voice caught and he stopped for a second.

"Foods you've never had, but we liked them for Christmas. I'd been off in California, raising funds to finish the station, but we'd made plans for the holidays. My father and mother were coming from Ohio. Nobody expected—"

He stopped to shake his head, lips shut tight.

"The station wasn't finished. Not yet ready for anything. We had left it on standby, with only the Robos there. Dr. Wu was coming out from Baltimore after the New Year, to bring more frozen cells for the maternity lab—"

"Her cells?" Tanya asked. "The cells I was born from?"

"Cloned," Arne muttered. "Clones aren't born."

"Dummies are," Tanya told him.

"Please," my father scolded them gently. "You did grow from the cells your parents left frozen in the cryostat. Your own lives did begin in the maternity lab. But clones aren't dummies."

"Your mother—" Arne poked his finger at Tanya. "Your mother was a machine."

"So was yours," she said.

"A wonderful machine," my father said. "Nearly as wonderful as a woman's body might have been."

"Why did we have to be clones?" Arne asked. "Why weren't we just born?"

"Cal's wife did want live people at the station," my father said. "But it's too small for any colony that could support itself. He planned the station to last a thousand years, or a million if it had to, with no aid from anywhere. The Robos and the master computer can wait here forever, with the frozen cells waiting to be cloned and cloned again, whenever you are needed."

"Now?" Arne scowled. "When all the Earth is dead?"

"Maybe not entirely dead." My father frowned, sucking the pipe as if he had tobacco in it. "It's time for a survey expedition to find that out. You must test the seas for microscopic life and test the air to find if you can breathe it. We can plan then for what your next generation can hope to do when their own time has come."

The image shivered, as if about to vanish.

"Wait!" Tanya called. "I hate to see you so sad. It must have been dreadful when the asteroid fell, but weren't you happy to get away?"

"Not really." My father froze for a moment as if the computer had stopped again. "Not when you think of all we had lost. Our families and our homes and our friends. All the good things we had ever known and loved and planned for. All—"

His face twitched, but he gave us a thin little smile.

"All but hope. Hope for you and what you can do."

The image stopped again till Pepe called, "Go on. Tell us all about the impact."

"All about it?" He sighed and shook his head, and put the pipe in his jacket pocket. "The people who really knew are dead. Nobody will ever know how it was for them, but I can tell you what I saw. We should have had a better warning. The big rock—asteroid or comet; nobody had time to fret about a name for it—was still two days off when the Robos picked it up. They did what they were programmed to do, which was to verify the sighting, compute the orbit, and estimate the time of impact, but they had been told our Earth base would be shut down for Christmas. We'd lost a whole day before they tried to signal Earth.

"Thirteen hours." My father's lips bent down over a neat little tuft of red-gray beard. "That's all we had left. Thirteen hours to get the survival team together. To load the ship and fuel it. To get us off alive. And at first DeFort was afraid to spread the news. Afraid of panic that would kill any chance at all.

"And his wife—"

He stopped to shake his head and suck at the dead pipe.

"She was Mayu Ryokan. A marine biologist, she was somewhere on the Indian Ocean, not far from where the impactor fell. She was drilling the sea floor for cores that might carry records of past impacts and mass extinctions. They'd spent their honeymoon on her research ship. He wanted to call her, but he couldn't tell her anything. She was too far for him to reach her anyhow. You can imagine how he felt."

"Why isn't he here?" Tanya asked. "Cloned like us?"

"Because of her. They were desperately in love. She had promised to give up her own career when the station was finished, and be with him, but she didn't want to be cloned. She said one of her was enough. We have his tissue in the cryostat, but she had never given hers. He didn't want to be cloned alone."

He made a stiff little face.

"I wasn't so eager myself. I did leave a cell specimen, but I'm no scientist. No expert at anything. I was arranging to give my place to a noted anthropologist, but he was out of reach when that day came, off on a dig in Chile. And, well—"

He drew a long breath when he moved again.

"I did get back to the base. So did your natural parents. We fueled the ship and loaded what we could. Kell stopped the mob. We got away in time. I'm not sure I was ever really glad, or anybody was."

He shook his head, looking down at Dian.

"I remember your mother, after we were safe in space. She had opened her laptop to write something and found she couldn't. She sat huddled over it till Dr. Wu gave her something that put her to sleep."

"Your silly mother." Arne made a face at Dian. "My father was braver."

"Maybe not." My father laughed. "Pepe's father was the cool one. He was our pilot. He took us all the way out to orbit before he gave the controls to Cal DeFort. He'd brought a liter of Mexican tequila. He shared it with Kell and Mona, and finally slept till we got to the Moon."

"It's dreadful to see." Dian gazing up at the Earth, speaking almost to herself. "The rivers all running red, like blood pouring into the oceans."

"Red mud," my father said. "Silt colored red by all the iron that came from the asteroid. Rain washes it off the land because there's no grass or anything to hold it."

"Sad." When she looked at him I saw tears in her eyes. "You had a sad time."

"Tell us," Tanya said. "Tell us how it really was."

"Bad enough." He nodded. "Climbing east from New Mexico, we met the surface wave coming around the Earth from the impact point. The solid planet was rippling like a liquid ocean. Buildings and fields and mountains were jumping toward the sky and dissolving into dust.

"The impact blew an enormous cloud of steam and shattered rock and white-hot vapor up through the stratosphere. Night had already fallen on Asia. We passed far north, but we could see the cloud, already fading and flattening, but still glowing dull red from the heat inside.

"Clouds had covered all the Earth by the time we came around again. A rusty brown at first, but the color faded as the dust settled out. Higher clouds condensed till the whole planet was bright and white as Venus. It was beautiful." His voice fell. "Beautiful and terrible."

"Everybody?" Whispering, Dian wiped at her tears. "Was everybody killed?"

"Except us." His plastic head nodded very slowly. "The Robos here at the station recorded the last broadcasts. The impact made a burst of radiation that burned out communications halfway around the planet. The surface wave spread silence farther.

"A few pilots in high-flying aircraft tried to report what they saw. The Robos picked them up, but I don't know who was left alive to hear anything. Radio and TV stations went off the air, but a few hardy souls kept on sending to the end. A cruise liner in the Indian Ocean had time to call for help. We picked up a reporter's video of the shattering Taj Mahal.

"An American astronomer had guessed the truth and called the media. We caught a White House spokesman trying to deny it. Just a sudden solar flare, he said. His voice was cut off before he finished. Watching from a thousand miles up, we saw the great wave rolling up out of the Atlantic. It washed all the old cities off the coast. The last words we heard came from White Sands. A drunk signal technician wishing us a merry Christmas."

Tanya asked, "What happened to Mr. DeFort?"

"I don't think he cared." My father shrugged. "He'd fought too long to get the station built and felt too sad for all he had lost. Most of all he grieved for his wife. He was never happy here. Never slept much. He spent half his time in the dome, looking back at Earth. It was still a huge white pearl, dazzling with sunlight but mottled with volcanic explosions. We never saw the surface. The third year, he decided to go back—"

Arne was startled. "Was he crazy?"

"We begged him to wait till the clouds broke enough to let him look for a safe spot to land. He kept imagining survivors somehow hanging on. Finally Pepe took us down. I went along to keep a video narrative. Under the clouds, all we saw was death. The heat of the impact had burned cities and forests and grasslands. Oceans had risen as the polar ice thawed. Lowlands were flooded, coastlines changed. The land looked like you see it now, black and barren, bleeding red mud into the seas. No spark of green anywhere.

"He had Pepe land us on the shore of a new sea that spread far into the Amazon valley. I got a whiff of the air when we opened the lock. It had a burnt-sulfur stink and set us all to coughing. In spite of it, he was determined to get samples of mud and water to test for any surviving microscopic life.

"We had no proper breathing gear. He tried to improvise, with a plastic bag around his head and an oxygen bottle with a tube to his mouth. Pepe and I watched from the plane. Jagged black lava sloped down from a smoking cone north of us. No sunlight anywhere. A thunderstorm was towering in the west, alive with lightning.

"Cal carried a radio. I tried to copy what he said, but the plastic made him hard to hear. He tramped down to the water, stooping to pick up rocks and drop them in his sample bucket. 'Nothing green,' I heard him say. 'Nothing moving.' He looked at the volcano behind him and the blood-colored waves ahead. 'Nothing anywhere.'

"Pepe was begging him to come back, but he muttered something I couldn't make out and stumbled on over the frozen lava, down to a muddy little stream. Squatting there at the edge of it, he scraped up something for his bucket. We saw him double up with a coughing fit. He got back to his feet and waded on down the beach, into a surf that was foaming pink.

" 'Sir!' Pepe called. 'You've gone too far.'

"He waved a sample bottle and slogged on into the foam.

" 'Our best chance for a new evolution,' he said. The plastic blurred his voice. 'If anything is left in the sea.'

" 'Please!' Pepe begged again. 'While you can. We need you.'

" 'Not to cry.' I heard his muffled laugh. 'Don't forget you're all immortal.'

"His voice was strangled from a new wave breaking over him. He tried to get his breath, tried to say something else I didn't get. He lost the radio and his bucket. He did turn back and stumble a few yards toward us before he tripped and fell. The oxygen bottle floated away. We saw him grabbing for it, but the next wave took it out of reach."

"You left him there?" Dian's voice rose sharply. "Left him to die?"

"He was already dead." My father shrugged. "His own choice, I think. He knew the danger, but his spirit was dead. He was grieving for his wife. He let that last wave carry him under. We saw him later, far out in the surf. Just a glimpse before he went under again. Pepe wanted to look for his body, but that could have killed us both. We had no oxygen gear."

"The air?" Arne asked. "What's wrong with the air?"

"Volcanic fumes, and maybe cyanide. I caught the scent."

"Cyanide?" Pepe frowned. "What put it there?"

"The impact object, I suppose. There's cyanogen in cometary gases."

"Poison air!" Arne turned pale. "And you want us to go back?"

"Not till you are grown, but that's why you were born. To help nature heal the planet." He looked down gravely at Arne. "Your father was the terraformer. He knew green plants could do our work. They use the energy of sunlight to generate free oxygen. If none of them are left, you must replant them."

5

We are a younger generation. Born in the maternity lab, growing up in our narrow pits and tunnels under the station dome, we have listened to our parents and read the letters and notes and diaries they left for us. We have studied the books and disks in Dian's library and the precious relics in her museum. The Robos have let us see the underground shops and hangars where they will build the spacecraft to take us home when the time for that has come. I think we have recovered some sense of our own identity and our noble mission.

How many years have passed since the great impactor fell? If the Robos and our holo parents know, they have never told us, but the clouds that veiled the Earth have cleared. An ice age has come and gone. The Robos, observing it through the instruments in the dome, have found it once more warm enough for human life.

The station is a lonely little prison, but our childhood has generally been happy enough. We know our parents only as images in the holo tank, but they always seemed alive and seemed to love us. My father's character had two sides. The impact hurt him as terribly as it hurt the Earth. He never wanted to talk about that dreadful last day on Earth, but he grew more cheerful in mood when he spoke about our mission.

"It's why we're here," he used to say. "Our kind of life on Earth had taken billions of years to evolve. The impact erased it, everything but us. We are all there is. You were born to build it back. The society. The culture. The civilization. The whole biocosm. A terrible responsibility. Maybe too big for you to understand till you know more about it."

More than once he had us stand in line before the holo

tank, the Robos who served us in a silent line behind us.
He made us raise our right hands and promise solemnly
to obey the mother computer, to return to Earth when she
commanded us, and to give our lives to our great task.

"It won't be easy," he told us, "but life is rare in the
universe. For all we know, we may be here alone. Promise
me that you'll never let it die."

We promised.

Our parents took turns in the tank, teaching us all they
could. Our Robos, never in the tank, were with us all the
time. My Robo taught me to spell, taught me science and
geometry, counted time when I was working out in the
centrifuge.

"Never mind the sweat," he used to tell me. "Build the
body you're going to need. I may last forever, but you're
only human. You must work to stay alive."

Pepe's Robo father taught him the multiplication tables
and rocket engineering and fighting skills that left him
quick with his wits and quick on his feet.

"To make you fit," he said, "to do what you must do."

Pepe liked to compete. He was always begging to try
his boxing skills on Arne and me. Better than I was, he
kept beating me till I'd had enough. Arne was big and
quick enough for punches that would send him sailing all
the way to the wall in the Moon's low gravity, but that
didn't matter. Not to Pepe. He always came back for
more.

Tanya's Robo cloned her a cat for a pet and taught her
how to care for a baby-sized doll, taught her biology and
the genetic science that might help her replant and repeople the Earth. Working in the maternity lab, she learned
to clone frogs and dissect them, but she refused to dissect
any kind of cat.

Arne's Robo helped him learn to walk, tried to teach
him the astronomy and geology he needed to understand
what the asteroid had done to Earth and what we must do

for its recovery. His first experimental project was a colony of cloned ants in a glass-walled ant farm.

"You'll learn from it," his holo father told him. "All life evolved as a single system, one great symbiotic biocosm. All its parts depend on the others, the way a human body does. Green plants free the oxygen we breathe. We exhale the carbon dioxide they need. The impact wiped nearly everything off the Earth. Our job is to carry back the seed and spores and cells and embryos that will bring it back to life."

Arne shrugged and grunted.

"I've made my own biocosm for my ants."

My own holo father, when he was my teacher, appeared as a slim man in a brown corduroy jacket, wearing a neat little beard. Counting push-ups when I worked out in the centrifuge, he looked younger and wore a red sweat suit and had no beard. He had a pipe but never smoked it, because his tobacco was gone and they had brought no seed. A good thing, he said, but still he missed the pipe.

Except for the gold plate on her flat chest, Tanya's Robo looked like all the others, but her holo mother was tall and beautiful, not flat-chested all. She had bright gray-green eyes and thick black hair that fell to her waist when she left it free.

In the classroom holo tank, teaching us biology, she wore a white lab jacket. In the gym tank, teaching us to dance, she was lovely in a long black gown. Down at the pool on the bottom level, she appeared in a red swimsuit she used to wear into my dreams.

There was no real piano, but she sometimes played a virtual grand piano, singing her own songs of life and love on Earth. Tanya grew up as tall as her mother, with the same bright greenish eyes and sleek black hair. She learned to sing in the same rich voice. We all loved her, or all of us but Dian, who never seemed to care if anybody loved her.

Dian's holo mother, Dr. Diana Lazard, was smaller than Tanya's, with a chest as flat as the nameplate on her Robo. She wore dark glasses that made her eyes hard to see. Her hair was a red-gold color that might have been beautiful if she'd let it grow longer, but she kept it short and commonly hid it under a tight black tam.

Her Robo cared for Dian deftly enough, but it was her holo mother who taught us French and Russian and Chinese, and tried to share her love of literature and art.

"Knowledge. Art. Culture." Her everyday voice was dry and flat, but it could ring with passion when she spoke of those treasures and her fear that they would be forever lost. "Guard them like your lives," she urged us. "They matter more than anything."

In her classes, we put on VR headsets that let her guide us over the world that had been. In a virtual airplane, we flew over the white-spired Himalayas and dived to skim the river that had cut the Grand Canyon and crossed the ice desert of Antarctica. We saw the pyramids and the Acropolis and the newer Sky Needle. She guided us through the Hermitage and the Louvre and the Prado.

She wanted us to love them, to love all the Earth had been. Dian surely did. Growing up in her mother's image, she cut her hair just as short, kept it under the same black tam, wore the same dark glasses. Glasses she needed to shield her eyes from the glare of Earth, she said, though she was seldom in the dome to see Earth at all.

If she cared for anybody, it was Arne.

His holo father, Dr. Linder, had been a football quarterback whose athletic scholarships had set him on his way to degrees in physics and geology. Just as combative and just as smart, Arne ran every day on the treadmill in the centrifuge. He learned all that our parents taught and wore the VR gear to tour the lost world and played chess with Dian. Perhaps they made love; I never knew.

We had no children. They had never been in DeFort's

plan. The maternity lab, as Tanya's mother explained, was only for us clones. The Robos gave us contraceptives when we needed them.

Tanya did. Our biologist, she understood sex and enjoyed it. So did Pepe. From their teens, they were always together, never hiding their affection. Yet Tanya was generous to me. Once, dancing with her in the gym, I was so overcome with her scent and her voice and her lithe body in my arms that I whispered what I felt. With Pepe glaring after us, she led me out of the room and up to the dome.

The Earth was new, a long curve of red fire slashed across the cold and soundless night, lighting the dead moonscape to a ghostly pink. In the dimness of the dome, she stripped to reveal her enchantment, and stripped me while I stood trembling with a dazed elation.

In the Moon's mild gravity, we needed no bed. She laughed at my ignorance and proceeded to teach me. Expert at it, she seemed to relish the lesson as keenly as I did. We were a long time there, the dance over and only the Robos awake when we went back down. Kissing me a long good night that I never forgot, she whispered that practice might make me be better than Pepe. Sadly, however, she never invited me to practice.

She must have given Pepe consolation enough, because he held me no grudge. Afterward, in fact, he seemed more amiable than ever, perhaps because of our shared devotion. He got on less well with Arne, who played his endless chess with Dian and roamed the old Earth in his VR cap to study DeFort's plan for restoring the planet. He wanted to be our leader.

The leader, of course, should have been DeFort's clone, but he had never wanted to be cloned without his wife. The Robo with his name on the white plate stood dead in its corner of the stockroom, gray beneath millennia of moondust.

The year we were twenty-five, our Robo parents gathered us into the tank room. We found our holo parents already there, all in their most formal images and looking very serious.

"The time has come for your first flight to Earth." My father spoke for them, or perhaps the master computer. "Your training is complete. Remote readings show the ice age ended. The Robos have fueled a two-place moon jumper and loaded it with seed pellets. Two of you will go down, taking off when you are ready."

"I am." Glancing at Tanya, Pepe raised his voice. "Today, if we can."

"You are the pilot." My father smiled and turned to Arne. "Linder, you will go to begin the reseeding."

Flushing pink, Arne shook his head.

"Have you forgotten who you are?" My father grew severe. "Our chief terraformer. Sowing new life is the vital first step, to rekindle evolution and let nature do her work. Or ours."

Arne's jaw set hard, and he shook his head again.

6

A rne was still shaking his head, scowling at our parents in the holo tank. Dian stepped to his side and slid her arm around him.

"We have to go," Pepe told him. "Have you forgotten why we're here?"

"Damn DeFort!" Arne's lip jutted stubbornly. "His crazy plan doesn't fit the facts. Maybe he was smart as anybody, but still he got surprised. The asteroid was bigger than he ever imagined. It not only sterilized the planet, but shattered a lot of the crust. That left seismic instabilities that still cause quakes and volcanoes. It's still recovering, the ice caps receding, but I think we ought to let it wait for another generation."

"Arne!" Tanya shook her head in pained reproof. "Its albedo says it's warm enough. Ready for us now.

"If you believe albedos."

Our holo parents stood frozen in the tank, their eyes fixed on Arne as if the master computer had never been programmed for such a rebellion, but Tanya made a face at him.

"Arny Barny!" Mocking him, her voice turned shrill as it was when she was three. "Under all the bluff, you've always been a fraidy cat. Or are you just a yellow-bellied coward?"

"Please, Tanny." Pepe touched her arm. "We're all grown up." He turned very soberly to Arne. "And we can't forget why Dr. DeFort put us here."

"DeFort's dead."

"Given time, we'll all be dead." Pepe shrugged. "But really, if you think what old DeFort meant us to be, we don't really have to care. No matter when and how we die, we can always be replaced by another generation."

"I'm not ready to be replaced." Arne had flushed with emotion, but he shook his head at Tanya with a sort of forced deliberation. "You call me a coward. I'd rather say prudent. I know geology and the science of terraforming. I've spent thousand of hours surveying the Earth with telescopes and spectroscopes and radar, studying oceans and floodplains and lowlands.

"And I've found nowhere fit for life. The seas are still contaminated with heavy metals from the asteroid, the rivers still leaching more lethal stuff off the continents. We'd find the atmosphere unbreathable, oxygen depleted, carbon dioxide levels that would kill you, sulfur dioxide from constant new eruptions: climates too severe to let life take root anywhere.

"I see no place for any kind of life, at least for now. If we've got to make some crazy effort in spite of all the odds, at least let's wait for another ten or twenty years—"

"Wait for what?" Tanya cut in more sharply. "If an ice age wasn't long enough to cleanse the planet, what kind of miracle do you expect in just another ten or twenty years?"

"We can gather data." Arne dropped his voice, appealing to reason. "We can update the plan to fit the Earth as we expect it to be in ten or twenty thousand years. We can train for our own mission, if we must finally undertake it."

"We've trained." Pepe waited for Tanya to nod. "We've studied. We're as ready as we'll ever be. We're going. I say now."

"Not me." Arne hugged Dian to him, and she smiled into his face. "Not us."

"We'll miss you." Pepe shrugged and turned to me. "How about it, Dunk?"

I gulped and caught my breath to say okay, but Tanya had already clutched his arm. "I'm the biologist. I understand the problems. I've found masks ready for us in the stockroom, if we do need oxygen masks. Just take me down. I know how to sow the seed."

They took off together, Pepe flying the spaceplane, Tanya filing radio reports as they surveyed the Earth from low orbit. She described the shrunken ice caps, the high sea levels, the shifted shorelines that made familiar features hard to recognize.

"We need soil where seed can grow," she said. "Hard to pinpoint from space if it does exist at all. Rocks do crumble into silt, but the rains are scouring most of that into the sea for lack of roots to hold it. We'll try to seed from orbit, but I want to land for a closer look."

Dian asked them to look for any relics of human civilization.

"We're a little late for that." Tanya sounded sardonic. "Ice and time have erased the great pyramids, the big dams, the great wall of China. Everything large enough to look for."

"No surprise," Arne muttered. "The impact has remade the Earth, but not for us. It may never be fit for human life."

"That's our job." Pepe's voice. "To make it fit."

"A brand-new world!" Tanya's irony was gone. "Waiting for the spark of life."

On the mike, Arne had technical questions about spectrometer readings of solar radiation reflected from the surface and refracted though the atmosphere, questions about polar ice, about air and ocean circulation. It was all data, he said, that we ought to record for the next generation.

"We're here to replant the planet." Tanya grew impatient. "And now we're too low over the equator to see all that much. So far there's nothing useful we can say about atmosphere or ocean circulation patterns. At least we can see that the planet is pretty wet. Heavy clouds hide most of the surface. We'll need the radar to search for a landing site."

Arne never said he wished he had gone down with them, but he kept on with his questions till I thought he felt guilty.

Dropping into an orbit that grazed the atmosphere, they sowed the planet with life-bombs, heat-shielded cylinders equipped with parachutes and loaded with seed pellets coated with fertilizer.

Clearing weather over east Africa revealed a narrow sea in the Great Rift Valley, which seemed to have deepened and opened wider. Tanya wanted to land there.

"The most likely spot we've seen. It ought to be warm and wet enough. The water looks blue, probably fresh, with no sign of any great pollution. Besides, it happens to be near the spot where Homo sapiens evolved. A symbolic location for a second creation, though Pepe says I was crazy to bother about it.

"He says our work is already finished. We've scattered seed on every continent and dropped algae bombs into all the major oceans. He says we'll have to let nature take care of the rest, but I'm still the biologist. I want to collect soil and air and water samples to help with the next attempt if we have to try again.

"Arne ought to be here." She was serious, with no sarcasm. "He's the geologist who would understand the consequences of the impact. He's the terraformer, more expert than we are. And he's missing the thrill of his life."

Elation bubbled in her voice.

"We feel like gods. Coming down from the sky with the gift of life for the stricken world. Pepe says we ought to head back to the Moon while we can, but I won't—I can't—give up the actual landing."

Beginning the final descent on the other side of Earth, they were out of contact while I bit my nails for an hour.

D own safe!" Tanya was exuberant when we heard her again. "Pepe set us down on the west shore of this Kenyan sea. A splendid day with a high sun and a great view across a neck of the water to a wall of dark cliffs and the slopes of a new volcanic mountain almost as tall as Kilimanjaro. A tower of smoke is climbing out of the cone. The sky above us is blue as the sea, though maybe not for long. I see a storm cloud rising in the west."

She was silent for a moment.

"Another thing—a very odd thing. Landing on its tail, the plane stands tall. From the cockpit we can see far out across the sea. Most of it calm, there's an odd little patch of whitecaps. Odd because they're moving toward us, with no sign of wind anywhere else.

"I can make out—"

Her voice broke off. I heard the quick catch of her breath and Pepe's muffled exclamation.

"Those whitecaps!" Her voice came back, lifted sharply. "Not whitecaps at all. They're something—something alive!"

She must have moved away from the microphone. Her voice faded, though I made out a few words of Pepe's.

". . . impossible . . . nothing green, which means no photosynthesis, no energy for our kind of life . . . with oxygen so depleted . . . we've got to know . . ."

I caught nothing else till at last Tanya was back at the mike.

"Something swimming!" Her voice was quick and breathless. "Swimming at the surface. We can't see much except the splashing, but it must have descended from something that survived the impact. Pepe doubts that any large creature could live with so little oxygen, but anaerobic life did evolve on Earth before there was free oxygen. Survivals were found in the thermal vents on the ocean floors. The black plumes, the giant tube worms, the bacteria that fed them—"

I heard Pepe's muted voice. The mike clicked, went dead, stayed dead while Dian and Arne came up to listen with me.

"Something has cut them off!" Dian shuddered. "An attack by those swimming things?"

"No way to know, but I did try to warn them." Arne must have repeated that a dozen times as the hours went by. "The planet simply isn't ready for us. It may never be."

I suggested that we think of a rescue flight.

"We'd be fools to go." Arne shook his head. "If they need help, they need it now, not next week. We don't know they're in trouble. We don't know anything. Our duty is to stay here, gather the data we can, record it for a generation that may have a better chance."

"I'm afraid," Dian whispered. "I wish—"

"Wish for what?" Arne snapped. "There's nothing we can do. Nothing but wait."

We waited forever, till the mike clicked at last and we heard Pepe's voice.

"Navarro here, on board alone. Tanya's been off the plane for hours. In her breathing mask, collecting whatever she can. With oxygen so low and all this carbon dioxide, she does need the mask. I've begged her to come back before her air runs out.

"But she's fascinated with those swimmers. We watched one crawling up out of the water. Something like a red octopus, though she says it looks no kin to any octopus that ever existed before the impact. A mass of thick, bloodred coils, too far off for us to see it well. It splayed itself on the beach and lay still in the sun.

"Its energy source is what puzzled her most. She wondered if it might have some kind of photosynthetic symbiote in its blood. Something red instead of green, that feeds on solar energy. I don't see any way for her to tell, but she's still out there with her binoculars and her video and her sample bucket.

"I've begged here to call it a day and come back with what she has, but she always needs a few more minutes. At first she stayed near the plane, but now she's working toward the beach. Taking crazy chances the way DeFort did so many million years ago.

"She wants a closer look. The red things are amphibians, she says. A dozen of them out there now. An unexpected life-form that she thinks could be a problem to the colonists when they come. Leave it to them, I told her, but she wants to learn all she can.

"The beach is mud, silt washed down off the hills in the west. She says the things are digging in it, maybe for something they eat. She wants to see. But now—"

His voice lifted and stopped while he must have been watching. I heard no more till he came back at last, his voice faint but urgent as he spoke to Tanya, begging her to get back to the plane. The future could wait. She had gone too far down the beach. The mud was deeper than it looked. Her air had run low. The creatures could be dangerous. She could watch them from the cockpit till she knew them better. More faintly still, I caught her answer.

"Just another minute."

For a long-seeming time I heard nothing at all.

" 'One more minute.' He echoed her words when he raised his voice for us again. "Too many minutes. She ought to get back while she can. It's close to night. That storm in the west is rolling down on us. The wind's getting up. A few raindrops already—

"Stop, Tanny! Stop!" His voice went high. "Mind the mud."

"Give me just another minute." Her radio voice, so faint I hardly heard it. "These creatures—they're a new evolution. We've got to know what they are before we come again. Never mind the risk."

"I mind it," he called again to her. "Tanny, please—"

He stopped for something from her that I failed to catch. For a time he was silent again, except for the rush of his rapid breath.

"Navarro again." His voice came back, bitterly resigned. "She keeps slogging on toward those queer things ahead. At first they sprawled motionless under the sun, but now they're moving. One of them rushing at another, jumping in a way you'd never expect. The other dodged and sprang to meet it. Now—"

He stopped to watch and shout another warning.

"She won't listen. The things are really quite a show. They look legless, maybe boneless, but amazingly active and quick. A riddle, if they need no oxygen. But I wish—"

He yelled again, and waited.

"What are they doing? From here they're a crazy tangle of long red tentacles roiling the mud. Fighting? Mating? She has to know. Binoculars now, then the camera. She's too close. Getting useful data, maybe, but I don't like this mud. Maybe bottomless, with no plant life to hold it. Her feet are sinking in it. She's stumbling, struggling—

"My God!" He was screaming into the microphone. "Hold still! I'm coming."

"Don't!" Her voice came thinly, desperate yet oddly calm. "Pepe, please! Get back to the Moon. Report what you can. Don't mind me. There'll be another clone."

I heard the whir and clang of the lock, and then nothing at all.

1

The robots slept. Perhaps another million years, or ten million; if the master computer counted years it never told us. Only it stayed awake to monitor the sensors and revive the Robos when it found the Earth green enough for us to be born again. Growing up again in the narrow cells carved so long ago into the Tycho rim, we listened to the Robos and the holos and struggled once more to understand what we were.

"Meat robots!" Arne was always the critic. "Created and programmed to play God for old DeFort."

"Hardly gods." Tanya was bright and beautiful and sure of nearly everything. "Maybe only clones, but we're at least alive."

"Only clones." Arne mocked her. "Meat copies of the holo ghosts in the tank."

"Better than copies," Tanya said. "Genes aren't everything. We're ourselves."

"Maybe," Arne muttered. "But still slaves of old DeFort and his idiot plan."

"So what?" Tanya wore a thick sheaf of sleek black hair, and she tossed it scornfully back. "Crazy or not, it's the reason we're here. I expect to do my bit."

"Maybe you, but why should I care?"

"If you really need to know, just listen to your father."

We all had seen his father's image in the tanks. Dr. Arne Linder, a bronze-bearded giant and a distinguished geologist back before the impact. We'd read his books in Dian's library. *Formation of the Earth-Moon System*, about how the Earth and the Moon had been created from impacting planetesimals. *Earth Two*, an optimistic proposal for terraforming and colonizing Mars.

Born in old Norway, he had married Sigrid Knutson, a

tall blond beauty he had known when they were children. We learned more about his life from Pepe's journal. The warning caught them in Iceland. Flying back to the Moon base, he begged Pepe to drop him off in Washington, where his wife was a translator in the Norwegian embassy.

He had left her pregnant, their first child due. He felt frantic to be with her, but Pepe said they had no time for a stop anywhere. They fought in the cockpit. Pepe was only a lightweight David to Arne's Goliath, but he had won his way out of the barrio in the boxing ring. He knocked Arne out and got them to the base in time.

"A dreadful thing for Arne," Dian said. "He never got over grieving for letting Sigrid die alone."

All that was long ages past, though it became vivid reality when we watched the old holos. We are a new generation, learning our destined roles once again from our holo parents and the records our vanished siblings had left in Dian's library files.

"Somos los mismos," Pepe used to say. We were never created quite the same, yet the mission of the station always helped us find old identities. Old garments, Pepe said, a comfortable fit when we put them on. At least for most of us. Arne never shed his clone father's bitterness. While the greener Earth had always beckoned the rest of us with its promise of magnificent adventure, he never learned to love the mission. Even as a child, he used to haunt the dome, scowling at the Earth through the big telescope.

"Those black spots," he used to mutter, and shake his head. "I don't know what they are. I don't want to know."

They were dark gray patches scattered here and there across all the continents. The instruments showed only naked rock and soil, bare of life.

"Only old lava flows, most likely," Tanya said.

"Cancers." He muttered and shook his head. "Cancers in the green."

"A silly notion," she scolded him. "We'll find the truth when we land."

"Land there?" He looked sick. "Not if I can help it!"

Our holo parents had been too long in the computers to show much concern with such current problems, yet the Earth they had known became very real to us. Working for DeFort's Robo Multiservice Corporation, my father had traveled all over the world. His videos of the monuments and history and culture of Russia and China and other old nations held an eerie fascination, yet I never much liked watching them. They left me too full of sadness for all that was gone.

He never spoke much about himself, but I found more about him from a long narrative, an odd mix of fact and fiction, that he had dictated to the computer. He called it *The Last Day*. Writing for a future he hoped might want to know about the past, he spoke of his family and everybody he had known, telling about their lives and what they had meant to him. That was the fact, as true as he could make it.

The fiction was their final moments. One chapter was about Linder's wife. Best man at their wedding and dancing with her at the reception, he felt haunted by her fate. The baby had come, he imagined, while Arne was in Iceland. She was already at home from the hospital, trying to reach him with her news, when DeFort called on that last morning.

Though he told her nothing about the falling asteroid, his haste and his tone of voice alarmed her. She tried and tried again to reach Arne at his hotel in Reykjavik. He was never there. Frantic, she tried to call friends at the White Sands Moon base. The phone lines were jammed. Listening to the radio, watching holo stations, she learned of the communications blackout spreading over Asia. The baby sensed her terror and began to cry. She nursed it and crooned to it and prayed for Arne to call or come home. When the holophone rang, it was a friend in flight operations at White Sands, who thought she would be relieved to know her husband was safe. He had just gotten aboard the escape plane.

She must have felt relief, my father thought, but also dreadful despair. She knew she and the baby were about to die. Trying not to feel that he had betrayed her, she prayed for him. With the wailing baby in her arms, she sang to it and prayed for its soul till the surface shock brought the building down upon them.

Hearing the emotion in my father's voice, I shared something of his sorrow, a grief that always touched me whenever we climbed into the dome to see the reborn Earth and talk of how to restore it. Pepe and Tanya never returned from that first attempt. When my clone self wanted to undertake a rescue flight, Arne balked. Twenty years later, however, another Pepe had dropped another clone of my own into low orbit to see what they could.

"A few tiny spots of green." The voice on the video was an eerie echo of my own. "On the Amazon and Mississippi deltas. On the new islands that ring the great crater the asteroid left. Even a green dot at the edge of that sea where Tanya and Pepe were lost. Lost for nothing, Arne says. He says our old biocosm was built of symbiotes, species that existed in harmony, dependent on one another. He thinks we'll never belong in the new one."

Listening to those words, it's strange to recall that another geologic age has passed since then. Our instruments have never revealed anything more of those anomalous creatures Tanya and Pepe had seen crawling out into the sun, but they did find that something green had grown.

The depleted oxygen had been replenished. Spinning its swift days and nights high in our black sky, Earth waxed and waned through our long months, dazzling when it was full on the jagged Tycho rim and the gray waste of pits and rocks below, waning slowly to a thin sliver of fire in our endless nights. Its seas looked clean and blue again. The polar caps and the great storm spirals shone white as they always had. Something green had belted the equatorial lands and spread far toward the poles in the summer hemispheres.

Though we shared the same genes as our clone siblings, we were never entirely like them. The elder Tanya and Arne had been cold to each other, she in love with Pepe, he playing a lot of chess with Dian, and perhaps a more intimate game they kept to themselves. Adoring Tanya myself, I'd had only that one miraculous moment with her.

Grown up again, all three of us were in love with Tanya. Perhaps Pepe was again her favorite, but she never seemed to favor him. Wanting no jealousies to cloud our mission, she gave us equal turns with her.

The elder Tanya and Pepe had left us no records. Dian, a very private person, had written only of the library, the museum and her legacy for the future. Arne had left his own cynical philosophy. Helping DeFort plan and equip the survival station, he had never hoped or wanted to survive any actual disaster.

"Arrogance!" he had written in his diary. "Anthropocentric arrogance. Pepe and Tanya found a new biocosm already blooming. We have no right to harm it. Doing so would be a crime worse than genocide."

The new Arne laughed when I asked what he thought of that passage.

"Another man writing, a million years ago. I've read the record of his life, but he's a stranger to me. Frankly, I don't get what he saw in Dian, if they really were in love. All she cares about now is her dusty books, her frozen art, and chess with her computer."

When the master computer had my father announce that the time had come for our return, he gathered us in the library reading room.

"First of all," Arne asked, "are we really going back?"

"Of course we are." Tanya spoke sharply, irked at him. "That's the reason we exist."

"An overblown dream." His nose tilted up. "The impact was not the first. It won't be the last. A new evolution has always replaced the loss with something better. That's nature working as it should. Why should we meddle?"

"Because we're human," Tanya said.

"Is that so great?" He sniffed at her. "When you look at the old Earth, at all the wanton savagery and genocide, our record's not so bright. Pepe and Tanya found a new evolution already in progress. It could flower into something better than we are."

"Those black monsters on the beach?" She shuddered. "I want our own kind to win."

Arne looked around the table and saw us all against him.

"If we're going back," he said, "I'm the leader. I know terraforming."

"Maybe." Tanya frowned. "But that's not enough. We'll have to get down into low orbit and make a new survey to select the landing site. Pepe is the space pilot." She smiled at him. "If we make a safe landing, we'll have things to build. Pepe is the engineer."

We voted for a leader. Dian raised her hand for Arne, Tanya for Pepe. When that left me to break the tie, I named Tanya. Arne sat scowling till she warmed him with a smile. Voting on the landing site, again we chose the coast of that same inland sea. Pepe picked the day. When it came, we gathered in space gear at the spaceport elevator. Only three of us at first, anxiously eager, impatiently waiting for Arne and Dian.

"She's gone!" Arne came running down the passage. "I've looked everywhere. Her rooms, the museum, the gym, the shops, the common rooms. I can't find her."

8

The robots found her in her space suit a thousand feet down the crater's inner wall. She had struck jagged ledges, bounced and rolled and struck again. Blood had sprayed the faceplate, and she was stiff as iron before they got her back inside. Arne found a note on her laptop.

"Farewell and good fortune, if any of you miss me. I've chosen not to go because I see no useful place for me at the Earth outpost, even it you get one set up. I lack the hardihood for pioneering, and even at the best, the colonists will have no time or need for libraries and museums before another crop of clones can grow."

"Hardly true." Gravely, Pepe shook his head. "She was caring for the seed of civilization. The mission means nothing without the heritage she was guarding."

"She loved what she loved," Tanya murmured. "She gave me a gift to carry with me back to Earth. A book of poems by Emily Dickinson. It meant a lot to her and I'll never give it up."

The Robos dug a new grave in the plot of rocks and dust outside the crater where our parents and our older siblings had lain so long, beside them the sad little mounds that covered my beagles. We buried her there, still rigid in her space gear. Arne spoke briefly, his voice hollow and somber in his helmet.

"I do miss her. It's a terrible time for me, because I think I killed her. I've read the diaries of our older selves. We have been in love. I think she loved me again, though she never really told me, or said much to anybody. Perhaps I should have guessed, but I'm myself. Not any elder brother. Maybe I'll do better if we're ever born again."

"I hope we'll all do better." Tanya tried to comfort him. "But we can't help being what we are."

We watched the robots fill the grave and delayed the launch again while he made a marker to set at the head of it, a metal plate that should stand forever here on the airless Moon, bearing only this legend:

DIAN
CLONE OF DIANA LAZARD

"Clone!" His voice in the helmet was a bitter rumble. "That's all we are."

"More than that," Tanya protested. "We're as human as anybody. More than human, if you think of our mission."

"Not by choice," he grumbled. "I wish old DeFort had left my father to die on Earth."

Muttering and swallowing whatever else he wanted to say, he knelt at the foot of the grave. The rest of us waited silently, isolated from one another in our clumsy armor, yet thinking of Dian.

I felt that I myself had failed her. Shut up in her own tiny world of the lost past, she had seemed content with the precious artifacts she cared for. I had spent many an hour with her there, but never really got to know her.

Arne got back to his feet and Tanya led us from the cemetery to the loaded plane. Our five individual Robos had to be left on the Moon to care for another generation, but the sixth, the one DeFort had not lived to program, came with us. We called it Calvin.

From orbit, we studied those dark blots again.

"They've changed since we were children," Arne said. "Moved and maybe grown. I can't image what they are, but I don't think the planet's ready for us."

"Ready or not—" Tanya grinned and leaned to slap his back. "Here we come."

"I can't imagine—" He muttered again, scowling at the

ulcerated Earth, ominous and huge on the telescope monitor. "I can't imagine what they are."

"Bare lavas, maybe, where the rains have left no soil where anything could grow?"

"Do bare lavas move?"

"Maybe burns?" She waited for her turn to study the readouts. "The spectrometers show oxygen levels higher now than before the impact. More oxygen could mean hotter forest fires."

"The air looks clear." He scowled and shook his head. "No smoke from any fires."

"So let's go down." She shrugged. "I want to find out."

She had Pepe drop us into a landing orbit above the equator. The great African rift had widened again in the ages since our elder twins landed there. The sea had risen, covering the mudflat where they died.

"We'll land there again," she decided, "on our next pass."

"Why?" Arne demanded. "Have you forgotten those red monsters?"

She shook her head. "I'd like to see how they've evolved."

"Another danger." He pointed at the monitor. "Don't you see that black area just west of the rift?"

"I do. Something else we have to see."

"So close? Can't we pick a safer spot till we've had time to look around?"

"If it's a challenge, I want to meet it and cope with it now."

Arne had been watching the spot for years as it crept out of central Africa, erasing what he thought was dense rain forest. He begged Tanya to let him study it longer from low orbit, but she had Pepe set us down on the bank of a new river, just a few miles from that narrow, cliff-walled sea.

We rolled dice to be first out of the plane. I won with

a seven and opened the air lock. The air was good, spiced with scents new to me. I stood a long time there, staring west across the grassy valley floor to the forested slope and sharp volcanic slopes that edged the rift, till Tanya nudged me to make room for her.

Pepe stayed on the plane, but the rest of us climbed down. Tanya picked blades from the grass at our feet and said they were almost the same Kentucky Blue she and Pepe had sowed so long ago. When we looked through binoculars, we saw nothing they had planted. Massive palmlike trees lifted feathery jade-green plumes and enormous trumpet-shaped purple blooms out of a dense tangle of thick crimson vines.

"A jungle of riddles," Tanya whispered as she studied it. "The trees could be descended from some cactus species. But the undergrowth?" She stared a long time and whispered again, "A jungle of snakes!"

I saw them at last, when she passed the binoculars to me. Writhing like rooted snakes, they wrapped the black stalks of things that looked like gigantic toadstools and kept striking out as if to catch invisible insects.

"A new evolution!" Tanya took the glasses back. "Maybe evolved from the swimming things we saw on that beach a million years ago? The color may be due to a red mutant photosynthetic symbiote. I want a closer look."

"Don't forget," Arne muttered. "Closer looks have killed you."

We saw nothing else moving till Pepe's radio voice came from the cockpit, high above us. "Look north! Along the edge of the jungle. Things hopping like kangaroos. Or maybe like oversize grasshoppers."

We found a creature venturing warily over a ridge, standing tall to look at us, sinking out of sight, hopping on toward us to stand and stare again while it purred like a huge cat. A biped, it had a thick tail that balanced its forequarters and made a third leg when it stood. Others came slowly on behind it, jumping high but pausing as if to graze.

"Our retrojets must have scared them away," Pepe called again. "But now! Farther up the slope. A couple of monsters that would dwarf the old elephants. And half a dozen smaller, maybe younger."

"Do you think they're a danger to us?" Arne called uneasily.

"Who knows? The big ones have stopped to look. And listen, too. They've spread ears as wide as they are. I hear the leader roaring at us. They do look able to smash us if they like."

"Should we take off?"

"Not yet."

Arne had reached for the binoculars, but Tanya kept them, sweeping the edge and the riverbank and the herd of hopping grazers while we waited.

"A wonderland!" She was elated. "And a puzzle box. We must have slept longer than I thought, for all this evolutionary change."

Arne climbed back into the plane when the larger creatures came into view and came back down with a heavy rifle he mounted on a tripod. A weapon DeFort had hoped we would never need. He aimed it at them, squinting through the telescopic sight.

"Don't shoot," Tanya said, "unless I tell you to."

"Okay, if you tell me in time."

He held the rifle on the things till they stopped a few hundred yards from us. Armored with slick purple-black plates that shimmered under the tropic sun, they looked a little like elephants, but more like military tanks. The tallest came ahead, spread its winglike ears again, opened enormous bright-fanged jaws, bellowed like a foghorn.

Arne crouched behind his gun.

"Don't," Tanya warned him. "You couldn't stop them."

"I could try. No time to take off."

He kept the gun level. We watched those great jaws yawning wider. A thunderous bellow scattered the hoppers. She caught his shoulder and pulled him away from his weapon. The monster stood there a long time, watching us through huge, black-slitted eyes as if waiting for an answer to its challenge, till finally it turned to lead its family on around us and down to the river. They splashed in and disappeared.

"Nothing I expected." Tanya stood frowning after them. "No large land animal survived the impact, but perhaps sea creatures did. The whales were prehistoric land dwellers that migrated into the sea. Perhaps something like them has returned to the land. Maybe to breed, if they're amphibian."

The alarmed hoppers settled down. Tanya had us stand still in the shadow of the plane as they grazed in toward us, till Pepe shouted again.

"If you want a killer, here it comes!"

The hopper leader stood tall again, with a kind of purring scream. The grazers reared and scattered in panic. Something swift and tiger-striped pounced out of the grass and darted to overtake a baby before it could leap again. Arne's rifle crashed, and the two tumbled down together.

"I told you," Tanya scolded him. "Don't do that."

"Specimens," he said. "You'll want to take a look."

He stayed with the gun while I went on with Tanya to study his kill. No larger than a dog, the infant hopper was hairless, covered with fine gray scales, its body torn open and entrails exposed. Tanya spread them on the grass for my video camera.

"It's well shaped for its apparent ecological niche." She shook her head in frustration. "But that's about all I can say. We must have had fifty or a hundred million years of change."

The killer was a compact mass of powerful muscle, clad

in sleek striped fur. She opened its bloody jaws to show the fangs to my cameras, had me move the body to show the teats and claws.

"A mammal." She spoke for the microphone. "Descended perhaps from rats or mice that somehow got through alive."

Still aglow with elation when we got back to plane, she forgave Arne for the killing.

"A wonderland waiting for us!" she told him. "An open home for the new humanity, but as new and strange as Mars used to look."

"And likely just as hostile," he muttered. "A brand new biology where I'm afraid we'll never belong."

"We'll see." She shrugged and looked around again at the sea where the great amphibians lived, and at the jungle that had bred the killer. "We're here to see."

She set the Robo to scraping soil from the top of a rocky knob to level a site for our lab and living quarters. We unloaded supplies and set up a geodesic dome while the robot began cutting stone for a defensive wall. She took me on short expeditions along the shore and up the ridge to record her reports on the flora and fauna we found. Only a few weeks had passed before she was asking Pepe about fuel for the plane.

"We're equipped to produce it here," he told her, "from nearly any organic stuff."

"The reserve still aboard?"

"It might get back to the Moon, with half a drop left in the tanks."

"With only two aboard?"

"Probably safe enough." He frowned at her. "But I like it here."

"So do I." She grinned at his puzzlement. "I think we've come home to stay. I want you to go back for what we need to replant our own biocosm. Seed, frozen ova and embryos, equipment for the lab."

"You call this home?" Arne scowled at her. "With that black spot just over the ridge."

She shrugged. "It's a risk. We'll always face risks. We must cope if we can. And leave our records for the next generation if we can't." She turned to me. "You'll go back with Pepe. Holograph the data you have and what we can send you. Stay there to hold the fort for another generation."

"And leave us?" Arne wasn't ready for this. "Just the two of us?"

"Pepe will be back," she told him. "You have work enough here. Testing soils for our first crops. Prospecting the area for oil and ores we'll need."

Pepe and I went back to the Moon. My beagle, Earthman, who had been left in the Robos' care, was happy to have me back. The Robos loaded and refueled the plane. Pepe took off again and left me alone with Earthman.

I wasn't used to solitude. The Robos were poor companions and the holos had nothing new to say, but Earthman was a comfort and the news from Earth kept me absorbed for a time.

Tanya reported that Pepe had inflated another geodome to house a hydroponic garden. Arne had surveyed land for a farm. When the rainy season ended, Robo built a diversion dam to draw irrigation water from the river.

"Arne enjoys shooting a yearling jumper when we need meat," Tanya said. "A tasty change from the irradiated stuff we brought from the Moon. The hippo-whales come and go between the river and the grass. They stopped twice to stare and bellow, but they ignore us now. I think our tiny human island really is secure, though Arne still frets about the black spot. He's gone now to climb the western cliffs for a look beyond the rim."

Her next transmission came only hours later.

"Arne's back." Her voice was tight and quick. "Exhausted and in panic. Something chased him. A storm, he calls it, but nothing we can understand. A cloud so dark it hides the sun. A roar that isn't wind. Something falling that isn't rain. He says our days on Earth are done."

9

The monitor went blank. All I heard was static. Outside the dome, Earth hung full in the lunar night. I saw Africa slide out of sight, watched the black-patched Americas crawl through an endless day, watched till Africa returned, and finally heard Tanya's voice.

"We're desperate."

Her face was drawn haggard and streaked with something black. In the window beyond her head, I saw a dead black slope reaching up to the dark lava flows that edged the rift valley.

"The bugs have overwhelmed us." Her voice was hoarse and hurried. "Bugs! They're what made the blighted areas that always worried Arne. You must preserve the few facts we've learned, information that will surely be important when our clone siblings are born to try again.

"These marauding insects have evolved, I imagine, from mutations that enabled some locust or cicada to survive the impact. Evidently they enter migratory phases like some of our ancient locusts. A strange life cycle, as I understand it. I believe they're periodic, like the seventeen-year cicada, though I think with a far longer period.

"I think they must spend decades or even centuries underground, feeding on plant roots or juices. Emergence is triggered, perhaps, when they begin to kill too many of their hosts. Emerging, they're voracious, consuming everything organic they can reach and then migrating to fresh territory to leave their eggs and begin another cycle.

"Their onslaught on us was sudden and dreadful. They darkened the sky, swarming over us. Their roar became deafening. Falling like hail, they ate anything that had ever been alive. Trees, brush, grass, live wood and dead wood, live animals and corpses. They coupled in their excrement, buried their eggs in it, died. Their bodies made a carpet of dark rot. The odor was unendurable.

"We're safe in the plane, at least for now, but total desolation surrounds us. The bugs ate the plastic geo-domes and all our supplies inside. They ate the forest and the grass. They killed and ate the hoppers, bones and all.

"They shed and ate their wings. They died and ate the dead. They're all gone now. Nothing alive but their eggs in the dust, waiting for wind and water to bring new seed from anywhere to let the land revive, while they hatch and multiply and wait to kill again.

"Dark dust rises when the wind blows now, bitter with the stink of death. The hippos came out of the river, wandered forlornly in search of anything to graze, and dived back in. Nothing alive is left in sight so far as we can see. Nothing but ourselves, in a silence as terrible as their bellowing.

"How long we can last, I don't know. Arne wanted to give up and get back to the Moon, but there's no fuel for it. We have no supplies for any long trek across this devastation, but Pepe has ripped metal off the plane and welded it into a makeshift boat. If the bugs didn't get across the sea, perhaps we can make a new start beyond it.

"The plane must be abandoned, with our radio gear. This will be our last transmission. Keep your eye on the Earth and record what you can.

"And Dunk—" With a catch in her voice, she stopped to wipe at a tear. "I can't wish you were with us, but I want you to know I miss you. Next time, whenever that comes, I hope to know you better. As Pepe likes to say, *Hasta la vista!*"

Till we meet again. The phrase was bitter irony, because she knew that would never happen. They may have a chance, if the bugs fail to follow them across that sea. They are resourceful. They will give it their best. I can beg the computer to have the Robos build another ship and take it down with fresh supplies, but it is unlikely to take orders from me.

I am here, alone with the computer, my beagle, and the Robos. The computer was never programmed for human company, although it does have all our records of the lost Earth and the efforts of our own generations to let it live again. I can watch the videos and listen to the holos. Earthman is a good companion, but he is already aging and I have no skills to make another clone. The Robos will try to care for me as long as I live, but they will feel no grief when I am gone.

A thousand years later, we are yet another generation. Much of Earth is still darkly scarred, but those dark spots are gone from Africa and Europe. We're going back again, all five of us, carrying a cryostat filled with seed and cells to replant the planet. Dian is bringing holo copies of her precious artifacts, along with a library of tapes and disks and cubes.

We're landing on the delta of the Nile. It drains into the Red Sea now, but its valley is still a vivid green slash across red-brown desert. Pepe has picked a landing spot a little north of where the pyramids stood.

We're overloaded. Pepe says we've had to spend so much fuel on survey and landing that we can't get back to the station, but we're prepared to stay. Dropping into low orbit, we've searched for life.

"Technology!" Pepe's shout of triumph rang from the cockpit on our first pass above the Nile. "They've got technology. I heard radio squeals and whistles, and then a burst of weird music. I think our job is done."

"If it is—" Staring through the telescope, Dian murmured the words in awe, almost to herself. "A new civilization ready for us. I hope—I do hope—"

"Maybe." Doubtfully waiting for his turn at the telescope, Arne shook his head. "We haven't met them yet."

"Maybe?" Pepe mocked him. "We came to meet them, and I think they'll have enough to show us. I see a lot of bright lines across the ancient delta. Some run all the way to the river. Canals, I imagine. And—"

His voice caught.

"*Mira!* Look at that! A pattern of closer lines. Maybe the streets of a city." He was silent as Earth rolled under us. "Buildings!" His voice lifted suddenly. "It is a city. With the sun shifting, I can make out a tower at the center. A new Alexandria!"

"Try for contact," Tanya told him. "Ask for permission for us to set down."

"Down to what?" Arne frowned. "They didn't ask us here."

"What's the risk?" Dian asked him. "What have we got to lose?"

Pepe tried when we came around again.

"Squeals." Frowning in the headphones, he made a face of wry frustration. "Whistles. Scraps of eerie music. Finally voices, but nothing I could understand. If it's still English, accents have changed."

"There!" Tanya was at the telescope. "Out in the edge of the desert, west of the city. A pattern like a wheel."

He studied it.

"I wonder—" His voice paused and quickened. "An airport! The wheel spokes are runways. And there's a wide white streak that must be a road into the city. If we knew how to ask for permission—"

"No matter," she told him. "We've no fuel to look much farther. Put us down, but out beyond the runways where we won't damage anything."

On the next pass, we glided down. The city roofs raced

beneath us. Red tile, yellow tile and blue, aligned along stately avenues. The airport skittered toward us. We were low above the tall control tower when I felt the heavy thrust of the retrorockets and we tipped down for a vertical landing. Thundering fire and steam hid everything till I felt the jolt that stopped us. The rocket thrust gone, we could breathe again. Tanya opened the cabin door to let us look out.

The steam was gone, though I caught its hot scent. I rubbed the sun dazzle out of my eyes and found spiny clumps of yellow-green desert brush around us. The terminal building towered far off in the east. We stayed aboard, uneasily waiting. At the radio, Pepe got hums and squawks and shouting voices.

"Probably yelling at us." He twirled his knobs, listened, tried to echo the voices he heard, shook his head again. "Could be English," he mustered. "Angry English, from the sound of it, but I can't make anything out."

We sat there under the desert blaze till the plane got too hot for comfort.

"They won't know—" Arne shrank back from the door. "They can't know we brought their forefathers here."

"If they don't," Tanya said, "we'll find a way to tell them."

"How?" Sweating from more than the heat, he asked Pepe if we could take off again.

"Not yet," Pepe said. "Not till we must."

Tanya and I climbed down to the ground. Spaceman came with us, running out to sniff and growl at something in the brush and slinking back to tremble against my knee. Arne followed a few minutes later, standing in the shade of the plane and staring across the brush at the distant tower. A bright red light began flashing there.

"Flashing to warn us off," he muttered.

I had brought my camera. Tanya had me shoot clumps

of the thorny brush and then a rock matted over with something like red moss.

"Data on that crimson symbiote reported by the last expedition." She spoke crisply into my mike. "Surviving now in a mutant Bryophyte—"

"Hear that?" Arne cupped his hand to his ear. "Something hooting."

What I heard was a pulsing mechanical scream. Spaceman growled and cowered closer to my leg till we saw an ungainly vehicle lurching over a hill and rolling toward us on tall wheels, flashing colored lights.

"Now's our chance," Tanya said. "To show them what we've brought. Show them we mean no harm."

Clumsy under the heavy gravity, we climbed back into the plane and came down with our offerings. Dian carried one of her precious books, the poems of Emily Dickinson, wrapped in brittle ancient plastic. Tanya had a little holo projector and a box of cubes. Arne brought a loudhailer, perhaps a copy of the same one Kell had used to warn the mob away from the escape craft. Pepe stayed in the cockpit.

"We come from the Moon." Arne pushed ahead of us to meet the vehicle, bawling through his hailer. "We come in peace. We come with gifts."

The vehicle had no windows, no operator we could see. Spaceman ran barking to meet it. Arne dropped the bull-horn and stood in front of it, waving his arms. Hooting louder, it almost ran over us before it swerved and rolled on around us to butt against the plane. Heavy metal arms reached out to grab and tip it. Pepe scrambled out as it was lifted off the ground. The hooting stopped, and the machine hauled it away, while Spaceman whimpered and huddled against my feet.

"Robotic, I guess." Pepe stared after it, scratching his head. "Sent out to salvage the wreck."

Baffled and afraid, we stood there sweating. Flying insects buzzed around us. Some of them stung. Tanya had me get a close-up of one on my arm. A hot wind blew out of the desert, sharp with a scent like burnt toast. We started walking toward the tower.

"We're idiots," Arne muttered at Tanya. "We should have stayed in orbit."

She gave him no answer.

We plodded on, battling the gravity and swatting at insects, till we came over a rocky rise and saw the wide white runways spread out ahead, the tower at the hub still miles away. Parked aircraft scattered the broad triangles between the flight strips. A few stood upright for vertical landing and ascent, like our own craft, but most had wings and landing gear like those I knew from pictures of the past.

We dropped flat when a huge machine with silver wings came roaring over us, stopped again when a silent vehicle came racing to meet us. Arne lifted his bullhorn and lowered it when Tanya shook her head. Brave again, Spaceman growled and bristled till it stopped. Three men in white got out, speaking together and staring at him. He stood barking at them till one of them pointed something like an ancient flashlight at him. He whined and crumpled down. They gathered him up, and took him away in the van.

"Why the dog?" Arne scowled in bafflement. "With no attention to us?"

"Dogs are extinct," Tanya said. "New to them."

"Hey!" A startled cry from Pepe. "We're moving!"

The parked aircraft beside the strip were gliding away from us. Flowing without ripples, without a sound, with no mechanism visible, the slick white pavement was carrying us toward the terminal building. Pepe bent to feel it with his fingers, dropped to put his ear against it.

"A thousand years of progress since we came to fight

the bugs!" He stood up and shrugged at Tanya. "Old DeFort would be happy."

Scores of people were leaving the parked aircraft for the pavement. Men in pants and skirtlike kilts, women in shorts and trailing gowns, and children in rainbow colors as if on holiday. Though I saw nothing much like our orange-yellow jumpsuits, nobody seemed to notice. People streamed out of the terminal ahead. Most of them, I saw, wore bright little silver balls on bracelets or necklaces.

"Sir?" Arne called to a man near us. "Can you tell us—"

With a hiss as if for silence, the man frowned and turned away. They all stood very quietly, alone or in couples or little family groups, gazing solemnly ahead. Pepe jogged my arm as we came around the building and onto a magnificent avenue that led toward the heart of the city. I caught my breath and stood gawking at a row of immense statues that stood down the middle of the avenue.

"Look at that!" Arne raised his arm to point ahead. "I think they do remember us."

A woman in a long white gown gestured sternly to hush him, and the pavement bore us on toward a tall metal needle that stabbed into the sky at the end of the avenue. A thin crescent at its point shone like a bright new moon. Statues, needle, crescent, they were all bright silver. A bell began to boom somewhere ahead, slow deep-toned notes like far thunder. The murmur of voices ceased. All eyes lifted toward the crescent. I saw Pepe cross himself.

"A ceremonial," he whispered. "I think they worship the Moon."

I heard him counting under his breath as the bell pealed. "Twenty-nine," he murmured. "The days in a lunar month."

The soundless pavement took us on till he started and jogged my arm again, pointing at the statue just ahead.

More than magnificent, a blinding silver dazzle in the slanting morning sun, it must have been a hundred feet tall. Shading my eyes, I blinked and looked and blinked again.

It was my father. In the same jacket his image had worn when it spoke from the tank, waving the same tobacco pipe the image had waved to punctuate the lectures. Pipes, I thought, should be no more than magic symbols now; DeFort had saved no tobacco seed.

Those nearest the statue dropped to their knees, kissing their lunar pendants. Eyes lifted, they breathed their prayers and rose again as we moved on toward the next monumental figure, even taller than my father's. It was Pepe himself, in the flight jacket his natural father had worn to the Moon, one gigantic arm lifted as if to beckon us toward the needle and the crescent. People pressed toward it as we passed, kneeling to kiss their pendants and pray.

"He never dreamed." His own eyes lifted, Pepe shook his head in awe. "Never dreamed that he might become a god."

Tanya came next, taller still, splendid in the sunlit shimmer of her lab jacket, flourishing an enormous test tube. Arne next, waving his rock-hunter's hammer. Finally Dian, the tallest, holding a silver book. I heard our actual Dian gasp when she read the title cut into the metal.

The Poems of Emily Dickinson.

Below the needle and the crescent, the pavement ended in a vast circle ringed with massive silver columns. Slowing, it crowded all of us closer together. At a single thunderous peal, people stood still, gazing up at a balcony high on the face of the spire.

A tiny-seeming figure in bright silver appeared there, arms raised high. The bell pealed again, echoes rolling from the columns. His voice thundered, louder than the bell. The worshipers sang an answer, a slow and solemn chant. He spoke again, and Pepe gripped my arm.

"English!" he whispered. "A queer accent, but it's got to be English!"

The speaker stopped, arms still lifted toward the sky. The bell pealed, its deep reverberations dying into silence. People around us fell to their knees, faces raised to the crescent. We knelt with them, all of us but Arne. He stalked on forward, bullhorn high.

"Hear this!" he bawled. "Now hear this!"

People around him hissed in protest, but he strode on toward the tower.

"We are your gods!" He paused to let his voice roll back from the columns. "We live on the Moon. We have returned with gifts—"

A tall woman in a silver robe came off her knees to shout at him, waving a silver baton. He turned to point at us.

"Look at us!" he shouted. "You must know us—"

She waved the baton at him. His voice choked off. Gasping for breath, he dropped the bullhorn and crumpled to the pavement. The woman swung the baton toward us. Dian rose, waving her book and declaiming Dickinson:

This is my letter to the world
That never wrote to me—

Dimly, I recall the desperate quaver in her voice, the hushed outrage on the woman's face. She swept us with the baton. A puff of mist chilled and stung my cheek. The pavement seemed to tilt, and I must have fallen.

10

For a long time I thought I was back at Tycho Station, on the bed in our tiny clinic. A robot stood over me, as patiently motionless as our old Robos. A fan hummed softly. The air was warm, with an odd fresh scent. I felt a sense of groggy comfort till a tingling on my face brought recollection back: that avenue of gigantic silver figures, the stern-faced woman in her silver robe, the icy mist from her silver baton.

Shocked wide awake, I tried to get off the bed and found no strength. The robot tipped its lenses, bent to catch my wrist and take my pulse. I saw the difference then; its slick plastic body was the pale blue of the walls, though it had nearly the same shape as our Robos on the Moon.

Earth gravity turned me giddy. The robot eased me back to the bed and seemed to listen when I spoke, though its answer was nothing I could understand. When I stirred again, it helped me to a chair and left the room to bring a human physician, a lean dark man who wore a silver crescent on a neat white jacket. Briskly efficient, he listened at my heart, felt my belly, shook his head at what I tried to say and turned to leave the room.

"My friends?" I shouted at him. "Where are they?"

He shrugged and walked out. The robot stood watching. When I was able to stand, it took my arm to guide me outside, into a circular garden ringed by a circular building. Its lenses followed intently while I walked gravel paths through strange plants that edged the air with odors new to me. The other doors, I thought, might be hiding my companions, but it caught my arm when I tried to knock. When I persisted, it drew a little silver baton clipped to its waist and beckoned me silently back into the room.

Under its guard, I was treated well enough—for a prisoner. Though my words meant nothing, it nodded when I rubbed on lips and my belly, and brought a tray of food: fruits that we had never seen on the Moon, a plate of crisp brown nut-flavored cakes, a glass of very good wine. I ate with a sudden appetite.

Silent most of the time, now and then it burst into speech. Clearly, it had questions. So did I, desperate questions about these remote children of ours and what they might do with us. It seemed to listen blankly when I spoke, and locked the door when it left the room, with no hint of any answers.

Haunted by our colossal images along that monumental avenue, I slept badly that night, dreaming that they were lumbering in hot pursuit while we fled across a lifeless landscape pitted with deep craters those black insects from a millennium earlier had eaten into the planet.

Terror of the huge icons chilled me. Did they want to sacrifice us in that sacred circle? Drown us in the Nile? Feed us to the insects? Freeze us into silver metal and stand us on guard against the next invasion of heretic clones? I woke up shivering, afraid to know.

Next morning the robot brought an odd-looking machine, and admitted a slim, quick little woman who looked a little like Dian, though she was wrinkled and dark from a sun that never shone below our Tycho dome. Perhaps a sort of nun, she wore a tall silver turban and fingered a silver moon pendant when anything irked or puzzled her. She set up the machine to project words on the wall.

The moon is distant from the sea,
And yet with amber hands
She leads him, docile as a boy,
Along appointed sands.

Familiar words. I'd had heard Dian recite them in a tone of adoration, though I was never sure just what they meant. They became stranger now, as the woman chanted them like a prayer. She repeated them two or three times in the same solemn tones and then read them more slowly, watching through dark-rimmed glasses to see my response, until at last I nodded to a spark of recognition. Vowel sounds had simply shifted. *Moon* was *mahan, sea* was *say*.

She came back again and again, using her machine to teach me like a child. Even as the words became familiar, everything else was baffling: plants and animals, clothing and tools, maps of the world and the symbols of math. Yet at last I was able to ask about my companions.

"Uhl-weese." She frowned and shook her head. *Unwise*.

When I tried to tell her we were visitors from the Moon, she scolded and pitied me. Fingering her sacred pendant, she spoke of the paradise the Almighty Five had made of the Moon, where the blessed dwelt in an everlasting joy not meant for such as me. Pretenders who unwisely tried to steal holy authority were to be consumed forever by the black demons in their hell beneath the earth.

In olden days, she told me darkly, my errant soul might have been cleansed with divine fire. In these more enlightened times, fortunately for me, those who attempted to misuse the Holy Book were regarded as either psychotics in need of treatment or sinners deserving eternal torment.

She tried to instruct me in the lunar truth and heal my invalid soul. Her medicine was a massive volume in silver boards with theological footnotes on almost every holy word. Dickinson's oriole had become the trickster god, Pepe, who cheated as he enchanted. Dian was not only the All-Mother but also the soul who selected her own society of those blessed to dwell with her in paradise. The book itself was her letter to the world that never wrote to her.

I was unconverted until the day I was walking with the robot in the garden and stepped off the path to pick a purple flower. The robot said "Noot, noot," and took the flower from me, but it had failed to see me palm a little ball of crumpled paper. When I was able to spread it out in the privacy of my bathroom, it was a note from Tanya, written on a blank page torn from her own ancient copy of Dickinson.

They want to think we're crazy, though they have trouble explaining how we got here in a sort of craft they never saw before. My doctor has a theory. He's trying to convince me that we came from South America, which has not yet been colonized. He talks of a lost expedition that set out a couple of centuries ago to fight the black insects there. It seems to have ended with a crash into the Amazon rain forest in an area the insects were just invading. Rescue efforts failed, but he believes we are descended from survivors. He thinks we somehow salvaged or repaired the wrecked craft that brought us back. If we want to get out of here, I think we'd better go along.

I rolled the paper up and dropped it next day where I had found it. In the end we all went along, though Arne held out until Dian was allowed to persuade him. He grumbled bitterly till he found work on a Nile dredge, improving the channel and turning a swamp into new land for docks and warehouses. He says he is happier now than he ever was twiddling his thumbs on the Moon.

Though the ages seem to have erased every relic of our own times, these people are searching their own past for evidence of the Holy Clones. They have given Dian a museum position, where she can make good use of her skills at restoring and preserving antiquities.

Pepe has qualified for a pilot's license, and Tanya has studied methods for the control of the predatory insects. They are gone now with a new expedition to reclaim the Americas.

Though all the history I know is heresy, sternly outlawed here, I've found a university job as a janitor. It gives me access to radio equipment that can reach the lunar station. We can't help hoping that our own silver colossi will endure to watch this new Egypt grow into a better world than our own ever was.

Yet that is far from certain. Arne says it will never happen. Dian has searched Dickinson for anything that might lead these people toward a new enlightenment, but they want no reinterpretation of the sacred text. Tanya says the best we can do is to learn the necessary ceremonials of our worship as the gods we never were, and live our lives out, remaining silent about the station and the truth.

The petty roles we have found here keep us busy. Though we try to stay well apart and avoid any attention that might put us back in danger, we do meet now and then for lunch or dinner in small eating places where common workers gather. We find comfort in one another and some consolation in the knowledge that Tycho Station stands intact on that far-off crater rim.

We like to think we have carried out our mission. The life of Earth has been revived again, after one more great extinction, with no need of another billion years of evolution, which in fact would probably never shape another species much like our own.

We still exist. So do our culture and our science, at least in altered fragments. This odd new world may survive. If not, if things here go badly wrong, if some new peril strikes from off the Earth, the master computer will surely clone us once more, to let us try again.

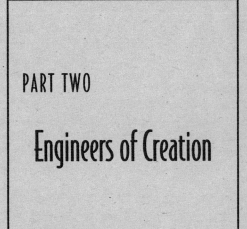

PART TWO

Engineers of Creation

11

Kids can be cruel.

"Hey, Slit-Eyes!" Arne used to yell at Casey. "You're nasty black all over. Go take a bath."

We were creators, my father used to say, cloned to recreate the Earth. One more generation, this time six of us, growing up at Tycho Station on the Moon, we were training for our great mission: to terraform the planet, which had been swept clean of life by the killer impact.

Casey had a Chinese face, black as the lunar sky. Arne liked to tease him for that, though the rest of us were just as different. Pepe was too brown to tan. Tanya had eyes as dark as his, and straight black hair. Arne and Dian were as pale as their holo parents. Casey took the kidding patiently till he heard about his natural father.

We were in the holo room. Speaking from the tank, my own holo father told us the story. The man who called himself K. C. Kell had been a night watchman at the White Sands Moon base in old New Mexico. The falling impactor caught him on duty at the launch site, defending the escape plane from the terrified mob fighting for space aboard. He abandoned that duty in the last frantic minutes and forced his own way aboard with his woman friend, who said her name was Mona Lisa Diamond.

"Casey had a gun," my father said. "His own ticket to the Moon. Cal DeFort had no time or way to get them off the plane. Or off the Moon. He made room for them at the station and finally decided that they had displayed useful genes for survival. He stored their cells in the cryonic vault." He nodded affectionately at Casey. "That's why you're here."

We knew our natural parents from their robots and their images, but we had never seen Kell or Mona until my father booted their holos into the tank. Kell stood there grinning at us, short and muscular like Casey, with the same black Chinese face. He was naked to the waist, the way my father said he came aboard. The tattooed flags of Mexico and China were crossed on his smooth black chest, the name El Chino red-lettered above them.

Mona stood close beside him, his arm around her. Wearing a yellow jumpsuit, she was half a head taller than he, her skin as white as Dian's. Pale gold hair fell around her shoulders. She looked older than Kell, with tired lines around eyes as blue as the seas we could see on Earth. To me she was beautiful. Casey loved her from that first moment. He asked why she hadn't been cloned along with him.

"Ask the computer." My father shrugged. "It makes the choices. But maybe—"

"Maybe what?" Casey asked when my father frowned and stopped.

"The original team members had all been scientists or experts, selected for their fitness for the mission." He frowned at Mona and Kell. "They didn't fit the pattern."

"Why not?"

My father frowned again, hesitating. "Kell didn't like to talk about himself, but he did admit that he had been a hit man for an international narcotics syndicate."

"Hit man? What's that?"

"A professional killer." Even though we had a lot of reference works about Earth, some of the darker aspects of society on the old Earth were strange to us, and my father had to explain. "Lawmakers had forbidden traffic in certain narcotics, drugs that many people wanted to use. Trade in them became an illegal but profitable business that underworld syndicates fought to control. Kell admitted that he had been a gunman and a spy for one of the syndicates.

"As for Mona—"

He nodded at her. Standing together in the tank, she and Kell looked as live as we were. Unlike our own natural parents, however, they had come aboard with no interface software installed in the computer. Their images lacked animation programs to make them interact with us, or even look entirely alive.

"She came from poor hill people on the east side of North America. The name on the passport she showed us was Fayreen Sutt. She had been a dancer. Her manager invented the Mona Lisa name to fit the da Vinci painting she had tattooed on her belly. She and Kell were in trouble with the law. They seem to have come to our New Mexico base with dreams of getting away to the Moon, even before the impactor gave them the opportunity."

"He killed people?" Dian whispered, backing away from Kell's dark and silent image in the tank, which was blind to her. "For money?"

"The old Earth was never peaceful." My father sighed. "People used to fight for power or territory or just because they worshiped different gods."

"Our new world will be better." Casey grinned at my father. "We'll make it better."

"You?" Arne scoffed at him. "You sneaky clone of a black hit man. He's what made the old world bad."

"Maybe he was a hit man." Casey shrugged, trying to be reasonable. "But the men he hit were worse. Men selling bad drugs to innocent people."

"Hah!" Arne snorted. "A hit man's a bad man."

"Maybe he had to be bad." Casey shrugged again. "Because his world was bad. We can make a world where I'll never have to kill anybody."

"So you want to be a coward?" Arne laughed. "Black outside, yellow inside?"

Tanya and Dian were staring at them. Tanya whispered something. Dian tittered. Arne grinned at them and shook his fist at Casey. "If you're afraid to be a hit man, I dare you to hit me."

Casey stood a minute looking hard at Kell and Mona and my father in the tank. I saw his lips quiver as if he wanted to cry, but then his black face set hard.

"Thank you, sir," he spoke very politely to my father. "I'm glad to know my father was El Chino, and proud to be his clone. If he had to be a hit man in that bad old world, I have to do what I have to do right here."

He balled a dark fist and sent Arne toppling across the room, blood streaming from his nose.

Though they were never really friends, Arne and Casey learned to get along, at least most of the time. We listened to our parents in the tank and read the records they had left for us, learning what we were and why we were here, learning science, learning to use the instruments in the dome. Casey studied with us, but he wanted more. He ran the holos of Mona and his natural father, ran them again and again, listening to every word they had recorded. Only ghosts in the tank, they never answered questions, or even seemed to know he was listening, but he made up his own romantic stories about them. He made them heroic.

"I think the bolide came because the old world was so bad," he told me. "People were starving when there was food, people were sick when there was medicine, people were fighting with no good cause. If El Chino and Mona were outlaws, that's because the laws were bad. If they took money from the rich, they gave it to the poor. They were in love, and hunted by evil men trying to kill them. They fought and risked their lives to get on the escape plane. Your father saw how great they were, and saved their genes because the mission needed them. Maybe El Chino was a hit man, but I'm glad to have his genes."

Casey always longed for a way out of our narrow tunnels. He used to climb into the dome and stand gazing down at the hangars and the spaceplanes on the mooncrete flight strip down below the crater rim. He pored over training manuals. When he'd grown large enough, he trained in the flight simulator. He used to get into space gear and cycle out through the air lock.

"I like to climb into a cockpit and study everything," he told me. "When it's time for us to go back to Earth, I want to be the pilot."

That, I thought, was how he meant to prove that he was born with El Chino's survival genes.

The whole staff, all five clones of the last generation, had gone down to Earth a thousand years ago, leaving only Robos to run the station. Now something had struck the planet again. Earth hung huge and still in our dead-black sky when we saw it from the dome, looking nearly close enough to touch. Waxing and waning as we swung around it in our slow lunar orbit, it spun faster through its own days and nights. The face of it was frightening. Even with naked eyes, we saw that green life was gone from the continents. The seas were blue as ever, but the land was white as the blazing spirals of cloud.

"From ice and snow?" Pepe asked my Robo father when he took us up to the telescopes to see the mystery for ourselves. "Another ice age?"

"Something stranger."

"Like what?" Arne asked.

My Robo father himself could seem strange enough to me. He was only a man-sized figure of stiff gray plastic till the computer activated the interaction software installed before the impact, but that could make me forget that he was not as live as I was. Now he stopped and stood frozen till the computer jerked him back to life.

"No data," he muttered. "No revealing data."

We gathered the data we could. Tanya and Pepe searched the computer records of the last thousand years, since our siblings of the last generation had found a human civilization restored at the mouth of the Nile.

"Something hit it," Pepe told us. "Hit it hard."

They had called us into the dome, high on the north rim of Tycho, for their briefing. The full Earth shone huge and deathly white in the dark night sky, the dead crater-scape below us a ghostly gray in its light. We were only in our teens by then, but he and Tanya were already very serious about the mission, with no time to waste.

Pepe was still boyish and slight, still shorter than Tanya, but intense and grave about the problem. Tanya was already a woman, fair-skinned and full-breasted, far more lovely than Dian. I was hopelessly in love with her, heartbroken because Pepe was the one she preferred.

We stood around the big telescope and the monitors with their images of Earth. Pepe reviewed the history of the last expedition. The whole team had gone down to Earth. They never returned. Though much of the planet had been infested with a deadly breed of mutant insects, their radio reports told of a thriving human colony at the mouth of the Nile, grown up around a towering Moon temple and colossal silver statues of five of us.

"Things seem to have gone well for the next four hundred years." Standing beside him at the monitor, Tanya showed us the Earth images the Robo had taken. "The killer insects were finally beaten."

Image by image, the black patches they infested shrank and finally disappeared. Green life spread over all the continents, and the colonists had followed. She magnified spots of East Asia and South America where Pepe pointed out what he said were roads and cities.

"It looked like our work was done," she said. "Till something went wrong. Terribly wrong. In just one year, all that green life was gone. The whole Earth turned to the white you see now."

"It's dead?" Arne glanced up at the bone-white Earth and shrank back from it. "What killed it?"

"We have a clue." She pulled up another image and let the tiny red arrow of her laser pointer dance around it. "Look at that. Tell me what it is."

The laser found a tiny bright dot on the white Earth. The image changed. She found the dot again, black now, on the white waste of tropical India. She twisted a knob to swell it from a dot to a tiny black globe.

"An asteroid?" Arne asked. "So close?"

"Too close," Tanya said. "Maybe it's no asteroid."

Pepe had her run three more frames that caught the object in transit across the full Earth.

"That's enough to bother us." He frowned at the monitor. "The rapid apparent motion puts it in low orbit, down near Earth. We can estimate the diameter, something under one kilometer."

"So?" Arne muttered. "If it's no asteroid?"

"I don't like the shape," Tanya said. "A perfect sphere. Any natural mass that small has too little gravity to shape it like that."

"Unless it's water ice," Pepe said. "Or formed from some other natural melt."

"Something artificial?" Arne glowered at the little black disk, now over the white spiral of a great typhoon on the blue Pacific. "An alien spacecraft? Space invaders that have devastated Earth?"

"We considered that." Tanya shook her head. "But we know we've been alone in the solar system. The stars are so far apart that space war is just too unlikely."

"What else?"

"Riddles," Pepe said. "Looking for answers, we've studied the spectrum of Earth. Atmospheric oxygen content has fallen, carbon dioxide risen. Ice caps have shrunk. Global temperatures are higher. Climates have changed, deserts grown. Though air and ocean circulation patterns showed little change, we see great clouds of white dust that hide whole mountain ranges.

"Riddles." He scowled and shook his head. "No solutions. We see nothing that should have killed the planet, but every sign says it's dead."

The day we turned twenty-one, we gathered again under the station dome. Ink-black shadow pooled in the crater pit. The full Earth stood where it always did, high in the black north sky, blazing down on the cragged wall that curved east and west of our high perch. Africa was a wide white patch on the sea-blue planet. Lake Victoria looked larger than the old maps showed it, a great blue jewel shining at its heart.

Searching again for any hint of humankind, we traced the Nile. Our maps showed the green streak of life it had drawn through the deserts to its delta and the sea. Now it was only a thin dark line. We found no dam, no city, no green of cultivated fields.

The Mediterranean was landlocked now, shrunk to a great salt lake since some geologic spasm had raised Gibraltar. A new bend had diverted the Nile into the Red Sea. The telescope showed a waste of long white dunes on the deserts west of the river, and a plume of white dust that reached far toward Asia. We scanned the site where our siblings had found a new city where Alexandria once stood, and found no hint of anything alive.

My holo father called us down to the tank in the dining room to talk about the mission. Standing at the head of the long table, Arne squinted into his laptop and read his latest data on air temperature, ocean circulation, ice cap retreat, planetary albedo. Casey asked what it all came to.

"I don't know." Big and blond as his Viking ancestors, but perhaps not so bold, Arne bristled as if the question offended him. "I'm afraid to know. I hope we never know."

"We had better know."

"Maybe not." Arne grew very grave. "Consider our responsibility. We've found no native life. The few of us here at the station are very likely the only life left in the solar system. So far as we know the only life in the universe. We must conserve it."

"Our duty to the mission." Very quietly, Casey agreed. "Whatever hit the Earth, we must cope with it. If life has been wiped out, we must bring it back."

"If we can." Arne made a stubborn face. "Whatever killed the planet would likely kill us."

"We've seen no proof of any invaders," Pepe said.

"Whatever happened to Earth," Casey said, "we're here to restore it."

"We're here for the mission." Arne's face had a stubborn set. "We must protect ourselves for its sake. Our duty right now is to gather the data we safely can and record it for later generations—if there are any later generations. We're still young; we have the rest of our lives to do that. Our first priority is to care for ourselves."

"We can do more." Casey shook his head. "We can design landing probes to look for data and send it back. But when the time comes, we'll have to go down to look for ourselves."

"No!" Arne blinked and stiffened. "Think of the danger. Even a probe might expose us. The invaders would have wiped us out if they'd ever found us."

"So?" Casey's voice grew sharp. "What do you want us to do?"

"Keep under cover. Do nothing to give ourselves away. Hope that future generations will know enough about the aliens to get a better break."

"Hope's not enough." Casey gestured to wave Arne's suggestion away. "We don't know that anything alien hit the Earth. If we do nothing, we ourselves defeat the mission. If there's a risk, we have to take it."

"Do we?" Arne tried to argue. "Let's not waste our lives. Certainly not until we've learned all we can. Don't forget that culture on the Nile. Those people were as smart as we are, armed with all our science and technology. They had their chance to save themselves. Till we know why they failed, we can't pretend that the station is immune."

"Suppose we die?" Casey shrugged. "We'll be cloned again."

He didn't mention Mona, but he must have been dreaming of another life with her.

"Unless—" Glaring, Arne shook his head. "Unless the aliens find us."

He demanded a vote. Dian sided with him, but the rest of us stood against them. We agreed to send a light plane with a crew of two to survey the Earth and its vicinity from low orbit, send back reports of what they found, and finally land in north Africa. Casey was eager to pilot the craft. Arne dealt cards to pick the other crewman. The first black jack fell to me.

12

We lifted off together, Casey and I. The crater behind us yawned deep in the Moon's gray face, the long white scars of the impact that formed it spread out to the blazing dark of space. It shrank as we lifted, shrank till the Moon was a dwindling gray ball adrift in infinity. Earth looked smaller still. The Milky Way wrapped us in a diamond-dusted belt of remote and ruthless splendor.

Staring from the cockpit, I cringed with a sudden sick longing for the comfort of our snug little burrow. The void around us was too vast for me, too old and complex and strange. How could the fate of mankind matter in this infinite cosmos where blind chance was king, where another chance bolide might strike at any moment to end all life forever?

"Great." Casey grinned and waved a lean black hand across the waste of stars. He liked to use El Chino's dialect. "Ain't they great?"

His elation was hard for me to share. Even before the takeoff, my own feelings for the expedition had been mixed. I wasn't exactly an eager volunteer. With no special skills of any sort, I was only the mission historian, my job simply to see that good records were kept for the clone generations to come after us. Thinking of the dead Earth and the mystery of its death, I had little hope that we would ever get back to the Moon with any useful records at all.

I'd voted for the effort, however, because the mission required it. And, like Casey, I had little to lose. The others had sorted themselves into affectionate couples: Arne and Dian, Pepe and Tanya. I had no lover to leave behind. Casey had only his dreams of Mona, if the master computer ever cloned them together. Though I sometimes felt that he was too conscious of his outlaw father and too anxious to prove the worth of his genes, we got on together.

His cheerful grin surprised me now.

"*Adiós* to Arne Linder!" He gestured as if to sweep the diminished Moon and Arne's blustery ego into oblivion. "Ain't it a great break for us? Shut up all our lives under the dome like bugs in a bottle, but look at all that!" He stopped for half a minute, turning in his seat to survey the diamond field of stars. "Our own vast playground now."

"Or battleground," I said.

"If we find anybody to fight." He shrugged. "Don't forget my dad. Anybody got in his way was just another job he got paid to do. I'm El Chino again and proud to be. Anybody don't like us there, we'll show 'em what we are."

I wasn't quite so ready, but still glad to have him with me.

Down to geosynchronous orbit, we floated for weeks over the Americas, weeks over East Asia, weeks over Africa. The ice-white land was hard to tell from the polar snows. Searching with binoculars and telescopes and spectrometers, we found no Earthly signs of life, but no alien monsters either.

"Dead," Casey muttered more than once, shaking his head at the bleached world beneath us. "Maybe it's dead forever." Yet his heart for the adventure was never lost for long. He always looked for new clues and explored new plans. "You know, Dunk, I've got the feel of the mission now. It's something great. Worth dying for. Dying a dozen times if that's what it takes. Tell Arne he ought to be with us."

Pepe had promised to track us and have somebody lis-

tening when we were in radio range of the Moon. We
described what we saw, transmitted our instrumental data,
asked for news from those we had left behind. Pepe answered whenever he got a message, but there was never
a word from Arne.

We dropped to lower orbits, rounding the planet every
three hours, then every ninety minutes, swinging north
and south to let us see far toward the poles. Still we discovered nothing green. Crossing North Africa, crossing it
again, we studied the site of that city our siblings had
found on the Nile.

The buildings had crumbled into a glaring white snow-
scape of wind-driven dust, but the streets had left a grid
of faint dark lines along the river's edge. We found the
radial runways at the airport and the road that led through
the city. The gigantic silver statues of our clones as gods
still stood in line along the avenue that led to the temple
of the Moon, though its tower had tumbled to rubble. My
recollection of what my clone father had written about the
landing gave me a strange feeling when I found his monumental figure towering out of the drifts.

"There's Arne, when he used to be a god." With a
sardonic smirk, Casey pointed at an age-stained colossus
that leaned into the dust. "Let's let him know."

The full Moon was out of range, above the dark side
of Earth. We called the station when it came back overhead, waited for an answer that never came, waited and
called again, heard only the rattle and crash of static.

"Tell the Robos," Casey said. "The computer will record it."

I called again, with a code to wake them.

"That's enough," Pepe's voice crackled out of the
speaker. "Sorry, Dunk, but Arne has taken charge. He's
hiding. He doesn't want you calling, doesn't want us to
answer."

"Why not? We've met no aliens."

Each reply took three long seconds to get back from the Moon.

"No matter. He's afraid they're listening."

"Still hunting us, after four hundred years?"

His hurried voice dropped lower. "If you thought you knew Arne, he's gone paranoid. He found Casey's gun. He's ugly with it. Trusts nobody. Orders us all around. He's taken Tanya as well as Dian. Treats me like a slave. Threatens to throw me out in the cold if I cross him. I wish—" His voice caught. "I wish I'd gone with you and Casey."

"Just hold out till we get back."

"Don't!" His voice came sharp. "Don't try to come back. Arne's afraid the aliens might see you and follow you back. Even if you got here, he wouldn't let you in."

Startled, I asked him why.

"He's the alpha male, since you and Casey are gone. He enjoys the job."

"Can't you compete?"

The three-second signal delay grew to half a minute.

"I tried." His voice was hoarse and low when it finally came. "I stole the gun while he was asleep, but Tanya—" Emotion choked him. "She was with him in the bed. She woke and got between us. You know how we were, but now she—she loves him, Dunk. And I can't do a thing."

I tried to ask if he could get away to join us, but his husky voice cut me off before my words had time to reach him.

"It's good-bye, Dunk. I'd like to think Arne's really as crazy as he acts, but—well, you can't really know. He could be right. You say you haven't encountered any aliens, but still you haven't found what killed the planet. The station may really be in danger."

"Or maybe not," I tried to say. "We've heard nothing electronic. I doubt that anything here has the technology to listen."

". . . sorry, Dunk." He hadn't waited for my reply. "Arne wants us off the air. And finally, Dunk—" His voice fell to a whisper. "I hope to know you again in later generations, if no aliens hit us now."

Airbraking to save fuel on the final orbit, we glided over the Indian Ocean and down into Africa's Great Rift valley to land at last on a wide white beach between the ancient cliffs and a freshwater sea. Waves danced on the water, but nothing else was moving.

We stayed aboard two days, gathering data we hoped to save for anybody who came to follow us. The spectroscope showed atmospheric oxygen a little low from lack of green life, carbon dioxide a little high, but nothing strange, no toxins, no microorganisms, nothing to alarm us.

On the third day, Casey ventured off the plane.

"Good luck, Dunk." He took my hand before he suited up. "It's been good fun. You'll soon know if Arne's right about his fatal agent. If I don't get back, keep your records and get them to the Robos. Whatever happens here, I want another chance for us. And my own chance—"

His voice caught.

"My chance to live again with Mona."

I watched while he dug a long furrow in the loose white sand, dropped seed pellets coated with fertilizer, covered them carefully, and knelt a long time at the end of the row. Plodding down to the beach, he brought buckets of water to fill his furrow.

"Test number one." He stood up to call on his helmet phone. "You'll see the results in a week. If life can exist here again, the seed will sprout. You'll see a show of green. If Arne's right, if the world's gone alien, you won't. Now, number two."

"Don't!" I saw him unsealing his helmet. "Wait to watch the seed."

He swept the helmet off and stood grinning up at me, breathing deep. I thought I saw him sway, but he was only bending to get at the seals on his boots. He stripped off the suit and the yellow liner under it. Nude and black, he raised two fingers in the V-signal we had seen DeFort make on the holo after the escape from Earth, shouted something that I couldn't hear, and ran down to the water.

Splashing out till it came to his waist, he dived, learned to stay afloat, paddled so far out I was frightened for him. Wading back at last, he waved at me and lay a long time basking under the sun before he gathered up his gear and climbed back into the air lock.

"A virgin Earth!" He bubbled with enthusiasm. "Swept clean of all the weeds and bugs and rival species our ancestors had to fight. A fresh field waiting for us to plant our own new Eden."

"And Arne's aliens perhaps the new Satan, waiting to hand us the apple."

"Maybe." He shrugged. "I hope not."

Next day I went out with him, our space gear left aboard. Earth! This was a moment I had dreamed about all my life, waiting for it with a mix of eagerness and dread. The sun was high. Its dazzle on the sand and the surf hurt my eyes. I turned my face and felt the wind, the first I ever felt. It was hot, with a dry bite of dust, yet I caught something of Casey's elation.

"Come along!" He darted ahead of me toward the sea. "Out of our little pit in the crater rim, into the universe!"

For all our work in the centrifuge, Earth gravity was still a heavy drag, but I trudged after him and helped carry water to fill the furrow again. I waded out with him when that was done, dived until I finally learned to swim, and then waded out again, and lay resting on the sand till a tingle of sunburn drove me back aboard the plane.

In just a few days the rising sun gave the furrow a faint tinge of green. Green blades thrust up. Leaves unfolded. A bright green line ran through white sand toward the sea. Casey spent his days feeding the plants, raking the soil around them, improvising making tiny tents to shelter any that seemed to wilt under too much sun. He made me call the station to let him rave about their swift growth and the sheer wonder of life. No response came back from the Moon.

We stayed there on the beach through a season of rain and another of sun. The white dust made fertile soil. Casey nursed the plants and rejoiced in the air and sea and sun. I got a tan and built strength to take the gravity. Our plants grew, hardy shrubs and grasses that bloomed and scattered seed. Fired with that promise, we took off again to spend our fuel reserve cruising the planet at stratospheric levels, sowing life-bombs loaded with seed over the continents and oceans.

That done, we came down again to wait out our current lives on the high plateau between the Rift and the Indian Ocean. It's a pleasant spot, though volcanic plumes sometimes tower over Kilimanjaro, far off in the south, and dust storms sometimes turn the sky to milk. Year by year, our small green island spreads wider across the barren plain.

We work together in the garden that feeds us. There's no frost here, and we've brought no pests other than those necessary to the ecology of the growing greenery; there are no weeds. Casey reads Shakespeare and enjoys declaiming great speeches in the style he learned from the holo dramas in the hall of treasures that Dian is hoarding for worlds to come. He is teaching me the martial skills he learned from a holo El Chino left him. Excellent exercise, though perhaps of little use for talk with any aliens that might appear.

We no longer expect trouble from them, but I suppose Arne does. We never get a response from test signals to the station, yet I continue keeping weather and seismic data, writing up the history of our work, beaming reports toward the Moon. Waiting Arne out, we trust that the robots will still be there after he is gone, the computer recording our transmissions for whoever follows us. Casey has sent a message—a love letter, I believe, though he didn't let me read it—intended to be waiting for some future Mona. We do expect to live again.

B

We are a new generation; I can't believe the computer has created them all.

I have died and died again, leaving my bones in unmarked and forgotten places, yet as I read the narratives of our holo parents and our own earlier lives, I can feel that I have always been the same individual self. Always cloned from identical cells in the identical maternity lab, growing up with identical companions in the same lonely pit in the Tycho rim, trained for the same great mission by the same robots and the same holos, we were free from the thousand distractions that used to draw identical twins apart in the old world. I always know that each new life will find its own new direction. Yet, after so many incarnations, I sometimes feel that I am a single immortal.

Often, as I tried to understand Tycho Station and our mission on the Earth, I have wondered about all the events since the great impact that left our natural parents alone with the Robos and the master computer here on the Moon, but I am seldom sure of anything. If the computer counted the past millennia, it has never told us. We study the records our past generations have left, but sometimes they seem incomplete.

Yet our duty seemed clear enough. We intend to do it.

A vast and unknown time has passed since Casey and I sowed new life across the dead planet. Our early years followed much the same track that our clone siblings recorded in their notes and their letters to us, but the Earth has changed enormously. An ice age has held it. Glaciers have spread south from the polar cap to the Himalayas and across most of North America.

Yet Casey and I had not failed. The white dust was gone. We found a broad belt of living green across Australia and southern Asia. Africa and the Americas bewildered us when we had grown old enough to be bewildered.

Our mission to restore Earth looked to be an awesome challenge, but this time the computer had cloned Cal DeFort to help us face it. Perhaps the last Arne, in his dread of possible alien invaders, had expected us to need DeFort, but the current Arne was never happy with him. Cal was a gangly redhead, freckled and pugnacious, bitter because he had no father.

His natural father died on the first landing on Earth, before programs had been created to keep anything of his mind alive in the tank. The robot father designed to care for him had been lost on Earth. When he was growing up, he always tried too hard to make believe he never needed them, yet always felt too proud of who he was.

"You know my dad," he used to boast. "The genius who built the station and saw the impact coming and brought us here to terraform the Earth. I'm him, alive again and still the boss. I always will be."

Arne never agreed. The battles began when they were five years old. They used to get black eyes and bloody noses from knocking each other off the floor in the Moon's light gravity. Arne was taller and bigger and stronger, but Cal was never willing to quit till Dian stopped them to let her look after Arne's bruises. She loved Arne. Cal never seemed to care if nobody loved him.

Our holo parents kept us busy as we grew up, studying the science and skills we would need on Earth. Cal was always eager to get there, to explore the planet and find a site for our first colony. Sad that the first expedition had not been able to leave any animals, because there would be no food for them till vegetation grew, he learned all he could about the frozen embryos and the equipment we would need to breed and nurture them.

His enthusiasm alarmed Arne, who was afraid for anybody to go back, afraid of the alien invaders his elder self had feared, afraid to do anything that might betray the existence of the station. What we saw in Africa and the Americas frightened him.

"Asia looks alive," my holo father said. "The plants we seeded are apparently thriving, ready to feed animals when we can breed them. I hope to feed us. But Africa?" He shook his head with an impatient frustration that made him look ready to climb out of the tank and take off to look at Earth himself. "And the Americas? What the hell has happened to them?"

Looking for answers, we haunted the dome through all our childhood, squinting into telescopes and spectroscopes, pestering the Robos and our parents, keyboarding queries to the master computer itself. The world no longer fit our maps. Glacial ice, piling up on land, had lowered the oceans, dried up the strait between Siberia and Alaska.

The sterile whiteness reported by the last Dunk and Pepe had vanished from Africa, but nothing green had grown to replace it. The Sahara was brown again, but the rest of the continent had turned dark red. The Nile was a narrow red line. Red rimmed the shrunken Mediterranean lake. Scanning the continent, we found grids of faint brown lines scattered over the south, one at the Red Sea mouth of the Nile.

"City streets?" Cal wondered. "And roads running from them, if Arne's aliens do build cities, running out into that red stuff, whatever it is."

"Which means they're still there!" Arne scowled uneasily. "They've killed our kind of life off the planet to let them take it over. They're ready to kill us if they ever detect us."

"Maybe." Cal shook his head. "But Earth's a quarter

million miles away. Too far off to tell us much."

The lower half of North America and most of South America looked just as strange, the land an odd greenish blue, spotted with islands of changing shades of red and orange and gold in patterns turned different every time we looked.

"Nothing I like." Arne scowled at the telescope. "We've studied the spectrographs, Dian and I. We've run computer records." He made an anxious face. "It's an ugly riddle. It may be life, but not our kind."

Casey asked how he knew. Arne had studied molecular biology. He tried to explain that some molecules twist polarized light. He said our kind of protoplasm gave it left-handed rotation. The tests were difficult, he said, and hard to interpret, but he and Dian claimed from their spectroscopic evidence that the life on the Americas was right-handed.

"Alien protoplasm! It must have come from outside the solar system. It could be poison to anybody crazy enough to go down there."

"Count me crazy," Cal told him. "I'm going down as soon as I can."

Cal first said that when he was hardly twelve years old. Arne never wanted anybody to go, but Cal's determination never failed. The year he was sixteen, he began asking the computer to permit an expedition. When we turned twenty-one, it agreed. He called us into the dome to announce that the Robos were getting a plane ready for it.

"Not yet." Arne looked around to see who might stand with him. Dian nodded. "We've got to be cautious. I don't know what has happened to America, but something alien is certainly established in Africa. The same aliens, likely, that sterilized the planet to let them take it over."

"Maybe." Cal shook his head. "We don't know."

"We know enough." Arne's jaw stuck out, covered with a pale yellow stubble. "And I'm afraid of them. Afraid of whatever it is in the Americas. There are too many questions that need more study. I see no reason to risk a landing. Or even to talk about it for another ten or twenty years."

"Ten or twenty years?" Cal snorted. "I'm taking off tomorrow."

"Think again." Arne's voice dropped. "I won't endanger the station and the mission till we know what we face."

"We'll never know unless we look." Casey turned to Cal. "I'll go with you."

"Sorry." Arne glared at then. "I can't allow—"

"Let them go," Pepe told him. "We've hidden long enough."

"I won't—" Arne scowled into Casey's black Chinese face, glanced uncertainly at Dian and saw that he was beaten. He turned abruptly to me. "Okay. Okay. You go with them, Dunk. Keep your records for the future, if we have a future. I'll stay with the girls. We'll keep the station going."

Tanya kissed me good-bye with tears in her eyes.

"Come back, Dunk." She held me close for a moment. "Come back if you can."

I hadn't known she cared.

Over the inviting green vastness of Asia, we considered possible landing sites. Over red Africa, we debated the nature of those faint gray lines. Over the Americas, we were baffled again when we turned the telescope on the blue-green lowlands and the many-colored highlands. Southern Asia welcomed us with vast reaches of rich familiar green.

When we finally landed, it was in the Vale of Kashmir.

"Paradise!" Cal whispered when he climbed down from the air lock and looked around him. "We ought to name it Eden."

The valley floor was a lush carpet of the grasses that last expedition had sowed. Dense forest clothed the lower mountain slopes. Naked cliffs beyond them climbed starkly to the Himalayan peaks that walled us in. We stood silent a long time there, staring up at the snow-crowned summits, inhaling the fresh scents of life, springing on the balls of our feet to test the gravity, stooping to pluck blades of green native grass.

"Damn! Damn!" Breathing deep, Casey stood craning his neck to look at the needle peaks and the azure sky. "I wish I had the words for it."

When the full Moon had climbed over the peaks into radio range, Cal called the station to report that we had found a perfect spot for the colony. A natural fortress, he said, safe from flood and drought and nearly anything but another impact. Its isolation should help secure it from discovery.

"That's enough!" Dian's sharp voice crackled to interrupt him. "Sign off! Arne ordered you not to alert the aliens."

"No aliens yet," Cal said. "No hint of any high technology. Only those lines across the red stuff, almost too faint to follow. We're taking off at dawn for a closer look. We'll let you know what we find."

"Don't!" Arne's angry voice. "Don't throw yourselves away."

"Our heirs will need to know—"

"Stop transmission." His voice rang higher. "Stay on the ground. We won't be coming down to plant any colony, not if you claim a hundred Edens. For the mission's sake, don't give us away."

"Dunk?" Tanya was on the speaker, her voice quick

and anxious. "You've done what you wanted. Can't you come back now? Do you have fuel?"

"Barely enough," Casey said. "If we take off now."

"We're taking off," Cal said. "For Africa and then the Americas. Not for the Moon."

"Dunk—Dunk—"

Her broken voice was cut off.

The ice-walled Vale was splendid by moonlight, but we took off at dawn. High in the stratosphere, alert for hostile action, we cruised over Africa. No radar locked on us. No missiles rose. No craft rose to challenge us. Searching with binoculars, we found dark dots in motion on those thin gray lines. Casey said he had made them out from orbit.

"Traffic," he said. "Roads with something moving on them. Nothing directed at us."

"Cities." He had sketched those puzzling lines and patches on a map of the continent as it had been. There were target patterns of tiny concentric circles, most of them near the coast, three near the mouths of the Limpopo, the Nile, and the Congo, one on the Kenyan plateau, another on the north shore of the Mediterranean lake.

"They have to be cities, because of geography. They stand where we used to live. On rivers or fertile plains."

"So Arne's aliens are really here?" Casey nodded. "And likely not to want us?"

"Could be." Cal frowned at his map. "We don't know. The mission's dead if we do nothing. They may have conquered Africa, but they're still a long way from any colony we might plant in Asia."

Casey was our pilot.

"Pick a point," he said. "And I'll set us down."

We came down at night on the Kenyan plateau near a line on Casey's map that he thought was a road running down to the Indian Ocean from what he thought might be an alien city. When day came, we found a flat plain around us, grown over with what looked like tall red grass. Kilimanjaro stood far off in the south, a mantle of cloud around the white summit. We waited there for hours, watching, listening. We heard no sound, nothing on the radio. A long red ridge cut off our view of the road.

"If anybody saw us," Cal said, "they don't seem to care."

Still in radio range, the waning Moon still high, we called the station. I reported the landing and described what we could see around us. We heard no answer. Cal took the mike.

"There's something here," he said. "We see no indication of any industrial culture, no sign of any technology able to cross space. Whatever they are, the creatures don't build long bridges; their roads don't cross large rivers. We get nothing on the electromagnetic spectrum. I doubt that they are detecting this signal."

We waited half a minute and heard nothing from the Moon.

"I hope for more to add," Cal went on. "We're down only two or three miles from the road. I saw something even closer as we came in. Something that could be a habitation. A circular clearing half a mile across, a dome-roofed building at the center. I'm going out to attempt some kind of contact."

Casey stayed aboard. I climbed down behind Cal, into red vegetation so dense that he disappeared just a few yards away. The air was motionless and oven-hot, almost suffocating. An acrid, bitter scent set me to coughing. In dread of too many strange unknowns, I retreated to the ladder. Thick clumps of saw-toothed blades crowded close round us. Narrow as rapiers and tipped with feathery purple plumes, they had the red-black hue of dried blood. They stood twice our height, and I felt lost among them.

"I've seen enough." Coughing again, I shouted at Cal. "It's no place for people."

"Okay." He looked back through the thorny tangle. "Stay here and report anything that happens. If I don't get back, go on to North America."

Picking a wary way through the blades, he vanished again.

14

Casey and I took turns in the cockpit, waiting for Cal to come back out of that tangle of thorns. The slow sun sank toward blue volcanic cones far west of us. A high anvil cloud rose over Kilimanjaro in the south and spread to hide the sky. A sudden wind whipped the red-black blades. Lightning flickered. Thunder crashed. Rain and hail battered us. The storm passed. Stars came out. I slept uneasily in the navigator's seat until Casey woke me to watch a red dawn break, to watch a red sun rise.

Kilimanjaro stood as serenely high over the crimson landscape as it had stood over our own green world before the impact. No aliens came out of the jungle, but Cal did not return. Our hope began to fade. At noon, over our lunch of the fruit and frozen stuff we had brought from the station, Casey peered bleakly at me.

"Without a weapon, without food or even water—" Gloomily, he shrugged. "I should have gone with him."

"We have his orders," I said. "Report to the station. Go on to look at America."

"So we will." He finished a banana and wiped his lips. "But right now I want to look for Cal." He pulled his boots on. "Give me twelve hours. If I'm not back, take off without me."

Those hours crawled on forever. The afternoon was bad enough, but when the evil spell of that red world began to overwhelm me, a glance at Kilimanjaro could always bring me back to the reality of Earth. After dark I found no escape from the monsters I imagined. Once, trying to break that intolerable anxiety, I opened the lock and looked out.

The blooms that tipped those rapier blades shone faintly, quilting the jungle with a ghostly violet. The night was deathly still till I heard a whisper of wind that scattered blood-red sparks, perhaps pollen grains. The humid air was fouled with a faint but sickening stench I found no name for.

I stood an hour there, listening for Casey's voice, shouting his name on the chance that he was lost and wandering through that alien jungle, until shadows began changing into shapes so monstrous that I shivered from a chill of dread and sealed the valve against them.

The dozen hours he asked for had doubled and more. Dusk was falling again, and my eyes were blurred and swollen, before I saw him stumbling out of that tangle of red-black blades. His clothing was ripped to shreds, his skin scarred and bleeding. He staggered to the ladder. I helped him through the lock. He reeled into the navigator's seat.

"Take us off," he gasped at me. "Take us off."

Of course I couldn't. He had studied astronautics with Pepe's holo father and trained in the simulator. I had not. All I could do was hand him a bottle of water when his haggard eyes fixed on it. He drained it and sank out of the world before he spoke another word.

I watched again as long as I could stay awake. Nothing came to follow him back. He lay snoring in his seat, muttering and jerking now and then as if fighting some invisible enemy. Groggy for sleep of my own, I dropped into the pilot's seat. Sometime in the night he jogged my arm to get me out of his way and lifted us off.

I found snack packets when we were safely in the air, and asked if he wanted to eat. He had me open an aid pack instead. Blood had dried black on long slashes down his arms. His ankle was bruised and swollen. The barbs had left scratches everywhere, swollen and inflamed. He was hot with fever when I touched him. He didn't want to talk, but he let me help him clean the scars and spray them with healant.

It did no good. He was shaking, yet he stayed hunched over the controls, eyes on the instruments. I asked no questions, but at last, when we were in the high stratosphere over the Atlantic, he drew a ragged breath and pulled himself straighter.

"If you want to know—" His voice at first was hoarse and broken. "If you want to know what became of Cal—"

"If you can talk."

"I never found him." His pale lips twisted. "Never did. But you'll need the story for the records—if we live to get them back."

I found the audiorecorder. He sat there a long time, clutching it in a quivering hand before he gathered himself to recite our names, our latitude and longitude, the date. He stopped to draw a long, unsteady breath and shake his head at me.

"We searched from orbit for evidence of possible extraterrestials in Africa." His words were labored and slow when he began, his tone painfully formal, but he spoke more freely as he went on. "Markings we observed from space appeared to be artificial. Down on the savanna between the Great Rift and the Indian Ocean, near what we took to be a traveled roadway, we found ourselves in a dense growth of unfamiliar vegetation. When Commander DeFort failed to return from a probe into our surroundings, I undertook—"

He closed his eyes and sank down in the seat, perhaps groping for the will to continue, perhaps to phrase his words for the computer and our heirs a thousand years from now. I saw him shiver, but he sat straighter and spoke with a clear and even voice.

"I undertook to follow him through that thorn jungle.

It was a dense tangle of dark-red three-edged spears armed with sharp barbs along the edges. It would have been impassable, but the spears stood in thick clumps with a little space between them, far enough apart that DeFort had been able the pick a way through them.

"The soil was loose and sandy. He had left footprints I thought I could follow, yet I had to nerve myself again for the search. The tropic sun burned at the zenith. The air was motionless and oven-hot, and the blooms that tipped the blades bore a nauseating odor that made it almost unbreathable. Sweat drenched me before I had taken a dozen steps. I stopped, looking back at the plane, unwilling to leave it.

"But of course I had to go on. DeFort had been kind to me, even back on Earth before we were cloned; our letters and diaries showed that. He had listened to my story, made a job for me at the station. Arne Linder may want to hear no more from us, but we must get all we could learn back to the master computer. For Cal's sake, anyhow. His own life seemed to matter more to me, there and then, than all the unknown future of the Earth.

"I traced his wandering tracks through the blades for maybe two hours, until I came out into a wide circular clearing that I think is a cultivated field. A small building roofed with a low black dome stands at the center. It's surrounded by curving rows of low-growing black-leafed plants. Plants like nothing in our botany books. The triangular leaves lie flat on the ground. They make star-shaped patterns centered with bright red, apple-sized fruits.

"The field looked empty, but I felt uneasy enough to want a better weapon. With my hunting knife, I cut a spear longer than my body and smoothed the barbs from the base of it to make a haft. Carrying that, I followed DeFort's footprints out across the field. Halfway to the building, I came to the end of the trail.

"He must have struggled. The black leaves were torn and splashed with something red. Perhaps the red was only juice from those red fruits crushed in the struggle, but I think it was his blood. I was kneeling there, trying to interpret the evidence, when I heard a strange bellow and stood up to see something coming fast from the building.

"A thing unearthly as the plants, it was perhaps as large as our old lions and tigers but not much like them. It came hopping high on two thick, long-taloned legs and glided down again on long leathery red bat wings. Its body was covered with slick black scales that glinted crimson when the high sun struck them. It had two heads.

"The larger head had long slit eyes and a great jaw filled with a double row of long fangs that shone like black glass when it yawned to bellow. The smaller, set far back on its shoulders, looked slick and black as the fangs. It had nearly the shape of a human skull, with huge white eyes that caught the sun like mirrors.

"I stared for a moment and turned to run, but it came at me too fast. On the last long glide, it dived around me and dropped ahead to cut me off from the jungle. The mirror eyes had yellow-rimmed pupils that glared at me with a force that paralyzed me. It roared again, with a gust of hot breath that stank like rotten meat. A thin red tongue stabbed at me like a striking snake.

"I crouched and drove my spear into its yawning throat. The tongue coiled around my ankle and jerked me off my feet, but the spear had found something vital. The bellow became a shriek that choked and faded. The creature crumpled down on its side, the black-scaled legs kicking convulsively. The tongue dragged me toward it, squeezing till it almost crushed my ankle, but then relaxed enough to let me jerk loose.

"Scrambling back to my feet, I thought I was free till I saw that skull-shaped second head come off the creature.

Riding the thing, it had held on with four long hooks, sharp red spikes that dripped dark blood when it pulled them out of the creature's back. It rolled to the ground and lay there staring up at me with those huge white eyes. It had a tiny, toothless mouth that mewed at me like a hungry kitten. Unnerved, I just stood there till I saw those spikes gathering under it.

"It was about to jump. I hauled at my spear, but the barbs had stuck it fast in the creature's throat. The spikes were legs, tipped like claws but muscular toward the base. The thing flexed them under it and sprang at me. I caught it with both hands, like a basketball. It felt slick and colder than anything alive ought to be.

"The spikes were slashing at my arms, trying to grab and hang on to me. I threw it like a ball, staggered back, and limped for the jungle. It came hopping after me, mewing louder. My ankle was throbbing, sprained from the grasp of that slimy tongue, but I got to the jungle far enough ahead. Glancing back, I saw it hopping back toward that black dome.

"Back among the thorns, I dropped flat in a little open space and lay there gasping for breath. I felt sick when I thought what must have happened to Cal. That thing's a parasite. A vampire. It drives those spikes into its victims, rides them, sucks life out of them."

He sat for a moment, silent, moodily shaking his blood-spattered head.

"They brought their own biocosm. Nothing in it ever evolved from what we planted in Asia. They're intelligent. And nothing that ought to be here." He stopped to stare at me, his eyes dark-lined and hollow. "I wonder how they got here. And if they didn't kill the planet to make space for themselves."

———

Getting back to what happened—" With a rueful shrug, he stopped to finger a long red scar across his forehead. "That black vampire had nearly done me in. My arms were bleeding from the slashes. I got lost. Cal had carried the only compass we had. I couldn't see the sun except for glimpses when it was straight overhead. I remember wandering on forever, till I must have I passed out.

"This morning I woke lying under one of those thorn-trees, aching all over, nearly too cold and stiff to move and still with no sense of where the plane might be. I stumbled on when I could walk and finally came to a rocky point where I could climb out of the jungle and look back to see the plane.

"I struck back toward it and got lost again. Somehow, I blundered back into that cleared circle where I'd met the monsters. I saw crawling things far across it. Machines or creatures harvesting those red fruits, I imagine. They stopped whatever they were doing and started toward me.

"Afraid I was done for, I ran along the edge of the field till I found our footprints, Cal's and mine, where I had followed him into the clearing. Night was close by then, and I felt all but dead, but I was able to follow them back." He grinned at me wanly. "Thanks for waiting."

His voice had grown husky and faint by then. He sank back in the seat, shivering again, stricken perhaps by poison from the thorns, perhaps by some alien virus. I had no idea what had hit him or what to do about it, but I found a blanket and spread it over him.

"Don't you fret," he whispered. "I'm okay. I'll get us down."

Certainly not okay, he snuggled into the blanket and lay there breathing heavily, his eyes closed. With the plane on autopilot, he seemed to sleep. Now and then he muttered words I didn't get, moaned as if in pain, struck out convulsively, dreaming perhaps of his battle with the parasite.

The plane droned on through the high stratosphere. We had taken off in the dark, but we overtook the sun. A flat infinity of slate-gray ocean lay beneath us till at last a thin dark line of land emerged across the horizon ahead. When I looked at Casey, he still lay huddled in the pilot's seat. His threshing movements had tossed the blanket off. I called his name to wake him.

"I think we're coming over America. Can you land us?"

He jerked bolt upright, caught a hissing breath and cowered back, staring at me with blind red eyes, his blood-smeared face contorted with terror.

"Casey? Don't you know me?"

He swayed away from me. His mouth opened as if he was trying to cry out, but I heard nothing.

"Wake up," I shouted at him. "You've got to take us down."

He flinched farther away, hands raising as if to fend me off.

"You damn—damn thing!" he gasped. "What did you do to Cal?"

I reached to catch his shoulder. He shuddered and twisted away. When I grasped again, he struck wildly back with doubled fists and then sank limply back and lay breathing hard.

"Casey, please!"

He flinched weakly away when I reached to touch his face. His skin was wet with sweat, still hot with fever, yet I saw him shivering.

"Casey," I begged again. "Don't you know me?"

He pulled himself a little straighter, gaping at me blankly.

"Please! We're close to America. You know I'm no pilot. You've got to get us down."

"Cal?" He shook his head, blinking in confusion. "Who

the hell—" His swollen eyes went wide in recognition. "Sorry, Dunk. I'm not myself." He nodded feebly, and groped for the edge of the blanket to wipe at his face. "I thought—I guess it was a nightmare. I'll try to take us down. I hope to something better than we found in Africa."

15

Half himself again, swaying unsteadily over the controls, Casey took us on toward North America. I brewed him a mug of the bitter tea we grew at the station. He sipped it absently, but still he couldn't eat. His dark jaw set hard, he kept his mind on his tasks, scanning the unknown world crawling back through the haze below, plotting our route on the maps we had redrawn from what we saw from orbit, estimating how far we could go on the fuel left in the tanks.

It must have taken desperate effort. I saw the sweat that filmed his tight, blood-flecked face, saw the tremor of his thorn-scarred hands. But he got us to the continent—one far different from anything on our ancient maps. Seas had shrunk as water froze. Glacial ice now covered ancient Canada and spread east from the Rockies, far across the upper Mississippi valley.

We reached the ice sheet in the latitude of old New England and flew south and west along its edge. With binoculars, I studied the uncovered land until the beige-brown flatness of the springtime tundra gave way to other vegetation. The lowlands looked green, a lighter, bluer green than we had found in Asia. Higher elevations were spotted and patched with a puzzling array of vivid color: red and gold, amber and emerald and blue, all in varied shades. I offered the glasses to Casey and tried to ask him what he thought. Sitting hunched and grim-faced at the controls, he shrugged and said nothing.

The ice retreated into the mountains as we went on south, but snow still capped the westward summits when he began a long descent. Watching those flecks and splashes of color as we came down, I began to make out trees. With no familiar look of oak or elm or pine, they grew in small groves and vast forests. Most of them stood straight and tall, spaced well apart, with no undergrowth around them. They were brick-red and cherry-red, orange and pink, gleaming gold, yellow and bright as flame.

Casey spent the last of our fuel for the landing, gliding low over that exotic landscape until a forest wall loomed close ahead, pulling the nose up to break our flight, dropping at last against the rocket cushion to blue-green velvet and sudden silence. The plane swayed and settled. He sagged weakly back, wiped his sleeve across his face and waved his map at me.

"Mexico . . ." He rasped words and phrases one by one as if each took a separate effort. "Old Chihuahua . . . Sierra Madre west of us . . . Tanks empty . . . We're here to stay." The map fluttered out of his quivering hand. "I'm done for, Dunk . . . Leaving the rest to you . . . Watch out . . . for anything . . ."

Eyes closed, he sank back in the seat, his breath a slow, wheezy snore. I reclined the seat, took off his boots, and spread the blanket over him before I turned to the windows. The flat blue plain spread far east and south. The forest stood a mile or so west of us, a towering wall of magnificent trees that seemed to reflect the crimson and gold of the sunset. Strange as it looked, I caught a comforting sense of quiet and peace.

Flying west, we had kept ahead of night, but it was overtaking us now, purple dusk climbing out of the east. Uneasy about the gathering darkness, I found the binoculars and scanned our surroundings. The level plain stretched east without a break to meet the falling dark. I saw no motion in the forest, felt no danger. With Casey seeming sound asleep, I opened the door and climbed down to the ground. The air was still and cool, sweet with a faint flower scent. I knelt to look at the turf and found a yielding carpet of blue-green fibers that felt warm and soft as fur.

The world was silent at first, as if hushed by alarm at our landing, but soon I heard a faint and far-off sound, a high pure tone that rose and trilled and finally died away. It seemed to come from the trees. I walked around the plane to look. Thickening shadow was already clotting the forest, but sunset crimson still brushed the treetops and outlined the dark peaks far beyond.

I listened till that note came again, higher, sweeter, quavering, throbbing with a melodic beat I had never heard, till it crested and sank and died away. A bird? I wondered for a moment. My father had played bird holos for us when we were small. We had bird cells in the cryostat. Tanya had begged her mother to clone a canary for her till Arne laughed and said Dian's cat would eat it.

Of course all those ancient birds were gone. Was this the voice of some new species as strange to Earth as the black vampires? Something perhaps alarmed by our landing and anxious to know what we were? I thought it had seemed somehow like a voice, though no human voice, that was calling to me. An insistent voice, almost urgent, that gave me a sense of some intended meaning, yet no meaning I could grasp.

It came again. I started toward it without thinking why. It rose louder when I moved. The timbre of it changed. It became a chorus of many voices, singing to a rhythm I had never heard, moving me with emotions I had never felt. A greeting? A welcome? A question about who or what we were?

I heard no menace in it. My haunting dread of the black vampires fell away. Africa was far behind us, and I felt sure they had no aircraft to carry them off the continent. Something hurried me faster till the strangeness of it checked me, and the thought of Casey left in the plane behind me, lying sick of something stranger. I turned back toward the plane, relieved to see the familiar beauty of it, a leanly tapered silver shard that shone against the purple night.

That eerie euphony followed me, rising with an urgency that drew me to a halt halfway to the plane. I stood rapt, utterly perplexed, searching to understand. Except in holos I had never heard a hurricane, never heard thunder boom, but that great harmony held me with the power I had always imagined in such natural forces.

Turning back to the forest, I searched for the source of that awed emotion. The huge tree trunks were lost in darkness now, but the high treetops still glowed dully red against a redder sunset. I saw no movement anywhere, but something eased my concern for Casey. It erased the pain of my awareness that we were here to live our lives and die, never to see the station and our friends again. It filled me, somehow, with new hope for the mission and the clone generations to come.

I stood there in the thickening dark, listening in vain for any familiar chord or cadence in the rise and fall of that mighty tide of sound, yet transfixed with a joy I couldn't understand. I forgot our quarrels with Arne, forgot the vampires in Africa, forgot myself and even my care for the future of Earth. I felt lifted into pure elation, beyond the need for thought or action.

Time ceased until that music, if I can call it music, peaked and died slowly into silence. It left me with an ache of longing for it to go on. The darkness turned to loneliness, and worry for Casey bit me again. I plodded heavily on to the plane. Glancing back when I reached the ladder, I saw something lifting out of the forest.

A balloon!

Only a flash of gold when it rose into the sunlight, it became a real balloon, a gondola swinging under it. Though I felt no wind, it drifted slowly toward me. I stood craning until it passed high above me and vanished at last in the failing night. It meant another breed of alien beings here, I thought, intelligent beings with an advanced technology. Yet I felt no alarm. Still intoxicated with that music, I was eager to know them.

Back on the plane, I found Casey sitting up and looking better. He let me heat a bowl of soup and open a packet of the squash-and-tofu wafers the robots made, stuff Arne called manna of the Moon. While he ate, I tried to tell him about that music and how it had changed my mood.

"I heard it, or something like it," he said, "in a crazy dream." He stopped with his spoon in the air to shake his head in wonder. "It made me feel—I can't say how—made me feel the mission has a chance in spite of those things in Africa. A dream that kept getting crazier."

He paused again to eye me as if I might be wondering if he himself was crazy.

"I thought I saw a golden balloon rising out of the forest. Mona was in it. She had come down from the Moon to look for me. She was pregnant, I guess you didn't know, when we got on the escape plane. Six months along, though she hardly showed it. With a boy we were going to name Leonardo. She miscarried after we got to the station. In the dream, I thought little Leo might have another chance.

"I remember—" Eyes half closed, he fell silent, remembering.

Or seeming to. Growing up, we had all known our clone parents through the holos in the tank and all the letters and diaries and journals and relics they had left for us. Waiting for me in my own lockers, I had found my father's pipe and the brittle leather pouch that had held his tobacco, his pocketknife, his wallet with faded photos I didn't recognize.

His life and his world had become more vivid and exciting to me than our tiny den on the crater rim, the stories of our clone parents as real as actual memories. And we shared the same flesh. My father spoke of racial memories, handed down through the unconscious to shape myth and habit. I think there were moments we really did recall from more than hearsay, though Arne never agreed.

"And you know, Dunk—" Dark eyes wide, Casey was smiling. "I remember how I found her. It happened in a nightspot in an old South American city called Medellin. I was there as a pilot and bodyguard, employed by a man named Hugo Carrasco, a dealer in outlawed narcotics. Mona—"

He paused and shook his head as if the dream had been a miracle. While Pepe and Arne and I had always loved Tanya and Dian, who were alive and with us at the station, Casey worshiped his vision of Mona. Once long ago he had showed me the picture of her he had found in the wallet El Chino brought to the Moon. A tiny photo, brittle and faded through the ages, it was holy to him, so precious that he had Dian put it back in the cold-storage vault.

"A stunner, Dunk!" His face lit up. "Long hair the color of honey, hanging loose behind her back. Eyes as blue as this Earth sky. A figure like those old statues of Venus. She was singing sad Spanish songs, and they hit me hard. I had our waiter take her a hundred-dollar bill. Her first quick wink changed to a smile when she saw how much it was, and she kept on looking. I knew right then that we belonged to each other, but my boss had his own ideas.

"He was a big hairy brute. They called him El Matador, because he had a habit of killing whoever crossed him. Swimming in too many piña coladas, he wanted to dance with Mona. She tried to tell him that her job was just to sing. He dragged her out on the floor. She slipped away from him and ran to me.

"He came after her, yelling at me to hold her for him." Haggard eyes staring off into the past, he shook his head

with a wicked grin. "No hard choice. He pulled his gun.
I shot first. Hit him in the shoulder. He fell, bawling on
the floor. I had the keys to his limo and his jet. We beat
the local cops to the airport. Lucky he had had me keep
it refueled for emergency flights; it was refueled already.
We flew north, and sold the jet in Mexico. She had an
American passport. I had connections to get one made.
We got back across at Juarez. We lay low till I finally
found another job, with Cal DeFort. It was at a fraction
what Carrasco used to pay, but Cal saved our lives."

I made us another pot of the robots' black tea and tried
to talk about that golden balloon. Did it mean we'd
found another breed of aliens here? Would they welcome
any colony we tried to plant? Hardly listening, Casey still
had Mona on his mind.

"That dream, Dunk." He shook his head, with a wryly
wistful shrug. "You know, it left me feeling that our little
Leo could really have a chance. In some future generation,
when Mona and I are cloned together."

He munched another squash-and-tofu wafer, finished
his tea, and lay back in his seat. He was soon snoring
softly. I felt groggy for sleep, but I lay a long time wondering about the singing trees and the soaring balloon.
Wondering too about the tale of Mona and El Matador.
Casey loved to talk about El Chino and the past he imagined. He told his stories well. I enjoyed them, even when
they seemed to be sheer imagination. Whatever the truth
of it all, his hope to know the lost little Leo in some future
life had left me aching for him.

He startled me awake, once in the night, with a cry of
anguish.

"Mona! Mona, wait for me!"

Day had come when I woke. A yellow sunbeam from
the window struck his seat. It was empty.

16

I called his name and got no answer. He had left the cabin door open. I climbed down to the ground and found no trace of him. The morning sun, hot and high in the east, showed no life on the great plain around us. The mossy turf held no footprints. No sound, not even a whisper of wind, came from the gold-and-crimson forest in the west. No golden balloon floated above it.

Wondering what to do, I climbed back aboard, rummaged through the food locker for a breakfast pack, then found that I had no appetite. Only desperate questions. Why was Casey gone? Was he in delirium from those poison thorns, or perhaps an alien virus on the vampire's fangs? Or maybe drawn into the singing forest by his fevered dreams of Mona? Without a clue, I had to look for answers.

First of all, I called the station to report on our landing and Casey's disappearance, trusting the robots to record it. I had no weapons. DeFort had brought no arsenal to the Moon, but my euphoria from the song of the trees was not entirely gone.

Carrying only the binoculars, I left the plane and walked toward the forest. It looked very open, parklike and clean, the floor matted with the same leafless blue-green turf. The trees stood wide apart, with no fallen leaves or branches under them. They towered higher and still higher as I came near. Even the saplings along the forest's edge reduced the plane to a toy. Those trees farther on seemed to rise endlessly. The ground beneath was strangely clean. I found only one fallen leaf, a blanket-sized sheet of copper-red tissue stretched over a kitelike frame.

Listening for any sound from Casey, all I heard was

silence, a stillness that somehow seemed alive and alert, watchful, waiting. Or so I felt. When I shouted once, my voice woke echoes from the towering trunks, sounds so faint and ghostly that I did not call again.

Walking farther, I heard a muffled thud and found a fruit that had fallen near me. I picked it up. A bright pink bubble, pear-shaped and heavy in my hand, it flexed as if filled with liquid. Was it fit to eat, or perhaps as poisonous as those jungle barbs? I weighed it again, considering that. We were here for the rest of our lives. The food in the locker would soon be gone. We had to take our chances, and its odd aroma woke my appetite.

The small end of the bubble tapered into a sort of nipple. I squeezed it. Fragrant wine-red drops oozed out. I caught them in my palm and sniffed again. Saliva wet my mouth. I touched them with my tongue. The taste was slightly salt, slightly sweet, and altogether good. I sucked at the nipple till the bubble was flat.

It satisfied my hunger, but left me with a question in botany. The fruits in our old world had been seeds covered with flesh, evolved to tempt more mobile organisms to eat and scatter them. The bubble had shrunk to a flat bladder with no seed in it. What was its biological function?

The forest looked darker and stranger when I looked ahead. The massive trunks, the color of time-darkened bronze, rose like the columns of an enormous temple. The branches spread so high I had to crane to make them out. The dense foliage shut out the sun to leave me in a heavy twilight. I had gone only a little way before I stopped, sensing that I was invading a sacred place where I had no right to be.

Turning back, I searched north along the fringe of the forest, cautiously keeping daylight in view. I must have gone two or three miles before I heard something sing again. Its voice seemed to come from treetops, far ahead at first and far away, then near, louder, till it had become a trilling lilt high above me, a melody so lively and eager that I quickened my pace to its beat.

Was it aware of me?

For a moment I thought so, but its song continued when I stood still. Was it addressed to Casey, not to me? Suddenly certain of that, with no rational reason, I stood wondering till it broke. After a moment of total silence, I heard a piercing note like a cry of pain that changed into a long-drawn wail that seemed to come from all around me. The glow of color in the treetops darkened as if from a sudden shadow, but I saw no cloud.

Overwhelmed by a wave of dread I knew no reason for, I retreated farther into the open and looked a little anxiously for the plane. It stood where I had left it, small and lonely in the distance, no more than a tiny silvery exclamation point to that dying wail. I was raising the binoculars to make sure it was safe when I saw another balloon.

A bright golden ball, small and far away, it came drifting over the forest toward the plane. A wave of darkness followed it, a shadow too large for it to cast. It was drifting too low. The gondola dragged the treetops, caught and broke free, caught and broke free again. That fading wail had sunk into a breathless hush, as if the forest itself felt anxious.

The glasses shaking in my hand, it took me a moment to get the balloon into a sharper focus. My breath stopped. It had snagged again on the splintered limb of a tree lightning must have blasted. Wind dragged it free again, but its fabric must have torn. Deflating, it sank fast. A door opened in the side of the gondola. Something jumped out.

I tried to steady the glasses, tried to get the focus sharper. The falling creature looked half human, half unearthly, yet clearly female. Her skin was hairless, smooth, almost the golden hue of the balloon. She had three-toed, dark-clawed chicken feet, made for perching, but her thighs curved nicely to a golden tuft of pubic hair. Her full golden breasts were nippled like the fruit I had sucked.

For an instant I caught her face. Smoothly oval, softly feminine, it was framed in flowing pale-gold hair. Her eyes were darker, golden green, wide with terror. Her mouth gaped as if with a scream too far off for me to hear.

Tumbling down, she spread wings, bright gold sails attached from her shoulders to her elbows. One seemed crooked, useless. She had opened them too late. Falling fast, she flapped them wildly, came down hard, staggered, stumbled, sank into a golden huddle, lay there not moving. On the impulse to help if she needed help, I started toward her and stopped when Casey came running out of the woods behind her.

He knelt beside her, felt her narrow wrist, bent his head against her breast to listen for her heart. I saw his lips moving as he spoke, saw stark fear fade into relief when her eyes blinked and stared at him and finally smiled. He leaned a long time over her, bending to listen when her lips moved, kneeling to examine that injured wing.

I saw her flinch and sink back when she tried to move it. He gathered her up to lift her. Her feathered arms went around his neck, the gold wings wrapping them both. I thought he was taking her aboard the plane. Instead, he carried her back into the forest. The treetops shone bright again. Something like a single voice pealed from them, grew and spread into a great chorus of rejoicing, I imagined, that she was safe.

More wonder than compassion urged me to follow, but I thought he wouldn't want me. He must have thought I was aboard the plane if he thought about me at all. Why hadn't he tried to reach me? Had the forest somehow possessed him, the way the black vampires possessed their hosts? Such riddles—all unanswered—haunted me.

The voice of the forest softened as he carried her into the shadows. A gentle melody that fitted no melodic pattern that Dr. Lazard had taught when she gave us music lessons at her holo piano, it became as quietly soothing as the wind sounds and brook sounds and surf sounds Tanya's mother used to play when we were young and she wanted us to sleep.

It quieted my anxieties enough to let me stop and inspect the deflated balloon, a great ragged sheet of something that looked a little like plastic film but was still altogether baffling. It had no metal in it, no rivets or grommets or cylinders of gas. I found no cords or ropes or any valves that they might have controlled. It was all one single piece. I found no seams or stitches, no mark of manufacture. And the gondola—

I had to stand and scratch my head and stare again into the forest, which was purring softly now, like ten thousand of Dian's cats. The gondola was a slick orange-red shell, hard as a pecan shell. It had split wide open to let that winged creature escape. I wondered how there had been space for her till I saw that it was lined with some soft pliant gray stuff shaped to fit the curves of her body. Leaning to look inside, I caught a hint of the winelike odor of the fruit I had found.

What was she?

Another fruit of the forest, grown on some singing tree? That was hard to imagine, but what else? Neither the trees nor the black vampires could have evolved here on Earth. My father had taught us words invented for such other-worlders. Panspermia. Extraterrestial. Xenobiology. The words were all I knew.

Hopeful for Casey's return, I stayed in or near the plane. Hunger and thirst, I thought, should bring him back, but he never did appear. Again and again I ventured out to the forest fringe to look for any sign of him, but I never went far. What kept me out was something greater than my concern for Casey, awe more than actual fear, a dread of some felt presence that I didn't know or understand. A presence aware of me, perhaps warily alert, perhaps merely curious, maybe unconcerned with me at all. The sense of that was not hostile or alarming, yet strong enough to stop me.

I found another great copper-colored leaf, fallen from that shattered tree at the forest's edge. I dragged it out into the open, brought a holocam, measured and described it for another report to the station. The long central vein was a hollow tube with something like a reed at the end. It squeaked faintly when I squeezed it. Were the leaves the voice boxes of the forest?

On another day I went back to study the balloon again. I found the empty shell of the gondola melting into the ground. The golden fabric had faded almost white, and a flap of it was stuck fast when I tried to pull it free. Dragging it loose, I found tiny yellow roots grown into it from the turf. One mystery solved. The forest needed no rangers or loggers to give it the look of a well-tended park. The mossy turf was doing that work, absorbing whatever fell.

Next morning I sat aboard the plane, trying to sum up our data and conclusions for transmission. I now had no doubt that Arne's terror of alien invasion was based on fact. Though we had seen no evidence of spacecraft in Africa, or any high technology at all, the black vampires were certainly not native to Earth. The singing trees? They remained an even greater riddle.

Waiting for the Moon to rise into radio range, I couldn't help feeling that the microphone was a black hole where my words would be lost forever. Though I hoped the Robos would be listening, I had no way to know. I confess a certain perverse satisfaction in the thought of Arne shaking in terror that the vampires might find him.

The cabin door was open. I heard a sudden clamor, a sound like a thousand voices screaming, with no music in it. It rose and fell and became a rapid cannon fire that to my ears had no harmony at all. Watching from the door, I saw the whole forest flickering as if from multicolored lightning.

In a moment Casey and the winged thing burst into view. They ran frantically. She was limping. He held her hand to help her, her wings wrapped around him. Out of the trees, she spread them and tried to fly. One wing buckled. She sprawled to the turf. He picked her up, her arms around his neck, and plunged on toward the plane. The forest boomed in time with his footfalls, and scarlet lightning blazed behind them.

Something followed out of the forest.

17

An ungainly, brown-furred beast, loping clumsily on long hind legs and shorter forelegs in a way that made it grotesquely tall behind and short ahead, it was already halfway to the plane. I first thought Casey had time enough to win his race, but he staggered weakly. The golden being seemed too heavy for him.

A dozen yards out of the woods, the beast stood up on its huge rear legs, trumpeted like the elephants I had seen in holos, and lumbered faster. I grabbed the binoculars and got them in focus to see the creature more clearly. Even as a biped, it looked more like a great ape than anything human, but really not much like anything ever evolved on Earth.

Two huge yellow eyes glared out of a slick hairless head ridged with a red, saw-toothed crest. Its hands were wicked claws. The three-toed feet were armed with longer claws and bright red spurs. A sharp black penis thrust out below its yellow-furred belly. It came on at a lurching run, as if more used to ambling on all fours.

Casey was still well ahead till he stumbled on the being's dragging wing. They sprawled together on the turf. She lay motionless under the twisted wings. He came up on hands and knees, stared up at the beast, struggled to his feet and stumbled to meet it. In his left hand he had a weapon, something that looked like one of the gray socks we wore in our boots, rocks packed in the toe.

The beast stopped once and turned back to bellow its rage into the forest. The forest echoed it with a great booming crescendo of discordant wrath. The beast swung back, howling like a hunting wolf. Casey raised his right hand, open palm out, in an appeal for peace.

The creature growled and came on to swipe its claws

across his chest, ripping off most of his tattered shirt. He shifted the sock to his right hand, swung it high, brought it down toward the thing's yellow-shelled head. It ducked and grappled him with both black-clawed hands. The sock swung again and struck beside the crimson crest.

The thing stopped as if dazed, the yellow eyes blinking at him. He stepped back to get his breath, bright blood running down his chest. It swayed and fell toward him. I thought he had knocked it out, but it grappled him again, snatched him off his feet, whirled his body, tossed him sprawling.

The sock went flying and bounced off a golden wing. He lay motionless till I saw his fingers groping at the turf. The creature stalked to him, kicked a scarlet spur into his side, stamped its three-clawed foot on his blood-stained chest, and turned with arms spread high to trumpet a raucous call of triumph into the forest. The forest answered with a thundering paean of victory.

It spurred his limp body again, leaned to gather the female with its crimson claws, and carried her back toward the forest, the injured wing dragging. The forest welcomed his return with a rumbling chant that kept time to his footfalls.

Casey tried to sit up before I reached him, and sank weakly back. A pitiful scarecrow, he was hollow-eyed and half naked, dried blood clotted black on the welted marks of the vampire's fangs, fresh blood oozing where the claws had slashed him.

"Damn, damn, damn!" He gave me a forlorn little grin. His voice turned anxious. "Did you see Mona?"

"I saw—saw something."

"Wasn't she beautiful?"

"Something strange," I said. "Out of a new biology."

"She is—different." He was panting for breath. "Wonderful! And strange enough till I found Mona in her."

He shook his head at my look of disbelief and tried again to rise. I helped him stand. He staggered after the creature swaggering away with the female, stumbled and nearly fell, stopped with a helpless shrug. He stood looking after them, getting back his breath, while the creature's razor crest shrank to a bright red point in the distance, bobbing along above her golden wings. They vanished at last in the shadows. He turned back to me, still swaying on his feet, something wild in his deep-sunk eyes.

"I guess you think I'm sick or crazy." He shook his head, with a faint little grin. "I know she's a different breed. Hard to understand. But she does have Mona in her. If you had seen her eyes—she has Mona's eyes." He was hoarsely whispering, an awed devotion on his haggard face. "Mona's voice when she sings. I love her, Dunk." His face set with stubborn purpose. "I've got to get her back."

"How? How can you hope—"

He wasn't listening.

"That—that hideous *thing*!" His voice went thick with baffled fury. "A devil from—from I don't know where. I believe it came down in that first balloon we saw. Hunting her. We've been hiding. Running from it." He stopped to calm his quivering voice. "I can't let it take her."

His scarred fists were knotted, but he was barely able to stand. He limped with me back to the plane and let me clean his wounds and spray them with healant. He must have been sick from some poison or virus, but half his weakness came from hunger.

"She found fruit for us," he said. "Something like big red grapes, full of juice we could suck. I liked the taste. It gave me a sort of high, but it wasn't meant for humans. There's no strength in it."

He devoured two meal packs and a banana the robots

had grown in our hothouse, and poured himself a stiff shot of the moonshine El Chino had taught him to distill. He said it eased his pain. Groggy with exhaustion, he was still too jittery to sleep. He wanted to talk about Mona. Or Monas. The human refugee who boarded the escape plane with El Chino and the gold-winged alien had somehow run together in his mind.

"She sang to me, Dunk. Not with words, her language has no words. Not even with any tune I ever heard. But she made me sense what she felt for me. We were speaking with something better than words." He paused to shrug at the questions on my face. "I don't know how. It doesn't matter. Listening, I saw what she saw. Heard what she heard. I understood the trees when they sang to her."

I got up to brew a pot of tea.

"Dunk!" His voice rose impatiently. "If you think I'm out of my head, it's because you never heard her sing. But damn those trees!" He made a bitter face. "They don't like me. Maybe because I'm not a tree. They say I don't belong. They're afraid I'll take her away. But she loves me, Dunk. She loves me."

His voice had fallen into silence, and he sat staring away at nothing till I touched his arm to offer the mug of hot tea. He jumped as if that startled him.

"Sorry, Dunk. I forget where I am." He gave me an apologetic grin and sloshed a shot of his moonshine into the tea. "She gave me dreams." Sipping at the tea, he let his voice fade absently. "Memories, really, at night when I slept with her arms around me."

He stopped to squint at my shock and doubt.

"It's real, Dunk." His voice fell soberly. "Nothing I can even try explain or understand, but it's real as anything. Don't you remember how it was when we were kids back at the station? How our holo parents used to talk about their lives before the impact? I listened to the holos and read the papers they had left for me. I used to dream that El Chino was alive again in me."

I had to nod. Growing up so close together, and so close to our holo parents, we knew each other very well. Tanya had known I loved her before I ever dared say so, and I'd felt sick because I already knew what she had decided to say. Dian used to call it telepathy. I doubted the reality of that because I knew no way to explain it. Casey had been another skeptic, until now.

"Mona—" He tipped his head and looked away as if he heard her speaking. "I used to dream about her pictures and all I heard and read. In the dreams I remembered things that happened back on Earth when we really were together. Remembered more than she and El Chino ever told me.

"Things like that fight—" He paused to nod as the recollections came. "The gunfight in that Medellin nightclub when El Matador was coming on to Mona. And then another gun battle with the men guarding his jet. One of them took my last bullet. Another murder rap on my record if they'd caught me, but we got off a minute or so ahead of the cops. We flew north in the dark out over the Pacific, around the fringe of a hurricane. The fuel tanks were empty when we glided down to a private strip near La Paz."

He reached for his map.

"That was a city in Baja California, here," he pointed, "near the tip of the peninsula. A center of the drug trade. I had an old friend there. El Yankee Rosa. Man I met in a Colombian jail. I swapped him the jet for the help we needed. He got our passports fixed and offered me a good spot in his own *grupo*.

"El Matador was offering to pay big money for our tattoos. Proof we'd been knocked off. El Yankee could have sold us out, but he knew him for the diamondback he was. He wanted to sign me on for his own war with

El Matador's gang. He promised to help Mona get back to the States.

"She wouldn't go." He turned to gaze through the window at the forest, a dark wall of shadow beneath the stain of a blood-colored sunset. "Because she loved me." He whispered that, turning slowly back to me. "Dunk, one night together on that flight, and she already loved me. Live or die, all I wanted was to keep her with me. El Yankee called us *dos locos* because we wouldn't split up, but he found us a car and told us *vayan bien*.

"Fifty kilometers up the peninsula we hit a roadblock. Had to leave the car and run for it. Blazing summer heat in a killer cactus desert. The cops gave up the chase, but the next three days were no fun. Mona passed out once, nearly dead for water. The hurricane rain saved her. Up the coast, we stole a fishing boat and headed out into ugly weather.

"The gulf was wider then, all the oceans higher, but we made it across. Beached the boat and limped into Los Mochis. A tourist spot. Mona had worked as a travel guide. Her wits and know-how got us into a tour group. We rode a train across Copper Canyon to Chihuahua." He pointed at his map. "A city that stood about where we are right now. We got a flight from there to El Paso and lay low till we heard El Yankee had knocked El Matador off. Finally, by great good luck, we were at Cal DeFort's Moon base when the bolide hit."

He tipped more moonshine into his mug, drained it straight, and turned to stare again into the silent forest and the fading sunset.

"Memories." He murmured the word and turned back to me. "Memories from a million years ago, but real as yesterday." His gaze grew piercing. "You don't believe me, Dunk? You think all that was just another crazy dream?"

"I don't know." I looked out into the thickening dark

and back at him. "I've heard the forest singing. I saw the balloon that brought that—brought your Mona, if you want to call her that. I watched that creature knock you out and take her away. They're nothing natural to this Earth. I've got no way to understand them or what they can do."

"No matter." He paused to sit up straighter. "They're here. Great stuff for your next report to the robots, if you think the Robos want to hear you. As for Mona—" He clenched his fists. "I won't give her up. Not to that beast, or those crazy woods. I'm going back after her.

"But not tonight—"

He yawned and stretched and sank into sleep.

His seat was empty again when I woke. I climbed down to the blue-green carpet. The air was still and cool, with a bracing scent a little like the wine Arne used to make from the grapes the robots grew. The forest was silent, a great wall of red and golden fire in the morning sunlight.

I found Casey lying on his back under the plane. He climbed out with a long metal bar he had cut out of the landing cradle. At work without a shirt, he looked gaunt. Drops of darkening blood had oozed through the healant film over his scars. Yet he was energetically busy, using his torch to trim one end of the bar to a jagged point and taping the other for a grip. Trying the balance of it, he turned to grin bleakly at the forest.

"*Viva!*" he muttered. "*Viva la Mona!*"

The forest darkened. I heard a faint, far-off sigh like wind in the treetops, though I felt no wind, then a deep-pitched rumble like distant thunder, altogether tuneless and coldly forbidding. I retreated to the ladder and Casey shook his lance.

"Any fuel left in the tanks?" I asked him. "Could you move us to a safer place?"

"Run from that hairy devil?"

His dark jaw sagged in astonishment, and stiffened instantly. He shrugged my reaching hand away, stood a moment looking into the silent forest, and shouldered his lance. His face worked, and his sober voice was almost apologetic when the spoke.

"You don't—you don't understand." His voice trembled and he made a quick wipe at his eyes. "I'm sorry for you, Dunk."

Before I could find anything to say, he lifted his free hand in a sort of salute and walked off toward the trees. Ahead of him, their alien voice rose in a solemn song that had no melody or harmony until a muffled drumbeat came into it, keeping time to his feet.

18

He never came back. I believe I am the only man on Earth; perhaps the only man alive anywhere. Or perhaps Arne Linder still reigns as the alpha male on the Moon, lording it over his three companions. I'll never know, but I intend to keep on transmitting these reports so long as I survive, trusting the Robos to receive and record them for our heirs.

My own will to live endures, even here and now. I exist in a kind of comfort. The seasons are so mild, without frost or drought, that I wonder if the trees don't influence the weather. My home is the disabled spaceplane. When the supplies ran short, I often thought of Daniel Defoe's marooned hero in the old paper book my holo father used to read aloud when we complained of loneliness.

I've learned to grow my own food. Needing tools to till the soil, I cut metal from the landing cradle to make spades and hoes. My first garden had to be abandoned because the nearer trees flashed red and cried out as if in pain when my spade bit into the velvet sod, but I found uncovered ground a mile or so south, where a cold spring flowed out across the floor of a shallow valley.

We had brought seed from the station: corn, beans, peanuts, squash, tomatoes, even peppers and the okra for the gumbo my father learned to love when he was a child in the old city of New Orleans. When my diet seems monotonous, I sometimes venture into the fringe of the woods to look for those red, juice-filled fruits. Though the forest floor is always clean, two or three often fall near where I am searching, almost as if dropped as a gift for me.

Though their bittersweet tang seemed sharp and strange at first, I have come to enjoy them more and more. Perhaps they contain some protein or vitamin lacking from my diet. They leave me with a renewed sense of vigor and well-being, though they never satisfy hunger, and the brief euphoria they bring is never enough to erase my longing for the station and the friends I left on the Moon.

I miss Pepe, always asking for another chess game and taking forever to decide his moves. I miss Dian, always eager to recite some trivial bit of ancient Earth history that nobody cared to hear. I miss even Arne. When he was in his better moods, he had a power of mind I admired. And Tanya—I long for her most of all.

I keep a picture of her over my bed in the plane, a little pencil drawing she let me make on the day we turned sixteen. Though I'm no artist, I thought it caught the sly quirk of her lips and the bright mischief in her smile. It can wake a haunting recollection of the kiss she gave me the day I dared to say I loved her, the taste of her lips, the scent and softness of her dark hair, the warmth of her body in my arms.

But that wistful recollection is hard to hold. Pepe was the one she loved. When I look up at the drawing, trying to bring that bright moment back, her image is likely to fade into Mona's as I used to see her in the holo tank, golden-haired, taller than Tanya, more alluringly shaped.

Though I never knew her except as that luminous ghost in the tank, smiling at El Chino and blind to us, I often dream of them. The gunfight in Medellin, the night flight to Mexico in the stolen jet, the desperate trek through the cactus desert, the battle to get on the escape plane before the impact: the drama of their lives is as vivid to me as if I had shared it with them.

Grown more tolerant now, the trees no longer growl or thunder at me. They seem to sense my moods. One night when I lay sunk in bitter despair, contemplating suicide, they sang to call me out of the plane and greet me with a symphony of light and sound that captured and restored me in a way I have never understood. It left me content with my exile, at least for the moment, and happy to have them near.

At dusk on another evening a year or so later they invited me away from the plane. Though I felt no wind, they sighed and whispered as if to one another. The gold and crimson splendor of the sunset flowed down into the treetops as darkness thickened, and their rising chorus spoke to me in a way I had never heard before.

Yielding to them without purpose or intention, I climbed down the ladder and started toward them. Their pealing voices rose. As if to hurry me on, a rosy light swept the shadows out of a majestic avenue through the towering trunks ahead. I followed it into an opening where a single young sapling stood. Its bronze bole, arrow-straight, was no thicker than my arms, but the glowing foliage rose to twice my height, pulsing with waves of vivid color that matched the rapid rhythm of my heart.

The gleam of metal caught my eyes. Casey's lance lay beside the trunk, between two white skulls. Two skeletons, when I looked more closely, had sunk half into the leafless turf. I saw objects it had not absorbed: Casey's boots, his pocketknife, the gold watch his clone father had brought to the Moon. The bones of his right arm extended to the lance; remnants of the finger bones were still curled around the hilt.

The other skeleton looked weirdly semihuman, but larger and heavier than his. Half gone, it still had the alien's three-toed chicken feet, the cruel black claws, the blood-red spurs. The skull was longer than Casey's, flatter, heavy-jawed, a sharp ridge across the crown. The lance had gone into the right eye socket; the jagged point jutted through a crack at the back of the skull.

I stood a long time there under the shimmering leaves, trying to imagine how they died. Casey must have been mauled, but when I knelt to search his bones for damage, they were half melted away and stuck fast in the turf. I found none broken, no clue to the actual manner of his death.

The voice of the little tree had fallen into a solemn monody that died slowly into silence. Its glowing leaves dimmed, their light gathering around its root. Getting off my knees, I found another, smaller skull among the brittle fragments of a slighter skeleton. The bones of Casey's gold-winged Mona. Thin scraps of the wings, not yet eaten by the turf, lay beside the bones of her arm. They were stretched toward Casey's skeleton.

The little tree had grown up through the slender relics of her rib cage. I stood there in the dark, groping to understand their story, till the voices of the forest rose again in a dirge that reflected my dazed bewilderment. The shimmer of the treetop dimmed and flickered out. The only light left to me was the glow along the avenue that had brought me there. I followed it back toward the ship.

That night the forest sang to me with a voice I knew, the human voice of Mona's image in the holo tank. I dreamed of the little tree. In the dream, I pulled my boots on and climbed down out of the plane. The night lay clear and bright under a full Moon that washed the immensity of the plain and the long forest wall with a mystic splendor I had never felt before. I stood spellbound until a great chorus rose to call me into the darkness under the trees. They glowed ahead to light a road for me.

I followed it again in the dream, back to that small tree in the clearing. The skeletons were gone. Mona stood with Casey where his bones had been. Not the gold-winged being who had come down in the balloon, but now the tall blond and lovely Mona whose holo ghost I had known. She looked lovely in a long crimson gown, with a red rose in her hair. A breathless hush filled the forest when she saw me, and she ran to throw her human arms around me.

I felt the warmth of her arms and caught the sweetness of the rose, the fragrance of those the Robos had grown for Tanya in the hothouse at the station. Her lips were warm and moist when she kissed me, her hand warm and strong when she caught my own to lead me on to Casey and the tree.

Casey was El Chino now. He was thick and black and naked to the waist as he had been when he brought her aboard the escape plane at the White Sands Moon base. He wore the same faded jeans, the same heavy work boots, the same jaunty crimson tam. The golden shimmer of the tree caught the tattooed flags of Mexico and China on his wide black chest. The red-ridged scars from the poison thorns and the vampire's fangs were gone.

"Hi, Dunk!" Grinning warmly, he strode to catch my hand in a grip that left my fingers aching. He stood a moment appraising me, a smile of affection in his narrow Chinese eyes. "For a Crusoe with no Friday, you're looking good." He caught Mona's hand and turned to look at the little tree. "Meet our son, Leonardo."

"Our little Leo." With a smile of tender adoration, Mona lifted her face to the tree. "Our child that never lived. We have him with us now."

Casey waved me closer.

"Our good friend Dunk," he told the tree. "Duncan Yare. He came with me down from the Moon. He may seem strange to you, but he's okay. Marooned here alone, he'll need a new companion."

I heard a whisper through the leaves above me, as if from wind I didn't feel. Light pulsed through it, brightening to match the rose in Mona's hair. The whisper became a singing voice, almost too soft for me to hear. I heard tones like Mona's, then like Casey's, but neither words I understood nor anything like the music I had learned to love when Dian played her holo records.

Sometimes it had a fleeting rhythm that matched my heartbeat, sometimes my breathing. The sheer strangeness of it held me till it was no longer strange at all. I began to feel comfort in it, and something more, perhaps even love. My father told me once that his mother used to speak and sing to him before he was born. Our own education begins in the maternity lab. We don't remember, but I'm sure it helps to make us what we are. In some way, I think, the tree was reaching me.

I don't know how long I stood there, awed and wondering. The forest picked up the small tree's song, faintly at first but finally with a rolling crescendo so great that it seemed to vibrate through me before it reach its peak and died away. The glowing treetops faded. The small tree was left silent and dark. When I looked around for Casey and Mona, they were gone.

And that was the end of the dream.

A shrill screech shocked me awake. I was in my bed on the plane, the old metal creaking from expansion as the morning sun warmed it. Bright sunlight glittered on the instrument panels. Beyond the window, a single bright golden balloon drifted low above the long forest wall. A pool of brightness crept across the treetops beneath it, following like the shadow of a cloud, but the wonder of the dream was gone.

I sat there on the side of the bed, dazed with the pain of loss. Casey alive again, the human Mona here on Earth, the shining tree they called a son: all illusion. Cold reality hit me with my recollection of the three turf-eaten skeletons, Casey's lance thrust through the alien skull, the brittle rib fragments around the root of the little tree. The forest lay silent and dark. The joy of the dream had vanished into utter loneliness. The bleak fact came back. I was here alone forever, the only man on the planet, maybe anywhere.

Yet the drive for life endures. With no appetite for breakfast, I plodded down for a cold plunge into the pool beneath my spring. A little revived by that, I spaded ground for another row of corn. I stopped for breath when that tired me, and searched the sky again for the balloon. It was gone. Had it brought another gold-winged fairy like Casey's Mona? Another alien creature like the thing that killed him? I never knew.

Time flows on. I watch the forest now and listen to it, longing for the sense of comfort and companionship I enjoyed in the dream. It never speaks to me, not in any human tongue, yet I now feel sure that it does hold something more than toleration for me. Sometimes when I think I've heard another invitation in its song, I have ventured into it to search again for that small tree.

On the first occasions, I never got far. The towering trunks seemed too vast, the roof too high, the shadows too dark, its whole alien presence overwhelming. Dread of being lost, as Casey was lost in that African jungle, turned me back toward daylight. As time has passed, however, that dread has dimmed.

Older now, changing slowly, I have begun to know and trust the forest. I have learned how to live here. Now I know when and what to plant, how to save and ration what I harvest. I have learned to repair worn boots and clothing, learned to make do and improvise. Though I will always wonder whether Arne and Tanya and Dian are still alive on the Moon, that no longer matters greatly. We shall all be cloned again.

On hot summer afternoons when I feel exhausted from work in my little field, I have fallen into a habit of walking into the shade of the nearer trees to escape the high sun's blaze on the open plain. I have come to like the stillness when the trees are silent and their voices when they sing. Sometimes I sleep and dream of the little tree called Leo. It speaks to me with dancing colors and wordless songs that have made it seem a friend. Feeling that it wanted to know me, I have told it the story of the great impact and the aftermath, the story of the station and our mission to restore the planet. I feel somehow that it understands, and even seems to welcome the promise of our return to Earth.

It has guided me back to the clearing where it stands. I find it grown taller now, its straight bole sturdier, its broader leaves more vividly splashed with crimson and gold. The skeletons are gone. The ground where they lay is clean now, since I carried Casey's lance and those other uneaten relics back to the plane.

I visit it often. Sometimes it sings very softly, just to me. Sometimes it is silent. Always it brings me a sense of quiet companionship. Near it, I no longer feel alone. Never using words, it has helped me begin to understand the exotic botany of the forest.

In their alien biology, I believe the trees bear those golden balloons as a means of dispersing their seed. The gold-winged being Casey loved was somewhat like a flower, more like a hatching egg. He was the first moving thing she saw after she emerged from the shell where she had grown. She bonded to him, as she would have bonded to the alien mate searching for her.

His own infatuation with her is harder to explain. I have come to believe that the trees are able to communicate with some means beyond their eerie music and the changing light and color of their leaves. Dian might call it telepathy, though I know no actual proof of that. Casey was still a sick man, sometimes hallucinating. Yet I think it was something in the forest itself that made him see her as El Chino's Mona.

Whatever the cause, it was a desperate and impossible love, its ending told by what I found beneath the tree. In the terms of what my father might have called exobiology, the male being must have carried something like pollen to fertilize the flower. The Leo tree must have sprung from something like a seed formed in her body by their union.

So I speculate, and I have time for speculation. The forest holds more mystery than I can ever hope to probe. Our parents on the Moon never made us pray, but they spoke often of the old world's religions and philosophies. The trees and even the black vampires are proof of life evolving beyond our solar system. The forest has become to me a temple, where I go not to worship or adore but to share an awed and solemn sense of kinship with life throughout the cosmos.

For I realize, astounded, that life is universal. The old astronomers found its basic molecules in the great clouds of interstellar dust and gas, the stuff of life created before the stars were formed. Life, it seems, creates and re-creates itself in an infinity of shapes. In my own wordless communion with the trees, I have come to sense a vast webwork of lives and minds existing all across the cosmos.

I catch a fleeting sense of beings often older and wiser and stranger than I can ever know, most of them good in the abstract sense that altruistic love is good, some of them evil, as I see the black vampires as evil in the way that blind self-regard is evil. The evil entities are often at war with one another, the best of the good at war with death.

I have come to see the trees as engines of creation, created as we have been not by any supernatural agency but by the processes of natural evolution with which life creates itself. Arne was justified, I believe, in his dread of alien conquest. There must be an evil power elsewhere in the cosmos that erased our reseeded life from Earth to make space for the black vampires. The singing trees must have been put here as instruments of good, sent to counter them.

Or so I feel.

Does this make us hapless puppets in an age-long war waged by vast and unknown powers far out across the galaxies? We have no way to know, but so long as we continue our mission of creation, what could be a better use for us? I expect to live out my own life here alone, and finally die here. Yet, sustained by the company of the trees, I no longer feel entirely alone, nor do I expect to die entirely. Creation is eternal. We ourselves, we clones at the station, are engines of life. Our mission must endure.

That is the message I have been transmitting toward the Moon. Our heirs in the next generation must be informed and warned. I recall the Vale of Kashmir, that lovely little Eden far from the vampire race in Africa and secure behind its majestic mountain walls. I trust that we will all be cloned again, Mona and Casey with us, to land there and plant mankind on Earth again.

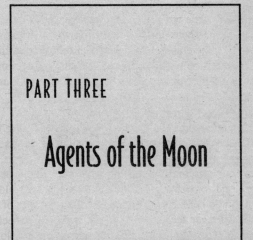

PART THREE

Agents of the Moon

19

Another generation of us was cloned again, perhaps within the next fifty years. Few records are left, and the Robos were never created to be historians. We grew up, Mona and Casey with us. The Robos built a spaceplane for us. We took off, all of us, planning to plant a colony in the Vale of Kashmir. The master computer preserves a call made as they were coming down to land.

"A perfect emerald!" I hear my own voice describing the Vale. "Set in a ring of shining ice!"

That was the last transmission received.

Another age had passed before the master computer let us live again. It husbands its resources, and runs on its own scale of time. It had waited for a reason of its own to wake us.

One day when we were nine or ten years old, my holo father called us into the tank room. Casey and Mona were holding hands as we waited, smiling at each other. Dian had brought her laptop to take notes. Tanya had her great dark eyes fixed on my father's image till Arne elbowed her aside.

"New riddles are waiting for you down on Earth." Speaking from the tank, he paused and waited for our eyes. "Perhaps a new threat to the Kashmir colony, if it still exists."

He paused to frown at Tanya as she jabbed her own elbow into Arne's ribs. He muttered something at her. Casey hissed for them to listen. Patiently, my father waved his empty pipe and cleared his throat in a way he had, a sort of cough meant to get attention.

"There's something you must know." He was very solemn. "The Robos have been watching, as they always do, for any new danger out of space. Over two hundred years ago, the Robos at the telescopes discovered an anomalous object approaching the sun. Its velocity was too great for it to have been a member of the solar system. It came from toward the galactic core."

Even Arne had raised his eyes to listen.

"It appeared to be something very massive, its estimated diameter nearly two hundred kilometers. At first it seemed to offer no danger to Earth, but then its motion changed in a strange way. It slowed instead of accelerating as it came deeper into the sun's gravity well. And it turned toward the Earth, seeming to threaten us with another devastating impact. But then it stopped completely, backed away, and lost its circular shape. Retreating from the sun, it has now disappeared."

"Not to worry," Arne muttered. "If it's gone."

My father shook the pipe at him.

"We believe it brought something that came on toward Earth. The Robo's observations seem to mean that the apparent object was an interstellar light-sail craft. It must have brought a payload."

"Light what?"

"A sail made of some ultrathin fabric, spread like a great parachute. The radiation pressure of its home star was used to launch it. It caught the radiation of our own sun to brake its motion and turn it toward Earth. The sail collapsed. It was finally driven away. But we suspect that the payload came on toward us."

"Invaders?" Pepe was startled. "Invaders from another star?"

"Quite possibly." My father nodded at him and Casey. "We believe, in fact, that this might explain the origins of the exotic vegetation you two found in North America or perhaps the vampiric monsters that killed or captured

DeFort in Africa. If one light-ship has reached us, others may have come before."

"Okay," Arne grunted. "So what's your problem now?"

"Or maybe yours." My father eyed him sharply. "You have all looked down at Earth, but now the computer wants a closer view. The areas of exotic vegetation in North America seem to have been shrinking in the last few decades. The red color of that thorn jungle in Africa has reached the Mediterranean lake and spread around it. We have never heard even once from the Kashmir colony since it landed. It may be in danger. We need to know what's going on."

"Can we?" Casey turned to Mona. She nodded, smiling into his eyes. "Can we go down to see?"

"Perhaps." My father nodded. "When you are grown up, if you are qualified and trained for the mission. The computer will be asking for volunteers."

They spoke in unison, "We'll be the volunteers."

They had been the odd couple among us. Cloned in the maternity units DeFort had meant for himself and his wife, they had no Robos programmed for their individual care. Their holo parents, created from fragmentary records made after the escape craft reached the Moon, were too incomplete to be well aware of them. Growing up together and very much in love, they lived in the past. They pored over the transmissions my elder clone self had sent back about the vampire things in the African jungle. Awe and longing in their voices, they used to quote what he said about the singing forests in North America. Casey used to ask her if she had really been incarnated in the winged being he had named for her. She shrugged and kissed him and said that it didn't matter. Their voices hushed with a wistful wonder when they spoke of the little sapling he had named Leonardo.

Grown up and still inseparable, they had Pepe's Robo train them for space. When the master computer called for volunteers for a look at the state of Earth, they were ready. It found them qualified. Casey shook our hands when they were ready to go. Mona kissed us all, even Arne. They got into their space gear and cycled through the lock.

The Robos had a spaceplane waiting for them down on the field below the crater rim. A neat little two-person craft, it was fueled for a landing on Earth, a cruise around the planet, and a flight back to the Moon. As we watched from the dome, the Robo escorted them aboard and stood clear. The steam cloud from the jets froze into a flurry of vanishing snow. The plane climbed fast and vanished in the black lunar sky.

Studying the Earth from low orbit, they sent back brief transmissions. The glaciers of the last ice age were still retreating. Southern Asia looked clear of ice and green enough to support human life. The high mountain summits around the Vale of Kashmir were still capped with white, but Casey said they had found signs of an active colony there. They were dropping out of orbit to attempt a landing.

Though we waited for months, we picked up nothing more. Pepe and I wanted to follow them down. Though they had never quite seemed to belong, we were fond of them. Mona had always been so gracious to me that her blond beauty could still give me dreams. We both felt anxious for them.

"You're fools to take the risk," Arne told us. "We've lost too many ships and too many of us. You want to waste another?"

"Por qué no?" Pepe shrugged. "DeFort built the station to keep Earth alive. We're here to take the risks."

Arne grumbled again. How many ships could the Robos

build for us to waste? If Casey and Mona had failed, how could we hope to do better? But Pepe was determined. Maybe they hadn't failed. Maybe they were simply away from the ship, with no radio. We had to know, had to find and help them if we could.

We begged my father to persuade the computer. He seemed as cynical as Arne, but in the end it had the Robos finish and fuel another two-person spaceplane for us. I had never been off the Moon, and the plane's sleek grace was a heady thrill to me.

Arne shook our hands and wished us luck, though I thought he was not unhappy to be rid of us. With a prim little smile, Dian gave us copies of ancient silver coins that she thought might help us prove we were really from the Moon. Tanya hugged us and kissed us and turned to hide her tears.

We climbed the ramp. Pepe sealed the lock. We took our seats, and the Robos waved us off. The jets coughed and roared. Condensing steam washed the field around us and fell in glittering flakes. The sudden thrust rammed me into my seat.

The Moon's gray-pocked face dwindled behind, and we looked into the starry dark ahead for the thin bright blade of the nascent Earth.

The flight to orbit took three days. We spent the time with maps and letters our earlier selves had left us. Pepe was haunted with the story of the death of the unearthly being Casey took for a reborn Mona, and the mystery of the young tree he called their son.

"Don't laugh." His voice went sharp. "It may sound strange, but they found the world gone strange. God knows what we'll find now in the Vale, or anywhere else, but I want to get to America and look for that tree."

In orbit at last, we listened for radio signals, for any kind of signal, and picked up nothing at all. We spent a week surveying Earth from orbit. Most of Africa south of the Sahara bore a dull red hue from the foreign biocosm established there. Both Americas were mottled with unearthly vegetation. The north half of Asia shone white with glacial ice that spread from the pole to the Himalayas.

With no sign of any high technology, I felt ready to search out a site for a fresh attempt. Pepe kept his eyes on southern Asia, which looked lush with the green native life we had restored. On our last low pass, he scanned it with the telescope.

"Lines!" Elation quickened his voice. "I see a web of narrow lines spread over the Indian subcontinent and on into China. Roads, they must be, or railways. I think we'll find a civilization."

I had to ask. "With no electricity?"

"Perhaps they use steam."

Seen from space, the Vale of Kashmir was a tiny green oasis nestled into that barrier of towering saw-toothed peaks that held back the ice.

"They're alive!" On our last low pass, Pepe reached for binoculars. "They really are!" He turned to grin happily at me. "The valley looks inhabited. The roads converge toward it. I make out rectangular patches that must be fields." He looked again. "There in the middle of the Vale!" His voice lifted. "That has to be a city!"

Airbraking on the final pass, we came down to land. I needed no binoculars to find roads and fields and scattered villages as the valley opened wider and wider beneath us. The city made an odd target pattern, the bull's-eye a white spot at the center of a green oval space that was ringed with circles of red and green and gray which became streets and trees and red-roofed buildings as we came lower.

Pepe brought us down to the white spot on a cushion of roaring steam. He killed the jets and opened the door. It swung down to make a narrow platform. Crowding outside, we stood there a long time, lost in awe. Pepe's hand was shaking when he gripped my arm. Our whole world had been the tiny nest of tunnels in the crater rim and the dome that looked out on the bleak and colorless Moon and its dead-black sky. The Vale was overwhelming.

"How fabulous!" Pepe whispered. "What a marvel!"

The wonder of it dazed me. A sky not black, but dazzling blue. A huge white mushroom was suspended in it. I shaded my eyes to look again.

"A cloud!" Pepe pointed at it. "That's a cloud."

The station had been a tiny dot of life on a world that had never lived. Here we stood out in open air that shielded us from killing radiation, gazing out across a sea of red rooftops toward a landscape not the dead gray of barren dust and naked stone, but vividly green. I felt cool wind and warming sun, inhaled sweet scents I had no words to name. A dark fleck soared overhead, trilling music. A songbird?

I breathed deeper and peered at everything. The open oval was a great amphitheater, rimmed with seats. Buildings walled it, only three or four stories tall but solidly made of some white stone. Far beyond, the valley floor sloped up to dark green forest. Farther still, bare cliffs climbed high to sunbright slopes of ice.

"Wouldn't Arne be surprised!" Pepe grinned. "His aliens never built this."

He handed the glasses to me. Toward the south, I found a cluster of tall stacks, smoke trailing from them. Off in the distant east, I saw a dark line creeping across a high green slope, a trail of smoke above its head.

"A train." I gave the glasses back. "They do have steam."

"But I think no electricity." He frowned. "That's why they couldn't call the station. I guess they had too much to do, building shelter. Clearing new land. Plowing farms to grow their food. Setting up labs to clone animals and

people. Defending themselves if they had to. But they—
they did it!"

He froze, staring through the glasses.

"Look at that!"

He pointed toward the end of the oval. A hundred yards
off, I saw another tall rocket craft, a twin of our own.
Painted bright red, it stood on a second white landing pad.

"The ship they came in." He lifted the glasses to study
it again, and awe slowed his voice. "I think they remember. I think they've kept this arena ready for us. I think
they've been expecting us for three hundred years."

He moved suddenly to unfold the landing stair.

"I'm going down to meet them."

I reached for the glasses and found people on rooftops
outside the arena. Only a handful at first, but more by the
dozens. Men in jackets like my holo father's. Men in
brightly patterned shirts. Women in slacks, women in
skirts, women with babies in their arms. Quiet children
neatly uniformed in white and blue. I heard a hushed hum
of voices.

"They're our colonists. Children of our clones?" His
voice sharpened uneasily. "Are they us?"

Frowning, he focused the glasses and grinned with relief.

"None of them is me. They had specimen cells from
hundreds of individuals. They didn't have to keep cloning
themselves."

He pointed to a wide gate opening in the side of the
arena. Two men came out, riding an odd little vehicle that
puffed white steam. He lifted the binoculars, and I heard
a sharp catch of his breath.

"Look at the driver." Whispering hoarsely, he pushed
the binoculars into my hand. "Look at his face."

The driver sat at the rear, over the engine. Naked to the
waist, he was black as Casey. He had the same high

cheeks and almond eyes, and a bright black bead on his forehead.

"He looks like another El Chino."

I studied the driver's face again, and found a thin red stain on the dark skin beneath the little bead. The passenger was a lean little man in silver and black sitting lower, above the single front wheel. They drove in a slow circle around us and stopped below our platform. The passenger stepped from the vehicle, dropped to one knee, stood again, shading his eyes to look up at us.

"Are you agents—" His quavery voice caught, and he began again. "Are you agents of the Moon?"

"We come from Tycho Station."

"Welcome to Kashmir." He knelt and rose again. His knobby Adam's apple rose and fell as he swallowed. He caught another breath and went on. "I am Thomas Drake, first secretary to Deputy Agent Eric Frye. I greet you in the name of First Agent Arne Stone, Regent for the Moon. We beg you to remain on your craft until a proper reception can be arranged."

I looked at Pepe.

"Why not?" He made a sad face at the black driver and shrugged uneasily. "Let's play their game."

"The First Agent will be honored to receive you," Drake said. "He regrets the inconvenience of this slight delay, but arrangements must be made." He raised his wrist to consult a bulky timepiece. "I'll be back two hours from now with transportation for you."

"Please thank the First Agent," Pepe called. "Tell him the honor is ours."

He dropped his voice. "Honor! I don't think so."

Drake knelt to us again and got back on the little vehicle. The black man drove them back through the gate. Pepe unfolded the landing stair and raised the glasses again to sweep the murmuring crowd on the rooftops, which was growing as we waited. He stood gazing around us in grim silence till suddenly he gripped my arm and pointed.

A young woman on a bicycle was riding out of a doorway on the opposite side of the empty field. Her blond head low, she pedaled rapidly toward us. "Mona!" he whispered. "She's Mona's clone."

20

S he stopped just below our platform, stepped off her bicycle, and looked up at us. Pepe shook his head and gave the glasses back to me.

"No, she isn't Mona." His voice fell in disappointment. "She has the same blue eyes, but not Mona's chin."

She leaned the cycle against the side of the stair, started up toward us, and paused to stare. In slacks and a neat green jacket, head bare and honey-colored hair cut short, she looked as enchanting as I thought the young Mona must have been when she came out of the east American hills to sing and dance for the ill-fated Earth. Nothing was wrong with her chin.

"May I climb up?"

Pepe grinned at her. "You're halfway already."

I stepped back into the doorway to make more room. She came up with us, flushed and a little breathless from her ride. She stood a moment staring at us, blue eyes wide with excitement.

"You are immortals?" Her voice was hushed with awe. "Truly immortals from the Moon."

I left the answer to Pepe. He simply grinned at her, looking more breathless than she was.

"I know your picture from the history books." She studied his face. "You are Space Pilot Pedro Navarro."

"Just call me Pepe."

She looked at me. "You—you must be Dr. Yare? I know your writing of the immortals. The great epic of the impact and the restoration. Though many call it fiction. I never understood how you became immortal."

"We aren't," Pepe said. "Only clones. But we do come from Tycho Station on the Moon."

"If you really do!" She was flushed with emotion.

"We've been waiting for hundreds of years, but I never really expected you now." She stopped to catch her breath and her gaze grew sharper. "If I may ask you to talk—"

"Okay," Pepe said. "We're talking."

"Okay?" She frowned. "Your words seem odd."

"So do yours." He grinned. "But let's talk."

She reached into a brown leather purse slung over her shoulder and turned to hand him a small white card. "I'm a watchbird," she said, "for *New World Reporter*. I have questions."

He examined the card and handed it to me. "What's a watchbird?"

"A writer of events." Her name on the card was Laura Grail. "Your coming is a historic event. Here is my great question." She looked searchingly at me and back at Pepe. "Do you bring a warning for our world?"

"Warning." Pepe shook his head, with a puzzled shrug. "No warning at all. We came just to survey the colony and report to the computer at the station. Your history. Your progress. Your problems, if you have problems. And most important to us, to find what became of the survey party we sent last year."

"No warning? You are certain?" She looked closely at me and back at him. "Don't you search the sky for danger?"

"The computer does."

"You see no threat of another impact? No great object coming out of space to strike the Earth?"

"Nothing at all." She seemed to relax, and Pepe went on, "Here is our own big question. About our lost expedition. Two of our people left the Moon not a year ago in a craft like this one."

She gave him a blank glance and shook her head, stepping back to look up in wonder at the shining silver tower of our hull.

"They planned to land here in this valley." He gestured

at the ice-crowned mountains that walled us in. "Do you know if they arrived?"

"I never heard—or maybe—" She blinked in a startled way. "There was a story nobody believed. An escaped slave who told the ridiculous tales such men invent. He claimed to be an immortal from the Moon."

"Only one?"

"A man and a female fugitive. Bounty hunters found them hiding on the ice."

"What happened to them?"

"Nothing unusual. Slaves escape. If no owners are found, they go to public auction."

"The woman?"

The girl turned from him to listen to the sound of distant music from somewhere beyond the open.

"I shouldn't be here." She frowned at the watchers on the rooftops and glanced uneasily around the empty field. "I must go."

"Not yet!" Pepe begged her. "We just arrived. We're desperate for answers. Everything is strange to us. Even the weather." He grinned at Laura Grail, trying to detain her, and gestured beyond her at the shining peaks, the indigo sky, the towering cloud. "On the Moon we have a hot sun and bitter nights, but no weather."

"It's spring." She stared at our distorted images reflected in the ship's ceramic skin and reached curiously to feel it. "Summer will be warmer, but we often have snow in the winters." Her voice quickened. "For the *Reporter,* may I ask about your plans here?"

"First," Pepe said, "we need help to locate our people. If they were that fugitive slave and the woman with him."

Her face grew grave.

"Slaves lie. The man spoke of a Moon ship that crashed on the glaciers, but no report of such a ship ever got past the censors. I advise you to forget the story."

"Is there a reason to forget?"

"The Scienteers." Gravely, she nodded. Though the watchers on the roofs were far away, she hushed her voice. "I should not have come here. If you are ever asked, you must not speak of me. Or speak of anything I say. Talk of agents of the Moon could put my life in danger."

"Not a word," he promised. "Cross my heart."

She looked puzzled.

He crossed his heart and asked, "What are Scienteers?"

"Enemies." Almost whispering, she stepped closer. "They call the regency a fraud and claim to be the only true agents of the Moon. Bounty hunters are employed to hunt them down. They are killed or fed to the riders."

"You say the slave and the convict were taken for Scienteers?"

"Perhaps." She looked uncomfortable. "Such events are never published. And please understand. I don't malign the regent. He has greater problems than the Scienteers."

"Yes?" Pepe asked. "Problems?"

"Everywhere. Rebels in America. Stalemate on the African front. Treason here at home. And he's no longer young."

"Are we another problem?"

Again I heard music from somewhere off the field, perhaps a military march. I saw her hands twist together as if in anxiety, but she smiled uneasily at Pepe.

"You should be safe," she told him, "unless you are taken to be Scienteers."

"We are not," he assured her. "But we need to know all you can tell us about what not to say. What not to do. We are waiting for a reception. What does that mean?"

"A great honor, if you are really from the Moon."

"What can we expect?"

"Questions, I'm sure." She frowned, considering. "You should speak with care. The regent sometimes has strange ideas. And strange advisors."

"Can you tell us more about him? About the history of the colony? About the situation now?"

"In the time I have." The military music rose again, and she glanced uneasily toward the gate. "If you will not speak of me."

"We'll say nothing." Pepe offered his hand. I wondered if a handshake still had meaning here, but she smiled and gripped his hand. "We need your help and we are grateful for it. If there are questions, what would they be?"

Listening to the voices from the rooftops, she stepped closer to him.

"The regent may want proof that you are actual agents of the Moon." Thinking, she paused to brush the fair hair off her face. "He may ask if you have a message from the immortals. He may ask if you bring help from them. And—" She frowned. "I never said so, if anybody asks, but he may fear that you threaten his authority."

"We didn't come to meddle."

"Our readers—" She paused again to listen. "They'll be asking for any kind of message, if they believe you're really from the Moon."

"I suppose you can tell them that Tycho Station still exists to continue its original mission."

"If that's true—if the regent believes it—he should welcome you. The Scienteers have never been certain of Tycho Station. They have suspected that it is only a myth, invented by the regents to support their authority."

"Don't you have records?"

"None accepted as authentic from the first century. The facts are all in question. Wars have been fought over tales nobody can prove. Scienteers have burned for what they believe."

"You yourself, what do you believe?"

She flushed and bit her lip.

"You should not ask such questions."

"Forgive me," he begged her. "What does anybody believe?"

She stood silent a moment, thoughtfully frowning, listening to the music from beyond the gate.

"Okay," she spoke at last, testing the new word. "Ask the regents. Ask the Scienteers, if you can find one. The regents like to call this field a holy spot. They believe that ancient spacecraft still stands where it landed. They have kept this space clear for a new craft to land here. Officially, they are eager to welcome new agents from the Moon." She hesitated and dropped her voice again. "Privately, I imagine they might prefer for things to stay as they are."

"And the Scienteers?"

"They doubt the official story. As that goes, the immortals quarreled after the landing, and fought for command. Arne Linder killed his male companions and had a natural son by the Immortal Dian. The son became Arne the First, legitimate founder of the dynasty."

"The Scienteers have another story?"

"The truth is hard to know, because old books and manuscripts are rare, perhaps destroyed by the early regents. The Scienteers have claimed that the colonists made a safe landing, but too high in the valley. Avalanches caught all three men off the ship. The women survived to build the first maternity lab and clone new children. The Scienteers have denied that the regents carry any immortal blood. That is the heart of their treason."

"That's our Arne." Pepe grinned at me. "He always had to be the top dog."

"Take care!" she warned him. "Care with what you say."

"Give us more history," he told her. "If our ignorance could kill us."

"It really could." Soberly, she glanced back toward that high-arched gateway. "The first century was difficult.

Even after it, Arne the Third was almost overthrown by the Chino wars. Yet a few of the later regents were able rulers. Our civilization has spread east to the Pacific. A hundred years ago, Arne the Eighth began shipping convicts to North America. A long voyage to a strange land, where trees are said to sing and strange creatures fly. The colony became profitable in spite of the distance and all the hazards, shipping exotic exports, but it's in rebellion now."

"You spoke of war with Africa?"

"War with the black riders and the red jungle where they live." She frowned. "It goes on forever. They're slow, but they never stop pushing out. We've studied them, traded with them, tried to make peace, but nobody understands them. The regent ought to hope that you have brought some better weapon."

The music was louder, and she moved to the stair. "Please forget me. I must go."

"We can't forget." Pepe reached to take her hand. "Will we see you again?"

"I hope." She caught his hand for a moment and ran back down the stair.

"Laura Grail." I heard him murmur her name as she jumped on the cycle and pedaled fast the way she had come. "A remarkable woman, and beautiful as Mona. Her eyes and her hair must come from Mona's genes."

We had both loved Mona, back at the station, though she had always chosen Casey. She had learned her mother's dances, watched El Chino's holo and had the robots teach her the art of defense, but she remained a free and charming spirit, ready for nearly anything.

"Great luck that Laura came." Pepe watched her vanish through that narrow doorway. "She told us a lot we need to know."

"And left us to wonder about all she had no time to say. Slaves, convict colonies . . ."

The music suddenly boomed louder. A big man in blue and gleaming gold came strutting out of the open gate pounding an enormous drum. A flag bearer followed, then a dozen men with instruments blazing music that had a familiar beat.

" 'The Stars and Stripes Forever,' " Pepe murmured. "Arne used to play a record of it. But that's a different flag."

When the wind caught the flag, I saw that it was blue, with a white crescent at the center. The band marched straight toward us and stopped twenty yards away. The players separated and spread out to form a single rank.

"What now?" Pepe looked uncertainly at me. "Shouldn't we go down to meet—"

He stopped when they turned away from us to face the gate and struck up another tune. Coming out of the gate was a huge sedan chair, gleaming with polished silver. It had seats for four. Eight men carried it. Black-skinned and bright with sweat, they were harnessed with straps to the poles, four men in front and four in the rear. They stopped at the foot of our stair.

Pepe snatched for the binoculars. The single passenger was Thomas Drake, the little man who had come in the steam-powered tricycle to meet us. He shouted a sharp command. The bearers bent to set the chair on the ground. He stepped out, knelt formally before us, rose again to face us.

"Your Worships—" His high voice paused. "Forgive me, I am ignorant of your proper titles."

Pepe stood silent, staring through the glasses.

"No matter," I called. "We are ready."

"Thank you, sire." Drake wiped a shaking hand across his forehead. "If you will descend, Deputy Regent Frye is waiting to receive you."

When Pepe didn't move, I caught his arm to urge him toward the stair and found him stiffly rigid. I heard the sharp catch of his breath.

21

Pepe kept the glasses on the men at the carriage poles. They looked identical. Naked except for blue loincloths, they were black as the man who drove the steam car. Waiting, they stood rigid, eyes fixed straight ahead, faces expressionless as our robots at the station.

"Look!" He was hoarse and breathless. "Look at their faces." His hand shaking, he gave the glasses to me. "They're all of them Casey!"

I got the faces in focus. Masks rather than anything alive, they were frozen copies of Casey's black Asian features, empty eyes blindly staring.

"The beads!" he whispered. "On their foreheads."

The men were bending in unison to set the chair down. I focused on the black foreheads and the blacker beads centered on them, each small bead with a thin red stain of blood around it. Not mere ornaments, they were hard-shelled bugs, skull-shaped, slick and bright. Almost more alive than the men they clung to, they were watching us with tiny white-rimmed eyes.

The sight recalled a thousand aching images of Casey as we had grown up together on the Moon. I remembered how he used to let Arne beat him at chess, just to keep Arne at the board for one more game. I remembered how he used to tease Mona about a little heart-shaped freckle on the side of her nose. I remembered how he used to coax us to read Shakespeare's plays aloud because he loved the language and the drama, always wanting the villain parts, Shylock and the Moor and Macbeth, for himself.

Looking down at the motionless, sweat-wet slaves, I felt sick.

"Don't you know those bugs?" Pepe was whispering.

"Or something like them. Remember that survey expedition before the colonists went down? What happened when you and Casey and Calvin landed in Africa?"

We had all read the transcripts and listened to the audios again and again, till in our minds we *were* the clone selves who had spent their last days here on Earth four centuries ago. I remembered the rust-red hue of the continent when we saw it from space, remembered the landing in the thorn jungle north of Kilimanjaro, remembered the thick tangle of saw-edged blades taller than we were.

Calvin DeFort had left the plane to look for whatever built the roads and cities we had seen from space. He never came back. Casey went out to look for him and met the thing that mauled and nearly killed him. A slick black creature the size of a human skull, it had clung with saberlike limbs driven into the alien creature it rode. It sprang at Casey when he killed the creature under it, sliced his arms with its talons, chased him back into the jungle, left an infection in his wounds that nearly killed him.

These beads were tiny copies of it.

"We called them vampires!" Pepe whispered again. "Aliens from somewhere off the Earth. Now . . ." He gripped my arm hard and stood a long time staring down at the eight identical black men standing robotlike at the poles. "Now riding us. Ruling our bodies and sucking our blood." A bitter grin twisted his face. "I think the colonists have somehow created their own hot little corner of hell."

Drake was waiting at the foot of the stair.

"Your Mercies?" He seemed impatient and uneasy. "Are you ready?"

Teeth gritted, Pepe led the way down. Drake gave us a sweaty handshake and gestured us into the chair. At a sharp word from him, the bearers picked it up and ran with us back through the gate and down a wide avenue.

"Moon Boulevard." Drake gestured. "It runs from the Moon Pad through the regency district."

Men in blue-black uniforms guarded street intersections. Brighter-clad people lined the sidewalks, waiting to watch us pass. Most fell silent as we came by. Now and then I heard a patter of applause or a child's voice, quickly hushed.

Looking around, wondering about the history and the present state of the colony, I saw no flashing signs, no trolley tracks, no high towers. Because there was no electricity? Yet everything looked well constructed, most of the buildings laid up from some white stone, roofed with red tile, set back from trees at the edge of the empty pavement. The city had an air of solid prosperity.

Beside me Pepe was silent, jaws set hard, eyes on the bearers. Shaved heads bent down, black muscles rippling and gleaming with sweat, they ran in step, calloused feet slapping the pavement in unison. Slave power instead of internal combustion engines.

Pepe leaned forward with a sort of grim intentness, pointing, asking Drake about everything. A few oaks and elms along the street we knew from videos of old Earth, but more of trees were unfamiliar. Towering toadstools had thick red-brown trunks crowned with masses of leaves that looked like fat, bloodred snakes. They filled the air with a heavy fragrance that had a hint of rotting fruit and set me to sneezing.

"African." Drake gestured at them. "Arne the Sixth sent an expedition that brought specimens back. He thought they were ornamental. I despise the bog rot stink, but they're historical monuments now."

Trying in a nervous way to play the genial host, he said our arrival had been awaited for hopeful generations. The regent was vastly honored by our visit. His voice turned anxious. Had we brought news of disaster or threat of disaster? Perhaps a second impact?

"No disaster," Pepe assured him. "The computer watches the sky, even while the station sleeps. It has reported no new impactor."

Drake seemed happy to hear that, happy that our arrival had happened in his lifetime. So many generations had died in disappointment. The regent was eager to know more about our mission. How long could we stay? What were our plans? What did we want to see? What changes had we brought to Earth?

Pepe answered cautiously. We had no plan to change the regency. All we wanted was information. The station existed simply to replenish the damaged Earth, not to rule it. We had come to survey the colony and return to the Moon with our data. Any future action would depend on what we learned.

Drake became the sly inquisitor, turning in his seat to smile and keep up his shrewd queries. Could our telescopes follow events on Earth? Did we know how the alien invaders had reached Africa? Had we been informed of the Scienteer rebellions in North America?

Careful not to betray Laura Grail, Pepe asked more question about the Scienteers.

Drake's smile faded and his voice grew angry. They were a cult of outlaw heretics, enemies of the regency. They had been almost extirpated from Asia, but lately their treason had grown new roots in North America.

"They claim to be secret agents of the Moon." He twisted in the seat to peer sharply at us. "Are you aware of any possible contacts?"

"No." Pepe's eyebrows lifted. "Never."

Drake sat back and asked for more about the station. If the Moon had no air and little water, if nothing grew there, how had anybody stayed alive there for hundreds of years?

"Make it millions," Pepe told him. "The robots maintain the computer and rebuild themselves. The computer never stops, but none of us are cloned till it has a new mission for us."

"Remarkable!" Drake shook his head as if he had never heard of robots or computers. "Remarkable!"

His own world seemed remarkable enough to me. Wondering how much had been done with only steam power, I thought of the Parthenon, the Roman aqueducts, the great Medieval cathedrals, all built with human power.

Drake called something to the bearers. They carried us off the street, through a gate guarded by half a dozen identical black men who looked like more clones of Casey. Uniformed in white and blue, they carried weapons that resembled the muskets we had seen in ancient drawings.

The wide courtyard beyond was filled with heavy chairs like our own, their black bearers standing frozen. Our own carriers ran with us up a long flight of marble steps and set us down between the white columns of a portico at the entrance of a monumental building.

"The Tycho Palace." Drake gestured. "Once the regent's residence. Now Deputy Regent Frye's."

Smiling broadly, Frye came down a strip of red carpet to greet us. A fleshy man with a gleaming silver band around a head of yellow curls, he wore a silvery garment that resembled the togas in drawings of ancient Rome. It looked stiff and heavy, as if actual metal wire had been woven into the fabric.

"Agent Navarro! Agent Yare!" He caught our hands as we climbed out of the chair. "Regent Arne regrets that he is not able to greet you himself. On his behalf, we are gathered to welcome you to Earth. He asked me to put every resource of the regency at your disposal for the duration of your visit."

His hand felt limp and clammy. He quickly drew it back, his shrewd eyes narrowed to scan us. Stolidly, Pepe asked him to give our thanks and greetings to the regent, and we followed him into a long hall that hummed with many voices.

"Agency people." Drake nodded toward the crowd. "Officials. Citizens of Kashmir. All eager to meet you before we go in to dinner."

The clamor of voices paused while a man with a foghorn voice announced our names. People stared toward us for a moment, but turned back to their groups. Their voices rose again. Any eagerness to receive us was well concealed. We stood there at the entrance, getting our bearings. In the huge room, the voices rang back from lofty walls and a vaulted ceiling.

My eye was caught by huge murals whose artist had tried to imagine the impact and its aftermath. On one wall, a blazing fireball was plunging into an ocean, the splash drowning a city, its people in panicked flight from a towering wave already curling high over them. The opposite wall carried his vision of a lunar landscape, with the cliffs of Tycho climbing to an enormous crystal dome. A gigantic figure, with Arne's face but no helmet or space gear, stalked from it along the crater rim, toward a red-painted spacecraft. A second Arne stared down from an enormous portrait at the end of the room, a cold smile on his heavy-jawed, square-chinned face.

"He ought to be here," Pepe murmured at my ear. "He'd be proud to meet his heirs." He shook his head and squinted at me. "Though I'm afraid the actual regent might see him as a problem."

Leading us into the hall, Frye nodded at a group of white-gowned men around a young woman in bright green.

"Someone you must meet." He raised an imperative hand. Laura Grail left her companions and came smiling to join us. "A watchgirl," he said. "She will want your story."

Blue eyes wide, she waited innocently for him to introduce us.

"Our distinguished guests," he told her. "Inspectors from the Moon. Agent Pepe Navarro." Pepe bowed over her offered hand. "Agent Duncan Yare. They may have a story for you."

"I'll have questions."

Pepe turned to a young girl standing near us with a tray of glasses. Naked to the waist and blond as Mona, she had the vacant face of a sleeping child. Her eyes were wide, unfocused, blankly staring. A small stain of blood was drying around the bright black skull-shaped bead on her forehead.

"Sire?" Still staring blankly away, she spoke in a child's high voice. "A cocktail?"

Frye took two drinks off the tray and offered them to us. Grimly, Pepe shook his head. I tasted the cocktail. It was something sharp as vinegar, raw with alcohol. I set it back.

"That button?" His voice suddenly harsh and violent, Pepe pointed to the skull-shaped bead. "What is it?"

"A rider," Frye said. "Something new to you?"

Pepe nodded, bleakly silent.

"There's the expert." He beckoned to a man half across the room. "Kroman Venn, the Agent for Energy."

Venn waddled to meet us. As soft and fleshy as Frye, he gave us a genial grin and offered his fat white hand.

"Our guests are inquiring about rider energy," Frye told him.

"I have inquiries of my own." Venn's pale eyes narrowed to scan our faces. "I suppose you have electricity on your flyer? Perhaps atomic energy? The ancient texts mention such technologies. If they ever did exist."

"They still do," Pepe said. "Tycho Station runs on nuclear power. But I want to know about those bugs."

"The riders?" He paused to study us again. "New to

you? Call them our compensation for all the electric magic the Scienteers say we have lost."

Pepe looked back at the girl with the tray of drinks. Still near us, she stood rigid as the wax figures I had seen in old holos. Venn reached for a drink to offer him. He gestured as if to knock it away. His face white with emotion, it took him another moment to control his anger, but at last he spoke reasonably.

"If you want electricity, we could teach you the science. Your people would need to develop the skills to use it." He pointed a quivering finger at the skull-shaped bead, which stared back at him with tiny, white-rimmed eyes. "That little monster? What is it?"

"A useful technology of our own." Venn smiled with satisfaction. "You may not know our history. Our first century was a time of troubles. We had problems and found solutions. We built windmills. We developed waterpower. Most useful of all, we learned to use the riders."

Pepe's fists had clenched. "Those black bugs?"

"A surprise to you?" Venn backed away and raised his hand defensively. "If I must explain, the rider seed are bartered from Africa. They are grown and trained on our own regency farms and planted in sterile labs by skilled surgeons. They are an essential economic resource. More precious than rubies, as the saying goes."

"Planted?" Pepe rasped. "Where?"

"Where you see them." Venn gestured at the girl. "In the brains of convicts and clones."

"You breed clones for slaves?"

"Why not?" Venn's voice sharpened impatiently. "We have no other use for them."

Pepe nodded at the girl. "Is she a clone?"

Venn swung to bark at the girl, "What was your crime?"

"Shoplifting, sire." Her high child's voice held no feeling. "I took fruit from a market because my mother was hungry."

"You see?" He turned back to Pepe. "The riders are instruments of social order. They keep convicted criminals removed from society without the cost of prisons or guards. The surgeons assure us that they feel no pain. Their labor serves the nation. Does that answer your question?"

"It certainly does." Venn was turning away. Pepe raised his voice. "Sir, if you don't mind, I have another."

Frowning impatiently, Venn turned back to listen

"Cloning technologies are complex and difficult. I wonder how you manage them without electricity."

Venn shrugged.

"Life itself is electric. You may have heard of electric eels. We're familiar enough with the theories, but we have never tried to rebuild your old devices. As I understand them, your technologies were mechanical. Ours are organic."

"Organic?"

"You may be ignorant of Africa." Venn raised his sharp nose with a scarcely veiled disdain. "The inhabitants are exotic. Their evolutionary origin is unknown. Some say they come from off the Earth. Their culture is as alien as their bodies. They use no machines. Instead they adapt living organisms to fit their needs.

"Quite successfully." A frown creased his narrow face. "They have occupied the entire continent and now spread beyond it. We have fought endless wars to contain them. They don't communicate with us. Their language, in fact, may be biochemical. But we have learned something of their peculiar bioscience. Enough, in fact, to breed the riders and clone the slaves."

He nodded at a little man across the room.

"There's Hibbly. A rider engineer. If you like, I can arrange for you to visit his breeding station."

Pepe thanked him, and he stalked away.

"Don't go." Laura dropped her voice. "I'd advise you not to talk about rider slavery. The Scienteers have always fought to get rid of the riders. That is their greatest treason. If you express too much concern it could earn you riders of your own."

22

N ice to meet you both." Laura Grail raised her voice
and smiled for those around us. "Welcome to the regency. When you have time, I want to get the whole
Tycho Station story for our readers."

"One more question," Pepe murmured. "How can we
find Mona?"

She shook her head and slipped away. He stood looking
after her till Frye caught his arm.

"Your Mercies, please." Frye nodded at the crowd,
scores of people talking and sipping their drinks, ignoring
us after those curious glances when we were introduced.
"Our guests are dignitaries invited to meet you."

"Happy about it?" Pepe grinned. "They're keeping their
distance."

"Hesitant, perhaps." Frye frowned in apology. "Please
understand that your sudden arrival has taken us by surprise. Created something of a crisis, in fact. Nobody is
certain what to expect from you."

"We are grateful for the welcome," Pepe assured him.
"We plan no trouble for anybody."

He gave us a narrow look and escorted us around the
hall. I listened and made mental notes for our reports.
Pepe spoke for us, wary with what he said.

The Agent of Trade was short fat man named Galt
Wickman, who wore a bright gold headband and a golden
fringe on his toga. Frye told us he owned the rail system.
He shook our hands and beckoned the girl with cocktails.
Moving as stiffly as a robot, she thrust her tray toward us
and stood rigid, the black bug on her forehead watching
us with tiny bright eyes till we refused the drinks and the
agent waved her away. He stood inspecting us in a silence
that had grown awkward before Frye broke it.

"Our guests are curious about our sources of power. They were asking if we understand electricity."

"Our engineers have looked at the theory." His mouth pursed thoughtfully. "I've seen them creating bolts of lightning, but we have steam. Our rail system spreads south to the Indian Ocean and east to the Pacific, and our ships reach the Americas. We've never needed anything better."

"Are you certain?" Pepe frowned after the girl with the drinks. "With electricity, you wouldn't need human power."

"Why bother?" He shrugged. "It's free."

Pepe blinked and looked again at the girl. "That thing on her forehead? A rider, I think you call it? I understand that they come from Africa?"

"The seeds do."

"So you grow the bugs?"

"I don't." Wickman flushed and looked uncomfortable. "If you want to inquire into rider culture, talk to Sheba Kingdom."

"There she is." Frye nodded at a woman half across the hall. "I'll introduce you. Her family controls the Africa Company. If you care about history, there's a historic drama."

Sheba Kingdom glanced at us and turned back to the group around her while Frye expanded on his drama.

"Her great-great-grandfather was an early explorer, back before the age of steam. A typhoon wrecked his sailing vessel on the east coast of Africa. He got ashore alive and escaped twenty years later, paddling across the Red Sea in a crude little skin-covered canoe.

"He had been captured by the strange creatures of the continent. Creatures he called the black masters. One of them had ridden him, its fangs driven into his skull and controlling his brain. He escaped when it died and went back in one of the first ocean-going steamers to bombard their coastal cities with his cannon. He then began the Africa Company. Its business methods are secret, but it has been profitable. Sheba Kingdom is said to be the richest woman in the world."

She left her admirers and strode toward us. A commanding presence, she was tall and muscular, her long dark hair bound in gold. A heavy rope of black pearls hung below her ample breasts. Gold paint shone on her lips and around her eyes. She stood silent, regarding us with cold curiosity, while Frye explained that we were the new agents from the Moon.

"Have you dictates from the Moon?" Her voice was hoarse, almost masculine. "Orders you expect us to obey?"

"None," Pepe told her. "We came only to look and report what we find."

"They were inquiring about rider cultivation," Frye added. "Perhaps you can explain it?"

"Why?" She fixed him with her gold-rimmed eyes. "Why are you concerned?"

"We see them everywhere." Pepe nodded at the girl with the drinks. "Our computer will want information about them."

She frowned impatiently, moved as if to leave us, swung abruptly back.

"You can tell your computer that the rider seed we import from Africa are eggs of the black masters. We hatch them in baths of human blood, sterilize them to prevent unwanted reproduction, select and drill them for designated services. If that's any business of your clever computer on the Moon."

She straightened her massive shoulders and left us.

Frye spread his hands and took us on to meet Deputy Houston Blackthorn, the agent for defense. A towering, black-bearded man in a dark blue uniform, he wore a long sword in a jeweled sheath and gleaming medals on a wide red ribbon across his barrel chest. Crushing our hands in a powerful fist, he told us to inform our computer that the regency was well prepared to defend itself from any hostile power. I wondered if he saw the Moon as a hostile power, but decided not to inquire.

Frye asked him about the war.

"Which war?" His bronze grin was gone. "We've run the nomads back into their desert and fed a thousand Indonesian pirates to the fish. We're holding like a stone wall on the African front. As for North America—" His lips set hard. "It's half the world away. Even steamships take forever. Those frammed Scienteers have sprung up like African poisonwarts. They have a new leader now."

He scowled though his beard.

"A woman who claims to be an actual agent of the Moon. Sent to warn the world of another impact due. So their poison rhetoric goes. Her spacecraft crashed on the glaciers up at the head of the valley, if anybody believes her. She should have been seized and bugged for such a tale, but Scienteer agents got her to America. She's sowing her treason there."

Mona. Pepe looked hard at me, his lips moving to shape the silent words. *She is Mona.*

"A problem for us." Blackthorn shook his head. "Too many colonists believed her crazy story. Rebellion spread. Our forces always outnumbered them a hundred to one, but driven clones don't fight like those madmen. We had losses, but now we have them on the run."

A gong boomed. Frye escorted us into another vast room. A long table ran down the center, a wide fan above it swinging lazily back and forth, driven by one of Casey's black clones hauling on a rope at each end of the room. Porcelain, silver, and glassware shone on a sea of white cloth. A white-clad waiter stood at attention behind each chair, a bright black bug gleaming on his vacant face.

I was seated between a sallow-faced bureaucrat from the Justice Agency and an attractive young woman with a crimson hairband and a crimson fringe on her gown. Her name was Ellen Teller; she said she was a broker. Pepe sat just beyond her, Frye at the head of the table.

The gong rang again. The guests rose, lifted glasses of a sour black wine, and drank to the greater glory of Regent Arne XIX, Agent of Earth. I was half expecting a toast to the guests from the Moon, but Frye did not propose it.

The waiters began serving us from wheeled tables. Though most life in Asia had sprung from our own seedings, the dishes were often strange to us. Ellen Teller explained them brightly when Pepe asked. Baffled by the silver, I was watching for clues from the people across the table till she laughed at me.

"Don't fret about your table manners, Agent Yare," she told me. "If you're awkward with your forks, it's the best evidence that you're really from the Moon."

When Pepe asked, she explained the murals. They were historic: gigantic figures of Arne the First climbing a Himalayan peak, Arne the Tenth carrying a flag ashore to conquer North America, Arne the Twelfth carving a path through a jungle of crimson blades to battle a double-headed monster.

"You're a broker?" Pepe inquired. "Can we talk about your business?"

"Certainly," she told him. "I deal in riddens."

"You do?" Silent for a moment, he turned to look at her. His voice grew sharper. "You mean clones? Ridden by those bugs?"

"Oh no!" She laughed. "Most black clones are grown on low-profit contracts for wholesale. We deal in fresh convicts from the Justice Agency. A speculative market, but far more profitable. The fresh convicts require individual attention, but many retain useful skills and abilities, well worth the care." Silent for a moment, she added brightly, "If you need any special services, I can probably supply them."

"I see," Pepe said, and sat staring moodily at the bugs on the foreheads of the waiters across the table until she began asking what Agent Frye was planning for us. He muttered that he had no idea.

"The regent will want to receive you," she told him, "as soon as he's certain you are really from the Moon."

"How could he doubt?"

"The Scienteers are always attempting to deceive us with claims of new messages and messengers from the Moon. Most recently in America."

Pepe sank into gloomy silence, and she chattered at me.

"You should visit America if your stay on Earth allows—a long voyage, but there's a good stop at Cape Town. That's our African treaty port, where we trade for the rider seed. The natives may have no language we can understand, but we get on. There are fascinating side trips you ought to take, to see the red thorn bush and the plantations where the masters work their own creatures. Even a zoo of exotics."

Pepe aroused himself to ask, "What do you trade for the seed?"

"Minerals," she said. "The masters, you see, are believed to have evolved somewhere off the Earth. They don't do much mining or chemistry. We supply them with fluorides, iodine, bromine. Elements their odd metabolism seems to require."

Pepe muttered something under his breath and subsided again.

"I went to America on a business trip, hoping to set up a branch office." She turned back to me with a face of distaste. "Horrid hotels, and the project came to nothing.

Hostility to rider labor, and now this female rebel who claims to be an actual agent of the Moon."

Pepe dropped a spoon. Instantly his waiter picked it up and placed another by his plate.

"If you don't have time for the voyage," Ellen Teller went on, "you must see the museums here in town. Splendid dioramas of African and American exotica, and fascinating relics of our own dark age and the early wars with the black masters."

"You fight them?" I asked. "And you trade with them? If you don't mind the question—"

She laughed.

"We have to fight, because their jungle keeps on spreading. A wall of tall red blades with poison thorns that rip a man to ribbons and infect him with a virus that kills him. The masters and their monsters keep breaking out to raid human settlers. You have to hate them." Philosophically, she shrugged. "Yet rider seed are my business. It has been very good to me."

The gong rang. The hall went silent. The guests rose, hands on their hearts. Frye led a pledge of devotion to Regent Arne. We stood in a reverential hush till the gong sounded again. Voices rose again and Frye came back to us.

"Great news for Your Mercies," he said. "The regent will receive you tomorrow at noon. In the meantime, I have reserved the government guest house for you."

I looked at Pepe. He shook his head.

"We are grateful to the regent and to you," I said. "But we prefer to live on our ship till we get accustomed to the gravity and atmosphere of Earth."

"The regent will be informed, and you may return to your craft."

Drake met us at the door with the eight-man chair and took us back through the unearthly trees and evil reeks of Moon Boulevard. A squad of black clones at the arena gate saluted and let us pass. He left us, with a promise to pick us up at noon next day for the reception.

At the foot of the stair, Pepe glanced across the arena and frowned at the narrow doorway where Laura Grail had entered. Beside it, I saw a rickshaw, overturned and abandoned. With a puzzled shrug, he turned to climb the stair and stopped abruptly, looking down at the steps. They were spattered with blood.

Inside the lock, we heard hoarse breathing and found a naked black man lying on the deck. When he heard us, he gasped again and turned his head. I saw Casey's familiar Chinese face, now with a wide red smear across the forehead.

"Casey?" Pepe whispered. "Casey?"

23

He moaned and sank back on the floor, eyes closed, a thin stream of blood still oozing from the narrow black pit on his forehead.

"Casey!" Pepe knelt to call his name. "Can you speak to me?"

Lying on his back, the sounds of his breath faint and slow, he made no response.

"It is Casey," Pepe whispered.

"Are you sure?"

"I saw it in his eyes. He knew me."

He lay still while we washed off the drying blood and sprayed healant on the wound. Pepe opened the aid kit, stuck the sensors to the vital points, made a face at the red-lettered readout.

"It knows no more than we do."

Rolling the body over, we found hard calluses on his hands and feet, but no other injuries. We folded the co-pilot's seat back to make a bed and lifted him into it. He lay there lifeless except for the faint slow wheeze of his breath. We took turns sitting with him and saw no change. I was at work on a report for the station when Pepe saw the gate opening.

A squad of uniformed men marched in and scattered to search the field. They found the overturned rickshaw and trundled it away. They climbed into the red-painted plane that stood on the other pad, came out again, and finally gathered around our craft. Their leader hailed us.

"Your Mercy, please forgive us. We are searching for an escaped slave. A black clone, desperate and dangerous. We have traced him here. Have you seen him?"

Pepe glanced at the blood on the stair and turned to me. I took a moment to think. Caught with Casey aboard, we could be branded as Scienteer agents and enemies of the regent. Yet I shook my head.

"You're hunting a runaway slave?" Pepe mimicked astonishment. "You won't find him here."

"Watch for him, Your Mercy. He is a danger to you and your machine. Any evidence must be reported at once."

He formed his men into a column and marched them away. Pepe shrugged uneasily and we went back inside to take Casey's pulse and try the aid kit again. With no medical skills, no equipment except the kit and the heal-ant, we knew nothing else to do.

The healant had stopped the oozing blood. All after-noon he lay flat, breathing heavily, with no response when we called his name or offered water. Sometime after sun-set, he sat up and looked around the cabin. I saw fleeting recognition, and then stark anxiety.

"Mona? Where's Mona?"

"I don't know," Pepe began, "but we've heard—"

With something like a sob, he sank back and lay still again. All that night we took turns napping and sitting beside him. Sometimes he rubbed at the healant on his wound. Sometimes he shouted words I didn't understand and thrashed out at some invisible foe. When I caught his hand, he clung to mine as if he needed human contact, and his rapid breathing slowed. He relaxed and finally seemed to sleep.

Early next morning I woke from a doze and found him standing by the bed. Swaying unsteadily till he got his balance, he padded to the bathroom. I heard the shower. He came back naked, his body drawn lean but good mus-cles rippling under his skin.

"Mona." He stood gazing at me, his features twisted with pain. "Have you found her?"

Pepe shook his head and asked about her.

"I don't know anything." His voice was a rusty rasp.

"We left the plane on the ice when they fired at us and tried to hide when they hunted us. They caught me. I don't know what became of her."

"I think—I hope she got away," I told him. "We've heard of a woman fighting with the rebels in America. A woman who claims she came from the Moon."

"If it's Mona." He fell silent, scowling grimly at ice-white peaks far beyond the window. "If we could reach her."

"If we could." I had to shake my head. "She's half around the world. If she's really Mona."

"But now, Casey—" Pepe hesitated. "Could you tell us what it was like? With the bug on your head?"

"Hell!" He shivered and tried to grin. "Later, maybe. If I can. Not just yet."

"Don't fret about it." Pepe shrugged. "You've lost blood. How do you feel?"

"Huh?" Fingering the healant on his forehead, he stared for a moment as if we had been unwelcome strangers. "Sorry, Pep." He grimaced and shook his head. "It was nightmare. I'd like to forget—" He drew a long, unsteady breath. "I'll be okay, I think. My head—" He frowned and touched the healant as if it puzzled him. "What I need is sleep."

"No breakfast? Can you eat?"

"Breakfast?" He frowned again. "I can try."

Pepe made a pot of the bitter brew the Robos called tea and heated three of the breakfast packs they had made for us. Casey tasted uncertainly, ate with a growing appetite, wanted another mug of tea.

"If you can talk?" Pepe asked again. "Can you tell us how it was?"

"If you want to know." He huddled in silence for a moment, pulled himself grimly straighter. "It was hell!" his voice exploded, but then he went on more evenly. "If you believe in hell. My head bursting with an ache that never stopped. Worse, the utter helplessness. I could feel everything, hear everything, see everything that came in front of my eyes, but I couldn't move a muscle. Even an itch on my nose was torment. I couldn't scratch it.

"Or even think, except in moments when the bug wasn't using me. I fought for freedom when I could. Fought to wink an eye, move a finger. Waited for a chance. Last night they had us sweeping streets. I was coming out of an alley with my broom when the bug stopped me to let a freight wagon pass. In that free second, I saw a storm drain at my feet, dropped the broom and managed to trip. Twisted my head as I fell. It fought—fought—"

His voice gone, he peered at us as if we were sudden enemies. Fists clenched, he blinked around the cabin as if he had forgotten where he was.

"Sorry." He grimaced and caught a ragged breath. "It tried to kill me. Hit me with its own pain when it struck the pavement. Knocked me cold. I don't know how long I lay there before I got back to myself enough to jerk the dead bug out of my head. And then—"

In a dazed way, he stopped to brush at the healant.

"The next I remember is the stink of those queer trees. The freight wagon was gone. The street looked empty. I had to lean on a wall till my head cleared. Ran up the alley when I could. Found the rickshaw outside a repair shop and used it for cover to get me here. Now—"

He stopped to scan us with anxious, bloodshot eyes.

"Can you hide me? Let me—let me sleep?"

His voice trailed off. He sank back on the bed, gently snoring.

"We've got to hide him," Pepe said. "If we can."

He found a spade and climbed down the stair to toss sand over the spatters of blood. I updated my report for the computers and found a pale Moon climbing behind the sun. It gave me a dreamlike imagine of the station,

Earth blazing out of the black north sky across the crater to light the dome. I sat filled with a wistful longing for it, while Pepe sent the report and we waited for an answer.

I had grown up half in love with Tanya, half with Mona, always sadly aware that they both loved Casey more. And never fond of Arne. Not yet any proud prince of Earth, but an arrogant snot nobody loved, though Dian had let him claim her.

I remembered how they all came to say farewell when we took off. Dian wished us luck. Tanya had kissed us and cried. I wondered how much they would care about us now. Would Arne let them mount a rescue expedition if we had to beg for it? I thought not.

When our message got no answer, we were not surprised.

Casey slept, seeming at last to be at rest, while we kept an anxious lookout from the windows. A few people came and went to stare at us from the roofs beyond the wall, but we saw nobody in the arena. When time for the reception drew near, I shook Casey's arm.

Still heavy with sleep, he stood up unsteadily, stumbled to the bathroom, and gulped another mug of tea. He seemed bewildered and alarmed that we had to leave him, but he let Pepe persuade him to climb down into the coffinlike cargo locker between the fuel tanks. We shut the door in the floor and spread a scrap of carpet over it.

Noon came. The gate opened. A silver-trimmed eight-man chair came out, Drake and Frye in the front seat. They stopped the carriers at a little distance and stepped out of the chair. We climbed down the steps to meet them.

"Take your time," Pepe murmured. "Don't forget who we are. Actual agents of the Moon."

"Your Mercies!" Frye shook our hands rather too heartily, while Drake hung diffidently back. "The regent is ready to receive you."

Yet he beckoned us farther away from the chair, glancing back as if he thought the bearers or their bugs might be eavesdropping. His voice fell confidentially.

"Your Mercies, I trust you." He glanced at me so narrowly that I thought he didn't. "You have been asking for information about regency affairs. May I presume to add a word of my own?"

"Please," Pepe told him. "Really, we need to know everything."

"There's a crisis in the making." He caught our arms to pull us closer, his voice almost a whisper. "You should know that Regent Arne is no longer what he was. You will meet his second wife, Fiona Faye. A bitch!" Dislike twisted his face. "Forget the word, but that's what she is. She flaunts her position and dishonors him. She is said to sleep with her black clones. Perhaps also with her current favorite, Labor Agent Ash. She's plotting to make him the next ruler.

"The rightful heir should be the regent's son, Harold. He is now in America, commanding our forces there and too far away to protect himself. As for Ash—" Frye's lip curled in contempt. "He deals in controlled convicts. Buys them through Teller. Keeps the best women for himself. Sells the rest or works them to death on his own plantations."

He stopped to study our faces.

"A precarious situation, made more urgent by your arrival. If you get in anybody's way, the outcome could be ugly. Ugly for you and all of us, if you get me."

Pepe nodded soberly to say we did.

He beckoned us into the chair and the bearers ran with us out of the arena and back through the wagons and chairs and rickshaws and the evil reeks of the red-crowned fungoids on Moon Boulevard, which ended at a fountain playing around the feet of a towering figure of Arne the First. A wide flight of white marble steps rose to the regent's palace: a monumental pile of black granite beyond a white marble colonnade.

A squad of Casey clones halted us and searched us before they escorted us down a long hall to an empty antechamber, a huge room with bare wooden benches along the sides. We waited uneasily there till at last a gold-clad guard beckoned Pepe and me into the regent's sanctum. Drake and Frye rose to go with us, but he gestured in hard-faced silence to leave them standing, trying to hide their discomposure.

Regent Arne sat waiting with his wife at the center of a long table on a raised dais. A huddle of failing flesh in a gold-fringed toga of woven silver, he blinked at us dimly. I saw no likeness to the Arne we had known on the Moon.

Fiona Faye was a thin little woman in a purple robe. She may have been a beauty once, in spite of a hawkbeak nose, though the golden mask painted around her eyes and the enameled coils of her black hair made that impossible to guess.

The table was bare except for a small glass of some dark liquid, set in front of the regent. He reached for it with a shaking hand, but pushed it clumsily away when she frowned. Alone with them in the silent chamber, we stood there a long time, waiting under his empty gaze and her predatory stare.

"You!" Moving suddenly, she stabbed a silver-nailed finger at Pepe and then at me. Sharp as a thrown knife, her voice clattered against the high bare walls. "Who are you?"

We gave our names.

"Where were you born?"

"At Tycho Station," Pepe said. "On the Moon."

"Can you prove it?"

I thought of the old coins Dian had given us, but saw no use for them here.

"You can see our spaceplane on the field," Pepe said. "Your people saw us land."

"If you did—" She let us wait half a minute, her gold-rimmed eyes squinted at us coldly. "Do you bring a message?"

Pepe glanced uneasily at me and took his own time to answer.

"Only that Tycho Station is still there, its mission still to keep humankind alive on Earth."

Her probing stare swung to me and back to Pepe.

"You bring no warning of some danger in the sky? Nothing of this demon stone the Scienteers rant about, falling out of the sky to kill us all?"

"No stone I've heard about." Pepe shook his head. "Our computer watches the sky. It follows many objects. It has reported nothing on a collision orbit."

She shrugged, with no sign of surprise or relief. "So why are you here?"

"We came to survey the progress of the colony since it was planted, to search for two people who came down ahead of us, and to offer help toward further progress if help is wanted."

"Help with what?"

"Information, if you want it." Pepe paused expectantly. I saw no change in her wolfish intentness or the regent's dull indifference. He tried again. "We should be able to bring you arts and skills that seem to have been lost. Technologies I think you could use. Electricity, perhaps."

"Electricity?" The regent blinked vacantly. "What's electricity?"

"A useful force. It creates light. It can give you power."

The regent's head was drooping. She jogged him with her elbow. He farted loudly and glared at me.

"You get heavy rains in the monsoon seasons." Pepe

swung back to her. "Snow on the mountains. From space we saw great rivers and magnificent waterfalls. We can bring you technology for hydroelectric—"

"Hydrowhat?"

"Energy," Pepe said. "Power to build a greater civilization." He raised his voice to penetrate the golden mask. "Electricity is more powerful than steam. Your technology has stalled. You would have to train engineers and build an infrastructure, but we can bring the science you seem to lack—"

"Liars!" The regent pointed a trembling finger at us. "Scheming Scienteers!"

"Not so, sir." Pepe grinned in desperation. "Give us a chance. We can prove who we are and help you change your world. Electric power could do a thousand times more than your driven slaves. You can get rid of those hideous bugs—"

"Treason!" She shrieked at the regent, her golden face a mask of hate. "They are Scienteers!"

With a dim smirk at her, the regent picked up the glass and tossed the black liquid down his throat. Alarm gongs crashed. A heavy wooden wall crashed down in our faces. We were suddenly surrounded by black clones swinging clubs and machetes.

24

Half a dozen black clones surrounded us, their leader white and blind. One eye was a shriveled pit. A dark patch hid the other. He saw us through the tiny black eyes of the bug on his forehead. He, or perhaps the bug, drove us with harsh staccato commands: *Walk! . . . Quick! . . . Right! . . . Left! . . . Halt!*

He marched us back up Moon Boulevard to the Agency of Justice, a modest red-brick building two blocks down a side street. Inside the building he left us locked in a long bare cell with a stone bench along one wall and a narrow ditch of reeking sewage across the end.

A thin blade of sunlight from a high window slashed through the shadows to pick out a little man in a dingy gray cloak slumped into a sobbing huddle on the end of the bench. The iron door clanged behind us. Feeling trapped and bewildered, stunned by disaster, I could only stare at Pepe.

"I wish we'd never landed." His voice dropped, though the weeping man had paid us no attention. "Or never left Casey alone on the plane. God knows what will happen to him now." Sunk into bitter despair, he was silent for a time. "If this is the best we can do," he muttered suddenly, "DeFort should have let the dead Earth alone."

Searching for any way to cheer him, I found nothing to say, but somehow he found spirit enough to sit beside our unfortunate companion and coax him to tell his story. Between sobs, the man whimpered that he had discovered his best friend in bed with his wife. Out of his head with grief and fury, he picked up a lamp and struck his friend. His wife screamed and grappled him. He struck again. His friend fell and died. His wife's arm was broken, but she ran out naked and called the law.

"What will happen to you now?"

"I don't care." He rubbed his red eyes. "They can bug me if they want. I should have died with Carlo."

With no cheer from him, Pepe probed for any hint of hope from other prisoners that came in throughout the rest of the day. One was a jittery little man in a dirty white toga, eager to tell his tale. He had been an honest businessman, selling tropical fruit from a stand on Regent Street. Arrested for robbing a silversmith, he was the innocent scapegoat of the actual thief.

"Early this morning I was walking as always to my little stand on the street. The thief dashed past me, a fat cop whistling behind him. He snatched my hat and tossed a handful of stolen silver at my feet. I followed him to recover my hat. He stopped, pointed back at the scattered silver, and swore that he had seen me tossing a brick through the shop window. The cop laughed at the truth and let him walk away with most of the loot still in his pockets."

The weeping man sat up to give Pepe a sardonic shrug.

"Believe him if you want. I'd say his bug is talking. It makes a man a fool, even before it grows into his brain, but his lies will never save him. The judge won't listen and his bug won't care."

He wiped at his swollen eyes with the back of his hand and sank back into dismal silence.

"How many get bugs?" Pepe turned back to the man in the dirty toga. "Don't some go to prison instead?"

"Prison? What is prison?"

He stared as if we had been strange animals while Pepe tried to explain what a prison was. "If such places ever existed, they are not needed now. The bugs are enough."

When the door clanged again, our next guest was a drunk in a blood-spattered toga and a rag around his head. He staggered to the end of the cell, vomited noisily into the ditch, fell back on the bench, and lay there in a reek of raw alcohol, snoring hoarsely.

The last to come in was better dressed, with a gold hairband and a gold-fringed garment that looked like silk. A swarthy fellow with a thick black mustache, he seated himself with an air of offended arrogance and ignored Pepe's first efforts at talk. When Pepe persisted, he exploded into a sudden diatribe.

"They call this the temple of justice, but I've been frammed! Frammed by my partner. We were in construction. Royce and Ryan, a fine old company, loyal to the regent, our buildings standing all over the city. We were bidding on contracts for the Asian Tower when my first partner died and his son replaced him.

"Mike Ryan, a cocky kid just out of college and full of tarky about civil rights. We'd always used contract labor. Black clones for heavy work, ridden convicts for skills with steel and fine masonry. Of course the freeman unions always fought us when we went to the brokers for their skilled ex-members who had been bugged for strikes and riots. Mike wanted us to hire freemen at twice the price. I told him that would ruin us, but the framhead wouldn't listen.

"Instead he schemed to fram me. Accused me of his own crimes. Forged evidence that I was in a big conspiracy to liberate convicts. Killing their riders with the juice of some poison weed smuggled out of Africa and running an underground railway to get them to freedom in America.

"A monstrous plot to get me out of his way and take the company over." He sighed forlornly. "The stupid justice agents raided our office, seized our records, arrested me. Look at me now! A convict myself, sentenced to sweat out the rest of my life with a bug in my head."

The tearful man roused himself again.

"Could be the other way round." He grinned mali-

ciously at Royce. "Could be you were the thief. Could be
your victim turned the tables on you. Could be you frammed yourself."

They sat glaring at each other with no more to say. That
thin blade of sunlight shifted and reddened and dimmed.
The guards brought a jar of water for us to pass around,
but no food. The stinking ditch was a latrine when we
had to use it. The drunk slid off the bench and lay snoring
on the floor.

Pepe paced the narrow floor and came back to whisper
to me.

"Think, Dunk! Think! We're dead if we don't."

I tried and thought of nothing.

The light faded. Pepe paced as long as he could see.
Stiff from sitting, I felt stiff and cold and hopeless. The
dark cell grew silent, except for coughs and snores and
the sad man moaning that he loved his wife and never
meant to kill Carlo. I slept at last, dreaming that we were
back in the plane, on our way to the Moon. The screech
of the iron hinges woke me.

The others had been given numbers, by some system I
never understood. Guards reading numbers off a slate
came to call them out, one by one. The drunk lay snoring
till the red-eyed man shook him awake, tried to vomit
again, and staggered out after the guard. Pepe and I waited
uneasily until at last we were taken down a gloomy corridor and into a room where sunlight dazzled me.

The wide window framed a walled garden of luxuriant
plants with thick purple cactuslike leaves and huge,
trumpet-shaped scarlet blooms. The sun shone across a
wide desk of some jet-black hardwood, polished till it
mirrored the glare. The air was sharp with an odd scent
of tiny golden flowers on a mosslike plant that filled a
crystal bowl.

"Gentlemen!"

The rider broker, Ellen Teller, greeted us genially, smiling across the desk. Dressed in something brighter and more revealing than her toga at the dinner, she looked bright and young and clean, almost as attractive as I remembered Mona and Tanya. She rose. I thought for an instant that she was coming around the desk to shake our hands, but she beckoned briskly at the chairs in front of the desk. "Please sit down."

We sat and waited.

Seated again, she eyed us thoughtfully. I felt cold and tired and grimy, stiff from trying to sleep on cold hard stone, hunger aching in my belly. She shook her head at me as if in sympathy for my discomfort and turned to Pepe.

"So you say you're agents of the Moon?"

"We are from Tycho Station," he told her, "but here only to look and report what we find. We claim no authority to meddle with anybody." He bent toward her desperately. "All we want is to get back on our plane and back to the Moon."

"Sorry." I thought I had seen a momentary flash of pity, but her smile was gone. "The regent permits no appeals. Our problem now is your future here. Your cellmates were easy enough to place, but you—" She paused to frown searchingly. "Do you have manual skills that might be useful here?"

In a moment of hope, I nodded at Pepe. "He's a space pilot."

She looked at him.

"A skill you may not need." He shrugged and added quickly, "Better than that, we can bring you knowledge. At the station, we have a library and museum filled with the art and history and science of the old Earth. Treasures of the old world that could transform yours."

She was shaking her head.

"We've seen the regent," he hastened desperately on. "Perhaps he doesn't want any major change, but we aren't here to threaten anybody. There must be bits of technological know-how that you could use."

"Perhaps somebody can use you." She glanced through the open door and nodded thoughtfully. "I'll inquire." She studied us again and asked abruptly, "Have you eaten?"

"Not lately," Pepe said.

She clapped her hands. A black Casey clone came in with a huge silver tray stacked with glasses, a pitcher, a bowl of ice, and a dish of little cakes that filled the air with a fragrance that wet my mouth. We watched avidly while the silent clone scooped ice into the glasses and filled them with a pale pink liquid.

"Glacier ice." Beaming expansively, she let the clone hand her the first glass. "A new luxury. The agent of trade has just opened a new road through the mountains all the way up to the glaciers. Clone runners are now able to get the ice to us before it melts."

The drink was the juice of an American fruit, she said. She had brought seedlings back from her visit there, and established them on her own plantation. Famished as I felt, its tangy sweetness was a delight. We drained the glasses and the clone offered the cakes. She watched with an evident amusement at our appetites till he was gone with the tray.

Ignoring Pepe's thanks, she picked up a slate, frowned at it, and shook her head.

"The regent sees no good in this electricity, whatever it is, or any of your magic off the Moon." Erasing something on the slate, she peered at Pepe. "Can't you do some useful work that might interest a buyer?"

"Don't you believe us?" he begged her desperately. "Don't you believe we're really from the Moon?"

"Who knows?" She shrugged. "I've seen your flying machine. We might do better if I knew more about you.

Tell me about this city on the Moon. How does anybody live there, with no air to breathe?"

She listened with apparent interest while he tried to describe the station.

"Get us back to our machine," he told her, "and we can fly you there." A flash of interest lit her face, and he hurried on. "We could freeze a tissue sample, if you like. You could be cloned to live again on future worlds. A kind of immortality—"

"Clone me?" She was offended. "I've seen clones enough. My problem is a place for you."

"A bug, you mean?" Pepe bent toward her, hoarse with dread. "You want to drill holes in our skulls? Plant those hideous little monsters in our heads, to ride us and torture us the rest of our lives?"

"Nothing you'll enjoy." She gave him a philosophic nod. "Life is seldom perfect. But you have already admitted that you are only clones, endowed with your own peculiar immortality. Whatever happens in one life, you can always look forward to another."

"Clones are people." He spread his hands, pleading. "Clones can hurt."

She marked something on the slate and rang a bell to call the guard.

"Miss Teller, please!" Desperately he raised his voice. "You look human. Have you no human feelings?"

She stiffened and flushed in anger, but then sank slowly back into her chair. The guard appeared in the doorway, glanced at her, and vanished. She sat a long time staring blankly at us. When at last she spoke, her voice was nearly too low to hear, as though she were speaking to herself.

"Of course I feel." Her lip was quivering. "I remember a friend, a man I cared for, condemned for a mere political blunder. I appealed, but he had enemies. Once I saw him pulling a wagon on the street. I called his name. He couldn't turn or speak, but his bug looked at me. I know he heard. I know what he felt."

Turned pale, she slammed her hand on the shining desk and slumped down over it as if about to cry. In a moment, however, she was on her feet.

"That was then." Her voice was hard and sharp. "This is now. I do have feelings, Agent Navarro, but they are no concern of yours."

She rang again for the guard.

25

T he iron door of our cell clanged again, and we were left there alone in the stifling reek of the sewer ditch. I walked the narrow floor while Pepe hunched miserably down on the hard stone bench.

"*Que cabrón*" He swayed back to his feet. "Damn the regent! Damn the bugs! Damn the whole stinking system! They'll find Casey and put the bug back on him." His fists knotted, relaxed, and clenched again. "He should take the plane and look for Mona." Hopelessly, he slumped down again. "There's nothing he could do for us here."

That thin blade of sunlight reddened and climbed the wall. I was still dismally wondering what sort of buyer Ellen Teller might find for us, when we heard the tramp of boots outside. The door screeched open. Two tight-faced guards in blue ordered us curtly out of the cell.

Sturdy white males, they wore no bugs. I saw Pepe stiffen as if to make a break, but they wore weapon-clipped belts and kept a wary distance. They marched us down a long corridor to the back of the building, unlocked a heavy door, and let us out into a narrow cul-de-sac where two empty rickshaws stood waiting.

With a signal for silence, they beckoned us into them. Stripping off their uniforms, they stuck black beads on their foreheads, picked up the shafts, trotted with us through a maze of alleys back to Moon Boulevard. Pepe grinned at me and raised two fingers in a gesture of elation. I sank back in the cushions, rejoicing in the fresh air and sunshine but hardly daring to hope for anything better.

Sirens were suddenly howling. The boom of a cannon echoed off the buildings around us. Our rescuers never looked back. As stolid and wordless as actual slaves of the bugs, they threaded a way through the rickshaws and cycles and lumbering wagons, back to the arena. Guards at the gate glanced at a scrap of slate one man showed him and waved us on toward the spaceplane. We jumped off the rickshaws. The sweating men were gone before we could thank them.

"All okay?" I heard Laura Grail calling from the top of the stair, smiling widely to greet us. Dressed in green-trimmed white and a green hairband, she was an unbelievable dream. "Let's go!"

We ran up the steps.

"Who are they?" Pepe gestured after the rickshaws.

"Friends." She beckoned us into the plane. "Or call them heroes of liberation."

"Okay!" Casey shouted from the pilot's seat. "*Adiós* to the bugs!"

The engines coughed and thundered. At the window, I watched the jet steam roaring out to hide the walls around us. The ship quivered and lifted. Slowly at first, but faster, faster, the arena and the red-tiled roofs of the city fell away below. When Casey turned from the instruments, I saw that he looked almost himself again. A glassy patch of healant still gleamed over the dark little wound on his forehead where the bug had been, but no blood was seeping through.

"Where to?" Pepe whispered. "Back to the Moon?"

"America," he said. "Back to where I found Mona when we were here before."

His voice slowed when he spoke her name. I saw the shine of tears and thought I had a hint of what he was feeling. Age after age, as we lived and died and lived again, the robots and our holo parents had given us a sense of immortality that left us very mortal. Cloned and brought up to be the selves we had been, we were never quite identical, yet those past lives lay vivid in my mind.

We had slept four centuries since our escape from those

vampirish black parasites in the red thorn jungle in Africa, yet our flight seemed as real as yesterday. Our great circle course had taken us north to the glaciers and then back south along the edge of the North American ice cap until flat brown tundra gave way to an exotic bluish green and we came down at last over the strangely varicolored forests of what had been Chihuahua.

I had read the old records and listened to the holos until the haunting songs of the trees and the winged being Casey called Mona were almost actual memories of my own. I recalled the young tree he named Leonardo and loved like their son. I asked Casey now if he meant to look for the Leo tree.

"After all that time—" He shrugged with misgivings, but old emotion glowed on his dark Asian face. "I don't know about the tree, Laura thinks my own Mona may be out there, fighting with the rebels to end rider slavery. We'll find her if we can."

He turned back to his instruments, plotting our path. Taking off from a different point, we were on another great circle route, flying far north of the diminished Mediterranean. We were already high. I found the rim of the north Asian ice cap. Laura was brewing tea and warming squash-and-tofu packs she had found in the food locker. Pepe asked for more about the friends who had freed us.

"We had heard of your date to meet the regent." She gave us an ironic smile. "My editor wanted another story on you if he could get it past the censors. I didn't want to see you with bugs on your faces. I slipped back for another look at your machine. Casey let me in. We talked. And then—"

She paused for a glance at the sky beyond the windows, dark purple now, the white glare of ice and cloud far beneath us.

"I've never dared say so," she went on, "but I'm with what they call the Scienteers. Or loonies. Or traitors to the regent. Names they use when they catch and bug us. We call ourselves colonials. If you care about our history, the first colonists had a hard start. They landed in the Vale. A lovely spot, fertile and well-watered, secure inside its mountain walls, but too near the ice as it lay at the time.

"The first winter was severe. Unexpected avalanches buried their original site and nearly wiped them out. The survivors were able to build a lab and clone new people. The Vale remained the center of what government there was as the colony grew, but communication was poor. The generations that began to settle farther south were at first independent. Those on the coast built ships and began exploring. Their future looked bright till they reached the shores of Africa and met the black masters.

"That began a different sort of prosperity. One of Arne Linder's descendants escaped from Africa with a live bug. Learning the science of the masters, they were finally able to hatch the eggs and plant them in people. Alfred Linder worked them on a plantation that covered Sri Lanka. His son Roscoe built a fleet of ships and found that trading with the masters paid better than war against them.

"The horrified colonial government outlawed slavery, but Roscoe stayed out of reach. He changed his name to Arne, declared himself Arne the First, regent of the Moon and legal ruler of Earth. His clone armies captured the Vale. A few colonials held out along the frontiers. More migrated to America and set up a free nation there. His successor sent expeditions to make them slave territory. Regency politics!"

She gave a sardonic shrug.

"The black masters need the regents now, and the regents need them. With their alien biochemistry, they need minerals to feed themselves, minerals hard to find in Africa. Their red thorn jungle keeps on spreading. They hide in it and ride their killer beasts out to snatch the men trying to burn it or hack it down, yet they can't afford to wipe the regents out. As for the American war, it's pure politics, fought to spread rider slavery to one more continent." She shrugged forlornly. "That war they're winning."

"But Mona!" Casey turned from the controls, his voice grown sharp. "She's out there. We've got to find her."

"If we can." Laura looked doubtful. "It's a big continent."

I asked Laura what else she knew.

"Not much. A mountain climber saw their flyer come down. He thought it must be from the Moon. His report alarmed the regent. They were hunted. Casey, of course, was taken for a runaway slave. The Scienteers found Mona and got her on the underground railway to America."

"That's where she is." Casey nodded hopefully. "Fighting with the rebels."

"Where she was." Laura shrugged. "News from America is hard to get. Our Freetown correspondent has disappeared. His last reports were censored and delayed for months. My friends were willing to risk their lives to get you on your ship, but there wasn't much else—"

"We'll find her." Casey bent back to his instruments. "We must."

We left the ice behind. Brown mountains rose out of gray haze, and brown desert turned an odd blue-green. I saw Casey frowning over his charts, copies of those we had faxed to the Moon before we died here.

"The forest," I heard him mutter. "I can't find the forest."

I remembered the singing trees that must have come from somewhere off the Earth, remembered the balloons they had grown to carry their seed, remembered the gold-winged seed that Casey called Mona and the little sapling that had grown from her body after she died.

He studied his maps and studied the ground ahead.

"The forest is gone," he muttered again. "The forest where we landed."

I searched for it. The earth below looked flat and brown and dead. I thought I saw flecks of color along the far horizon, a gleam of snow on a mountain cone farther still, but not much else.

"See those lines?" He pointed, but I found no lines. "Railways, I think. They run south. Toward seaports, I imagine." He squinted ahead. "Confusing, but the rivers and the lay of the land should show us the spot where we came down."

He dropped us at last into bellowing steam. It cleared to reveal a bleak landscape. Huge stumps where trees had stood were all charred black, black ash around them. Bitterly silent, he opened the door and unfolded the landing stair. We followed him down into blazing sun and an acrid reek of fire.

Not far off, steel rails gleamed. He pointed north across the stumps, toward a plume of white smoke. We waited in silence while a steam locomotive thundered past us. I saw a line of smoke-grimed clones passing great blocks of wood from the tender to feed the boiler. The engineer leaned out of his cab to stare and blew a whistle blast that startled me.

Enormous logs were loaded on the long train of flatcars behind it. We stood there with Casey in the hot wet reek of smoke till the last car had rumbled past. Then, without another word, he stalked across the tracks. We stumbled after him along the bank of a narrow stream till he stopped to stare down at one wide stump.

"That was Leo." His face had twisted under the glassy glint of the sealant over his rider wound, and his voice was hoarse and slow. "Our son."

Pepe reached to touch his shoulder. A flash of anger set his face, as if he thought we were about to laugh.

"I'm sorry," Pepe whispered. "Terribly sorry."

The anger gone, he turned back to the stump.

"I had to come," he muttered. "I had to know." He stood there a long time, staring down at the charred stump, and finally shrugged and swung back to us. "Not that it matters." He shook his head, and I saw tears in his eyes. "When you hear what I have to tell you now, you'll understand that it no longer matters at all."

26

Casey stood there a long time, silent, bent down over the black stump. Smoke and dust had turned the cloudless sky to copper, and a red sun blazed hot on the charred desolation around us. The motionless air had an acrid taint of fire. Far off, a dust devil lifted a small black spiral. The only sound was the rush of the little stream over a rocky ledge behind us.

"Come." Pepe finally caught Casey's arm. "Let's go."

"Go on," Casey snapped harshly at him. "Leave me here."

We clambered back across the rails and climbed aboard the plane. When I looked from the landing he was kneeling by the stump as if in prayer. Laura had stayed aboard. She made a fresh pot of tea and we sipped it while we waited.

"What now?" I asked.

Pepe shrugged. "*Quién sabe?*"

"Our correspondent reported the Moon Lady leading the rebels in this area," Laura said. "But that was months ago."

Casey came plodding back at last. He stopped on the landing for another long look back across the burnt past before he came inside. Yet, seeming dry-eyed and composed, he sat down, and accepted a mug of tea.

"I'm sorry if I was sharp with you." Wryly, he shook his head at Pepe. "It's hard to say how hard this hit me. I've known the Leo story all my life, but I never quite believed it. Not till now." He nodded at the dark waste beyond the windows. "Not till I recognized that crook in the creek and found the little waterfall where the tree had stood." He grinned and sipped his tea. "It was nearly too much, but I'm okay now."

"Ready to look for Mona?" Pepe asked. "If you have a clue?"

"No clue." He shrugged. "Not really. But rebel refugees were reported hiding in the forest still standing west of us. I saw the color of live trees on the highlands to the west. We can hope she saw us. If she's still there. If she has time enough to get here."

"Time?" Pepe raised his voice. "You had something else to tell us?"

"Something I don't like to say." Casey drained his mug, set it down, and took a moment more before he went on. "You know Tycho Station was set up to watch for approaching objects that might impact the Earth. The computer is programmed to carry the mission on while we sleep—"

Sharply, Pepe broke in. "It has found something new?"

"Nearly forty years ago." Soberly, Casey nodded. "That's why we were cloned—the computer had meant to give the colony another thousand years before it sent us back to look."

"Why weren't we told?"

Casey shrugged. "It makes its own decisions."

"What about this object?"

"It's probably a drifter from the Kuiper Belt, out beyond Neptune." Casey frowned, careful with his words. "Some thirty miles in mean diameter. Big enough for the impact to devastate the planet, maybe erase all life. Any impact was uncertain at first. We were awakened just to be ready for whatever happened."

His face set harder.

"It's going to happen." He glanced at me. "Dunk, you know your holo father is the computer's voice. He told Mona and me before we left the Moon—"

"You knew?" Pepe stared at him. "And didn't tell us?"

"He said the computer would inform you of whatever you needed to know."

"The danger?" Laura whispered. "That's certain now?"

"He said it is. The early observations had been refined. The destruction is predicted to be total, with no chance for human survival. The truth was hard for us to take. I know it's hard for you. Tycho Station, out on the Moon, ought to survive, but this means that all our past efforts have been wasted. The master computer will be there to assess the damage and keep on cloning us, but it will have to start all over again.

"But for us, right now—For all the Earth—For you—" His scarred face grimly set, Casey reached to touch Laura's shoulder. "It's the end."

She had listened in silence, her own face white. Her lips quivering, she tried to speak and gulped, and gave him a feeble smile. He turned back to me.

"Your father advised us not to try to warn the colonists. There's nothing they could do. Our errand was simply to file a bit of history that ought to be remembered."

"When?" She stared into his face. "How much time before the impact?"

He glanced at the watch on my wrist.

"Today is August 14," he said. "The impact is forecast for noon on August 17, Kashmir time. That would be about midnight here."

We sat in dazed silence for a time.

Three days." Laura shook her head. "Just three days. So much to think about." She shrugged. "No use to think of anything. I need to walk."

Pepe and I went with her down the stair. We walked along the rail line, our feet stirring little clouds of soot-black dust. We didn't talk until I heard her brittle laugh.

"World to end in three days!" She laughed again, too loudly. "A great headline. Anybody that dared print it back at home would have been branded a Scienteer and bugged for high treason."

Pepe caught her hand, and they walked on together.

Casey had stayed on the plane, watching the dark horizon. Back there with him, we prepared a final transmission to the station. Laura dictated a brief history of the colony. Pepe reported our meetings with the regent and the rider broker. Casey gave a terse description of his experience under the bug. I summed up our situation and sent the message when the Moon had risen.

That night we took turns on guard. We saw nothing till, early next morning, Casey found a smudge of smoke up the railway north of us. It became another train, approaching slowly as if wary of us and halting a few miles away. With binoculars we made out half a dozen flatcars crowded with black clones in military gear, a long-barreled cannon on the last car. The gun crew trained it on us.

"We're dead," Pepe muttered. "If they fire."

They didn't fire, but presently a little rail car came on toward us, flying the blue-and-white regency flag. It carried a white officer and two black clones pumping handlebars to drive it.

"They're here to kill us." Pepe looked at Laura with a sudden grin, and turned anxiously to Casey and me. "Let's take off for the Moon while we can."

"Not quite yet." Casey shook his head. "I won't leave Mona. Go on if you like. I'm heading into the standing forest to the west on the chance she's there." He looked at me. "Coming with me, Dunk?"

"I'm coming."

We found a canteen and a few ration packs. Laura hugged us both. Pepe shook our hands and wished us luck. The officer on the handcar fired a handgun as we crossed the track. The bullets sang past our heads and we tramped on. A few miles across the stumps we came into trees still standing, but dead.

"You should have seen them live." Casey shook his

head in dismal regret. "They were magnificent. Somehow sacred."

They had been magnificent. The straight black trunks, thicker than the body of our plane, towered up forever, and my neck ached from craning to trace the dense web of dead black branches that laced the sky. A thick carpet of unburned leaves covered the ground, spicing the air with an odd fragrance of decay. In the heavy and depressing silence, I felt an awed sense that we were entering an abandoned temple, built for the worship of some dead and forgotten deity.

There was no sign of fire here. I wondered what had killed the trees.

"They were sentient," Casey said. "Sentient and all of them kin. I think they were all a single conscious being. Even the ground cover somehow belonged to it. If you won't call me crazy, I'd say it died of grief."

Tramping on, we came through a stand of trees where leaves still hung, though yellowed and bleached. Farther, we climbed a rise and came out of that dead silence into a murmur of life. The ground was still covered with a soft, mosslike, blue-green carpet, the high canopy still bright with live and varied color. Though there was no wind, I heard a faint sighing in the treetops and then a note of song, high and faint and far away.

"They know us." Casey stopped. "They remember Leo."

We stood there a long time, listening. The song swelled louder till it filled the forest, a changing melody I had never heard, somehow touching me with emotions I had never felt. I saw rapture on Casey's upturned face, as if it moved him deeply. Fading finally into silence, it left me with a painful ache of emptiness and loss.

He turned solemnly to me.

"They know Mona," he whispered. "They are reaching to find her. If we wait, they will try to guide her."

We waited. When I asked how long she would be on the way, he shrugged and said the trees had no language of words or numbers, no human sense of time. Later in the day they sang again, still with no meaning I could catch though sometimes I caught a sense of aching sorrow. We drained the canteen and finished our ration packs. When darkness began to thicken, we went back a little way to gather armfuls of the great dry leaves to make a bed. The voice of the trees had faded into a stillness that seemed hushed with expectation. I listened uneasily for anything, for Mona's voice, the boom of the cannon on the flatcar, the thunder of the plane lifting off without us. I heard nothing at all.

All next day we waited. The trees sang again, sometimes with slow and solemn rhythms that pierced me with wordless pangs of loss and death and left my mind filled with sharpened images of the desolate desert of dead stumps and the fires that had charred the land. Yet toward the end they puzzled me with a thunderous chorus that seemed to echo a solemn triumph.

"They know about the asteroid," Casey said. "Perhaps they sensed it. Perhaps Mona told them. They are grieving for themselves and their failure here, but not for us or the future of Earth. They have felt the evil of the black masters and sensed a sort of justice in their coming destruction. Happy with that, they will live on in the greater being that set them here. Though the loss is painful to them, they can accept death as the dark side of life. They expect the future of Earth to be better than its past."

That second night was endless. I heard no wind, no voice from the trees, yet sometimes I thought I felt a ghostly presence in the faint moonlight that filtered though their branches, something so elusive that it vanished when I tried to grasp it. Listening in vain for any sound at all, I dozed and woke to a sad conviction that we were insane, trusting our lives to the imagined mind of a dying forest.

"It's the last day," I reminded Casey when he woke. "If Pepe and Laura still have the plane, they can't afford to wait till the impact kills them. Shouldn't we get back?"

He got to his feet, stretching the stiffness out of his bones.

"Mona's on her way," he insisted. "We have till midnight."

That brought me small comfort, but I waited with him and felt a little relieved when I heard a soothing crooning from the trees and then the plop of something falling. He walked away and came back with two of the big juice-filled fruits that I recalled from our lives here. Their tangy sweetness eased my thirst and hunger, but the day seemed a century. Daylight was fading from the treetops when we heard a distant shout.

Casey answered, and a little band of ragged, wildly bearded men emerged from the thickening dusk. They carried crudely forged swords, rough lances, a few stolen military weapons. One had his arm in a blood-clotted sling, another was stumbling on a broken branch. Two or three were black clones, dirty headbands hiding the scars where their bugs had been. Cautious of us, they stopped under a tree some distance off.

"Casey?" A hoarse and anxious voice. A woman's. "Is it you?"

"Mona!" Casey yelled. "Thank God! Or thank the trees."

Her companions stared at us for a moment and melted back into the forest.

She limped on toward us. In tattered fragments of a jacket and jeans, she was drawn thin, dark with soot and dried blood, her filthy hair jaggedly clipped. Yet her white teeth flashed in the dusk with a smile as bright as it had been on the Moon.

She hugged me briefly before Casey took her in his arms. With no time for talk, we helped her back through the dying trees and the dead into open moonlight. The spaceplane stood where we had left it, a thin silver pillar on the stark waste of stumps. Before we reached the stair I heard a faint and far-off chant from the trees behind us and thought I caught a monody of fond farewell.

Laura opened the door to let us in. Grinning with relief, Pepe shook our hands, sealed the door, tumbled into the pilot's seat. The jets bellowed. The ship shuddered. We lifted toward the Moon. When we were safely aloft, I asked Laura what had become of the regency force.

"The officer was after the plane," she said. "He offered to let us go free if we surrendered it intact. He didn't want to believe me when I tried to tell him why he didn't need it. Pepe invited him aboard and let him call the Moon. The answer convinced him. He got back on his train and went back the way he had come."

Pepe glanced at his watch and turned back from the instruments.

"We're on our way." He nodded at Laura, with a grim little grin. "Time enough left to get us well clear of the ejecta and give us a good view of the impact from high orbit." He made a wry face at me. "A black chapter, Dunk, but we'll be alive to try again."

Casey and Mona sat close together on the narrow rear seat, holding hands. He murmured something to her and leaned against the window to look back down at the shrinking Earth. Night had drowned the wasted forest behind us, but over the Pacific white reefs of cloud were still bright with sun. He stared a long time before he sighed and turned again to Mona.

"Our colonists, once our last best hope." Sadly, he shook his head. "Only hours left, if they knew. A dreadful end, too dreadful to imagine. But yet—" His lips set hard. "We couldn't help. And there's a terrible justice in it. They had gone too far wrong."

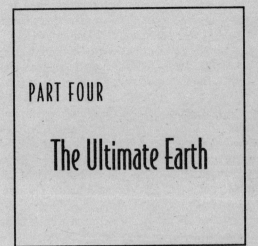

PART FOUR

The Ultimate Earth

27

We loved Uncle Pen. We all called him that, though the name he gave us was something like Sandor Pen, spoken with an accent we never learned to imitate. Though the robots and our holo parents kept us busy with our lessons and our chores and our workouts in the big centrifuge, life was dull in our narrow quarters. His visits were our best excitement.

He never told us when he was coming. We used to watch for him, looking from the high dome on the Tycho rim, down across the field the digging machines had leveled. Standing huge on the edge of it, they were dark monsters out of space, casting long black shadows across the gray waste of rocks and dust and crater pits.

His visit on our seventh birthday was a wonderful surprise. Tanya saw him landing and called us up to the dome. His ship was a bright teardrop, shining in the black shadow of a gigantic metal insect. He jumped out of it in a sleek silvery suit that fit like his skin. We waited at the air lock to watch him peel it off. He was a small lean man, who looked graceful as a girl but still very strong. Even his body was exciting to see, though Dian ran and hid because he looked so strange.

Naked, he had a light golden tan that darkened in the sunlit dome and faded when he went below. His face was a narrow heart shape, his brown eyes enormous. He required no clothing, he had always told us, because his sex organs were internal.

He called Dian when he missed her, and she crept back to share the gifts be had brought from Earth. There were sweet fruits we had never tasted, strange toys, stranger games that he had to show us how to play. For Tanya and Dian there were dolls that sang strange songs in voices we couldn't understand and played loud music on tiny instruments we had never heard.

The best part was just the visit with him in the dome. Pepe and Casey had eager questions about life on the new Earth. Were there cities? Wild animals? Alien creatures? Did people live in houses, or underground in tunnels like ours? What did he do for a living? Did he have a wife? Children like us?

He wouldn't tell us much. Earth, he said, had changed since our parents knew it. It was now so different that he wouldn't know where to begin. He let us take turns to see it through the big telescope. Later, he promised, if he could find space gear for us, he would take us up to orbit the Moon and loop toward it for a closer look. Now, however, he was working to learn all he could about the old Earth, the way it had been before the last great impacts.

He showed it to us in the holo tanks and the old paper books, back when it still had white ice caps over the poles and bare brown deserts on the continents. The new Earth had no deserts and no ice. Under the bright cloud spirals, the land was green where the sun struck it, all the way over the poles. It looked so wonderful that Casey and Pepe begged him to take us back with him to let us see it for ourselves.

"I'm sorry." He shook his head, which was covered with short gold-brown fur. "Terribly sorry, but you can't even think of a trip to Earth."

We were looking from the dome. The mysterious Earth stood high in the black north, where it always stood. Low in the west, the slow sun blazed hot on the new mountains the machines had piled up around the field, and filled the craters with ink.

Dian had learned to trust Uncle Pen. She sat on his knee, gazing up in adoration at his face. Tanya stood behind him, playing a little game. She held her hand against his back to bleach the golden tan, and took it away to watch the sun erase the print.

Looking hurt, Casey asked why we couldn't think of a trip to Earth.

"You aren't like me." That was very true. Casey has a wide black face with narrow Chinese eyes and straight black hair. "And you belong right here."

"I don't look like anybody." Casey shrugged. "Or belong to anybody."

"But you do belong here at the station." Uncle Pen was gently patient. "You were cloned for your job here, to watch the sky for any danger to Earth and restore its life in case of any danger."

"We've finished that." Casey looked at me. "Tell him, Dunk."

My holo father is Duncan Yare. The master computer that runs the station often speaks with his voice. He had told us how we had been cloned again and again from the cells our live parents had left in the cryostat.

"Sir, that's true." I felt a little afraid of Uncle Pen, but proud of all we had done. "My holo father says the big impacts killed Earth and killed it again. He says we have always brought it back to life." My throat felt dry. I had to gulp, but I went on. "If Earth's alive now, that's because of us."

"True. Very true." He nodded, with an odd little smile. "But perhaps you don't know that your little Moon has suffered a heavy impact of its own. If you are now alive, you owe your lives to us."

We all stared at him.

"The digging machines?" Casey was nodding. "I've watched them and wondered why they were here. When did the impact happen?"

"*Quién sabe?*" He shrugged at Pepe, imitating the gesture and the voice Pepe had learned from his holo father.

"It was long ago. Perhaps a hundred thousand years, perhaps a million. I haven't found a clue."

"Something hit the station?"

"A narrow miss." Uncle Pen nodded at the great dark pit in the crater rim just west of us. "The ejecta smashed the dome and buried everything. The station was lost and almost forgotten. Only a myth till I happened on it."

"The diggers?" Casey turned to stare down at the landing field where Uncle Pen had left his flyer in the shadows of those great machines and the mountains they had built. "How did you know where to dig?"

"The power plant was still running," Uncle Pen said. "Keeping the computer alive. I was able to detect its metal shielding and then its radiation."

"We thank you." Pepe came gravely to shake his hand. "I'm glad to be alive."

"So am I," Casey said. "If I can get to Earth." He saw Uncle Pen beginning to shake his head, and went on quickly, "Tell us what you know about the last impact and how we came down to terraform the Earth again that last time."

"I don't know what you did."

"We've seen the difference," Casey said. "The land is all green now, with no deserts or ice."

"Certainly it has been transformed." Nodding, Uncle Pen stopped to smile at Tanya while she left her game with the sun on his back and came to sit cross-legged at his feet. "Ages ago. But our historians are convinced that we've done much more ourselves."

"You did?" Casey was disappointed and a little doubtful. "How?"

"They believe we removed undersea ledges and widened straits to change the ocean circulation. We diverted rivers to fill new lakes and water the deserts, changing atmospheric circulation. We engineered new life-forms to fit new climatic patterns."

"If Earth was dead, we must have put you there."

"Of course," Uncle Pen said. "Excavating the station, I was looking for answers I never found, but authorities agree that the second impact was more severe than the first. It annihilated life and even destroyed most geologic records of it. The story I recovered here was cut short by the lunar impact, but it does confirm that you were re-planting the planet and landing new colonists."

Pepe had gone to stand at the edge of the dome, looking down at the monster machines and Uncle Pen's little ship, which was strangely different from the rocket spaceplanes we had seen in the old video holos. "Can it go to the other planets?"

"It can." He nodded. "It can reach the planets of other suns."

"Other stars!" Tanya's eyes went wide, and Pepe asked, "How does it fly in space with no rocket engines?"

"It doesn't," he said. "It's called a slipship. It slides around space, not through it."

"The stars?" Tanya whispered. "You've been to other stars?"

"To the planets of other stars." He nodded gravely. "I may go again, though I still have work to finish here. And space flight plays tricks that might surprise you. I could fly to our closest interstellar colony in an instant of my own time and come back in another instant, but twenty years would pass here while I was away."

"I didn't know." Her eyes went wider still. "Your friends would all be old."

"We don't get old."

She shrank away as if suddenly afraid of him. Pepe opened his mouth to ask something, and shut it without a word.

"Or die." He chuckled at our startlement. "We've en-gineered ourselves, you see, more than we've engineered the Earth."

Casey turned to look out across the shadowed craters at the huge globe of Earth, the green Americas blazing on the sunlit face, Europe and Africa only a shadow against the dark. He stood there a long time and came slowly back to stand in front of Uncle Pen.

"I'm going down there when I grow up." His face hardened stubbornly. "No matter what you say."

"Are you growing wings?" Uncle Pen laughed and reached a golden arm to pat him on the head. "If you didn't know, the impact smashed your old rocket craft to junk."

He drew quickly back.

"Really, my boy, you do belong here." Seeing his hurt, Uncle Pen spoke more gently. "You were cloned for your job here at the station, to watch for danger to Earth, and to repair any harm that occurs. It's a job that ought to make you proud."

Pepe swallowed hard, but he kept his voice even. "Maybe so. But where's any danger now? Why do you need us here on the Moon?"

Uncle Pen had an odd look. He took a long moment to answer.

"We are not aware of any actual threat from another impacting bolide. All the asteroids that used to approach Earth's orbit have been diverted, most of them steered into the sun."

"So?" Casey's dark chin had a defiant jut. "Why did you want to dig us up?"

"For history." Uncle Pen looked away from us, up at the huge, far-off Earth. "The resurfaced Earth had lost nearly every trace of our beginning. People tried to prove we had evolved on some other planet and migrated here to colonize the solar system. Tycho Station is proof that Earth is the actual mother world. Its excavation has been the work of my life."

He turned back to us with a smile of satisfaction.

"Others may quarrel, but I found our roots here under the rubble. The true story, that even the skeptics will have to accept."

"If that is the true story," Casey asked, "who needs the station now?"

"Nobody, really." He shrugged, with an odd little twist of his golden lips, and I thought he felt sorry for Casey. "If another disaster did strike the mother planet, which isn't likely at all, it could be repeopled by the colonies."

"So you dug us up for nothing?"

"Please try to understand." Uncle Pen leaned and reached as if to hug him, but he shrank farther away. "The station was almost obliterated. Restoration has been a long and difficult task. We've often had to invent and improvise. We had to test the tissue cells still preserved in the cryostat, and build new equipment in the maternity lab." He smiled down into Tanya's face, which was beaming with devotion. "The tests have turned out well."

"Maybe for you," Casey muttered bitterly. "Not so well for us. Do you expect us to sit here till we die, waiting for nothing at all?"

Looking uncomfortable, Uncle Pen had nothing to say. He just reached down to lift Tanya up in his arms.

"I want to live," Casey told him. "Any way I can."

"Please, my dear boy, you must try to understand." Patiently, Uncle Pen shook his golden head. "The station is a precious historic monument, our sole surviving relic of the early Earth and early man. You are part of it. I'm sorry if you take that for a misfortune, but there is certainly no place for you on Earth."

28

Sandor Pen's visits continued as we grew older, though they came further and further apart. His tantalizing gifts always delighted as much as they puzzled us. Exotic fruits that had to be eaten before they spoiled. New games and new music that gave us strange dreams. Little holo cubes that had held living pictures of us caught while we were younger. He was always genial and kind, though I sometimes thought he found us less interesting than we had been.

His main concern was clearly the station itself. He cleared junk and debris out of the deepest tunnels, which had been used for workshops and storage, and stocked them again with new tools and spare parts that the robots called Robos had used to repair themselves and maintain the station.

Most of his time was spent in the library and museum with Dian and her holo mother. He studied the old books and holos and paintings and sculptures, carried them away, brought copies back to replace them. For a time he had the digging machines busy again, removing loose rubble from around the station and grinding it up to make concrete for a massive new retaining wall poured to reinforce the foundation.

For our twenty-first birthday, he had the robots measure us for space suits like his own. Sleek and mirror-bright, they fitted like our skins and let us feel at home outside the dome. We wore them down to see one of our old rocket spaceplanes, standing now on the field beside his little slider. His robots had dug it out of a smashed hangar, and he had them rebuilding it with new parts from Earth.

One of the great digging machines held it upright. A robot was replacing a broken landing strut, fusing it smoothly in place with some process that made no glow of heat. Casey spoke to the robot, but it ignored him. He climbed up to knock on the door. It responded with a brittle computer voice that was only a rattle in our helmets.

"Open up," he told it. "Let us in."

"Admission denied." Its hard machine voice had Sandor's accent.

"By what authority?"

"By the authority of Director Sandor Pen, Lunar Research Site."

"Ask the director to let us in."

"Admission denied."

"So you think." Casey shook his head, his words a sardonic whisper in my helmet. "If these new robots can think."

B ack inside the air lock, Sandor had waited to help us shuck off the mirror suits. Casey thanked him for the gift and asked if the old spaceplane would be left here on the Moon.

"Forget what you're thinking." He gave Casey a penetrating glance. "We're taking it down to Earth."

"I wish I could come."

"I'm sorry you can't." His face was firmly set, but a glow of satisfaction turned it a richer gold. "It's to stand at the center of our new historic memorial, located on the Australian subcontinent. It's part of our reconstruction of the prehistoric past. The whole story of the pre-impact planet and pre-impact man."

He paused, with a warm smile for Tanya. She flushed pink, smiling back.

"It's really magnificent! Finding the lunar site was my great good fortune, and working it has been my life for many years. It has filled a gap in human history. Answered questions that scholars had fought over for ages. You yourselves have a place in a replicate station, with a holographic diorama of your childhood."

Casey asked again why we couldn't go down to visit it.

"Because you belong here." Impatience edged his voice. "And because of the charter that allowed us to work the site. We agreed to restore the station to its state before the impact, with no trace of ourselves. It has to be sealed, protected and secured from any future trespass."

We all felt sick with loss on the day he told us his work at the site was done. As a farewell gift, he took us two by two to orbit the Moon. Casey and I went up together, sitting behind him in his tiny slider. We had seen space and Earth from the dome all our lives, but the flight was still an exciting adventure.

The mirror hull was nearly invisible from inside, so we seemed to float free in open space. The Moon's gray desolation spread wider as we rose, and then dwindled to become a bright bubble floating in a gulf of darkness. Though Sandor touched nothing I saw, our view was changed.

The stars blazed suddenly brighter, the Milky Way a broad belt of gem-strewn splendor all around the sky. The sun was dimmed and hugely magnified to let us see the dark spots across its face. Hit with a fearful sense that I was falling into it, I had to clutch at the edge of my seat. Still he touched nothing and I felt no new motion, but now Australia expanded. The deserts were gone. A long new sea lay across the center of the continent, crescent-shaped and vividly blue.

"The memorial." He pointed to a broad tongue of green land thrust into the crescent. "If you ever get to Earth—

which I don't expect—you could meet your doubles there in the Tycho exhibit."

Casey asked, "Will Mona be there?"

"Ask the computer," Sandor said. "Her tissue specimens are still preserved in the cryostat."

"If I'm worth cloning," Casey said, "Mona ought to be." His voice softened wistfully. "Someday she will be."

"Nunca." Sandor smiled at him, aping Pepe again, but *nunca* meant never.

Sandor gathered us in the station dome for his final farewell. He seemed happy to go, though he failed to say why. We thanked him for that exciting glimpse of the far-off Earth, for the space suits and all his gifts, for restoring us to life. It was a trifling repayment, he said, for all he had found at the station. He shook our hands, kissed Tanya and Dian, and got into his silvery suit. We followed him down to the air lock. Tanya must have loved him more than I knew. She broke into tears and ran off to her room as the rest of us watched his bright little teardrop float away toward Earth.

"We put them on the Earth," Casey muttered. "We have a right to see what we have done there."

He turned to stare down at the restored spaceplane, standing now on its own landing gear. Busy again, the big machines were digging a row of deep pits, burying themselves under the rubble, leaving only a row of new craters that might become a puzzle, I thought, to later astronomers.

Next morning he called us back to the dome to watch a tank truck crawling out of the underground hangars dug into the crater rim.

"We're off to Earth!" He slid his arm around Pepe. "Who's with us?"

Arne scowled at him. "Didn't you hear Mr. Pen?"

"Sandor's gone." He grinned at Pepe. "We have a plan of our own."

He and Casey hadn't talked about it, but I had heard their whispers and seen them busy in the shops. Though the space-skipping science of the slider was still a mystery to us, I knew they had studied astronautics and electronics. I knew they had worn bugs to record Sandor's voice, always begging him to say more about the new Earth than he ever would.

"I know what Mr. Pen told us." Arne made a guttural grunt. "I can guess your crazy plan, but it's not for me. I've seen the reports of people who went down in the past to evaluate our terraforming. They've never found anything they liked, and never got back to the Moon."

"Que le hace." Pepe shrugged. "Better that than wasting our lives waiting here in our little pit *por nada.*"

"We belong here." Angry at him, Arne echoed what Sandor had said. "Our mission is just to keep the station alive. Certainly not to throw ourselves away on some insane adventure."

Dian chose to stay with him, though I don't think they were in love. Her love was the station itself, with all its relics of the old Earth. Even as a little child, she had always wanted to work with her holo mother, recording everything that Sandor took away to be copied and returned.

Tanya had set her heart on Sandor. I think she had always dreamed that someday he would take her with him back to Earth. She was desolate and bitter when he left without her, her pride in herself deeply hurt.

"He did love us when we were little," she sobbed when Pepe begged her to join him and Casey. "But I think just because we were children. Or maybe interesting pets. Interesting because we aren't his kind of human. People that live forever don't need to have children."

Pepe begged again, I think because he loved her. Whatever they found on Earth, it would be bigger than our tunnels, and surely more exciting. She cried and kissed him and chose to stay. The new Earth had no place for her. Sandor wouldn't want her, even if she found him. She promised to listen for their radio and pray they came back safe.

I had always been the station historian. Earth was where history was happening. I was glad to go.

"You won't belong," Tanya warned us. "And you can't come back."

Yet she found water canteens and ration packs for us, and reminded us to pack safari garments to wear when we got out of our space gear. We took turns in the dome, watching the tank truck till it reached the plane and the robots began pumping fuel.

"Time." Casey wore a grin of eager expectation. "Time to say good-bye."

Dian and Arne shook our hands, wearing very solemn faces. Tanya clung a long time to Pepe and kissed me and Casey, her face so tear-stained and drawn that I ached with pity for her. We got into our shining suits, went out to the plane, climbed the landing stair. Again the door refused to open.

Casey stepped back to speak on his helmet radio.

"Priority message from Director Sandor Pen." His crackling voice was almost Sandor's. "Special orders for restored spaceplane SP2469."

The door responded with a clatter of speech that was alien to me.

"Orders effective now," Casey snapped. "Tycho Station personnel K. C. Kell, Pedro Navarro, and Duncan Yare are authorized to board for immediate passage to Earth."

Silently, the door swung open.

I had expected to find a robot at the controls, but we found ourselves alone in the nose cone, the pilot's seat empty. Awed by whatever the plane had become, we watched it operate itself. The door swung shut. Air seals hissed. The engines snorted and roared. The ship trembled, and we lifted off the Moon.

Looking back for the station, all I found was the dome, a bright little eye peering into space from the rugged gray peaks of the crater rim. It shrank till I lost it in the great lake of black shadow in the crater and the bright black peak at its center. The Moon shrank till we saw it whole, gray and impact-battered, dropping behind us into a black and bottomless pit.

Sandor's flight in the slider may have taken only an instant. In the old rocket ship, we had time to watch three full rotations of the slowly swelling planet ahead. The jets were silent through most of the flight, with only an occasional whisper to correct our course. We floated in free fall, careful not to blunder against the controls. Taking turns belted in the seats, we tried to sleep but seldom did. Most of the time we spent searching Earth with binoculars, searching for signs of civilization.

"Nothing," Casey muttered again and again. "Nothing that looks like a city, a railway, a canal, a dam. Nothing but green. Only forest, jungle, grassland. Have they let the planet return to nature?"

"*Tal vez.*" Pepe always shrugged. "*Sí o no.* We are still too high to tell."

At last the jets came back to life, steering us down into airbraking orbit. Twice around the puzzling planet, and Australia exploded ahead. The jets thundered. We fell again, toward the wide tongue of green land between the narrow cusps of that long crescent lake.

29

Looking from the windows, we found the spaceplane standing on an elevated pad at the center of a long quadrangle covered with tended lawns, shrubs and banks of brilliant flowers. Wide avenues all around it were walled with buildings that awed and amazed me.

"Sandor's Tycho Memorial!" Pepe jogged my ribs. "There's the old monument at the American capital! I know it from Dian's videos."

"Ancient history." Casey shrugged as if it hardly mattered. "I want to see Earth today."

Pepe opened the door. In our safari suits, we went out on the landing for a better view. The door shut. I heard it hiss behind us, sealing itself. He turned to stare again. The monument towered at the end of the quadrangle, towering above its image in a long reflecting pool, flanked on one side by a Stonehenge in gleaming silver, on the other by a sand-banked Sphinx with the nose restored.

We stood goggling at the old American Capitol at the other end of the mall, the British Houses of Parliament to its right, and Big Ben tolling the time. The Kremlin adjoined them, gilded onion domes gleaming above the grim red-brick walls. The Parthenon, roofed and magnificently new, stood beyond them on a rocky hill.

Across the quadrangle I found the splendid domes of the Taj Mahal, Saint Peter's Basilica, the Hagia Sophia from ancient Istanbul. On higher ground in the distance, I recognized the Chrysler Building from old New York, the Eiffel Tower from Paris, a Chinese pagoda, the Great Pyramid clad once again in smooth white marble. Farther off, I found a gray mountain ridge that copied the familiar curve of Tycho's rim, topped with the shine of our own native dome.

"We got here!" Elated, Pepe slapped Casey's back. "Now what?"

"They owe us." Casey turned to look again. "We put them here, whenever it was. This ought to remind them of all we've given them."

"If they care." Pepe turned back to the door. "Let's see if we can call Sandor."

"Facility closed." We heard the door's toneless robot voice. "Admission denied by order of Tycho Authority."

"Let us in!" Casey shouted. "We want the stuff we left aboard. Clothing, backpacks, canteens. Open the door so we can get them."

"Admission denied."

He hit the door with his fist and kissed his bruised knuckles.

"Admission denied."

"We're here, anyhow."

Pepe shrugged and started down the landing stair. A strange bellow stopped him, rolling back from the walls around us. It took us a moment to see that it came from a locomotive chuffing slowly past the Washington Monument, puffing white steam. Hauling a train of open cars filled with seated passengers, it crept around the quadrangle, stopping often to let riders off and on.

The sun was high, and we shaded our eyes to study them. All as lean and trim as Sandor, and often nude, they had the same nut-brown skins. Many carried bags or backpacks. A few scattered across the lawns and gardens, most waited at the corners for signal lights to let them cross the avenue.

"Tourists, maybe?" I guessed. "Here to see Sandor's recovered history?"

"But I see no children." Casey shook his head. "You'd think they'd bring the children."

"They're people, anyhow." Pepe grinned hopefully. "We'll find somebody to tell us more than Sandor did."

We climbed down the stair, on down a wide flight of steps to a walk that curved through banks of strange and fragrant blooms. Ahead of us a couple had stopped. The woman looked a little odd, I thought, with her head of short ginger-hued fur instead of hair, yet as lovely as Mona had looked in the holos made when she and El Chino reached the Moon. The man was youthful and handsome as Sandor. I thought they were in love.

Laughing at something he had said, she ran a little way ahead and turned to pose for his camera, framed between the monument and the Sphinx. She had worn a scarlet shawl around her shoulders. At a word from him, she whipped it off and smiled for his lens. Her daintily nippled breasts had been pale beneath the shawl, and he waited for the sun to color them.

We watched till he had snapped the camera. Laughing again, she ran back to toss the shawl around his shoulders and throw her arms around him. They clung together for a long kiss. We had stopped a dozen yards away. Casey spoke hopefully when they turned to face us.

"Hello?"

They stared blankly at us. Casey managed an uncertain smile, but a nervous sweat had filmed his dark Oriental face.

"Forgive us, please. Do you speak English? *Français? Español?*"

They frowned at him, and the man answered with a stream of vowels that were almost music and a rattle of consonants I knew I could never learn to imitate. I caught a hint of Sandor's odd accent but nothing like our English. They moved closer. The man pulled the little camera out of his bag, clicked it at Casey, stepped nearer to get his head. Laughing at him, the woman came to pose again beside Casey, slipping a golden arm around him for a final shot.

"We came in that machine. Down from the Moon!" Desperation on his face, he gestured at the spaceplane behind us, turned to point toward the Moon's pale disk in the sky above the Parthenon, waved to show our flight from it to the pedestal. "We've just landed from Tycho Station. If you understand—"

Laughing at him, they caught hands and ran on toward the Sphinx.

"What the hell!" Staring after them, he shook his head. "What the bloody hell!"

"They don't know we're real." Pepe chuckled bitterly. "They take us for dummies. Part of the show."

We followed a path that led toward the Parthenon and stopped at the curb to watch the traffic flowing around the quadrangle. Cars, buses, vans, occasional trucks; they reminded me of street scenes in pre-impact videos. A Yellow Cab pulled up beside us. A woman sprang out. Slim and golden-skinned, she was almost a twin of the tourist who had posed with Casey.

The driver, however, might have been an unlikely survivor from the old Earth. Heavy, swarthy, wheezing for his breath, he wore dark glasses and a grimy leather jacket. Lighting a cigarette, he hauled himself out of the cab, waddled around to open the trunk, handed the woman a folded tripod, and grunted sullenly when she tipped him.

Casey walked up to him as he was climbing back into the cab.

"Sir!" He seemed not to hear, and Casey called louder. "Sir!"

Ignoring us, he got into the cab and pulled away. Casey turned with a baffled frown to Pepe and me.

"Did you see his face? It was dead! Some stiff plastic.

His eyes are blind, behind those glasses. He's some kind of robot, no more alive than our Robos on the Moon."

Keeping a cautious distance, we followed the woman with the tripod. Ignoring us, she stopped to set it up to support a flat round plate of some black stuff. As she stepped away, a big transparent bubble swelled out of the plate, clouded, turned to silver. She leaned to peer into it.

Venturing closer, I saw that the bubble had become a circular window that framed the Washington Monument, the Statue of Liberty, and the Sphinx. They seemed oddly changed, magnified and brighter. Suddenly they moved. Everything shook. The monument leaned and toppled, crushing the statue. The Sphinx looked down across the fragments, intact and forever enigmatic.

I must have come too close. The woman turned with an irritated frown to brush me away as if I had been an annoying fly. Retreating, I looked again. As she bent again to the window, the sky in it changed. The sun exploded into a huge, dull-red ball that turned the whole scene pink. Close beside it was a tiny, bright blue star. Our spaceplane took shape in the foreground, the motors firing and white flame washing the pedestal, as if it were taking off to escape catastrophe.

Awed into silence, Casey gestured us away.

"An artist!" Pepe whispered. "A dramatist at work."

We walked on past the Parthenon and waited at the corner to cross the avenue. Pepe nodded at the blue-clad cop standing out on the pavement with a whistle and a white baton, directing traffic.

"Watch him. He's mechanical."

So were most of the drivers. The passengers, however, riding in the taxies and buses or arriving on the train, looked entirely human, as live as Sandor himself, eager as the tourists of the pre-impact Earth to see these monumental re-creations of their forgotten past.

They flocked the sidewalks, climbed the Capitol steps

to photograph the quadrangle and one another, wandered around the corner and on down the avenue. We fell in with them. They seldom noticed Pepe or me, but sometimes stopped to stare at Casey or take his picture.

"One more robot!" he muttered. "That's what they take me for."

We spent the rest of the day wandering replicated streets, passing banks, broker's offices, shops, bars, hairdressers, restaurants, police stations. A robot driver had parked his van in front of a bookstore to unload cartons stamped ENCYCLOPAEDIA BRITANNICA. A robot beggar was rattling coins in a tin cup. A robot cop was pounding in pursuit of a red-spattered robot fugitive. We saw slim gold-skinned people, gracefully alive, entering restaurants and bars, trooping into shops, emerging with their purchases.

Footsore and hungry before the day was over, we followed a tantalizing aroma that led us to a line of golden folk waiting under a sign that read:

STEAK PLUS!
PRIME ANGUS BEEF
DONE TO YOUR ORDER

Pepe fretted that we had no money for a meal.

"We'll eat before we tell them," Casey said.

"They're human, anyhow." Pepe grasped for some crumb of comfort. "They like food."

"I hope they're human."

Standing in line, I watched and listened to those ahead of us, hoping for any link of human contact, finding none at all. A few turned to give us puzzled glances. One man stared at Casey till I saw his fists clenching. Their speech sometimes had rhythm and pitch that made an eerie music, but I never caught a hint of anything familiar.

A robot at the door was admitting people a few at a time. Its bright-lensed eyes looked past us when we reached it. Finding nobody else, it shut the door.

Limping under Earth gravity, growing hungrier and thirstier, we drifted on until the avenue ended at a high wall of something clear as glass, which cut the memorial off like a slicing blade. Beyond the wall lay an open landscape that recalled Dian's travel videos of tropical Africa. A line of trees marked a watercourse that wound down a shallow valley. Zebras and antelope grazed near us, unalarmed by a dark-maned lion watching sleepily from a little hill.

"There's water we could drink." Pepe nodded at the stream. "If we can get past the wall."

We walked on till it stopped us. Seamless, hard and slick, too tall for us to climb, it ran on in both directions as far as we could see. Too tired to go farther, we sat there on the curb watching the freedom of the creatures beyond, till dusk and a chill in the air drove us back to look for shelter. What we found was a stack of empty cartons behind a discount furniture outlet. We flattened a few of them to make a bed, ripped up the largest to cover us, and tried to sleep.

"You can't blame Sandor," Pepe muttered as we lay there shivering under our cardboard. "He told us we'd never belong."

30

We dozed on our cardboard pallet, aching under the heavy drag of Earth's gravity, through a never-ending night, and woke stiff and cold and desperate. I almost wished we were back on the Moon.

"There has to be a hole in the fence," Casey tried to cheer us. "To let the tourists in."

The train had come from the north. Back at the wall, we limped that way along a narrow road inside it, our spirits lifting a little as exercise warmed us. Beyond a bend, the railway ran out of a tunnel, across a long steel bridge over a cliff-rimmed gorge the stream had cut, and into our prison through a narrow archway in the barrier.

"We'd have to walk the bridge." Pepe stopped uneasily to shake his head at the ribbon of water on the canyon's rocky floor, far below. "A train could catch us on the track."

"We'll just wait for it to pass before we cross," Casey said.

We waited, lying hidden in a drainage ditch beside the track till the engine burst out of the tunnel, steam whistle howling. The cars rattled past us, riders leaning to stare at Sandor's restorations ahead. We clambered out of the ditch and sprinted across the bridge. Jumping off the track at the tunnel mouth, we rolled down a grass slope, got our breath, and tramped southwest away from the wall and into country that looked open.

The memorial sank behind a wooded ridge until all we could see was Sandor's replica of our own lookout dome on his replica of Tycho's rugged rim. We came out across a wide valley floor, scattered with clumps of trees and grazing animals I recognized, wildebeest, gazelles, and a little herd of graceful impala.

"Thanks to old Calvin DeFort. Another Noah saving Earth from a different deluge." Casey shaded his eyes to watch a pair of ostriches running from us across the empty land. "But where are the people?"

"Where's any water?" Pepe muttered. "No deluge, please. Just water we can drink."

We plodded on through tall green grass till I saw elephants marching out of a stand of trees off to our right: a magnificent bull with great white tusks, half a dozen others behind him, a baby with its mother. They came straight toward us. I wanted to run, but Casey simply beckoned for us to move aside. They ambled past us to drink from a pool we hadn't seen. Waiting till they had moved on, we turned toward the pool. Pepe pushed ahead and bent to scoop water up in his cupped hands.

"Don't!" a child's voice called behind us. "Unclean water might harm you."

A small girl came running toward us from the trees where the elephants had been. The first child we had seen, she was daintily lovely in a white blouse and a short blue skirt, her fair face half hidden under a wide-brimmed hat tied under her chin with a bright red ribbon.

"Hello." She stopped a few yards away, her blue eyes wide with wonder. "You are the Moon men?"

"And strangers here." Casey gave her our names. "Strangers in trouble."

"You deceived the ancient spaceship," she accused us soberly. "You should not be here on Earth."

We gaped at her. "How did you know?"

"The ship informed my father."

We stood silent, lost in wonder of our own. A charming picture of childish innocence, but she had shaken me with a chill of terror. Pepe stepped warily back from her, but after a moment Casey caught his breath to ask, "Who is your father?"

"You called him your uncle when you knew him on

the Moon." Pride lit her face. "He is a very great and famous man. He discovered the lunar site and recovered the lost history of humankind. He rebuilt the ancient structures you saw around you where the ship came down."

"I get it." Casey nodded, looking crestfallen and dazed. "I think I begin to get it."

"We can't be sorry we came." Blinking at her, Pepe caught a long breath. "We'd had too much of the Moon. But now we're lost here, in a world I don't begin to understand. Do you know what will happen to us?"

"My father isn't sure." She looked away toward the replicated Tycho dome. "I used to beg him to take me with him to the Moon. He said the station had no place for me." She turned to study us again. "You are interesting to see. My name is—"

She uttered a string of rhythmic consonants and singing vowels, and smiled at Pepe's failure when he tried to imitate them.

"Just call me Tling," she said. "That will be easier for you to say." She turned to Pepe. "If you want water, come with me."

We followed her back to a little circle of square stones in the shade of the nearest tree. Beckoning us to sit, she opened a basket, found a bottle of water, and filled a cup for Pepe. Amused at the eager way he drained it, she filled it again for him, and then for Casey and me.

"I came out to visit the elephants," she told us. "I love elephants. I am very grateful to you Moon people for preserving the tissue specimens that have kept so many ancient creatures alive."

I had caught a tantalizing fragrance when she opened the basket. She saw Pepe's eyes still on it.

"I brought food for some of my forest friends," she said. "If you are hungry."

Pepe said we were starving. She spread a white napkin on one of the stones and began laying out what she had brought. Fruits I thought were peachlike and grapelike and pearlike, but wonderfully sweet and different. Small brown cakes with aromas that wet my mouth. We devoured them so avidly that she seemed amused.

"Where are the people?" Casey waved his arm at the empty landscape. "Don't you have cities?"

"We do," she said. "Though my father says they are far smaller than those you built on the prehistoric Earth." She gestured toward the elephants. "We share the planet with other beings. He says you damaged it when you let your own biology run out of control."

"Maybe we did, but that's not what brought the impactor." Casey frowned again. "You are the only child we have seen."

"There's not much room for children. You see, we don't die."

I was listening desperately, hoping for something that might help us find or make a place for ourselves, but everything I heard was making her new world stranger. Casey gazed at her.

"Why don't you die?"

"If I can explain—" She paused as if looking for an answer we might understand. "My father says I should tell you that we have changed ourselves since the clones came back to colonize the dead Earth. We have altered the genes and invented the microbots."

"Microbots?"

She paused again, staring at the far-off elephants.

"My father calls them artificial symbiotes. They are tiny things that live like bacteria in our bodies but do good instead of harm. They are partly organic, partly diamond, partly gold. They move in the blood to repair or replace injured cells, or regrow a missing organ. They assist our nerves and our brain cells."

The food forgotten, we were staring at her. A picture of innocent simplicity in the simple skirt and blouse and floppy hat, she was suddenly so frightening that I trembled. She reached to put her small hand on mine before she went on.

"My father says I should tell you that they are tiny robots, half machine and half alive. They are electronic. They can be programmed to store digital information. They pulse in unison, making their own waves in the brain and turning the whole body into a radio antenna. Sitting here speaking to you, I can also use them to speak to my father."

She looked up to smile at me, her small hand closing on my fingers.

"Mr. Dunk, please don't be afraid of me. I know we seem different. I know I seem strange to you, but I would never harm you."

She was so charming that I wanted to take her in my arms, but my awe had grown to a dread. We all shrank from her and sat wordless till hunger drove us to attack the fruit and cakes again. Pepe began asking questions as we ate.

Where did she live?

"On that hill." She nodded toward the west, but I couldn't tell which hill she meant. "My father selected a place where he could look out across the memorial."

Did she go to school?

"School?" The word seemed to puzzle her for a moment, and then she shook her head. "We do not require the schools my father says you had in the prehistoric world. He says your schools existed to program the brains of young people. Our microbots can be reprogrammed instantly. That is how I learned your English when I needed it."

She smiled at our dazed faces and selected a plump purple berry for herself.

"Our bodies, however, do need training." Delicately, she wiped her lips on a white napkin. "We form social groups, play games, practice skills. We fly our sliders all around the Earth. I love to ski on high mountains where snow falls. I've dived off coral reefs to observe sea things. I like music, art, drama, games of creation."

"That should be fun." Pepe's eyes were wide. "More fun than life in our tunnels on the Moon." His face went suddenly dark. "I hope your father doesn't send us back there."

"He can't, even if he wanted to." She laughed at his alarm. "He's finally done with the excavation. The charter site is closed and protected for future ages. All intrusion prohibited."

"So what will he do with us?"

"Does he have to do anything?" Seeming faintly vexed, she looked off toward the station dome on the crater ridge. "He says he has no place ready for you. There are humanoid replicates playing your roles there in the Tycho simulation. I suppose you could replace them, if that would make you happy."

"Pretending we were back on the Moon?" Casey turned grim. "I don't think so."

"If you don't want that—"

She stopped, tipped her head as if to listen, and began gathering the water bottle and the rest of the fruit into the basket. Anxiously, Pepe asked if something was wrong.

"My mother." Frowning, she shook her head. "She's calling me home."

"Please!" Casey begged her. "Can't you stay a little longer? You are the only friend we've found. I don't know what we can do without you."

"I wish I could help you, but my mother is afraid for me."

"I wondered if you weren't in danger." He glanced out across the valley. "We saw a lion. You really shouldn't be out here alone."

"It's not the lion." She shook her head. "I know him.

A wonderful friend, so fast and strong and fierce." Her eyes shone at the recollection. "And I know a Bengal tiger. He was hiding in the brush because he was afraid of people. I taught him that we would never hurt him. Once he let me ride him when he chased a gazelle. It was wonderfully exciting."

Her voice grew solemn.

"I'm glad the gazelle got away, though the tiger was hungry and very disappointed. I try to forgive him, because I know he has to kill for food, like all the lions and leopards. They must kill, to stay alive. My mother says it is the way of nature, and entirely necessary. Too many grazing things would destroy the grass and finally starve themselves."

We stared again, wondering at her.

"How did you tame the tiger?"

"I think the microbots help me reach his mind, the way I touch yours. He learned that I respect him. We are good friends. He would fight to protect me, even from you."

"Is your mother afraid of us?"

She picked up the basket and stood shifting on her feet, frowning at us uncertainly.

"The microbots—" She hesitated. "I trust you, but the microbots—"

She stopped again.

"I thought you said microbots were good."

"That's the problem." She hesitated, trouble on her face. "My mother says you have none. She can't reach your minds. You do not hear when she speaks to you. She says you don't belong, because you are not one of us. What she fears—what she fears is you."

Speechless, Casey blinked at her sadly.

"I am sorry to go so soon." With a solemn little bow for each of us, she shook our hands. "Sorry you have no microbots. Sorry my mother is so anxious. Sorry to say good-bye."

"Please tell your father—" Casey began.

"He knows," she said. "He is sorry you came here."

Walking away with her basket, she turned to wave her hand at us, her face framed for a moment by the wide-brimmed hat. I thought she was going to speak, but in a moment she was gone.

"Beautiful!" Casey whispered. "She'll grow up to be another Mona."

Looking back toward the copied monuments of the old Earth, the copied station dome shining on the copied Tycho rim, I saw a dark-maned lion striding across the valley toward the pool where the elephants had drunk. Three smaller females followed, none of them our friends. I shivered.

31

We wandered on up the valley after Tling left us, keeping clear of the trees and trying to stay alert for danger or any hint of help.

"If Sandor lives out here," Casey said, "there must be others. People, I hope, who won't take us for robots."

We stopped to watch impala drinking at a water hole. They simply raised their heads to look at us, but fled when a cheetah burst out of a thicket. The smallest was too slow. The cheetah knocked it down and carried it back into the brush.

"No microbots for them," Pepe muttered. "Or us."

We tramped on, finding no sign of anything human. By mid-afternoon, hungry and thirsty again, with nothing human in view ahead, we sat down to rest on an outcropping rock. Pepe dug a little holo of Tanya out of his breast pocket and passed it to show us her dark-eyed smile.

"If we hadn't lost the radio—" He caught himself, with a stiff little grin. "Still I guess we wouldn't call. I'd love to hear her voice. I know she's anxious, but I wouldn't want her to know the fix we're in—"

He stopped when a shadow flickered across the holo. Looking up, we found a silvery slider craft gliding to the grass a few yards from us. An oval door dilated in the side of it. Tling jumped out.

"We found you!" she cried. "Even with no microbots. Here is my mother."

A slender woman came out behind her, laughing at Pepe when he tried to repeat the name she gave us.

"She says you can just call her Lo."

Tling still wore the blouse and skirt, with her wide-brimmed hat, but Lo was nude except for a gauzy blue sash worn over her shoulder. As graceful and trim, and nearly as sexless, as Sandor, she had the same cream-colored skin, already darkening where the sun struck it, but she had a thick crown of bright red-brown curls instead of Sandor's cap of sleek fur.

"Dr. Yare." Tling spoke carefully to let us hear. "Mr. Navarro. Mr. Kell, who is also called El Chino. They were cloned at Tycho Station from prehistoric tissue specimens."

"You were cloned for duty there." Lo eyed us severely, her English as precise as Tling's. "How did you get here?"

"We lied to the ship." Casey straightened wryly to face her. "We did it because we didn't want to live out our lives in that pit on the Moon. I won't say I'm not sorry, but now we are in trouble. I don't want to die."

"You will die," she told him bluntly. "Like all your kind. You carry no microbots."

"I guess." He shrugged. "But first we want a chance to live."

"Mother, please!" Tling caught her hand. "With no microbots, they are in immediate danger here. Can we help them stay alive?"

"That depends on your father."

"I tried to ask him," Tling said. "He didn't answer."

We watched Lo's solemn frown, saw Tling's deepening trouble.

"I wish you had microbots." She turned at last to translate for us. "My father has gone out to meet an interstellar ship that has just come back after eight hundred years away. The officers are telling him a very strange story."

She looked up at her mother, as if listening.

"It carried colonists for the planets of the star Enthel, which is four hundred light-years toward the galactic core. They had taken off with no warning of trouble. The destination planet had been surveyed and opened for settlement. It had rich natural resources, with no native life to be protected. Navigation algorithms for the flight had been tested, occupation priorities secured."

She stared up at the sky, in baffled dismay.

"Now the ship has returned, two thousand colonists still aboard."

Casey asked what had gone wrong. We waited, watching their anxious frowns.

"My father is inquiring." Tling turned back to us. "He's afraid of something dreadful."

"It must have been dreadful," Pepe whispered. "Imagine eight hundred years on a ship in space!"

"Only instants for them." Tling shook her head, smiling at him. "Time stops, remember, at the speed of light. By their own time, they left only yesterday. Yet their situation is still hard enough. Their friends are scattered away. Their whole world is gone. They feel lost and desperate."

She turned to her mother. "Why couldn't they land?"

Her mother listened again. Far out across the valley I saw a little herd of zebras running. I couldn't see what had frightened them.

"My father is asking," she told us at last. "The passengers were not told why the ship had to turn back. The officers have promised a statement, but my father says they can't agree on what to say. They aren't sure what they found on the destination planet. He believes they're afraid to say what they believe."

The running zebras veered aside. I saw the tawny flash of a lion charging to meet them, saw a limping zebra go down. My own ankle was aching from a stone that had turned under my foot, and I felt as helpless as the zebra.

"Don't worry, Mr. Dunk." Tling reached to touch my arm. "My father is very busy with the ship. I don't know what he can do with you, but I don't want the animals to kill you. I think we can keep you safe till he comes home. Can't we, mother?"

Her lips pressed tight, Lo shrugged as if she had forgotten us.

"Please, mother. I know they are primitives, but they would never harm me. I can understand them the way I understand the animals. They are hungry and afraid, with nowhere else to go."

Lo stood motionless for a moment, frowning at us.

"Get in."

She beckoned us into the flyer and lifted her face again as if listening to the sky.

We soared toward a rocky hill and landed on a level ledge near the summit. Climbing out, we looked down across the grassy valley and over the ridge to Sandor's memorial just beyond. Closer than I expected, I found the bright metal glint of the rebuilt spaceplane on the mall, the Capitol dome and the Washington obelisk, the white marble sheen of the Egyptian pyramid looming out of green forest beyond.

"My father picked this spot." Tling nodded toward the cliff. "He wanted to watch the memorial built."

While her mother stood listening intently at the sky, Tling inspected our mud-stained safari suits.

"You need a bath," she decided, "before you eat."

Running ahead, she took us down an arched tunnel into the hill and showed me into a room far larger than my cell below the station dome. Warm water sprayed me when I stepped into the shower, warm air dried me. When I came out a human-shaped robot handed me my clothing, clean and neatly folded. It guided me to a room where Tling was already sitting with Pepe and Casey at a table set with plates around a pyramid of fragrant fruit.

"Mr. Chino asked about my mother." She looked up to smile at me. "You saw that she's different, with different microbots. She comes from the Garenkrake system, three hundred light-years away. Its people had forgotten where they came from. She wanted to know. When her search for the mother planet brought her here, she found my father already digging at the Tycho site. They've worked together ever since."

Pepe and Casey were already eating. Casey turned to Tling, who was nibbling delicately at something that looked like a huge purple orchid.

"What do you think will happen to us?"

"I'll ask my father when I can." She glanced toward the ceiling. "He is still busy with the ship's officers. I'm sorry you're afraid of my mother. She doesn't hate you, not really. If she seems cool to you, it's just because she has worked so long at the site, digging up relics of the first world. She thinks you seem so—so primitive."

She shook her head at our uneasy frowns.

"You told her you lied to the ship." She looked at Casey. "That bothers her, because the microbots do not transmit untruths or let people hurt each other. She feels sorry for you."

Pepe winced. "We feel sorry for ourselves."

Tling sat for a minute, silently, frowning, and turned back to us.

"The ship is big trouble for my father," she told us. "It leaves him no time for you. He says you should have stayed on the Moon."

"I know." Casey shrugged. "But we're here. We can't go back. We want to stay alive."

"I feel your fear." She gave us an uneasy smile. "My father's too busy to talk to you, but if you'll come to my room, there is news about the ship."

The room must have been her nursery. In one corner was a child's bed piled with dolls and toys, a cradle on the floor beside it. The wall above was alive with a scenic holo. Long-legged birds flew away from a water hole when a tiger came out of tall grass to drink. A zebra stallion ventured warily close, snuffing at us. A prowling leopard froze and ran from a bull elephant. She gestured at the wall.

"I was a baby here, learning to love the animals."

That green landscape was suddenly gone. The wall had become a wide window that showed us a great spacecraft drifting through empty blackness. Blinding highlights glared where the sun struck it. The rest was lost in shadow, but I made out a thick bright metal disk, slowly turning. Tiny-looking sliders clung around a bulging dome at its center.

"It's in parking orbit, waiting for anywhere to go," Tling said. "Let's look inside."

She gave us glimpses of the curving floors where the spin created a false gravity. People sat in rows of seats like those in holos of ancient aircraft. More stood crowded in aisles and corridors. I heard scrap of hushed and anxious talk.

". . . home on a Pacific island."

The camera caught a woman with a crown of what looked like bright golden feathers instead of hair. Holding a whimpering baby in one arm, the other around a grim-faced man, she was answering questions from someone we didn't see. The voice we heard was Tling's.

"It's hard for us." The woman's lips were not moving, but the voice went sharp with her distress. "We had a good life there. Mark's an imagineer. I was earning a good living as a genetic artist, designing ornamentals to special order. We are not the pioneer type, but we did want Baby." An ironic wry smile twisted her lips. "A dream come true!"

She lifted the infant to kiss its gold-capped head.

"Look at us now." She smiled sadly at the child. "We spent our savings for a vision of paradise on Fendris Four.

A tropical beachfront between the surf and a bamboo forest, snow on a volcanic cone behind it. A hundred families of us, all friends forever."

She sighed and rocked the baby.

"They didn't let us off the ship. Or even tell us why. We're desperate, with our money gone and Baby to care for. Now they say there's nowhere else we can go."

The wall flickered and the holos came back with monkeys chattering in jungle treetops.

"That's the problem," Tling said. "Two thousand people like them, stuck on the ship with nowhere to live. My father's problem now, since the council voted to put him in charge."

Casey asked, "Why can't they leave the ship?"

"If you don't understand—" She was silent for a moment. "My mother says it's the way of the microbots. They won't let people overrun the planet and use it up like my mother says the primitives did, back before the impacts. Births must be balanced by migration. Those unlucky people lost their space when they left Earth."

"Eight hundred years ago?"

"Eight hundred of our time." She shrugged. "A day or so of theirs."

"What can your father do for them?"

"My mother says he's still searching for a safe destination."

"If he can't find one—" Casey frowned. "And they can't come home. It seems terribly unfair. Do you let the microbots rule you?"

"Rule us?" Puzzled, she turned her head to listen and nodded at the wall. "You don't understand. They do unite us, but there is no conflict. They live in all of us, acting to keep us alive and well, guiding us to stay free and happy, but moving us only by our own consent. My mother says they are part of what you used to call the unconscious."

"Those people on the ship?" Doubtfully, Casey frowned. "Still alive, I guess, but not free to get off or happy at all."

"They are troubled." Nodding soberly, she listened again. "But my mother says I should explain the microbot way. She says the old primitives lived in what she calls the way of the jungle genes, back when survival required traits of selfish aggression. The microbots have let us change our genes to escape the greed and jealousy and violence that led to so much crime and war and pain on the ancient Earth. They guide us toward what is best for all. My mother says the people on the ship will be content to follow the microbot way when my father has helped them find it."

She turned her head. "I heard my mother call."

I hadn't heard a thing, but she ran out of the room. In the holo wall, high-shouldered wildebeest were leaping off a cliff to swim across a river. One stumbled, toppled, vanished under the rapid water. We watched in dismal silence till Casey turned to frown at Pepe and me.

"I don't think I like the microbot way."

We had begun to understand why Sandor had no place on Earth for us.

32

D ear sirs, I must beg you to excuse us."

Tling made a careful little bow and explained that her mother was taking her to dance and music practice, then going on to a meeting about the people on the stranded ship. We were left alone with the robots. They were man-shaped, ivory-colored, blank-faced. Lacking microbots, they were voice-controlled.

Casey tried to question them about the population, cities, and industries of the new Earth, but they had been programmed only for domestic service, with no English or facts about anything else. Defeated by their blank-lensed stares, we sat out on the terrace, looking down across the memorial and contemplating our own uncertain future, till they called us in for dinner.

The dishes they served us were strange, but Pepe urged us to eat while we could.

"Mañana? Quién sabe?"

Night was falling before we got back to the terrace. A thin Moon was setting in the west. In the east, a locomotive headlight crept into the memorial. The mall was brightly lit for evening tours, the Taj Mahal a glowing gem, the Great Pyramid an ivory island in the creeping dusk. The robots had our beds ready when the mall went dark. They had served wine with dinner, and I slept without a dream.

Awake early next morning, rested again and full of unreasonable hope, I found Tling standing outside at the end of the terrace, looking down across the valley. She had hair like her mother's, not scales or fur, but blond and cropped short. Despite the awesome power of her microbots, I thought she looked very small and vulnerable. She started when I spoke.

"Good morning, Mr. Dunk." She wiped at her face with the back of her hand and tried to smile. I saw that her eyes were puffy and red. "How is your ankle?"

"Better."

"I was worried." She found a pale smile. "Because you have no symbiotes to help repair such injuries."

I asked if she had heard from her father and the emigrant ship. She turned silently to look again across the sunlit valley and the monument. I saw the far plume of steam from an early train crawling over the bridge toward the Washington Monument.

"I watched a baby giraffe." Her voice was slow and faint, almost as if she was speaking to herself. "I saw it born. I watched it learning to stand, learning to suck. It finally followed its mother away, wobbling on its legs. It was beautiful—"

Her voice failed. Her hand darted to her lips. She stood trembling, staring at me, her eyes wide and dark with pain. She gasped for breath.

"My father!" Her voice came suddenly sharp and thin, almost a scream. "He's going away. I'll never see him again."

She ran back inside.

When the robots called us to breakfast, we found her sitting between her parents. She had washed her tear-streaked face, but the food on her plate had not been touched. Here out of the sun, Sandor's face was pale and grim. He seemed not to see us till Tling turned to frown at him. He rose then, and came around the table to shake our hands.

"Good morning, Dr. Pen." Casey gave him a wry smile. "I see why you didn't want us here, but I can't apologize. We'll never be sorry we came."

"Sit down." He spoke shortly. "Let's eat."

We sat. The robots brought us plates loaded with foods we had never tasted. Saying no more to us, Sandor signaled a robot to refill his cup of the bitter black tea and bent over a bowl of crimson berries. Tling sat looking up at him in anguished devotion till Casey spoke.

"Sir, we heard about your problem with the stranded colonists. Can you tell us what's happening?"

"Nothing anybody understands." He shook his head and gave Tling a tender smile before he pushed the berries aside and turned gravely back to us. His voice was quick and crisp. "The initial survey expedition had found their destination planet quite habitable and seeded it with terran-type life. Expeditions had followed to settle the three major continents. This group was to occupy the third.

"They arrived safely but got no answer when they called the planet from orbit. The atmosphere was hazed with dust that obscured the surface, but a search in the infrared found relics of a very successful occupation. Pavements, bridges, masonry, steel skeletons that had been buildings. All half buried under dunes of red, wind-blown dust. No green life anywhere. A derelict craft from one of the pioneer expeditions was still in orbit, but dead as the planet.

"They never learned what killed the planet. No news of the disaster seems to have reached any other world, which suggests that it happened unexpectedly and spread fast. The medical officers believe the killer may have been some organism that attacks organic life, but the captain refused to allow any investigation. She elected to turn back at once, attempting no contact. A choice that probably saved their lives."

He picked up his spoon and bent again to his bowl of berries. I tasted one. It was tart, sweet, with a heady tang I can't describe.

"Sir," Casey spoke again, "those people looked desperate. What will happen to them now?"

"A dilemma." Sandor looked at Tling, with a sad little shrug. She turned her head to hide a sob. "Habitable planets are relatively rare. They must be discovered, surveyed, terraformed, approved for settlement. These people are fortunate. It took an emergency waiver, but we've cleared the way for them to occupy a very promising new planet, five hundred light-years in toward Sagittarius. Fuel and fresh supplies are being loaded now."

"And my father—" Tling looked up at me, her voice almost a wail. "He has to go with them. All because of me."

He put his arm around her and bent his face to hers. Whatever he said was silent. She climbed into his arms. He hugged her, rocking her back and forth like a baby, till her weeping ceased. With a smile that broke my heart, she kissed him and slid out of his arms.

"Excuse us, please." Her voice quivering, she caught his hand. "We must say good-bye."

She led him out of the room.

Lo stared silently after them till Pepe tapped his bowl to signal the robots for a second serving of the crimson berries.

"It's true." With a long sigh, she turned back to us. "A painful thing for Tling. For all three of us. This is not what we planned."

Absently, she took a little brown cake from a tray the robot was passing and laid it on her plate, untasted.

"*Qué importa?*" Pepe gave her a puzzled look.

"We hoped to stay together," she said. "Sandor and I have worked for most of the century, excavating the site and restoring what we could here at the memorial. With that done, I wanted to see my home world again. We were going back there together, Tling with us. Taking the history we had learned, we were planning to replicate the memorial there."

Bleakly, she shook her head.

"This changes everything. Sandor feels a duty to help the colonists find a home. Tling begged him to take us with him, but—" She shrugged in resignation, her lips drawn tight. "He's afraid of what killed that planet. He thinks we're safer here.

"And there's something else. His brother—"

She looked away for a moment.

"He has a twin brother. His father emigrated, and took the twin. His mother had a career in microbot genetics she couldn't leave. Sandor stayed here with her till he was grown. He left Earth then to look for his brother. He never found the twin. He did find me. That's the happy side."

Her brief smile faded.

"It's hopeless, I've told him. There are too many worlds. Star flights take too long. But he won't give up the dream." Her words slowed. "He's afraid his brother was on that planet."

"Can we—" Casey checked himself to look at Pepe and me. We nodded, and he turned anxiously back to Lo. "If Sandor does go out on the emigrant ship, would he take us with him?"

She shook her head and sat staring at nothing till Pepe asked, *"Porqué no?"*

"Reasons enough." Frowning, she picked up the little brown cake, broke it in half, dropped the fragments on her plate. "First of all, the danger. He says it's real. He doesn't want to kill you."

"Aren't there always risks?" Casey shrugged at them. "When you have to jump across hundreds of years of space and time, how can anything be certain?"

"Nothing is." She shrugged unhappily. "But that dead planet is toward the galactic core. So is this new one. If the killer is coming from the core—"

Her words broke off.

"Risk enough." Casey glanced again at us and gave her a stiff little grin. "But you might remind him that we weren't cloned to live forever. He has more at stake than we do."

Her body stiffened, fading slowly white.

"We begged him not to go." Her voice was faint. "But his microbots command him. And he is still looking for his brother."

"Is he their slave? Can't he think of you and Tling?"

Her answer took a long time to come.

"We are not slaves." She seemed composed again; I wondered if her own microbots had eased her pain. "You may see the microbots as micromachines, but they don't make us mechanical. We've kept all the feelings and impulses the primitives had. The microbots simply make us better humans. Sandor is going out with the ship not just to help the people aboard, but for me and Tling, for people everywhere."

"If the odds are as bad as they look—" Casey squinted doubtfully. "What can one man hope to do?"

"Nothing, perhaps." She made a bleak little shrug. "But he has an idea. Long ago, before he ever searched for the lunar site, he worked with his mother on her microbot research. If the killer is some kind of virulent organism, he thinks the microbots might be modified into a shield against it."

"Speak to him," Casey begged her. "Get him to take us with him. We'll help him any way we can."

"You?" Astonishment widened her eyes. "How?"

"We put you here on Earth," he told her. "Even with no microbots at all."

"So you did." Golden color flushed her skin. "I'll speak

to him." Silent for a moment, she shook her head. "Impossible. He says every seat on the ship is filled."

She paused, frowning at the ceiling. The robot was moving around the table, offering a bowl of huge flesh-colored mushrooms that had a tempting scent of frying ham.

"We are trying to plan a future for Tling." Her pixie face was suddenly tight, her voice hushed with feeling. "A thousand years will pass before he gets back. He grieves to leave Tling."

"I saw her this morning," I said. "She's terribly hurt."

"We are trying to make it up. I've promised that she will see him again."

Pepe looked startled. "How can that happen?"

She took a mushroom, sniffed it with a nod of approval, and laid it on her plate.

"We must manage the time," she told him. "I plan to stay here in charge of the memorial, at least till she is grown. Then we'll travel. I want to see what the centuries have done to my own home world. It will take good calculation and the right star flights, but Tling and I can plan to meet him at Tycho Station when he gets back."

"If he gets—"

He cut off the words. Her face went pale, but after a moment she gave us a stiff little smile and had the robot offer the mushrooms again. They had a name I never learned, and a flavor more like bittersweet chocolate than ham. The meal ended. She left us there alone with the robots, with nowhere to go, no future in sight.

"A thousand years!" Pepe muttered. "I wish they'd give us microbots."

"Or else—"

Casey turned to the door.

"News for you." Lo stood there, smiling at us. "News from the emigrant ship. Uneasy passengers have arranged for new destinations, leaving empty places. Sandor has found seats for you."

33

Sandor took us to our seats on the emigrant ship. Wheel-shaped and slowly spinning, it held us against the rim with a force weaker than Earth's gravity, stronger than the Moon's. A blue light flashed to warn us of the space-time jump. Restraints folded around us, I felt a gut-wrenching tug, and then the restraints released us. With no sense of any other change, we sat uneasily waiting.

The big cabin was hushed at first. Watching the faces of other passengers, I saw eager expectation give way to disappointment, then distress. I heard a baby crying, someone shouting at a robot attendant, then a rising clamor of voices sharp-edged with panic. Sandor sat looking gravely away till I asked him what was wrong.

"We don't know." He grinned at our dazed wonderment. "At least we've made the skip to orbit. Five hundred light-years. You're old men now."

He let us follow him to the lounge, where a ceiling dome imaged a new sky. The Milky Way looked familiar. I found the Orion Nebula, but all the nearer stars had shifted beyond recognition. I felt nothing from the ship's rotation; the whole sky seemed to turn around us. Two suns rose, one smaller than our own, the brighter a hot blue dazzle. The planet climbed behind them, a huge round blot on the field of unfamiliar constellations. Red fire rimmed it, edged with the blue sun's glare. Looking for the glow of cities, all I saw was darkness.

Anxious passengers were clustering around a few crew members uniformed in the ship's blue-and-gold caps and sashes. Most of their questions were in the silent language of the microbots, but their faces revealed dismay. I heard high-pitched voices, cries of shock and dread.

We turned to Sandor.

"The telescopes pick up no artificial lights." His lean face was bleakly set. "Radio calls get no answer. The electronic signal spectrum appears dead." He shook his head, with a heavy sigh. "I was thinking of my brother. I'd hoped to find him here."

With gestures of apology, a group of uneasy people pushed between us and surrounded him. He seemed to listen, frowning at the planet's dark shadow, and forlornly waved them away. He spoke his final words for us.

"We'll be looking for survivors."

We watched the planet crawl and crawl again across the ceiling dome as the spinning ship carried us around it. That crescent of blue-and-orange fire widened with each passage till we saw its whole globe. Swirls and streamers of high cloud shone brilliantly beneath the blue sun's light, but thick red dust dulled everything beneath.

One hemisphere was all ocean, except for the gray dot of an isolated island. A single huge continent covered most of the other, extending far south of the equator and north across the pole. Mountain ranges walled the west coast. A single river system drained the vast valley eastward. From arctic ice to polar sea it was all rust-red, no green anywhere.

"A rich world once." Sandor gave a dismal shrug. "But now—"

He turned to watch a woman marching into the room. A woman so flat-chested, masculine, and strange that I had to look again. Bright red-black scales covered her angular body, even her hairless head. Her face was a narrow triangle, her chin sharply pointed, her eyes huge and green. We stared as she sprang to a circular platform in the center of the room.

"Captain Vlix," he murmured. "She's old, born back in the days when microbots were new and body forms experimental. I sailed with her once, centuries ago. She had known my brother, but had no clues to give me."

Heads were turning in attention. I saw uneasy hope yield to bitter disappointment. Sandor stood frozen, widened eyes fixed on her, till she turned to face another officer joining her on the platform.

"What is it?" Casey whispered. Sandor seemed deaf till Casey touched his arm and asked again, "What did she say?"

"Nothing good." Sandor spoke at last, his voice hushed and hurried. "She was summing up a preliminary report from the science staff. This is our second discovery of a dead planet. The first is many light-years away. The implications are—"

He hunched his shoulders, his skin gone pale.

"Yes? What are they?"

With a painful smile, he tried to gather himself.

"At this point, only speculation. The killer has reached two worlds. How many more? Its nature is not yet known. The science chief suggests that it could possibly be a malignant microbot, designed to attack all organic life. It certainly seems aggressive, advancing on an interstellar front from the galactic core."

"It can't be stopped?"

"Certainly not unless we come to understand it. Microbots are designed to survive and reproduce themselves. They could be impossible to stop. They are complex, half life, half machine, more efficient than either. It's possible they have mutated into something malignant. It's possible some madman has reprogrammed them for military use, though they themselves should have prevented that."

"We're helpless?"

"The captain is doing what she can. A robotic drone is being prepared to attempt a low-level survey of surface damage. A search has already begun for any spacecraft that might remain in orbit. And—"

He broke off to watch a thin man with a gray cap and

sash who darted out of the crowd and jumped to join the officers on the platform.

"That's Benkar Rokehut." He made a wry face. "A fellow Earthman, born in my own century. An entrepreneur who has opened half a dozen worlds, made and lost a dozen fortunes. He funded the surveys and initial settlements here. He has his future at stake."

He gave us an ironic shrug.

"And he doesn't want to die."

Rokehut faced the captain for a moment, and turned silently to address the room. Gesturing at the planet, pointing at features on the surface, he turned to follow as it crept overhead, set, and rose again. When Captain Vlix moved as if to stop him, he burst suddenly into speech, shouting vehemently at her, his pale skin flushing redder than the planet.

"His emotions have overcome his microbots." Sandor frowned and drew us closer. "All he sees is danger. Though that first lost planet is a hundred light-years from this one, they both lie toward the core from Earth. He believes the killer pathogen is spreading from somewhere toward the core, possibly carried by refugees. He wants us to head out for the frontier stars toward the rim."

The officers moved to confront him. What they said was silent, but I saw Rokehut's face fade almost to the gray of his cap and sash. He snatched them off, threw them off the platform, waved his fists and shouted. Yielding at last, he shuffled aside and stood glaring, fists still clenched with a purely human fury.

Captain Vlix turned silently back to face the room, speaking with a calm control.

"The officers agree that we do seem to face an interstellar invasion," Sandor said. "But blind flight can only spread the contagion, if frightened refugees carry it. In the end, unless we get some better break—"

With a sad little shrug, he paused to look hard at us.

"Tycho Station could become the last human hope. It is sealed, shielded, well concealed. The Moon has no surface life to attract or sustain any kind of pathogen." His lips twisted to a quirk of bitter humor. "Even if the pathogen wins, there's still one hope. It should die when no hosts are left to carry it. You clones may have another book to write before your epic ends."

Captain Vlix left the room, Rokehut and his people close behind her. The robot attendants were circulating with trays of hard brown biscuits and plastic bubbles of juice.

"The best we can do," Sandor said. "With zero times in transit, the ship carries no supplies or provisions for any prolonged stay aboard. We must move, yet the officers agree that we can't turn back until we get whatever information we can from the drone."

It descended over the glaciers that fringed the polar cap and flew south along the west coast. Its cameras projected their images on the dome and the edge of the floor. Watching, I could feel that I was riding in its nose. It must have flown high and fast, but the images were processed to make it seem that we hovered low and motionless over a deserted seaport or the ruin of a city and climbed to soar on to the next.

All we saw was dust and desolation: broken walls of stone or brick, where roofs had fallen in; tangles of twisted steel where towers had stood; concrete seawalls around empty harbors. And everywhere, wind-drifted dunes of dead red dust and wind-whipped clouds of rust-colored dust, sometimes so dense it hid the ground.

The drone turned east near the equator, soaring over mountain peaks capped with snows dyed the color of drying blood. It paused over broken dams in high mountain canyons and crossed a network of dust-choked irrigation canals.

"I've dreamed my brother was here." Sandor made a solemn face. "Dreamed I might find him here." He stopped to sigh and gaze across an endless sea of wave-shaped dunes. "Dreams! All of us dreaming of endless life and time for everything. And now this, the pathogen."

The drone had reached the dead coast and flown on east across the empty ocean. The lounge was silent again, disheartened people drifting away. Casey asked if we were turning back.

"Not quite yet." Sandor tipped his head, listening. "Captain Vlix reports that the search team has found something in low polar orbit. Maybe a ship. Maybe just a rock. Maybe something else entirely. She's launching a pilot pod to inspect it."

Back in the lounge, strange music was playing. Strange at least to me. Unfamiliar trills and runs and strains were broken by long gaps of silence. A woman with a baby in her arms was swaying to a rhythm I couldn't hear. Silent people were dozing or wandering the aisles. A silent group had gathered around Rokehut at the end of the room, listening and gesticulating.

"He still wants us to run for our lives," Sandor said. "For a star two thousand light-years out toward the rim. An idiot's dream! To complete the jump he'd have to calculate the exact relative position of the star two thousand years from now. Nobody has the data."

The attendants came back with juice and little white wafers. Rokehut and his group refused them, with angry gestures, and trooped away to confront the captain again.

"A mild sedative." Sandor waved the robot away. "If you need to relax."

I accepted a wafer. It had a vinegary taste and it hit me with sudden fatigue. I slept in my seat till Casey shook my arm.

"The pod has reached that object in orbit," Sandor told us. "The pilot identifies it as the craft that brought the last colonists. His attempts at contact get no response. He asked permission to go aboard. That has been granted, with the warning that he won't be allowed back on our ship. He reports that his service robot is now cutting the security bolts to let him into the air lock."

I watched the people around us, silently listening, frowning intently, expectantly nodding, frowning again.

"He's inside." Head tipped aside, eyes fixed on something far away, Sandor spoke at last. "The pathogen has been there. He has found red dust on the decks, but he hopes for protection from his space gear. He believes the killer was already on the planet before the ship arrived. The cargo was never unloaded. All organics have crumbled, but metal remains unchanged.

"He's pushing on—"

Sandor stopped to listen and shake his head.

"The pilot was on his way to the control room, searching for records or clues. He never got there." He leaned his head and nodded. "The science chief is summing up what evidence he has. It points to something airborne, fast-acting, totally lethal. It likely killed anybody who ever knew what it is."

Captain Vlix allowed Rokehut and his partisans to poll the passengers. Overwhelmingly, they voted to turn back toward Earth at once. The lounge became a bedlam of angry protest when departure was delayed, hushed a little when Captain Vlix came back to the platform.

"She says Earth is out," Sandor told us, "for two sufficient reasons. We might find that the pathogen is already there. Even if we beat it, she says we would certainly be regarded as a suspected carrier, warned away and subject to attack."

"That recalls a legend of the old Earth." Casey nodded bleakly. "The legend of a ghost ship called the Flying Dutchman, that sailed forever and never reached a port."

The strange constellations flickered out of the ceiling dome, and the drone's images returned. The limitless ocean beneath it looked blue as Earth's when we glimpsed it through rifts in the clouds, but the sky was yellow, the larger sun a sullen red, the blue one now a hot pink point.

"The island's somewhere ahead." Sandor stood with us in the lounge, frowning at the horizon. "If the drone ever gets there. It's losing altitude. Losing speed. Probably damaged by the dust."

White-capped waves rose closer as it glided down through scattered puffs of cumulus.

"There it is!" Sandor whispered before I had seen it. "Just to the right."

I strained to see. The image dimmed and flickered as the drone bored through a tuft of pink-tinted cloud. Something blurred the far horizon. At first a faint dark streak, it faded and came back as we searched it for color.

"Green?" A sharp cry from Casey. "Isn't it green?"

"It was," Sandor said. "We're going down."

A foam-capped mountain of blue-green water climbed ahead of the drone. It crashed with an impact I almost felt, but I thought I had caught a flash of green.

34

The ceiling dome had gone dark when the drone broke up. After a moment it was spangled again with those new constellations. The dead ship, immense and high overhead, was a fire-edged silhouette against the Milky Way.

"You saw it!" Casey shouted at Sandor. "Something green. Something alive!"

Frowning, Sandor shook his head.

"I saw a brief greenish flash. Probably from some malfunction as the drone went down."

"It was green," Casey insisted. "Aren't they landing anybody to take a look?"

"No time for that."

"But if the island is alive—"

"How could that be?" He was sharply impatient. "We've seen the whole planet dead. Whatever killed it killed the drone before it ever touched the surface. The captain isn't going to risk any sort of contact."

"If she would let us land—" Casey waited for Pepe and me to nod. "We could radio a report."

"Send you down to die?" Sandor's eyes went wide. "She cares too much for life. She would never consider it."

"Don't you think we care for life? Tell her we were cloned to keep the Earth and humankind alive. But tell her we were also cloned to die. If we must, I don't know a better way."

Sandor took us to meet Captain Vlix, and translated for us. Our visit was brief, but still enough to let me glimpse a spark of humanity beneath her gleaming crimson scales. I don't know what he told her, but it caught her interest. She had him question us about Tycho Station and our lives there.

"You like it?" Her huge green eyes probed us with a disturbing intensity. "Life without microbots? Knowing you must die?"

"We know." Casey nodded. "I don't dwell on it."

"I must admire your idealism." A frown creased her crimson scales. "But the science staff reports no credible evidence of life on the planet. I can't waste your lives."

"We saw evidence we believe," Casey said. "In that last second as the drone went down. Considering the stakes, we're ready to take the risk."

"The stakes are great." Her eyes on Sandor, she frowned and finally nodded her red-scaled head. "You may go."

There were no space suits to fit us. That didn't matter, Casey said; space gear had not saved the pilot who boarded the derelict. With Sandor translating, the service robots showed Pepe how to operate the flight pod, a streamlined bubble much like the slider that had brought Sandor to the Moon. He shook our hands and wished us well.

"Make it quick," he told us. "Captain Vlix expects no good news from you. No news at all, in fact, after you touch down. Our next destination is still under debate. None looks safe, or satisfies everybody, but we can't delay."

Pepe made it quick, and we found the island green.

Rising out of the haze of dust as we dived, the shallow sea around it faded from the blue of open water through a hundred shades of jade and turquoise to the vivid green of life. The island was bowl-shaped, the great caldera left by an ancient volcanic explosion. Low hills rimmed a cir-

cular valley with a small blue lake at the center. A line
of green trees showed the course of a stream that ran
through a gap in the hills from the lake down to the sea.

"Kell?" Sandor's voice crackled from the radio before
we touched the ground. "Navarro? Yare? Answer if you
can."

"Tell him!" Casey grinned at Pepe as he dropped our
slider pod to a wide white beach that looked like coral
sand. "It looks a lot better than our pits in the Moon. No
matter what."

Pepe echoed him, "No matter what."

"Tell him we're opening the air lock," Casey said. "If
we can breathe the air, we're heading inland."

Pepe opened the air lock. I held my breath till I had to
inhale. The air was fresh and cool, but I caught a faint
acrid bite. In a moment my eyes were burning. Pepe
sneezed and clapped a handkerchief over his nose. Casey
smothered a cough and peered at us sharply.

"Can you report?" Sandor's anxious voice. "Can you
breathe?"

Casey coughed and blew his nose.

"Breathing," he gasped. "Still breathing."

I thought we were inhaling the pathogen. I hadn't
known the pilot who died on the derelict, or the millions
or billions it had killed. I felt no personal pain for them,
but Pepe and Casey were almost part of me. I put my
arms around them. We huddled there together, sneezing
and wheezing, till Pepe laughed and pulled away.

"If this is death, it ain't so bad." He jogged me in the
ribs. "Let's get out and take a closer look."

We stumbled out of the lock and stood there on the
hard wet sand beside the pod, breathing hard and peering
around us. The sky was a dusty pink, the suns a tiny red
moon and a bright pink spark. The beach sloped up to
low green hills. Perhaps half a mile south along the beach,
green jungle covered the delta at the mouth of the little

river. Pepe picked up a scrap of seaweed the waves had left.

"Still green." He studied it, sniffed it. "It smells alive."

My lungs were burning. Every breath, I thought, might be my last, yet I always stayed able to struggle for another. Pepe dropped the handkerchief and climbed back in the slider to move it higher on the beach, farther from the water. He returned with a portable radio. Casey blew his nose again, and started south along the beach, toward the delta. We followed him, breathing easier as we went.

The little river had cut its way between two great black basaltic cliffs. Casey stopped before we reached them, frowning up at the nearest. I looked and caught a deeper breath. The summit had been carved into a face. The unfinished head of a giant struggling out of the stone.

"Sandor!" Casey walked closer, staring up at the great dark face. "It's Sandor."

"It is." Shading his eyes, Pepe whispered huskily. "Unless we're crazy."

I had to sneeze again, and wondered what the dust was doing to us.

Sandor called again from the ship, but Pepe seemed too stunned to speak. A rope ladder hung across the face, down to the beach. Black and gigantic, gazing out at the sky, lips curved in a puckish smile, the head was certainly Sandor's.

"We're okay." Rasping hoarsely into the phone, Pepe answered at last. "Still breathing."

Walking closer to the cliff, we found a narrow cave. A jutting ledge sheltered a long workbench hewn from an untrimmed log, a forge with a pedal to work the bellows, a basket of charcoal, a heavy anvil, a long shelf cluttered with roughly made hammers and chisels and drills.

"The sculptor's workshop." Casey stepped back across a reef of glassy black chips on the sand, litter fallen from the chisel. "Who is the sculptor?"

He touched his lips at Pepe when Sandor called again.

"Tell him to hold the ship. Tell him we're alive and pushing inland. Tell him we've found human life, or strong evidence for it. But not a word about the face. Not till we have something Captain Vlix might believe."

We hiked inland, following a smooth-worn footpath along the river bank. The valley widened. We came out between two rows of trees, neatly spaced, bearing bright red fruit.

"*Cerezas!*" Pepe cried. "Cherries! A cherry orchard."

He picked a handful and shared them, tart, sweet, hard to believe. We came to an apple orchard, to rows of peach and pear trees, all laden with unripe fruit. We found a garden farther on, watered by a narrow ditch that diverted water from the river. Tomato vines, yams, squash, beans, tall green corn.

Casey caught his breath and stopped. I stared past him at a man—a man who might have been Sandor's double—who came striding up the path to meet us.

"Sandor?" His eager voice was almost Sandor's, though the accent made it strange. "Sandor?"

We waited, hardly breathing, while he came on to us. The image of Sandor, bronzed dark from the sun, he had the same trim frame, the same sleek brown fur crowning his head, the same pixie face and golden eyes. He stopped to scan us with evident disappointment, and pointed suddenly when he saw Pepe's radio.

Pepe let him have it. Eagerly, hands shaking, he made a call. The other Sandor answered with a quick and breathless voice. Their excited words meant nothing to me, no more than their silent communion after they fell silent, but I could read the flow of feeling on the stranger's weathered face. Wonder, fear, hope, tears of joy.

At last the Sandor on the ship had a moment for us.

"You've found my brother. Call him Corath if you need a name. Captain Vlix is ready for a jump toward the rim. She is slow to believe what you're saying, with her ship at risk, but Rokehut is demanding a chance for confirmation and I must see my brother. She's letting me come down."

Corath beckoned. We followed him down the path till we could see the distant lake and a ruined building on a hill. Once it must have been impressive, but the stone walls were roofless now, windows and doorways black and gaping. He stopped us at his very simple residence, a thatched roof over a bare wooden floor with a small stone-walled enclosure at the rear. Waiting for Sandor, we sat at a table under the thatch. He poured cherry wine for us from a black ceramic jug and stood waiting, staring away at the sky.

Sandor landed his silvery flight pod on the grass in front of the dwelling. Corath ran to meet him. They stopped to gaze at each other, to touch each other, to grip each other's hands. They hugged and stepped apart and stood a long time face-to-face without a word I could hear, laughing and crying, hugging again, until at last Sandor rubbed his wet eyes and turned to us.

"I saw—saw the head." Breathing hard, he stopped to clear his throat and peer again into Corath's face as if to verify that he was real. "It was meant to be my own, though at first I thought it was his. He has been here almost two hundred years, marooned by the pathogen. With no way to search for me, he says, except inside the mountain."

A spasm of coughing bent him over. Corath held his arm till he drew himself upright and turned soberly back to us.

"We were coughing," Pepe said. "Sneezing. Wheezing. We thought we had the killer pathogen."

"Something kin to it, my brother says. But benign. He says it saved your lives."

We had to hold our questions. They forgot us, standing together a long time in silence before they laughed and embraced again. Sandor wiped at his tears at last and turned back to us.

"The pathogen got here two hundred years ago. Corath knows no more than we do about its origin or history. It caught him here on the island, at work on the same sort of microbot research I once hoped to undertake. He was testing immunities and looking for quantum effects that might extend the contact range. The range effect is still not fully tested, but his new microbot did make him immune. Too late to save the rest of the planet, it did wipe the pathogen off the island."

Captain Vlix was still a stubborn skeptic, terrified of contamination. She refused to let Sandor bring his brother aboard, or even to come back himself. Yet, with Rokehut and some of the other passengers still at odds over a new destination, she let the second officer bring a little group of desperate volunteers down to see the live island for themselves.

They came off the pod jittery and pale. Fits of coughing and sneezing turned them whiter still, until Corath and his news of their new immunity brought their color back. To make his own survival sure, the officer drew a drop of Corath's blood and scratched it into his arm with a needle. Still breathing, but not yet entirely certain, he wanted to see the research station.

Corath took us to tour the ruin on the hill. The pathogen had destroyed wood and plastic, leaving only bare stone and naked steel. A quake had toppled one roofless wall, but the isolation chamber was still intact. An enormous windowless concrete box, it had heavy steel doors with an airlock between them.

Black with rust, the doors yawned open now, darkness beyond them. He struck fire with flint, steel, and tinder, lit a torch, led us inside. The chamber was empty, except for the clutter of abandoned equipment on the work-benches and a thick carpet of harmless gray dust on the floor.

We found nothing to reveal the structure of his new microbot, nothing to explain how its wind-borne spores had set us to sneezing and made us safe. Corath answered with only a noncommittal shrug when Pepe dared to ask if the infection had made us immortal.

"At least the dust hasn't killed us," Casey said. "Good enough for me."

The officer went back to the ship with a bottle of Corath's healing blood. Captain Vlix agreed to hold the ship in orbit. Rokehut brought his engineers to survey the island and stake out a settlement site on the plateau beyond the lake. Passengers came down with their luggage and crates of freight, ready now to stake their futures on the island and Corath's promise that the red dust could make fertile soil.

He decided to stay there with them.

Sandor took us back aboard with him. Convinced at last, Captain Vlix was waiting to greet us at the air lock, embracing him almost as tearfully as his brother had. When she had finally wiped her eyes and turned away, he spoke to us.

"Our job now is to fight the pathogen with Corath's microbot. Volunteers in flight pods are setting out to carry it to all the nearest worlds. I am taking it to Lo and Tling back on Earth. Do you want to come?"

We did.

PART FIVE

Farewell to Earth

35

Sandor Pen brought us home to Earth: Casey, Pepe, and me, sitting with him in the slider pod. Its hull was nearly invisible, so that we seemed to float among constellations that jumped and jumped again into different patterns as we skipped back across the light-years. For us, having grown up in the tiny slice of old Earth preserved at Tycho Station on the Moon, the flight was a strange adventure. Our plunge into his far-future universe had been a shock to us, and he tried to make us feel at home.

"We've had a long day." A quizzical smile on his pixie face, he reminded us of the time paradox. "A good thousand years when we get home."

A thousand years! I felt numb from too much wonder. Sandor was made little jokes that might help us adjust to his new world. His own Spanish perfect from the microbots in his brain, he gently kidded Pepe for trying to use the broken bits of it he had picked up from his holo father. He held his own chameleon hand beside Casey's black one in the blue glare of a passing star until their colors matched. He tried to tease me about what he said were gaps in what I had learned about Tycho Station. Certainly he knew our history better than I did.

Sandor's small talk stopped. Though his microbots required no visible controls to direct the slider, he was leaning intently forward to search our way toward a faint white star I found ahead, flashing brighter with each skip. We felt his anxiety, and the riddles of relativistic time still astonished us. I saw Pepe's troubled frown at the gem-cased timepiece the grateful emigrants had given him after our landing on that dead Sagittarian planet.

"Do these keep Earth time as well as ship time?" he

asked. "Or how will Lo and Tling know when to expect you?"

"They will know," he said. "The microbots account for time."

He leaned again to scan our path through the stars. Their slow, slow creep had dissolved familiar constellations, but I found the Pleiades. I was still looking for the Big Dipper when the sun exploded out of the dark ahead. Shading my eyes from it, I found a hot red spark.

"Earth?" Pepe went hoarse with dismay. "Dead? Turned red with dust?"

"Mars." Sandor laughed. "Earth was hiding behind the sun."

The sun jumped aside. The red spark was gone. I saw a blue-white point, a fainter dot beside it. They leaped closer till the dot became the Moon's gray face and I found the two Americas on Earth, still green with life.

"*Bien!*" Pepe relaxed. "*Todo lo mismo!*"

"The same?" Casey shook his head. "After a thousand years?"

"Quite a day!" Grinning, Pepe glanced again at his diamond-dialed gift. "Ten centuries since we got out of bed, and a trip to a star too far to see from here. I'm glad to see the Earth again."

A long day, and strange indeed. On the dead planet where we landed, Sandor had met his lost twin brother and found the microbots that brought a new immunity from the contagion that killed the planet. I knew nothing of their chemistry, but they had saved us. I felt grateful to have them flowing in my own blood.

The pod slid again, toward the Moon's gray and battered face. Tycho lay below us, its central peak a craggy islet in a lake of ink-black shadow, the pale rays splayed around it, the station a bright silver bead on the north rim wall.

"Still secure." Sandor smiled at us, with a nod of satisfaction. "Ready to clone you again, if Earth ever needs reseeding."

"Can we land?" Casey was suddenly eager. "Can we look inside?"

"It's asleep." Sandor shook his head. "Nothing alive inside except the master computer, set to wake it if danger is ever detected."

"Can't we wake it now?" Casey asked. "Can't Mona be cloned?"

They sat face-to-face in the sun's harsh glare, empty blackness behind them. Casey had come out of the past, his genes preserved since the first great impact erased most life from the early Earth. A stocky black man with thick black hair and stolid Oriental features, he was slack-jawed, shaken with emotion.

Sandor's genes came down from ours in the station, but ages of evolution and genetic engineering had made them almost alien. His microbots made him more than merely human. Nearly nude, tanned golden-brown where the sun struck and pale in the shadows, he was slim and graceful. He had a narrow impish face, a crown of sleek brown fur where we had hair.

"Mona?" Casey's voice rose sharply. "She should have been cloned when we were. Do you know why she wasn't?"

"She wasn't necessary." Sandor shrugged. "Tycho Station is a priceless bit of history, but only history now."

"Only history?" Casey muttered bitterly. "Don't forget the history. We clones reseeded the planet and reseeded it again, back when it was still the only human world. You all owe your lives to us. Don't you know my holo father's story?"

"As well as you do." Sandor gave him a quizzical

shrug. "Don't forget what I've done. Your station had been lost and forgotten, buried under ejecta from the lunar impact, till I discovered the site."

His dark face stubbornly set, Casey turned back to Sandor. "If you cloned us just to test the new maternity lab, why can't you test it again? Long enough to let her live again?"

Sandor shook his furry head.

"Now?" His voice had an impatient edge. "No time to waste. Lo may be there already, waiting for me in the Stonehenge circle."

"Can we come back?"

Sandor shrugged again, and the Moon slid away.

We were suddenly high over Asia. The eastern coasts were hidden under night. India was white with monsoon cloud, the Himalayas bright with ice, but north and east the land was vividly green, all the way to the open seas around the sunlit pole. The terraformed Earth was still temperate, still alive.

"It looks okay." Casey glanced at Sandor and his voice fell. "Isn't it?"

Sandor had tipped his head to listen. I saw him shake his head, saw the color draining from his golden face. The pod had no controls he ever touched, but the round Earth spun and lifted till we were floating high above the Mediterranean. It had changed since our old maps were made, grown wider as thawing ice raised sea levels. Shading his eyes against the sun, he leaned to peer again.

Casey asked, "Is something wrong?"

"I don't know." He paused to shake his elfish head. "I'm glad to see the green. No red dust. But I can't hear anything."

"No radio?"

He listened again and the frown bit deeper before he shook his head.

"None. The microbots link us all by radio. We're still too far to let me make out individual voices, but the millions should create an electronic hum. All I hear is silence."

Skipping around the planet, we overtook the falling night. The Americas were dark, but we made them out by moonlight. Hovering low over spots where I remembered cities, we saw no lights except for the ragged red line of a great forest fire across the plains along the eastern foot of the Rockies.

"People?" Pepe murmured hopefully. "People make fire."

"So does lightning," Sandor said, and slid us again.

The ancient terraformers had made Australia hard to recognize. As it rolled into sunlight ahead, I saw old coastlines redrawn, old deserts green, a new blue sea in the heart of the continent. Sandor dropped us toward the great memorial he had built to display the forgotten history he had recovered on the Moon.

"*Qué cabrón!*" Pepe gasped when we began to make it out. "*Qué lástima!*"

The wall around the memorial was gone. The Washington Monument still towered in solitary majesty, but the dome of Saint Peter's had fallen in. The Taj Mahal had crumbed into a mountain of broken marble. The Sphinx, its restored nose still intact, crouched like a beast ready to spring out of a lush new jungle. The Great Pyramid was a clean white marble peak in a dense forest that had climbed the slope of the replicated Tycho rim wall, almost to the replicated dome.

Stricken silent, Sandor dived to search for Stonehenge, which had stood at the edge of the mall. It took time to find. Copied in something that looked like solid silver, its massive rough-edged pillars still stood where he had set them, but now they were hidden under a tangle of climbing vines. A great tree with strange red leaves towered out of the central circle, far taller than the stones.

"Lo." I heard Sandor's faint whisper. "Lo and Tling. They were to be here."

I searched beneath that huge-leafed tree for the mirror glint of a slider pod, for anything alive. When at last I did find something moving, it was a little monkey scolding at us from the treetop. Sandor held us a long time there. His skin gone paper white, even where the sun should have gilded it, he sat grimly silent till Casey dared to ask, "Sir, what do you think?"

"They should be here." His face was a lifeless mask. "Let's look at my place."

His home had been dug into the side of a hilltop overlooking the memorial. He lifted us away from Stonehenge and the blindly staring Sphinx, soared over a wooded ridge and the open valley beyond. It looked unchanged since we left, still a slice of prehistoric Africa. Wildebeest and zebras grazed toward long-legged birds standing in a shallow lakelet. Half a dozen elephants followed a long-tusked bull marching out of the trees along a narrow stream.

Only days ago by our own space-twisted time, the three of us had wandered here along that same stream, strangers from the Moon, lost and hungry in a world we had never expected. Little Tling, here to visit her animal friends, had found us, fed us, and brought her mother to our rescue.

Just yesterday to us, but still a thousand years ago. A great tree had grown on the rocky shelf below the cliff. Dead now, fallen and crumbling into mold, its trunk blocked the doorway. Sandor hovered over it, finally set us down beside it. He sat there in the pod, listening, watching the sky for Lo and Tling.

"Can't they be somewhere here?" Pepe asked. "Looking for you?"

"I should feel them." His tone was dismal, but he finally moved in his seat. "Let's look inside."

He opened the door. We scrambled out and found a way around the great tree's rotting roots and the pit they had torn when it came down. He stopped again to listen at the archway in the cliff and pushed on into the darkness. Following, I felt my foot strike something that rattled and rolled away. Peering into the gloom, I found a bleached and broken human skull.

"Osos!" Pepe whispered. "Bears."

He had leaned to point at huge footprints in the muddy floor. In the dark ahead, I heard a hoarse animal grunt. A rank animal stink was suddenly overwhelming. My stomach roiling, I stumbled back into the open. We stood there, gasping for clean air, until abruptly Sandor turned and stared again into the sky.

I saw a thin bright line sliced suddenly across a cotton puff of cumulus. It widened silently and became a mirror-bright slider pod, dropping to the grass beside us.

36

The slider came down beside the fallen tree. The oval door stretched open and I saw Lo standing inside, her pale skin growing slowly golden as the light struck her. Nearly nude, she looked unchanged by whatever time had passed for her. Flat-breasted, almost boyish with short red-brown hair falling around her pixie face, she was still somehow gracefully alluring. She stood for a moment gazing at Sandor and darted out into his arms. They hugged a long time and then pushed apart, looking at each other in silent adoration.

"Mona!" I heard Casey's startled gasp. "Mona Lisa!"

Another woman stood in the slider door. Clad in some gauzy, half-transparent stuff, honey-hued hair falling to her shoulders, she looked more womanly than Lo, maybe more lovely. He had grown up in love with Mona's image. Here she was, identical and quite alive.

Recognition lit her face.

"Mr. Kell! Mr. Navarro. Mr. Yare. Mother was afraid you'd never get here."

Casey stood open-mouthed and speechless, gaping at her.

"You do know us?" Pepe whispered. "You look like Mona. Mona Lisa Live, in our holo tank on the Moon."

"I'm her clone." Laughing at our astonishment, she nodded. "I met you when I was a child. Remember the little girl who was out in the bush with the elephants when she found you?"

"Tling?" Pepe shook his head. "You are Tling?"

"I never guessed!" Breathless, Casey stumbled toward her. "I can't believe!"

She stepped toward him out of the pod. His arms had spread as if to embrace her, but he checked himself and let them fall. She laughed again, and offered her hand. He stood paralyzed for a moment, grinned sheepishly, and seized it.

"I was cloned to be an experimental guinea pig." She turned with a teasing smile at Sandor. "He wanted to see if the microbots would thrive in prehistoric flesh." She raised a bare arm to let us see its instant tan where the sun struck it. "Apparently they do."

"Mona!" Casey murmured the name, still clinging to her hand. "Where have you been?"

"With Mother. She took me to her birth world. I grew up there. We've traveled since, timing the flights to meet my father here."

"Do you remember the station? Your holo mother?" His eager eyes were still drinking her in. "You look just like her. I've always dreamed—"

His voice stopped when she shrugged.

"An identical twin." His elation had faded when he saw she had failed to share it. "I don't recall the Moon at all, though my father used to talk about his excavation there. I do remember when Mother took me to see the memorial and told me about Mona Lisa Live and El Chino."

"My father," Casey whispered. "I am El Chino's clone."

"Mother told me." She nodded. "Criminals, she said, in their violent prehistoric world. They had killed a man. They were escaping the law as well as the impact when they got off the Earth on the escape plane. That's hard to imagine." She stared hard at Casey. "I know we wouldn't be here if they hadn't got away, but now—"

She shrugged again, inspecting Casey as if he was a puzzling stranger.

ʃandor and Lo had moved apart and turned to gaze across the memorial's jungle-clotted ruin. She left

Casey and ran to hug them. All three huddled together in soundless communion. We stood waiting until at last Mona came back to us, smiling at Casey now.

"The hero!" She threw her arms around him and kissed his startled lips. "Father has told me how you found his brother."

He looked breathless when she let him go, shaking his head as if stunned with too much emotion.

"We heard a rumor on the last planet where we stopped," she said. "A tale too wild to believe, about three prehistoric clones who landed on a dead world and came back with a cure for the pandemic that had killed it."

She paused to shake Pepe's hand and mine, and slip her arm around Casey, who gave her another silly grin.

"We didn't know you were the three. Or that it was Father's lost twin brother you found there, along with this new microbot that had kept him alive. Father says it wiped out the killer pathogen and saved all our lives. But now—"

She shook her head, her fine skin grown pale again.

"We never expected this. We've seen the jungle and the ruined memorial. Something has hit the Earth. It can't be the same pathogen, because plants and animals are evidently immune, but we don't see any people. We can't hear any voices. Father's afraid the whole Earth is dead."

They huddled together again, Sandor's arms around Lo and Mona. We waited uneasily till Mona turned back to us.

"We must search for the killer, whatever it is. Father says the odds are better if we separate. He and Mother are going out to look at a space station we passed on the way in. It's still in geosynchronous orbit, but it didn't respond to our signals. We sensed no life about it, but Father hopes it can tell us something."

"And you?" Casey peered at her, his dark faced tensed. "You?"

"I'm staying here on Earth. First of all, I want to look for Akyar, the old world capital. It was located on the equator in east Africa, under that satellite station."

"May I go with you?" Casey begged her instantly.

"I see no need." She shook her head. "We have no notion what it is. We can't assume that we're immune."

"We've breathed the air here, and nothing has struck us yet. Whatever happened was long ago. Centuries, maybe, if you look at the jungle over the ruins. The killer's likely dead. If it isn't—" His dark face set, he moved closer to her. "Let me come with you. Please!"

She hesitated, frowning down across the ruins. Casey turned to Sandor, hands spread in silent appeal. I saw no sign from him, but after a moment she nodded at Casey.

"Father says you may be needed, as you were on the Sagittarian planet. Get your baggage."

We had very little baggage, only our space suits and a few gifts from the grateful emigrants. Casey rushed to get his bag from Sandor's pod and came back to wait with Mona. She was lost once more in silent talk with her parents. At last she hugged them again, wiped at her eyes with the loose end of her sash, and beckoned Casey into her slider. It lifted soundlessly, floated briefly over our heads, and slid out of space-time. Lo and Sandor watched till they were gone, and then stood gazing somberly down across the valley. A magnificent lion lay on a hill, looking down across a little herd of impala grazing toward the waterhole.

"I'm sorry for Casey," Pepe murmured to me. "He's in love with a dream. His world is the cave in the Moon where we grew up. Mona's lovely as a dream, but she grew up without her past." He shrugged uncomfortably.

"He's smart enough, but crazy over her. Too crazy to know they'll never get together."

He brightened when Sandor spoke to us.

"Do you want to come along to the satellite station?".

"Seguro!" he whispered. *"Seguro qui sí."*

He and I climbed into the pod to sit behind Sandor and Lo. The door flicked shut. The rotting log and the doorway in the cliff fell away and vanished. With no motion I felt, we were back out in space, the sun so dazzling that we saw no stars.

Moving as the Earth turned, the station hung stationary over what had been Kenya. It was suddenly only a mile or two ahead, a great silver wheel slowly rotating, blazing where the sun struck it. Sandor and Lo sat frowning at it, listening, I suppose, for radio voices. I looked back at Earth, searching for Akyar. Twenty-odd thousand miles under us, Africa was on the planet's dark side, lost in night.

"No visible damage." Sandor turned at last to speak to us. "No minds we can sense. No hint of any life surviving." He paused to glance at Lo. "We're going inside."

The pod slid to a dome that covered the axis of the wheel. I felt a gentle impact, and we were motionless against it.

"We're suiting up," he told us. "The air inside may be harmless, or it may be lethal."

They helped us seal our suits, and we went in with them. The rear end of the pod was a small air lock that let us through, one by one. I found myself in silent darkness, afloat in free fall. Reaching around me for Pepe or Sandor or anything at all, I discovered there was nothing within my reach.

Cut off from light or sound, from all sensation, I felt helpless as a bug on a pin. A wave of utter panic struck me. I wanted to call out, to hear a human voice, but my trembling fingers failed to find the button for the helmet radio. I was all alone, drowning in the silence and darkness and death of the station, calling myself a fool and a coward . . . till lights came on.

At first they were only dim and unfamiliar symbols, burning faintly through the blackness, but they let me breathe again. I found a shadow near me, Pepe's shoulder when I reached to touch it. Stronger lights came on to fill a vast empty cylinder. Glowing cords ran from us to points about the walls. We hung there for a time, seeing no motion, hearing no sound.

"Nothing," Sandor muttered. "No damage. No sign of accident or violence. Nothing to show what the killer was. Let's get out to the rim."

He caught a bright green cord that pulled him away. Lo and I followed. It brought us to a closed door in the cylinder's side wall. It opened when Sandor glanced at a green symbol on it. I followed into a tiny chamber that swung and gave us weight as it dropped toward the rim. It stopped, and we stepped out into an endless corridor that curved up ahead of us and behind, a circular tunnel that ran around the rim.

"*La calle mayor!*" Pepe's spirits were higher than mine. "Main street."

It was the only street of a little city in space. Signs along it began to flicker and flash with dancing characters in an alphabet unknown to me. Sandor and Lo led us on. Centrifugal gravity was an odd experience. Though the pavement always rose ahead, we never had to climb. The great wheel of the station seemed to roll as we walked, the pavement always level underfoot.

Sandor and Lo warily ventured forward, pausing and pausing again to study everything, saying nothing of whatever they concluded. Pepe and I followed nervously.

I didn't know what to expect. Battle debris? Dead bodies? Alien monsters?

We discovered no bodies, saw no life or motion. The pavement was bare and clean. We passed a dead machine that Sandor called a street sweeper. Dead, he said, because its power had failed. He stopped at a closed door. Symbols on it shone bright green when he looked at them.

"The captain's office," Lo told us. "The door says he is in."

It slid open. We followed them into what might almost have been the reception room of an office on old Earth, furnished with seats along the walls and a wide desk facing us, all made of something that looked like pale green plastic. The only other color was a glitter of diamond beads on the rim of a long golden bowl on a little table. It must have held an ornamental plant. Dead earth filled it now, and dead leaves littered the table.

Lo and Sandor explored the room, shook their heads, opened an inside door. The room beyond held four empty chairs, behind four empty desks. I saw no books or papers I could recognize, no office machines or files, but a big black globe hung over each desk. One of them glowed when Lo looked into it. Peering past her, I looked into another office room, where another empty chair sat behind another empty desk.

Pepe reached to touch the globe, and his hand went through it.

"A holographic contact device," Lo told us. "Still connected to an office down in Akyar. Nobody there."

Sandor opened another door and stopped to stare. Pressing after him, we stopped and retreated. A dozen people had been seated around a long conference table, though not at any business meeting. The table was covered with dishes, empty cups and glasses, odd-shaped forks and spoons, gem-bright bottles, bowls filled with dusty fragments of what must have been food.

"Una fiesta!" Pepe murmured. "I think they died *muy contentos*."

"Whatever hit them," Sandor said, "it must have been sudden."

Men and women, they had belonged to his fine-boned and graceful race, but they were not handsome now. They had dried to mummies, the flesh brown and shriveled, black empty sockets in empty skulls staring blindly across the table at the other empty skulls. I felt grateful for my helmet. The odor must have been overwhelming.

"Los pobres!" Pepe crossed himself. "I hope they got to heaven."

37

Mona called from Earth.

"She and Casey have reached Akyar," Sandor told us. "On the way, they flew north over the cities along the American coast and south again over Europe and the Mediterranean. Plants and animals seemed abundant, but the cities—" Lips set hard, he seemed to shrink into himself. "All tumbled into rubble and grown over with forest. They heard no radio, saw no open roads, no lights at night, nothing in motion."

Silent for a moment, he shrugged and went on.

"They've landed in an open park near the Crown. That's the Nexus building. There's life there, Mona says, monkeys in the trees and birds overhead. Most of the city fell into ruin long ago, but she says the Crown building appears to be intact, with no damage visible. They are leaving the pod. She wants to get inside if she can. They'll be out of touch till they get back to the radio in the pod. We'll wait here till she calls again."

We waited forever.

With Earth seeming stationary under us, time seemed to stop. We had no days or nights. Sandor and Lo spent endless time aboard the satellite, searching for clues they never seemed to find. Once I went back aboard with them, but all their talk was silent and I made nothing of anything I saw. I felt shut in, depressed by the strangeness and darkness of the station, the presence of too much death.

I preferred the stars, the illusion that we were floating free in open space, and Pepe's familiar company. Life in the pod was easy enough, so long as we could forget the dark riddles around us. There was food in the lockers, little brown cubes that water expanded into something I learned to eat. The seats reclined when we wanted to sleep.

Empty time on our hands, we watched the Moon's deliberate creep around the Earth, the sun's faster passage across the face of Earth. Though Tycho and the station were too far to see, I found myself grieving for Tanya and the others we had left there, alive and well when we left them but surely dead centuries ago. Or had they all been cloned again, and us with them, when the computer saw that Earth was dead?

We watched the monsoon clouds clear over Africa and waited for whatever Lo and Sandor might discover. Though they seldom slept, they came back to the pod now and then to eat and rest and try again to reach Mona. She never answered. Pepe urged Sandor to follow them to Akyar, to help if they were in trouble.

"They expected trouble." Frowning, Sandor shook his head. "That's why we separated. To double our chances. And we still have work to do here. We're confirming a date for the disaster. Whatever happened, it was a bit over two hundred forty Earth years ago.

"It certainly was not the Sagittarian pathogen, which was spread by interstellar travel and killed all organic life. We've read the records in the operations section here. Interstellar craft and Earth shuttles were still arriving and departing in a very normal way till that last moment."

His elfish face twisted as if with pain.

"We entered the room of an operations clerk who had just returned from a vacation on Earth. She had bought gifts for her friends. A neat little model of the prehistoric rocket craft from Tycho Station. A toy elephant still able to spread its ears, trumpet, and charge across a tabletop. Holo cubes of life in motion around the restored Taj Mahal and the Parthenon. All still wrapped and labeled with names, but never delivered."

With no time of our own, we counted days by the sunlight that marched and marched again over motionless Africa beneath us. Thirteen had passed before Sandor got a call from Earth.

"They're safe." His thin-chinned face had lit. "Back in their own pod. Ready to tell us what kept them so long."

Gliding down to Africa, we found Kilimanjaro grown taller since the great impact, a new caldera at the summit filled with snow. A chain of narrow lakes filled the long valley of the Great Rift, stretched deeper now as the continent was torn apart. Akyar stood east of the Rift, on the high plain that sloped toward the Indian Ocean. Seen from the air, the city made a target pattern, a bull's-eye surrounded by circular streets cut into blocks by wide radiant boulevards.

"Akyar." Sandor gestured at the bull's-eye as we slid past it. "That's the Nexus building at the center. Called the Crown for its shape."

It was magnificent. White columns that looked tall as the Washington Monument supported a vast golden dome topped by a needle spire that flashed with lances of rainbow color like a single enormous diamond. Gigantic animal figures marched around the base of the dome. A tyrannosaur, a mammoth, a saber-tooth tiger. Ahead of them a horse and a camel, a lion and a llama, a gorilla and a man.

"The lords of the universe!" From Pepe, a bitterly ironic laugh.

"At least the center of civilization." Peering down at the spire's prismatic splendor, Sandor shook his sleek-furred head. "That's our riddle. In a world that that spanned so many planets, so free from trouble or any hint of trouble, what could go so terribly wrong?

"I hope Mona has the answer."

He took us low over the diamond needle and turned in his seat to point at the silver gleam of Mona's slider pod, landed in a little park beside a broad avenue that ran west from the Crown. We landed near it. Looking around us through the transparent hull, we saw nothing of her or Casey, but Sandor opened the door. We tumbled out.

I heard a high-pitched bark. The grass around us was scattered with ring-shaped mounds of bare brown earth. A small brown animal stood upright on the nearest mound, barked again, and vanished down a hole in the middle of it.

"A cunning little creature," Lo murmured. "Mona would love it."

"A prairie dog," Pepe said. "My father used to see their towns in Texas when he was a kid. Dr. DeFort was trying to preserve what he called biodiversity. He tried to save tissue specimens from all the creatures—"

"*Amigos!*" Casey's shout stopped him. "*Qué pasa?*"

He and Mona were climbing out of their pod. They amazed me. Holding hands, they wore bright green loincloths and garlands of huge scarlet flowers, and nothing else. His broad black face shone with a happiness I had never seen on it, though he turned a little sheepish when she dropped his hand and ran to hug Lo and Sandor.

"Pep, Dunk, I'm glad you got here."

He shook our hands and looked back at Mona. She stood with her arms around Lo and Sandor. They were laughing, absorbed with one another. He stood a long moment watching them before he turned back to us.

"I never expected—" He checked his eager voice as if

abashed by his own emotion. "Never expected this."

Near us was a very solid table, made of what looked like green-veined jade, with seats on either side. He gestured for us to sit. Still heavy under Earth gravity, Pepe and I were glad to comply. After another fond glance at Mona, Casey joined us. We asked what they had found.

"Not a clue. Nothing I could understand."

Seeming untroubled by that failure, or even the death of Earth, he let his gaze drift back to Mona. She waved, with a smile that seemed to enchant him, and escorted Lo and Sandor into her pod. Casey sat staring dreamily after them till Pepe touched his arm.

"Sorry." He blinked as if he had forgotten us. "I was thinking."

"We got inside the satellite," Pepe told him, though he hardly seemed to care. "All we found was dried-up bodies, with nothing to show what killed them." He gestured at the towering Crown. "You've been in there?"

His answer was only a nod.

"Tell us about it."

"It's too big." Yet he shrugged as if its vastness hardly mattered. "We didn't see a tenth of it."

"Anything alive?"

"Nothing." At last he gave his attention back to us. "Though there is a staff of robot caretakers and janitors still active. If people died there, their bodies must have been removed."

We sat there, craning our heads to look up at the diamond spire and the animals marching around the great golden dome till Pepe pressed him to tell us more.

"It was really something wonderful." Awe slowed his voice. "It had a computer system linked to all the microbots everywhere. That made it a sort of super-mind, Mona says, in contact with similar centers on all the settled worlds. The mind of all humankind."

"Is it still alive?" Pepe asked. "Does it know what hit the people?"

He shook his head. "The robots keep the computer running. All the old data is still there, but Mona says nothing has been added since the blackout."

Another prairie dog had popped up to bark at us again.

"I'm glad something is alive." He grinned as if it cheered him. "No matter what struck us, evolution can happen again."

Pepe asked if they were going back to the building.

"No point." The grin gone, he shook his head. "Too much death! It wore on my nerves. I was glad to get out."

"Won't Sandor want to see it?"

"I guess there's plenty to see." He seemed to shrink from its towering mass. "Half of it is underground, level after level. Mazes of corridors go on and on forever. We got lost once, and had to find a robot to show us back to anything we recognized. The robots try to follow orders, but they never tell you anything. You won't see them outside, though they keep up the building."

He paused, something like dread in his eyes.

"It's too much! Too much of everything. Embassies from all the settled planets, with holo exhibits to tell all about them, all tied in to the main computer. Libraries, museums, laboratories, businesses, tourist and information offices, art galleries, theaters, facilities for sports I never heard of. Even a sort of luxury hotel, with a robot staff ready to put us up."

Grinning again, he touched his floral necklace as if in apology for it.

"And Mona!" He intoned the name almost with worship, and leaned very earnestly toward us. "You know I've dreamed we'd somehow be together, but I never thought it would really happen."

He drew a long breath.

"It did." His dark face shone. "You've seen her. She loves me. We've been together in paradise!"

Mona had stepped out of the other pod, carrying a basket. He darted to take it from her and set it on the table. She opened it, spread a cloth and began laying out dishes and glasses, bowls of food, a flagon of amber wine.

"The robots packed it for us," Casey said. "They do remember what they were."

Lo and Sandor came to join us at the table. Mona was pouring the wine. Casey handed out round golden fruits.

"They're different from anything we ever had on the Moon. I don't know a name for them, but just try them."

"Peaches." Sandor bit into one. "From cell specimens I found at the lunar dig. I had them in my orchard at the memorial."

Mona split another and shared it with Casey. Mine was delightful. There were cups of soup, cakes, nuts, jellies. Some I didn't like at first, but the amber wine enhanced the flavors till I relished everything. Lo and Sandor glanced at each other when we had finished, and stepped away from the table.

"Excuse us, please. We have things to think about."

Mona caught Casey's hand and led him after them. The four stood for a little time gazing up at the dome, then put their heads together, lost in silent talk. There was enough, I thought, for them to think about.

"Dos locos!" Pepe shook his head at Casey, a shadow on his face. "I was wrong to think they'd never get together. They've forgotten the world is dead."

38

The four stood together in silent contact, until Lo and Sandor abruptly broke away and walked fast toward Sandor's slider pod. Without a word, Mona dropped Casey's hand and followed them. He stood frozen, staring after her with fear etched on his face.

"Mona?" A breathless, voiceless whisper. "Why?"

"There's no time." She darted back to touch his gaping lips with a kiss. "No time at all."

She slipped away before he could embrace her, and ran after Lo and Sandor into the pod. The door snapped shut behind her. He turned to look at us, empty hands spread in mute appeal. I felt his shock but had no help for him.

"Demonios!" Pepe muttered. *"Fantasmas de los muertos!"*

Ghosts of the dead.

Darkness was thickening around us, the prairie dogs fallen silent. The spire on the Crown glowed softly, lighting the dome and throwing long black shadows across the trees and rubble mounds around us. Far off in the forest, I heard a strange, quavering scream. Only some night thing, I thought, calling for a mate, yet I felt the hair bristle on the back of my neck.

The pod simply sat there.

"Why?" Casey stood staring at it, stricken and dumbfounded. "Why did she leave me?"

"Dios sabe." Pepe shuddered. "God knows. Or has Satan claimed the world?"

We stood there a long time, shivering in the night wind, waiting for them to come out of the pod, for it to lift, for anything. The pod lay silent and motionless, a mirror-shelled mystery, gleaming faintly in the glow of the spire. Casey shouted at it once, begging hoarsely for Mona to open the door. It didn't open.

Tired of standing, Pepe and I went back to the table. A handful of biscuits were left in Mona's basket, along with a little wine in the flagon. Sitting there hunched against the wind, we called Casey to join us. He stood deaf to us, fists clenched, shaking his head at the slider, while we finished the biscuits and wine.

The door of the other pod was still open. To escape the wind, Pepe and I crept inside. I reclined a seat and lay there a long time, staring out through the glass-clear hull at Casey and the motionless pod, watching the slow Moon climb past the shining spire. Pepe kept muttering Spanish profanities in his uneasy dreams. Thanks to the wine, at last I slept.

Casey was inside with us when I woke. He lay snoring on the floor, hollow-eyed and haggard, black stubble on his chin. The prairie dogs greeted me with a chorus of barks when I climbed out. Sandor's pod still lay where it had been, a mirror-bright enigma under the morning sun. Pepe rummaged though a locker and found hard dry slabs of something that tasted like burnt oatmeal. We ate a little of that. Casey went out to listen at the other pod, his ear against the mirror hull, and came back dismally silent.

"*Qué le hace?*" Pepe frowned at it. "We can't wait here forever."

"I dreamed." Casey was moodily grim. "I dreamed they were dead."

"If they are." Pepe shuddered and crossed himself. "We ought to see."

He walked away toward the street and came back with a heavy chunk of broken pavement and lifted it with both hands to smash at the side of the pod.

"Don't!" Casey called to stop him. "There was more of the dream. I was trying to get inside. I heard Mona calling words I remember. 'Gold eight, red six, black four.' The door came open. That's when I saw they were dead."

Pepe dropped his rock and bent closer, staring at the side of the pod.

"*Mira!*" he whispered. *La cerradura!*"

He had found three colored dots on the mirror shell. Gold, red, and black. He tapped them carefully one by one, counting the taps aloud. The door yawned suddenly wide. We followed him inside.

They lay in the seats, lying flat and still. Mona's eyes were open, glazed and blindly staring, her beauty distorted into a frozen grimace. Her arm was cold and hard when I touched it, set in rigor mortis. Casey dropped to his knees beside her. We went out and left him there.

"*Cabrón!*" Pepe muttered. "*Madre de cabrones!* How can God allow such things?"

Or was there any God at all? What sort of power would murder innocent and unsuspecting planets without warning or cause? I had no answer.

Casey staggered out of the pod at last. He looked pale and shattered, as if life had bled out of him, yet he was fighting to recover himself, his hollowed eyes dry, his jaw set hard.

"What killed them?" Pepe asked.

He shrugged and shook his head.

"I think Mona knew, when she came back to kiss me good-bye. I think she wanted to tell me, but it gave her no time to say."

He wanted to bury the bodies. The soil was too hard, Pepe said, for us to dig the graves without any tools. The pod, he thought, should be tomb enough, but the dried-up mummies we'd found on the satellite still haunted Casey.

"We'll burn them," he said. "We'll build a funeral pyre."

We had no axe to cut timber for it, but storms had shattered old trees along the neglected streets. We spent most of the day lugging and dragging and piling fallen limbs, the annoyed prairie dogs scolding at us. When Casey declared we had enough, we brought the bodies out with as much respect as we could and laid them side by side on the pile.

We realized then that we had no way to ignite it. Pepe wanted to search for flint and steel, but Casey recalled a science exhibit he and Mona had seen in the Crown. He went back there and returned with a concave mirror. A dead leaf under it smoked and burst into flame. Pepe bent his head and murmured a Spanish prayer. We threw more wood into the blaze till sunset.

Next morning the ashes were dead. We gathered the flakes of bone into Mona's basket. When I wondered what to do with them, Pepe offered to scatter them out of the pod. That astonished me, because Sandor had seemed to fly with magic, never touching any controls. No magic, Pepe said; his microbots had done it with their magnetic and electrostatic fields. Sandor had taught him how to use the control stick.

"The Serengeti." Casey nodded gratefully. "I saw a herd of wildebeest there. Mona loved animals."

Pepe flew us high over the ice-filled crater at the top of Kilimanjaro's enormous new cone and back down to skim the eastern shore of a wider Lake Victoria. Gliding low over the lush green grasslands of the Serengeti, we opened the door. Wildebeest, gazelle and zebra fled ahead of us, and wide-winged birds scattered from a waterhole. Casey stood in the open door, scattering the ashes.

"Immortals." Pepe shook his head sadly as he closed the door and stopped the roaring wind. "I wish they had been."

He brought us back into the long shadow of the Crown and landed again among the scolding prairie dogs. Still in his seat, he looked around at Casey and me.

"*Y ahora qué?* What next?"

Casey shrugged. I felt crushed under black despair. We three were here alone with the animals now, without friends or food or the instincts that kept them alive. Groping for purpose or even sanity, I asked Pepe if he could take us back to the Moon.

"The computer will surely be cloning us again," I told him, "when it knows the Earth is dead. Whenever that happens, our new brothers ought to have our account of what we have seen."

"The station wouldn't let us in." He shook his head. "Sandor left it sealed."

Still I felt desperate to escape all the riddles of ruin and death that hung over us. Could he fly us to Lo's home planet? Or maybe on a flight that would take another thousand years? I thought we might hope to find ourselves cloned again when we got back, and Earth restored to life.

He brightened for a moment, but then shook his head again.

"I'm not an interplanetary pilot. Even if I were, we might not find any world alive. Anybody who thought we might carry contagion would shoot us out of the sky."

He landed us again among the startled prairie dogs. By sunset we were out of the pod, sitting again at the jade table, making another meal out of the hard biscuits Pepe had found in the locker and wondering how to stay alive.

"We can live in the pod, but this—" He stopped to scowl at a bitten biscuit. "Even this pig feed won't last us long."

We talked of trying to farm or hunt, but we had no seed or tools to turn the soil, no weapons to kill the game around us, not even the prairie dogs, no skills for any-thing. Casey kept moodily silent, gazing up at the spire above the Crown, till Pepe asked if he knew any way for us to stay alive.

"We carry the Sagittarian microbots." I heard his bitter irony. "They ought to make us immortal."

"So did Sandor," Pepe said. "They didn't save him."

"We don't know what they are." He nodded, looking up at the Crown, its golden dome, a huge half moon rising into the dusk. When he spoke again, it was more to him-self than to us. "Mona thought she had picked up those microbots from me. She was searching to understand them, hoping they would shield us from whatever killed the planet. I think she was finally in sight of something that had begun to terrify her."

Lips compressed, he shook his head.

"What she was finding, or thought she was, I never knew. She'd learned to read my mind, but hers was blank to me. We were in love, and she seemed happier and more hopeful toward the end. I was happy with her."

With a long sigh, he shook his head and sat a long time remembering.

"We hoped to live forever," he went on at last, his tone wistfully forlorn. "We used to laugh and talk about the good times of our lives. She wanted to know what her life might have been if Sandor had let her grow up with us on the Moon. She was fascinated with the story of the great impact and the history of the station. She talked about her travels with her mother, and all the odd crea-tures she had seen. She loved every new species, every sort of life. And the Crown—"

A momentary smile lit his face.

"While it lasted, we had a great life there. She enjoyed everything the robots gave us to eat and drink. We had wonderful nights in bed. She was always searching.

Happy, toward the end, with whatever she thought she was finding."

He looked up at the spire, a new determination of purpose in his eyes.

"I'm going back inside."

Next morning he did. Pepe and I followed him out of the pod to a broad avenue that once had been magnificent. Great trees had stood along it, most of them dead or dying now. A tall tangle of vines and brush walled the crumbling pavement. We had to scramble around fallen logs and clamber through a rocky gully that floods had cut.

Towering at the end of the avenue, the building was farther away than it had looked, and even more colossal. We took most of an hour to reach the jungle-clotted gardens around it. Weeds and brambles filled a long crescent pool below the entrance. A gigantic golden figure towered out of it, one great arm lifted to hurl a wheel-shaped ship into space.

We stopped again and again to gaze in awe at the topless columns, the great animals marching around the dome, the fire in the diamond spire. Their immense dimensions and the sense of death and long decay hit me with a sudden ache of longing for our safe little digs in the Moon, but Casey plunged doggedly on.

We followed him around the end of the crescent pool and up a ramp of something like white marble to a monumental doorway. The door was an enormous golden slab, deeply engraved with another gigantic figure, this one lifting a planetary globe toward the sky.

The globe held me hypnotized.

An island of life on this ocean of death, it glowed with vivid color. Spinning, it glowed with cloudless blue seas and strange green continents patterned with what I thought must be roads and cities, sometimes a flash of polar ice.

It changed as it turned. The hemispheres that vanished never came back. With every rotation, it revealed another world.

I stood gawking at it till a narrow panel opened at the bottom of the door. A bone-white robot stepped out to meet us, a human-shaped figure so graceful in form and motion that for an instant I took it to be alive. It stopped to block the entrance, stood still for a moment to inspect us, raised a silent arm to motion us away.

Pepe and I backed off uneasily, but Casey stood his ground, calling out something that echoed the intonations of Sandor's speech. The robot stood frozen for half a minute, then glided aside and beckoned us to enter.

mptiness met us. Emptiness, darkness, silence. Yet the great building had a life of its own. Light brightened around us. Another bone-white robot came noiselessly to meet us across a vast, vacant floor. It stopped when Casey uttered some command he must have learned from Mona, and we stood gazing around us.

We had come into a lofty hallway that curved around the building. The outside wall was suddenly lit with holo murals. Panel after panel, they were windows into worlds beyond the Earth. Alien landscapes and monumental buildings, spaceports and spacecraft, strange plants and stranger animals, figures and faces of human stocks that varied from planet to planet.

Casey gestured at them.

"The colonized planets. They all had people here. Delegations, traders, tourists, what have you. This was the nexus of interstellar civilization. You can see the problems, with relative time lost on space flights, but they made it. Centers like this bound the worlds together."

"And they're dead."

Pepe paused to frown into another holo window at a rugged landscape as red and lifeless as Mars. A huge blue balloon rolled across it on a wide roadway that led into dusty distance. Three smaller blue globes rolled along behind it.

"Are they dead?" He hunched to a shudder and turned back to Casey. "All dead? Did the contagion get here from another planet? Or maybe spread from Earth?"

"That's what Mona was trying to discover." Casey shrugged. "She'd found no evidence of any ship arriving since Earth died. Two hundred forty years ago. She was afraid that meant that other worlds had died, and even the crews of ships in interstellar flight. Meant that the human enterprise was over."

"How could that happen?" Pepe shook his head, staring again at the rolling balloons. "All at once, if it did? On planets and ships so many light-years apart?"

"I can't imagine." Casey peered blankly past us, down the empty hall. "But that's our problem now. I think we've got to crack it if we want to stay alive."

"If Mona couldn't do it, or Lo and Sandor on the satellite—"

Pepe let his voice trail off into the haunting stillness.

"Another thing that puzzles me." Casey turned back to frown at us. "I don't think Mona ever found an actual hint, not that she told me, but she did seem happier toward the end. I don't know why."

The robot had stood waiting. Casey spoke to it now. It answered with accents we had first heard from Sandor when we were children on the Moon. He nodded, and it beckoned us along the endless curve of that hushed and empty hall. Wide archways were spaced along the inner wall, signs above them glowing with symbols hieroglyphic to me.

The empty stillness was getting to Pepe. He looked at Casey, hesitating.

"The robots know us," Casey told him. "Mona introduced me."

It turned to lead us through a tall arch, into black darkness. As lights came on ahead, I saw that we were in another great hall, running toward the center of the building. Far along it I saw another robot pushing some silent device that must have been sweeping the floor. I heard no sound, saw nothing alive.

"There were people here?" Pepe asked uneasily. "Not just machines?"

"Many thousands of people," Casey said. "From two thousand planets."

"And they died?"

"The robotic staff removed the bodies."

He spoke to the robot again, and it led us through a door into an elevator that surged silently upward.

"I want to show you the sections Mona and I explored," he said. "The Earth section. And the section from Lo's planet, where she grew up. A tiny fraction of the Crown, but enough to give you an idea what it is. As likely as any, I suppose, to give some useful clue."

We spent a long day trudging though the Earth section, trying to understand what we saw. These centers were built, Casey told us, to share knowledge and culture, and to unify humanity. And of course for business. Tourism and trading.

"Interstellar trading must have been real adventure," he said. "The trader had to pack up his goods and take off for some distant star, knowing he would never get back to the world he had known—time would have turned it strange. With luck, he might make friends and find a market for his cargo. He was just as likely to find nobody who wanted his goods, or even that the new planet had no place for him."

I felt lost. Casey had learned scraps of Mona's language, enough to give the robots simple commands and understand simple replies. I caught a little of his driving purpose, but understood only a little of what he tried to show us. We walked through laboratories devoted to sciences I didn't know, museums filled with artifacts that were mostly riddles to me, libraries filled with information in a hundred formats I couldn't read.

We looked into splendid theaters without players, great lecture halls without speakers, enormous stadiums where thousands of empty seats looked down on bare arenas. There were endless galleries of art that left only blurs of cold confusion in my mind, great empty chambers that greeted us with a roar of music that was merely noise to me, shops filled with items I didn't recognize. There were universities where we might have mastered all the arts and crafts and sciences of all the worlds, if we had carried microbots to let us learn them.

We didn't.

The place was a haystack of baffling straws. I came to feel that we were searching for an invisible needle that might not exist, one that I thought we would never recognize even if we found it. I was footsore and relieved when at last Casey said he had showed us enough.

antasmas!" Pepe shivered.

We had seen no actual apparitions, but the silence and the emptiness had begun to people my own imagination with all the thousands from a thousand different races on a thousand far-scattered planets who had lived and worked here, died and disappeared.

The robots treated us like prehistoric royalty. They had taken us to the spacious quarters where Mona and Casey had been put up. A magnificent lobby was walled with live holos of the long Terran history. A forest of live plants perfumed the air in the great dining room. We each had private chambers, and always sleek white robots waiting silently to serve us.

There was a pool where they taught us to swim, a gym where they massaged us and watched us work out. Though no galactic encyclopedia had been programmed into them, they answered simple questions and obeyed simple commands. They were expert chefs. Under Pepe's coaching, they were able to make a fair copy of the *huevos rancheros* his father used to cook on the Moon.

I don't know how long we were there. Never outside, we never saw the sun. Pepe's gift timepiece could show the days and dates on several hundred planets. Toying with its magic, he had lost the setting for Earth. Casey became our clock. He was nearly always out, wandering through the labyrinths around us in search of any thread of meaning he could follow.

Sometimes in the beginning Pepe and I went with him, but the stillness and the sense of universal death overcame our hope for anything we could understand. Our own days began when he came in to eat or nap. That was never long. He was soon gone again.

"I'm learning," he insisted. "I think my microbots are beginning to kick in. I can decipher simple inscriptions and talk to the robots. Not that they've had anything useful to say."

"What can you hope for?" Pepe asked him. "There's no sign that anybody ever saw the cataclysm coming. What could their records possibly tell us?"

"Mona had a theory." Thinking, he frowned at the wall. "In the early ages of interstellar flight, there was a revolt against the microbots. The rebels felt that they were stealing our freedom, turning us into machines."

Pepe was nodding. I had felt the same way. Casey grinned and went on.

"The conflict became a sort of religious war. At the worst of it thousands of them died from battle wounds their microbots couldn't repair. Defeated, the survivors seized spacecraft and went out to settle new worlds of their own. Mona was searching ancient history for records of those attempts.

"So far as she had found, they'd all gone bad. Without microbots, the rebels were unfit. The lacked our community of knowledge and skills. Their new worlds were often hostile. Terraforming failed. New diseases killed them. Yet toward the end she was wondering if some hadn't survived to renew the war and try to wipe us out.

"The animals are still alive, while bearers of the microbots are dead. She suspected that something had made them a lethal weapon. Unlikely on the face of it, but what else could explain the sudden death of so many wearers at the same time on worlds so far apart?"

He frowned at us as if asking for an answer.

"She never found any actual proof of that, not that she told me, but toward the end, I think she was on to something. What it was, she never said, but still I hope to find what killed her. And everybody."

"Whatever it was," Pepe muttered. "I don't think I want to know."

"At the end, something had made her happy," Casey said. "I'm not afraid to learn it, if I can."

He went out again and came back grim with one more defeat. He ate a silent meal with us when the robots served it and went to his room without a word. Next morning he wanted no breakfast. He shook his head moodily when Pepe urged him to come with us to the pool and let the robots teach him how to swim.

"You're killing yourself," Pepe told him. "All for nothing, so far as I can tell. You'll live longer if you relax and get some exercise."

"Will I?"

He watched in bleak silence while we ate, but took coffee when the robots offered it, a better brew than we had ever tasted on the Moon. When they had slipped away, he spoke abruptly.

"I dreamed last night." He pushed his empty cup away, and paused to shake his head in bafflement. "A dream I can't explain or understand. It seemed too near and real to be any sort of dream. I thought—it's hard to explain, but I thought I could see everything that ever happened."

He squinted to see if we thought he had come unhinged.

"Mona." He looked away, the words coming slowly. "Her clone mother, Mona Lisa Live." His face lit with wonder. "I saw her with my clone father. That was back in Medellin, the hot spot where he was a hired gunman for the drug lord they called El Matador. She was there to sing. I saw El Matador drag her off the stage, trying to rape her. I saw El Chino shoot him down."

He was staring past us, dark eyes shining as if he saw them now.

"Matador had guards all around him, but my father's shot caught them by surprise. He got away with Mona. Got to the airport in his armored car. Got off the ground in his private jet. Skirted the Pacific coast from Columbia to Baja. Found friends there. In the dream I was with them all the way. I felt their desperate love."

His dark face quivered with emotion.

"I was proud of my father. He had cunning. He had guts. The Matador cartel had men waiting in Baja, hired to kill him, but he got away to *el norte*. Got another job as a night watchman at DeFort's White Sands Moon base. When the asteroid was coming in, he got Mona on the escape plane. Got her to the Moon. Got DeFort to keep them there, and save their cells in the cryostat. I'm still proud of him. Time and again, I've pored over the records he left at the station. I've longed to live my life the way he did. But now—"

He shook his head and sat in silence till Pepe asked, "Is that all the dream?"

"It went on forever." His eyes shone again. "You remember that holo panel with the blue balloons rolling across the desert? They were real. Real and alive. I saw one of those baby balloons bouncing across those red sand dunes. It was lost and panicked, looking for its mother. I could see her searching for it, but back behind it, rolling in the wrong direction. I wanted to tell her, but I couldn't."

He stopped to frown at Pepe.

"That made me feel furious in the dream, and bothered me when I woke. Wondering about it now, I think I know why. The incident happened in the past. The past is fixed."

His tone was flat and factual, as if he felt certain of it.

"The past is fixed?" Pepe echoed the words. "You think you really saw those balloon things. Ages ago, on a world a lot of light-years off?" His eyebrows had risen. "How could that be?"

"All I know is what I remember from the dream." Casey shook his head, staring off at nothing. "I don't know how it happened. I can't expect you to believe— but it did seem terribly real. And there's something more."

Abruptly, he stood up from the table.

"At the end of the dream, Mona was there with me. The clone Mona. The Mona I loved. The Mona we burned on the woodpile." A strange smile wiped the pain from his face. "I thought she was alive again, somehow, calling me from somewhere out in space. If she is, if she really is, I've got to find her."

40

Casey drained another cup of coffee, went back to his room, and returned in the work togs the robots had provided, a snug-fitting jumpsuit cut of some sleek, bright orange stuff. We were still at the breakfast table.

"You think I'm crazy?" He grinned when Pepe looked up at him. "Could be, but I'm going to look for Mona."

Pepe asked where.

"Where else?" He shrugged. "Toward the end, she thought she was on the trail to something more than those antimicrobot rebels. She never said what it was. She was frightened at first, trying to deny it and afraid to say. Toward the end, it seemed to make her hopeful."

"Casey, please." Pepe raised an anxious hand. "I'm not calling you crazy, but we've all been through hell. Let's take a break and look at the odds."

"If we knew the odds—"

"We know enough. The Crown's too big. A great haystack. You'll be looking for a needle you wouldn't recognize when you found it. I doubt it's there at all. Better eat your breakfast. Let the robots rub you down. Sleep tonight. Wait for Mona to come back in another dream, with maybe more to say."

"Thank you, Pep." Casey came around the table to shake his hand. "It's true I don't know what I'm looking for, but I can't stop now. Maybe Mona was wrong to fear the microbots. Maybe they can help us. We carry those we picked on the Sagittarian planet. I think mine are still working their way into my system."

"Huh?" Pepe blinked in alarm. "Doing what?"

"I think they're getting into my brain."

"Driving you mad?"

"Who knows if I am?" He shrugged. "But they've begun to teach me facts I never learned. Mona was speaking Sandor's language in the dream, but still I understood her. I hope she'll help me find her now."

When he moved to leave, Pepe asked if we could come with him.

"Okay." He shrugged, with an ironic grin. "If you think I need looking after."

"I do." Pepe nodded soberly. "If your microbots are waking up, I'm afraid they'll kill you."

He waited for us to dress. We followed him through the jungle-grown rubble back to the Crown. The robots let us in. We tramped after him all day, through endless corridors that lit as we entered, and countless empty rooms that depressed me with the hush of death. Now and again he stopped to watch a blank holo wall come to life, to question a robot for an answer I couldn't understand, or to stand waiting as if expecting inspiration that never seemed to come.

Yet he blundered on, finally through a bewildering maze of offices that he said had been the administrative complex. We came out at last on a balcony that looked into a pit of darkness. I shrank back from a railing that seemed too low. Pepe caught his breath and shouted, his voice a little quavery.

"Viva! Viva! Viva!"

We stood waiting a long time in silence before the faint echo whispered back. His voice lit stars overhead. Faint at first, they blazed into constellations brighter than any we had seen in space. They revealed an enormous hollow space at the center of the building.

The immense curve of its wall was lined with balconies like ours, rising level after level toward the dome, and falling level after level below us, so far that I caught a giddy grip on the railing. Peering down, I found a circular floor, vast and bare, ringed with row upon row of desks on a slope that rose to the wall.

"*Que grande!*" Pepe murmured in awe. "The council of the stars! Imagine the leaders of two thousand worlds gathered here, with all their science and wisdom, debating the future of the universe!"

"Wisdom?" Casey grunted. "They never knew they were about to die."

He shrugged and led us off the balcony, back into the labyrinth. Grimly determined, he watched holos that spoke in silence if they spoke at all, queried robots for replies that were only noise to me, paused again and again to listen for a voice he never seemed to hear. Worn out, we stopped at last to say we'd had enough.

"We're going home for supper," Pepe told him. "If we can call it home. Better come with us."

Stubbornly, he shook his head.

We ate a meal I hardly tasted, our robot servers standing behind us, Casey's empty chair across the table. The holo wall shone with scenes I hardly saw, landscapes on other worlds, far away and long ago. I was asleep before Casey came in. At breakfast his chair was empty again.

"He was here," Pepe said. "I heard him speaking to the robots, but now I just looked in his room. He isn't there."

Longing for distraction from problems too big for us to solve, we turned back to the holo wall. A strange seascape had filled it: yellow surf foaming on the shore of an endless yellow ocean under a lurid yellow sky. Huge ungainly creatures the color of blood came crawling out of the foam and up a broad beach of orange sand.

"Huh?"

I heard Pepe gasp. The wall flickered. The beach and the creatures were gone. Instead, I saw the world around us and Casey running desperately through the prairie dog mounds. His eyes on Lo's slider pod, he failed to see a dirt-rimmed hole. His foot went in it. He fell on his face, staggered to his feet, limped on till his injured leg collapsed. On all fours, he scrambled on to the pod. The door sprang open. He tumbled in. The door snapped shut. It darted away.

"*Caramba!*" Pepe muttered. "*Pobrecito! Él es loco!*"

The sky in the holo turned yellow again. The prairie dogs were gone. Once more the great lizard-things came crawling through the surf. Dragging long crimson tail fins, they were stumbling clumsily to stand on wide-webbed rear feet. One by one, they bowed their long-jawed heads toward a huge black globe, waddled into a circle, and shuffled slowly around it.

We sat there a long time, cringing from a dread we didn't want to face, watching what seemed to be a ceremony of worship. The robot brought Pepe a stack of something like tortillas he had taught them to make, with a bowl of something like frijoles seasoned with something like chili. He waved the robot away.

"They're probably still alive. The explorers never settled worlds with any kind of intelligent life, and the creatures had no microbots to kill them. If microbots can be killers. No matter what becomes of us, evolution still has a chance."

He had the robots erase that yellow sky to let us see the rubble and jungle arround us and Kilimanjaro towering in the south, cumulus piling up around lower slopes below the snow-crowned double cone. A small brown prairie dog stood guard on a mound where Casey's pod had been.

We left the table at last, to search his room for a farewell note or any hint of what had changed him. We found nothing at all. Pepe tried to question the robots. They kept repeating that they were ready to serve us, but they had been programmed for nothing more.

I told Pepe that I was going outside.

"Why?" He gave a narrow glance, as if to appraise my sanity. "Casey's gone. God knows where."

But I had to get out of the Crown. It was too big, too empty, haunted with too many riddles, too much death. Pepe must have felt the same way; he came out with me down the ruined avenue, back to the prairie dogs. They barked a greeting and scurried into their dens. We sat down at the jade table, and Pepe kept glancing at the empty pod where Sandor and Lo and Mona had died.

"I could fly it." He sighed and shook his head. "But where could we go?"

We looked for alternatives. With the station asleep, we couldn't go back. He was not qualified for interstellar flight. Could we get away to some nearer planet? Maybe Mars?

"Dead as Earth." Pepe shook his head. "Sandor told us about an early project to terraform it by steering ice asteroids into collision orbits. That was given up when the interstellar sliders opened better worlds. We're stuck here with the robots, so long as they tolerate us."

With nothing else worth doing, we sat there watching the prairie dogs spy on us from their pits, stand upright to bark at us, scurry again about their business. Noon passed. I was feeling a pinch of hunger, hating to go back into the tomblike Crown. A concussion sent the little animals darting back to their dens. A sound like nearby thunder boomed out of the western sky.

"Casey." Pepe made a dismal face. *"Pobrecito."*

We found him a mile or so down an avenue that ran toward Kilimanjaro. The impact had dug a deep pit beside the pavement. In the bottom of it we found twisted fragments of the pod, and red stains of Casey's blood.

"The Sagittarian microbots." Standing on the crater rim, Pepe stared at me and shook his head. "He said they were getting into his brain. I guess they did."

We went back to the Crown, brought shovels from an exhibit on the history of mining, and spent a long afternoon shoveling dirt back into the crater, finally covering the mound with rocks from the debris. I wanted to find something to mark the grave. Pepe shrugged.

"Who's left to read it?"

The robot guards let us back into the Crown. Our robot servers set out a meal we barely tasted. The holo wall was alive again, showing a tourist train crawling around Sandor's memorial as it had been when it was new, chuffing past the Washington Monument. The crouching Sphinx stared across the mall at the Acropolis and the Great Pyramid. I found the gleam of our replicated station dome on the replicated Tycho rim, and felt a pang of longing for its familiar tunnels and all we had lost.

Pepe shook his head at a robot who was offering glasses of a bright red wine.

"I guess we're here to spend what's left of our lives." Gloomily, he shrugged. "So long as they want to look after us."

I was half asleep and aching from our labor with the spades, but I didn't want to be alone. Neither did Pepe. When the robots offered wine again, he let me persuade him to take another glass. We sat there half the night, sipping glass after glass, sometimes teary with grief and nostalgia, watching holos of Sandor's excavations at the lunar site and the whole human story as he had pieced it back together from what he uncovered there.

"Maybe that's just the way it happened. Maybe not." Pepe shrugged. "*Cómo le hace?* Who's alive to tell the difference?"

We saw ape-men leaping out of the forest to grassy

savanna, learning to walk upright and carry food or weapons in their hands. We saw a naked woman running from a river of red-hot lava, loose hair flying, a smoking stick in her hand, saw her kneeling to pile dry leaves and twigs on the stick and blow on them till she had a fire. We saw shaggy men working in caves by the light of smoky torches, painting on the limestone walls images of the animals they hunted. We saw men with sharpened reeds pressing marks into soft clay tablets. We saw chains of men and women hauling on long ropes, dragging great rough stones on log rollers to build Stonehenge, and smoother stones to build pyramids in Egypt. We saw Christ on the cross, Mohammed riding a camel toward a mosque, Buddha smiling.

We saw men with stone axes felling trees and burning the hearts out of dry logs to make dugout canoes. We saw men building sailing ships and locomotives and rocket craft. We saw rockets landing on the Moon, saw old Calvin Defort building Tycho Station and Sandor's great digging machines plowing it out of the crater slope where the lunar impact had buried it.

Finally we saw ourselves, as Sandor had restored us. Awkward stiff-faced Robos carried sleeping babies out of the maternity lab. We recognized ourselves as toddlers learning to walk, laughing at one another when we made great leaps to the ceiling of the gym and fell sprawling on the floor. We wiped our eyes when we saw Tanya and Dian as small girls, sitting on Sandor's knee and giggling at the antics of a doll he had given them.

We saw our clone brothers returning to Earth through the ages, saw our own colossal silver statues standing along the avenue to the temple of the Moon in that lost city at the Red Sea mouth of the Nile. We saw the singing trees in North America, the gold-winged being Casey rescued from the fallen balloon, the young tree he called Leonardo. We saw Casey enslaved, running with a rickshaw through the streets of the Kashmir capital.

Finally, when the wall went blank, Pepe embraced me. We clung together, weeping with loneliness and grief, till at last he pulled away and begged the robots for more wine. Instead, they helped us to our rooms. I let them undress me and get me into bed. I woke late from a dream where I was still at the station, at odds with Arne over an illegal move he had made in a game of chess. My head splitting, I stumbled out to the dining room to beg for coffee. The breakfast table was set, the sleek white robots standing behind our chairs, but Pepe's chair was empty.

When I went to his room, he was gone.

41

The robots had made Pepe's bed, but they stood silent, cold eyes blindly staring, when I asked them where he was. In panic, I searched every room and closet in our apartments, finding nothing at all. Still half drunk from too much wine, I stumbled out to see if he had taken the remaining slider pod. It lay in the dog town where we had left it, empty when I looked inside.

A savage anger stunned me. I loved Pepe, my loyal companion since the days back at the station when Arne tried to bully us. Why had he left me abandoned and alone, the last man on Earth, perhaps the only man alive in all the universe? Betrayed, bitterly bewildered, I sat at the jade table till that irrational anger had faded into sobs of helpless grief. Finally I lay back on the bench and slept off the wine.

That long afternoon I walked out to the cairn where we had buried Casey and the wreck of his slider, hoping dimly to find Pepe there. He was not, but I knelt by the mound, groping in my memory for the Lord's Prayer and the Twenty-third Psalm, which my holo father had tried to teach us. I myself have no belief in life after death or anything supernatural, but with no will to leave, I knelt there for hours, droning the words I could recall, my last link with the old Earth.

A purple dusk was darkening in the east before I stood up and plodded back toward the Crown. Lit by a red sunset, its golden dome towered over me like a fallen Moon, half buried when it fell. I stopped and stood there, shivering in a cold night wind. It was too huge, too long dead, haunted with the ghosts of too many worlds.

Yet it was now my only home, my prison too, so long as the white robots wanted to feed and house me. Was

Pepe somewhere there, lost in its endless warrens, perhaps ill or injured or driven mad? I had to find and help him if I could.

The robot guards let me in. The dark halls lit my way to our apartments. The robot staff served me a solitary meal and followed to my lonely room. That night I slept badly, tormented by a bizarre dream that Pepe was calling me back to the dining room.

He said the robots had dinner waiting for us both. Finally wakened, I knew it was only a dream, yet I dragged myself out of bed and stumbled back to the table. Lights came on as I went, but no dinner was set. The room was empty till a silent white robot glided silently to stand behind the single chair.

I sat there till my eyes ached, staring at the holo wall, where a swarm of monsters never born on Earth was swimming though a jungle of enormous crimson worms grown up around a mushroom of black smoke spewing out of an undersea vent. I sat there till a robot shook my arm and asked how it could serve me. Half awake, I thought I heard Pepe's urgent voice.

"*Escuche*, Dunk. Listen! I'll reach you if I can."

I rubbed my eyes and tried to listen, but all I heard was silence. Stiff and cold from sitting there too long, I stumbled to my feet and let the robot escort me back to bed.

Next morning I ate alone, facing Pepe's empty chair and hardly aware of what the robots offered me. With no purpose or hope for anything better, I let them massage me and spent a long time in the shower. At last, searching for a better grip on my own sanity, I went back to the Earth sector.

Could Pepe be there? As much as I hated its empty stillness and all the riddles of its death, I had nowhere else to look. It had been a city in itself, the main street a great, high-arched hall. Black darkness faced me it as I entered, but hieroglyphic signs flashed to greet me and the ceilings began to glow. Section by section, they lit my way past dark doorways and across darker intersections, until I came out again on that high balcony that looked down into the vast black chamber at the city's core.

Vertigo froze me. Waiting for those strange constellations to light the dome above, I had to fight a sudden mad impulse to jump the railing. Had Pepe chosen that escape? I could hardly blame him if he had, but I wasn't ready to die.

Shivering from the chill of panic, I swayed against the railing, feeling suddenly so weak that I thought I might topple over it in spite of myself. I gripped it till I got my balance back, pushed myself away, and stumbled off the balcony before there was light enough to let me look for his body on the distant floor.

Back in the lighted corridor, I leaned against a wall, breathing hard and gulping against a sour nausea, till at last I found the will to move along. With no hope left of finding Pepe or his body, or anything at all, I blundered on though an endless maze that always lit to greet me and fell dark again behind me.

The lights around me were suddenly red, so dim I felt blinded. Signs were fainter, stranger. Shop windows held nothing I could recognize. The icy air had a strange, bitter bite that troubled my stomach again, and a sudden gust sent a shudder through me.

I had strayed into a sector whose people had come from some colder star. Lost from anything I knew, with no sense of where I was or how to find myself, I was paralyzed with a senseless terror. I was left with no interest in who they had been or how they had died. All I wanted was to get out. All sense of direction was gone; I stood there, sick and shivering, till a noiseless robot loomed out of the red shadows.

It had the shape and grace of the white humanoids in our quarters, but bright black scales covered it, instead of simulated skin. It stood motionless before me, speaking, perhaps, in some electronic language I did not hear. Its blind lenses unnerved me. When I tried to move aside, it glided to block my path again.

I turned to run. It caught my arm and held me with an iron grip until a more familiar white robot came at last to guide me back to our apartments. Another stood waiting to serve me dinner. I left the meal untasted, drank all the wine it offered, and finally let it assist me to bed. I lay there, hopelessly mourning all I had lost and feeling that I would never sleep, till I heard Pepe calling me.

I thought it was another dream.

D unk?" His anxious shout came through a rattle of static, as if from somewhere far away. "Dunk, can you hear me now?"

Groggily, I tried to answer.

"Dunk!" His voice was suddenly loud, near me in the dark. "Are you okay?"

I sat up on the side of the bed, fumbling for the light switch. The room lit before I found it, something shining from the door. A little cloud of milk-white mist, it glowed with swirling points of many-colored frost. It drifted around the room as if searching and finally paused to hang near my face. I reached out to see if it could be real. A hot spark from it stung my hand.

"Don't!" It spoke sharply. "*Por favor!* That hurt. Don't try to touch me."

"Pepe?" Searching for him, I scanned the empty floor, peered into the empty corners of the room, blinked into the empty air around the cloud. "Is this you?"

"*Verdad. Soy su compadre*, Pepe Navarro."

"Pepe?" The voice was his own, but I cringed away

from the cloud. "I was afraid—" I had to gasp for my breath. "Where have you been?"

"Everywhere. Or nowhere. If I can make you understand."

I sat there on the edge of the bed, shivering and trying to see some shape in the cloud, perhaps Pepe's face. It was almost the size of his head, but all I found was the dance and swirl of those diamond sparks. They made a faint frying hiss.

"How?" I whispered. "What is there to understand?"

"The microbots," he said. "They've simply learned to reprogram themselves."

I leaned closer, listening. The cloud drew back.

"*Cuidado!* Not too near. The atmosphere is smothering me. Even your breath gives me a twinge."

"I thought—" This was nothing I could understand. "I was afraid you were dead."

"*Estoy vivo.*" The voice had Pepe's slight Spanish accent, but edged with a faint electronic hum, and now I began to catch something of Sandor's dry precision. "More alive than ever."

The cloud dimmed suddenly and darted away, toward the far corner of the room.

"Sir?" A white robot was calling from the doorway. Another came behind it. "Have you trouble? May we assist you?"

"Get them out!" The voice had weakened. "*Pronto!*"

"No trouble," I called to the robots. "Please leave the room."

"Sir, you should be sleeping." They glided on to seize my arms and lift me off the bed. "Are you in pain?"

The cloud had dimmed till I could hardly see it.

"Now!" Pepe's voice came faintly. "Their radiation! It's killing—"

"I'm okay." I wrestled free. "I need no help."

"Sir, you seem—"

"Get out!" I waved them away. "Now!"

They looked at the flickering cloud, swung to face each other, and finally glided out of the room. I sat back on the bed and watched the cloud brighten and drift back to me.

"*Gracias*. Their radio spectrum interferes with mine."

"Can you—?" I tried to swallow the rasp in my throat. "Can you tell me what happened to you?"

"I come—come to do that." He spoke in brief phrases, as if each took an effort. "Not easy. Hurts like hell. But had to let you know what I can."

"If you're real." I had to shake my head. "If you can."

"I'll try. But Earth's alien now. Hard to push through to you. I can't—can't last—"

The cloud dimmed and sank toward the floor.

"Pepe?" I leaned closer, groping for anything I could believe. "Come back! Tell me where you are."

"Out in space." The cloud brightened and the voice came faintly back. "With Casey and Mona and all the others. Sandor tried to explain how we came up. More than I understand."

I leaned closer, trying to hear. It darted back.

"Not too close. I don't belong here."

I drew back and heard Pepe laugh.

"*Compadre mío!* If you could see your face. Remember all the times you frowned when I crossed myself or spoke of *fantasmas*? Life after death was only superstition, you said, born when primitive people tried to explain the dead loved ones they saw in their dreams? Maybe it was, but we are alive."

I did remember.

"If Sandor explained—" I shivered and swallowed again. "What did he say?"

The diamond flakes spun faster.

"The microbots?"

"You know their history." The voice spoke slowly but

more clearly. "They were microscopic robots, created to assist our bodies and our brains with everything we did. They were self-replicating, half mechanical, half alive. They depended, as we did, on biochemical processes, yet their energies were always electronic. Sandor says they evolved as we carried them out to space, till they could do more for us. Do it better, finally do it all. Our bodies were no longer necessary."

I shrank from the cloud.

"Still the skeptic, Dunk?" I heard Pepe chuckle. The diamond atoms burned brighter and his words flowed more freely. "Sandor says their silicon and diamond and gold were never more than vehicles for complexes of electromagnetic energy. Sandor thinks the evolutionary jump took place in the bodies of people dying in space. The microbots adapted and lived on, in the charged particles and magnetic forces in the interstellar clouds of dust and gas. They feed on sunlight, sense through hyperspace."

"If they were doing all that—" I thought of the dead Earth, the ghostly emptiness of the Crown, the mummies we had found at the satellite station. "Why didn't somebody tell us what was killing all the planets?"

"Nobody knew." The dance of light slowed for a moment and spun fast again. "The microbots were designed to be part of us, Sandor says, but never a conscious part. Never with a voice to tell us anything. One by one, flowing with the cells in our blood or working in our brains, they were nearly nothing. All their strength came from their unity. They had to act in unison to make the change, and never in any conscious way."

The diamond sparks dimmed a little as he paused.

"So they killed you?" I tried to believe. "Killed everybody? And you like it?"

"They've set us free!" His voice quickened. "You should see Casey and Mona! They are splendid! Larger than they were on Earth, with no air drowning them.

Changing shape as their feelings change. Spreading wings of light that shine like rainbows. I was with them when they found little Leonardo. You remember little Leo, their son who was cut down too soon? He sang to them. They all glowed with love, and they long for you to join us."

I pinched my arm and felt the twinge of pain.

"You will, Dunk." The spinning sparks had paled, his urgent voice speaking faster. "You will believe when you get here. When you find your new senses, test your new perceptions. You can look out to the edge of the universe and back through time to the big bang that made it. You can feel space expanding."

The cloud was hard to see.

"I felt your shock and sadness." His fading voice was hard to hear. "I had to try. To tell you what I can. To ease your pain if I can. I've stayed too long. *Hasta su muerte.*"

"Until I die?"

"Till you live again." The bright mist contracted, the diamond sparks only a fading point at its heart. *"Adiós, compadre."* His voice died into a crackle of static as I caught his last words. *"Vaya bien."*

The cloud was gone, like a blown-out candle.

42

That glowing cloudlet still haunts me. I hated to believe that the microscopic machines in my blood were destined to kill me, but the sting of the spark and the crackle of static had been too real to doubt. Wrestling with dread of it for the rest of that night, I felt desolate. Life all alone was no life, yet I wasn't ready to die.

A sleek white robot was standing by the bed when I woke, silently ready to massage me, to watch me through the exercises our own ungainly Robos had taught us in the big centrifuge on the Moon, to hand me a heated towel when I came out of the shower. Another was waiting in the dining room to pull out my chair and offer a breakfast I failed to enjoy.

I felt glad to get out of the building, even into the ruins around it, relieved to feel the morning sun and hear live birds chirping in the trees. I needed the company of anything alive. On my way out to the prairie dog town, I clambered again through that water-worn gap in the pavement and stopped to watch a sparrow flying with a twig to its nest. I felt a faint pleasure in the shimmer of the rising sun on the clean curves of the slider pod, even if there was nowhere for it to take me. I sat a long time at the table beside it, watching the tiny dogs. They had barked and hidden from me, but soon they were back again, sometimes standing up to watch me, but most of them scurrying about their business in the grass. I envied them.

My time goes on, even though I have no calendar or clock to keep account of it, nor any reason to. I live alone in this magnificent monument to human achievement, now the tomb of its builders. The white robots tend me well. Thanks to the microbots flowing in my blood, my health is excellent. Pepe keeps calling in my dreams, begging me to follow him into a finer paradise than any of the old religions ever promised. He says he is rejoicing in the wonders of new sciences, new arts, new philosophies, though I can seldom grasp anything he says about them.

He says his own senses are still expanding with his growing grasp of space and time. He has seen his parents alive and watched his own birth. He speaks of Casey and Mona, of Sandor and Lo, of multitudes of happy friends he found.

He says we'll all of us be merging with one another in the vast cosmic mind, which will have a place for every intelligence that ever existed, anywhere. That prospect frightens me, but he laughs at my alarm. He says we have no loss to dread, says everything that ever lived is still alive, eternal, says we will still be ourselves, keeping our own conscious identities, our individual freedoms of thought and action.

Perhaps. I want to deny it, but he insists that my own Sagittarian microbots will grow to convince me. He urges me to hasten the time when I can tell him I am ready. If that is left to me, I want to live forever. Though a desperate loneliness still haunts me, life is far too precious to be surrendered for any dream of endless enchantment somewhere off in the sky.

I enjoy the birds and squirrels that are old friends now, the little dogs barking around me, the little owls that live with us in our little town. The larger animals seem wary of the ruins, but sometimes on good days I walk out to watch the elephants and impala and zebras trailing toward the water hole. A sleepy lion is often watching from some high place. A leopard or a cheetah now and then dashes out of cover in pursuit of its next meal, but they all ignore me. Perhaps the microbots somehow protect me.

Though the immensity and the strangeness of the building is still overwhelming, I have set out to explore the Earth sector, mapping it as I go. I have begun to learn the simple oral talk of the robots. Electronic speech still baffles me, but now and then a street hieroglyph reveals itself, inviting me to visit a gallery of interstellar art, a lecture on galactic history, a sale of prehistoric antiquities, a symposium on the future of nanobiology. My own microbots may finally teach me their electronic language. The great building is a world of wonders I can never exhaust. Lonely as I am, I should never be bored.

I have a small telescope I found in a science museum. Sometimes on a clear night I take it outside. When I see the stars of Sagittarius, I find it hard to believe that I have been there among them, and skipped a millennium of time. More often I wait for moonlight for another look at Tycho and the rays spread around it.

I know the station is still there; we saw the mirrored dome on the crater rim from Sandor's slider pod. It is now dormant, but I know its instruments are still scanning the Earth for evidences of human life. When they warn the master computer that the Earth is empty, we may be cloned once more, to repeople it again.

If that takes place, I may be alive to greet my own clone sibling, arriving from the Moon. Though I feel a certain unease in the contemplation of that possible event, I expect to make him welcome. From the beginning, my own clone brothers have been the station historians. I am leaving this narrative for his information.

It must wait here for his arrival. I have no radio that can reach the Moon. Even preparing this manuscript has been a problem. People in instant contact and endowed with permanent memories have little need for paper or pens. I had to search a vanished artist's studio for pencils and drawing paper. I will leave the finished document in my room, with the robots instructed to show it to anybody who enters the building. I believe they have understood me.

Living in my own fading recollections, I know Tanya has been dead these thousand years, buried under the gray moondust down below the Tycho wall, along with all our other siblings who have died there, and dogs I used to own. Yet I don't forget her tears, her tight embrace, our last passionate kiss when we had to say good-bye. Sometimes in my dreams she has been cloned again, and returned to Earth again, as fresh and bright and lovely as she always was.

Life has always been uncertain, but it renews itself.

Or so I dream.

About the Author

Jack Williamson has been in the forefront of science fiction since his first published story appeared in 1928. Now in his seventy-third year as a published author, Williamson is the acclaimed author of such trailblazing science fiction as *The Humanoids* and *The Legion of Time*. Williamson won the Hugo and the Nebula awards for Best Novella for "Ultimate Earth," a section of his novel *Terraforming Earth*. The novel itself won the John W. Campbell Memorial Award for Best Science Fiction Novel of the year. Williamson's memoir, *Wonder's Child*, also won him a Hugo Award, for Best Non-Fiction Book Relating to Science Fiction. *The Oxford English Dictionary* credits Williamson with inventing the terms *genetic engineering* (in *Dragon's Island*) and *terraforming* (in *Seetee Ship*). His novel *Darker than You Think* was a seminal work of fiction dealing with shape-changing, and still ranks as a great achievement in horror. This and other horror works garnered Williamson a Bram Stoker Award for Life Achievement. He was the second science fiction author (after Robert A. Heinlein) to be named Grand Master by the Science Fiction Writers of America. His recent works include *The Silicon Dagger* and *The Black Sun*.

Williamson also has been active academically. A pioneer in the field of teaching science fiction as part of a university curriculum, Williamson has taught since the 1950s and is professor emeritus at Eastern New Mexico University. He lives and works in Portales, New Mexico.